"This book is an affirmation of the power of joy to transform the world, and reading it will make you sing like a bird while wishing for wings with which to fly."
—Nisi Shawl

"An amazing journey of struggle and spirit, love and loss."   —Pearl Cleage

"It's immediate, it's unflinching, and it's wonderful."
—*BookPage* (starred review)

"Hairston captures an impressive depth of tenderness between her leads and makes a moving argument for the power of stories and songs in the face of bigotry. The novel unfurls slowly, allowing each character the space to come into their own fully. It's a spectacular feat."   —*Publishers Weekly*

"A tender but explosive novel about friendship, magic, and the pain and power that come with not belonging."
—*BuzzFeed*

Praise for Andrea Hairston

"A beautifully multifaceted story . . . with deep, layered, powerful characters. Highly recommended."
—*The New York Times*
on *Will Do Magic for Small Change*

"Sheer, undiluted brilliance. Epic, courageous, unapologetically fierce. The world needed an epic fantasy from the unstoppably creative mind of Andrea Hairston, and it's right on time. This is a prayer hymn, a battle cry, a love song, a legendary call-and-response bonfire talisman tale. This is medicine for a broken world."   —Daniel José Older on *Master of Poisons*

"*Master of Poisons* makes me laugh, gasp, and dream of the world we are so desperately holding on to and of a better world yet to come. . . . I am so grateful Andrea hasn't given up on us! May she keep gifting our world with her expansive imagination throughout the years!"
—Sheree Renée Thomas

"Andrea Hairston's writing is not to be missed. Her fantasy is rich with evocative detail, stunning and original, and her characters are deeply humane and engaging. This is the kind of fantasy that expands your mind and warms your heart."   —Martha Wells on *Master of Poisons*

ALSO BY ANDREA HAIRSTON

Master of Poisons

Will Do Magic for Small Change

Mindscape

ANDREA HAIRSTON

REDWOOD
AND WILDFIRE

A TOM DOHERTY ASSOCIATES BOOK
NEW YORK

REDWOOD AND WILDFIRE

Copyright © 2011 by Andrea Hairston

A Tordotcom Book
Published by Tom Doherty Associates
120 Broadway
New York, NY 10271

www.tor.com

Tor® is a registered trademark of Macmillan Publishing Group, LLC.

The Library of Congress has cataloged the hardcover edition as follows:

Names: Hairston, Andrea, author.
Title: Redwood and wildfire / Andrea Hairston.
Description: First Tordotcom Edition. | New York : Tom Doherty
    Associates Book, 2022.
Identifiers: LCCN 2021041160 (print) | LCCN 2021041161 (ebook) |
    ISBN 9781250808707 (hardcover) | ISBN 9781250808721 (ebook)
Classification: LCC PS3608.A54534 R43 2022 (print) |
    LCC PS3608.A54534 (ebook) | DDC 813/.6—dc23
LC record available at https://lccn.loc.gov/2021041160
LC ebook record available at https://lccn.loc.gov/2021041161

ISBN 978-1-250-80871-4 (trade paperback)

Our books may be purchased in bulk for promotional, educational, or business use.
Please contact your local bookseller or the Macmillan Corporate and Premium Sales
Department at 1-800-221-7945, extension 5442, or by email at
MacmillanSpecialMarkets@macmillan.com.

Originally published by Aqueduct Press

First Edition: 2011
First Tordotcom Paperback Edition: 2022

Printed in the United States of America

0 9 8 7 6 5 4 3 2 1

FOR TWO WOMEN WHO REHEARSED THE IMPOSSIBLE:

Zitkala-Sa (1876–1938), writer and activist

*Aida Overton Walker (1880–1914),
performer and choreographer*

AND

*For my grandfather and great-aunt—
I am the song they sung.*

BOOK I

All our stars have not yet risen.

ONE

"I can't keep running."

Christmas moonbeams snuck through a break in the live oak trees, and Redwood Phipps planted her eleven-year-old self in the cold silvery light. Long legs and all, she was bone tired. Big brother George, her teary cousins, and wild-eyed grown-ups were leapfrogging through grandmother oaks, much wider than they were tall and so tangled up in one another, could have been a square mile of one tree. A maze of moss-covered boughs going every which way at once tripped up any fool aiming for speed. Redwood pressed her feet into the muck and felt fat ole roots holding down the ground. She leaned against gnarled branches holding back the sky. Warm as an ember in the small of her back, little sister Iris cooed in her sleep and burped sweet baby breath. Redwood turned her face to the stars, shivered, and closed her eyes.

The wind picked up. Sharp oak leaves sliced at her arms. She wanted to conjure herself somewhere else and give her poor legs a rest. But she'd just have to drop back into this mad dash to nowhere. And why try for some other where and when, without Mama to catch her if she got lost, without anybody to *believe*.

Redwood sank down on a mossy bough and rubbed an angry calf.

All they'd been doing for days was run: down dusty roads, through cold swamp mud, over the dead stocks of winter oats. Since a week ago, must be. Mama woke her up in the middle of a sweet singing and dancing dream. Then they raced out into a nightmare. Red flames flared against the black sky, babies screamed, and pale nightriders pumped shotguns at shadows darting through the trees. A posse of white men were going buck mad all over colored Peach Grove.

Whose fault was that?

Yellow fever took Daddy to Glory this past summer. Otherwise the family wouldn't have been running at all. That's what George said.

Redwood tried not to be mad at Daddy for leaving or at Mama for letting him go. When it was *really* your time, even a powerful conjure woman like Mama couldn't cheat the boneyard baron from his due.

First it was just them running—Mama with baby Iris on her back and big brother George holding Redwood's hand. Then two days ago, after the sun sank into mustardy mist, Miz Subie lurched out of the swamp grass, gray hair rioting 'cross her head, whiskers on her jaw twitching. "Demon posse going wild, and I was high and dry, out of harm's way. Why you calling me into this swamp between a hoot and a holler?"

Redwood snorted as Mama and Miz Subie hid behind the domed roots of a cypress tree to argue. Posse tracking them wouldn't get nowhere but lost. Mama's hoodoo spells kept them safe. She had secret places nobody could hardly find. Miz Subie had that cataract eye—wasn't too good at seeing in daylight, get lost in her own front yard. She never wanted to bother with gators or snakes or mosquitoes. Mama must've left a hoodoo trail Miz Subie could follow with her eyes closed. *Had* to follow, probably. Didn't she teach Mama conjuring? Why all the fussing and cussing?

"Garnett Phipps, you can run through fire and not get burnt," Miz Subie raised her voice loud enough for Redwood and George to hear, "but that won't put it out!"

"What you asking me to do?" Mama shouted too. "Stay here and what?"

"I'm not asking you to do anything," Subie replied. Redwood had never heard her sound so shaky. "If you're going, go. Otherwise—you running these little ones ragged."

Mama didn't say much after that. She hugged and kissed Iris and Redwood and fixed them in her eyes, but when it come to George, he pretended he was too grown for Mama still loving him like her baby. "I'm sixteen New Year's Day, 1899. A man now, ain't I?" he said. "Why we been running in circles? What you plan to do now?" Mama glared at George, but he kept on. "Why can't you tell me what's what?"

"Can't nobody tell you what's what." All the mad drained out of Mama's eyes. "You got to figure that for yourself." Mama hugged him hard, and he didn't want to let her go. She pulled away. "Y'all watch over each other. You hear me?" She squeezed Redwood's hand till it hurt. "Keep a look out, Subie. For my children. Keep a look out." Then Mama took off on her own, mud up to her thighs, tiddies dripping milk, tears aching in her eyes.

"We goin' catch up with your mama later," Subie said. "She got hard business to take care of."

"I could help," Redwood said. "If she's doing a tricky spell."

Subie didn't answer right off. "No. We need you to stay with us."

Redwood wanted to run after Mama but knew better than to make a big fuss. Didn't she have to sing to keep baby Iris from howling? Indeed, Redwood sang till they found Aunt Elisa who let Iris suck 'cause—

"Auntie be trying to wean your cousin, so drink me dry, gal."

Two days gone by since then, the whole raggedy family on the run—Uncle Ladd, Aunt Elisa, the five cousins too—sniffling, stumbling, and ain't nobody seen another sign of Mama, not Uncle Ladd who could track anything walking nor Miz Subie on the lookout for a hoodoo trail. Mama's hard business was taking too long.

Redwood peered through scraggly oak leaves curling against the chill. At least no more red fires danced 'cross the black face of night. Redwood tasted the air, drawing it slowly 'cross her tongue: cold ashes, cold soot. Maybe the nightmare was over. Maybe nobody needed to be running in circles no more, and she could lie down and catch a good sleep. Maybe Mama would come take them home . . .

"What you doing? We gotta keep ahead of those nightriders, till it's safe to go back. Get up." George pulled her off the old oak bough. His arms were thick with muscle. He shook Redwood once, twice, and rattled her teeth the third time. "Follow me. Should I take Iris?"

"No." Iris wailed if she wasn't sucking on Aunt Elisa or riding Redwood's back. Half an hour ago, despite bumping and jiggling through the woods, she got Iris to sleep singing. Why mess up that? In the moonlight, George found a way through the crisscross of boughs, but Redwood lagged behind. Each step, her feet throbbed and her legs wobbled. Wet, heavy air choked aching lungs, like she was breathing everybody's sweat. Her heart banged against her chest.

"Take your sister's hand, George, and keep a lookout." Aunt Elisa talked like Mama for a moment.

Redwood could've bust out crying. Nobody was *really* like Mama.

George reached out grubby fingers and pulled her along. His heart wasn't in it. Redwood stopped again. She wasn't running like them hound dogs who kept going even after their hearts stopped, even after they were dead.

"You feel something, sugar, the rest of us don't?" Miz Subie placed a cool palm on Redwood's hot brow and drew the fever, drew the weary right to her fingers. "A sign all right." Her milky eye twitched. "You think you can help us find your mama now?"

The whole family stood 'round Redwood, gawking.

"You know how to track her," George said.

"Can't find Mama if she don't want to be found." Redwood wondered what trick they were playing on her. Grown-ups were always hoarding the truth and lying, even though they said that was sin. "She'll find us, when she want to. I'm too tired."

"Why you got to be so stubborn? Have *your* way every time?" George just wanted her to do what he wanted.

"I can't run no more." Redwood pouted.

"Garnett's communing with . . . the angels," Aunt Elisa said. "She's too busy to find us. We got to find her."

Miz Subie scowled, but her rough palms on Redwood's cheeks pressed strength right into her. "George is right. Garnett don't hide from you. We follow you, chile. Go how fast you go. We counting on you." Everybody nodded, even George. Subie wasn't one to sneak in the back door. She just spoke plain and true.

"Angels." Redwood sighed. What did the angels want with Mama? "Well . . ."

"Play some music, Ladd," Subie said. "You know the gal like that."

"You think that's a good idea?" Uncle Ladd asked, looking 'round the shadows.

"Why she say play, if she don't mean it?" Aunt Elisa was 'bout to be through with everybody. So Uncle Ladd strummed his ratty banjo. He couldn't play worth a damn, and George had wondered why he'd dragged the ole thing along when they were on the run, life and death. Ladd kept strumming till he found *Joy to the World*. Redwood was done pouting then. She started singing loud. Nobody hushed her.

———

Aidan Cooper heard the Christmas music and stumbled to a halt.

And heaven and nature sing!

Thick strands of sweaty black hair obscured his line of sight. A hoot owl screeched, and he almost dropped the heavy burden that dug into his shoulder. He tried to breathe blood into constricted muscles. The alligator pouch dangling on his belt was caught between his thighs. He danced it free, juggling all that remained of Garnett Phipps's body. Not an hour ago, he'd cut her down from a Georgia pine that didn't burn when she did. He'd wrapped her in the white cloth his Aunt Caitlin used for bedsheets.

Thinking on her flesh crackling and boiling away, Aidan gagged. A foul stink leaked through the layers of rough cotton. Despite the powerful roots and herbs he'd gathered, Aidan smelled dried semen and spit, burnt hair, charred bones, and all Miz Garnett's screams; and those upstanding men, Christians, hooting and hollering, having a rip-roaring, good ole time. All still ringing in Aidan's ears, in his bones.

"Do right," Miz Garnett whispered—a spear right through his heart.

"How?" Aidan spoke out loud to a ghost. Eighteen and going out his mind, he ought to know better. He ought to know something.

Take her to somewhere before it's too late!

"It's already too late." Aidan told ancestors talking at him on the wind. "I saw Miz Garnett's face go up in flames." He wanted to fall over and not get up. His heart throbbed, like he'd been run through for sure. "What good is anything now?" He couldn't just leave Miz Garnett on somebody's doorstep. How awful for anyone to find her that way. "Well, I couldn't leave her hanging in that pine tree, could I?"

The fellow banging at the banjo on *Joy to the World* played more wrong notes than right, but he didn't lose the tune altogether. The music calmed Aidan's heart. He cleared his sinuses and spit mucous and blood at the sandy ground. Longleaf pine needles gouged his bare arms. The night was unusually chill, near to freezing, and he was drenched in cold sweat, shivering in a north wind. Without meaning to, he was running again. Not heading anywhere in particular, he just couldn't stand still. Miz Garnett was lighter when he was on the move. Bay branches smacked his face, but the scratches on his cheek barely registered. He was lost in a spell.

The church loomed out of the dark. The clean white oak gleaming in moonbeams startled Aidan back to hisself. Eighty-five years ago, after sweating and groaning all day in the fields, slaves built this house of the Lord by starlight. When the very first prayer meeting in the new church came to a rousing end, half these devout slaves, filled with the spirit of the Holy Ghost, took their freedom into the swamps and on to Florida, to live and die with the Seminoles. Paddy rollers chasing behind them got struck down by lightning, and their hound dogs got fried too. Overseer aimed to torch the church but set fire to his ownself—man run 'round for hours, burning everybody he touch, and nobody could put him out. They say, he still be burning in Hell. Even if this was a tall tale, the angry God of the Baptists made Aidan nervous. He was a sinner for sure, and no Hail Marys would help him here. God, Jesus, and the heavenly host had seen Aidan crouched up in that hunting perch doing squat, while Miz Garnett . . . while those men . . .

The door to the church was half-open, and Aidan nudged it the rest of the way. Plain wooden pews and altar were bathed in a silvery glow coming in a window that was as clear as fresh air. Aidan couldn't remember this church ever being empty on Christmas Eve before. Squinting down the aisle, he saw a mouse run from a crèche in front of the altar. Black bead eyes flashed a fleck of light. A carved wooden Mary cradled baby Jesus and smiled at Aidan. A few donkeys and sheep stared at him expectantly. One of the wise men dressed in a Seminole patchwork coat had a broken leg and was tipped on his side. Indian ancestors had their eye on him for sure.

Aidan lurched past pews worn smooth by devout behinds and headed toward the crèche. He laid his burden down gently, despite the tremble in his muscles. He wanted to say some words, speak a prayer, but didn't know what he believed. Singers joined the banjo on *Joy to the World,* coming closer now. Aidan scattered a bundle of sweet bay branches and violet orchids 'cross Miz Garnett's body.

Outside the window, twelve riders in dark robes tore through the night, pounding the ground, raising a thick haze of dust. The singers and banjo player went silent. Aidan slid his daddy's hunting knife out the scabbard on his thigh. The horses were wall-eyed and sweaty, tongues lolling and frothy. One rider's pale face blurred in the shadows as they disappeared. Aidan hugged hisself and bent over Miz Garnett's body trying not to scream or weep or break apart. The musicians started in again. A child singer soloed, and *Joy to the World* approached the church.

And wonders of his love . . .

A young gal stood in the doorway and sang her heart out. The music tore at Aidan's gut. He dashed behind the altar. A blur of grown-ups rushed by the gal to Garnett's body. Someone wailed and covered any noise Aidan made struggling out the back.

"Subie, the child led us right to her mama," Miz Garnett's sister, Elisa Glover said, her voice cracking. Must have been Ladd banging on the banjo beside her.

Clouds crossed the moon as Aidan sprinted to the trees. Subie, a dark woman in her sixties with a milky eye and wrinkled gnarled fingers, stood in the doorway, her hands on the singer's shoulder. Aidan couldn't make out the young one—her face swam in shadows. Taller than Subie, most likely it was Garnett's gal. Aidan was covered in shadows too. Still and all, Subie spied him with that blind eye. She nodded once to him and ushered the gal into the church. Aidan raced on. Banging through brush, he didn't feel hisself. But even deep in the old oaks, he felt the family grieving as the child sang a verse of *Joy to the World* Aidan didn't know.

Everybody was hollering on top of Redwood's singing.

"Garnett's in Heaven . . ." Aunt Elisa faltered, "communing with the angels."

"She's dead," Miz Subie talked over her.

Redwood didn't want to believe it. An acrid smell filled the church, like green pinewood burning. She felt as if scorched roots were coming apart beneath her feet, tearing through dirt, spraying bugs and mucky old leaves in the air. If she hadn't been singing, she'd have fallen over or worse. She clung to each note, longer than she should, louder than the pounding hooves drumming the road. Miz Subie didn't lie. Mama was dead and gone and never coming back. Redwood didn't know how she could stand it. She shook Miz Subie's cold, heavy hand off her shoulder. Singing loud helped her walk the aisle between the pews and push past her cousins, aunt, and uncle to George. He couldn't holler no more and stood at the crèche, staring at orchids on dusty white cloth wrapped 'round all that was left of Mama.

Redwood took George's hand. He squeezed hard. On her back, Iris fussed. Redwood was full of tears too, howling through *Joy to the World* louder than a baby, for Mama going off with the angels and leaving them behind.

"You singing like her!" George shook so, till he almost knocked Redwood down. "Just like Mama."

Hope burned through the hurt and held Redwood up. Everybody always said she was the spitting image of Mama. Sounded and acted like her too. So Mama wasn't all the way dead—Redwood was a spell she left behind. Spells only worked if you filled your heart, did them proper, and *believed*. So right then and there, she decided, no matter what, to sing, dance, and conjure up a storm, just like Garnett Phipps. It was what she wanted to do anyhow, but now she *had* to do it. For Mama's sake. Redwood's voice broke into wrong notes and lost words, wailing and sobbing out of tune, for she didn't know how long, but then she got a good breath and sang on:

> *No more let sins and sorrows grow*
> *Nor thorns infest the ground*
> *He comes to make his blessings flow*
> *Far as the curse is found*
> *Far as the curse is found*
> *Far as, far as, the curse is found*

TWO

Redwood Phipps squirmed in the last and only empty pew of the Baptist church. Folks had been smaller back in the day when her ornery ancestors built this church and decided how much legroom you needed to praise the Lord. Her knees pressed into splintery wood. At fifteen, Redwood was taller than a lot of grown men. Still, anybody would tell you, she was a beautiful gal with caramel skin, midnight eyes, and hair fluffy as a dandelion gone to seed. They'd also tell you she was a natural hoodoo child, beloved by the spirit in everything, wiry, spooky, working the conqueror root. And nobody—young folk or grown-ups— wanted to sit with her.

"You see clean through shady grins and lying skins. Of course they're 'fraid of you, of course ain't nobody goin' sit next to you," Miz Subie said, taking her side. Big brother George beat up Bubba Jackson yesterday for calling Redwood a ghost gal, a haint child. But George and Miz Subie didn't never come to church no more.

The preacher was always railing against conjuring. "A hoodoo witch sells her soul to the devil, and she has to keep someone in her power all the time; if not, the devil will make her suffer untold agony."

Despite all Miz Subie's supposed devil work, God didn't strike her down, and everybody sick kept on coming to her for healing. Preacher didn't sermonize against George, but why should he sit half the day praying for good times to roll *after* he was dead? "Ain't no time like now. Smile at them hinkty fools, Red, and you be surprised."

Before heading to service, Redwood had braided her hair in neat plaits, scrubbed her skin raw, and put on one of Mama's fancy dresses. Unfortunately, when she smiled and a few folks smiled back, there wasn't no more room in their pews.

The choir slid off-key—so many bad notes, it hurt. Members of the congregation wondered if the spirit could really be with such awful singers. That was the only reason the choir director wanted Redwood to join, desperate for any kind of help, even hoodoo.

The preacher grimaced and intoned over the wayward melody. "Have you swept your spirit clean? God sees to every black corner of your heart. He knows every black deed." The preacher mopped his brow and smiled at the widow in the first row who was swooning from the heat of the Holy Ghost—or pretending to. "Repent! Spill out your sins. Tell God your dark secrets."

"If God knows all," Redwood whispered to nobody, "why I got to tell him, too?" That was a good one to save for George later. Four-year-old Iris turned from two rows up and grinned. Redwood and Baby Sister could speak heart to heart even with Iris squished between Uncle Ladd and Aunt Elisa praising the Holy Ghost.

"HE sends us signs every day. Jesus wept, yes he did, for each one of us." The preacher hadn't said anything new for weeks but nobody noticed. Aunt Elisa, Uncle Ladd, and then the cousins were swaying with the hymn. Iris moved to her own music. Redwood stared out the open window. The sun was almost gone.

"Hoodoo conjure man only lead you astray." Preacher was riding his high horse now. "Singing *the* blues and telling you only what you want to hear. Easy lies. But the road to Heaven is uphill all the way. Have mercy!" he screamed, and the congregation jumped to their feet, shouting *amen!*

Redwood clutched a postcard that Mama sent from the Chicago Fair. The words written on the back changed from time to time. "We bear witness for redemption." She quoted the latest message under the *amen*s and have *mercy*s. She spoke Mama's words every chance she got, so she wouldn't forget herself or where she come from. "We speak truth that it may come true." She slipped out the side door into the twilight, certain that when the church sat back down, no one would notice the empty pew.

Aidan Cooper was sweating and spitting as he angled the plow into hard ground. The Lord's Day didn't bring rest. Aunt Caitlin's patch of dirt farm was his now. And he was a married man, responsible for two lives, not just his ownself. Who could say, maybe a baby, a new life was on the way. If he managed another good crop, he could afford to hire an extra hand—one of the Glover boys, whoever Ladd could spare. And if not, at least he wouldn't lose his land like the Jessups, the Crawfords, and half the poor colored and white folk this side of the creek. Determined to get one more row ready for winter oats, he ignored the sun sneaking down behind the trees. The mule had other ideas. She stopped mid-row and turned to stare into Aidan's smoky green eyes. An evening wind tangled his long black hair.

"Come on now, let's move, Princess. Just one more furrow and then supper." Tall and vibrant, a handsome man with burnished skin, Aidan whistled and shouted at Princess. The alligator pouch banged against Aidan's hip. His daddy's hunting knife sparkled in the fading light. The mule glared back at him, unimpressed. Princess was as red as the sunset, 'cept for a white nose and a patch of black shaped in a feather on her forehead. She snorted and twitched long, luxurious ears.

"What do you want out of me?" Aidan sighed, shook his head. He found a melody for just this moment, a haunting tune in a minor key. No words as yet, just nonsense sounds, whistles, click-clacks and *heya bob*s, which suited the mule just fine. With him singing, Princess plodded on into the twilight for three more rows.

"Anybody, please." A voice rustled through the stalks and leaves.

Aidan choked on the last of his song. Princess trudged on, dragging him along.

The voice blew through the trees. "Somebody!"

Horrified, Aidan twisted and turned in every direction—not a soul to be seen.

"Do right," the voice begged as an owl hooted.

How the hell was he ever goin' do that?

It was Christmas 1898 again, and hooded men—nightriders— blazed 'cross the newly plowed earth or through Aidan's mind. Either way, the horses' hooves stamped on his nerves. Something hung from a pine tree. He could smell the foul sweat, feel hot blood rising. A turkey buzzard circled with a string of flesh dangling from its beak.

Garnett Phipps groaned with the wind. "Do right, for the sickness cured, for the babies born true, for evil spirits chased from your gates. Have mercy."

Aidan slumped against the plow. Princess stopped and turned, flicking her velvet ears toward him. 'Cross the purple sky, bats swooped through a cloud of bugs, feasting. Aidan pulled his weary self up, un-hitched Princess, and reached for his jug. "What can I tell you? Wide awake hearing the voice of a dead woman."

Even if nobody sat next to her and she didn't last the whole sermon, talking to God always put Redwood in a grand mood. Sitting in church with a whole crowd of sinners and saints, *believing*, calling down the spirit, she felt right as rain, good as dirt, and wide open like the sky. She felt as ancient as the old oaks, as new as the falling dew—just how Mama said. "Listen hard, Red, and you can hear everything, all over creation."

This Sunday evening, creation was so loud with all the hooting, squealing, slithering, hollering, slurping, and buzzing, it was a wonder she could hear her own footfall. But cutting through the woods and taking the long way home, Redwood tracked the sound of good music. So faint at first, it could've just been wishful thinking. Yet a throb under her toes called her to dance. A twang vibrating her breastbone begged her to sing. Real professionals were passing through Peach Grove. That was the talk 'round town. Storm had washed them out Saturday evening. Sounded like they were goin' give it another go tonight—blasphemy or not.

The burning flavor of moonshine tinged the air. Redwood also smelled sweet potatoes boiling, chicken and ribs roasting, biscuits and skillet bread too, melting fresh butter. A peach cobbler bubbled and popped, and she picked up speed. Laughter and love talk echoed through the trees. Lanterns swung from oak branches and winked at her. Spanish moss danced in the warm beams of light. Redwood dashed through evergreen magnolias into a clearing just as a guitar got coaxed back in tune and a washboard was wiped down. She squatted under a flickering light to catch her breath.

Eyeing the steaming food on rough wooden tables, her stomach growled. A nickel for what you could eat and drink, but she didn't have a cent on her. Young folk from all over, from thirty miles away even, sat on splintery benches dressed in silky fabrics and starched collars. They smelled sweet as spring. Redwood smoothed her stiff cotton dress, something Mama made ten years ago to wear to the Chicago World's Columbian Exposition. It was old and faded, thin and patched, but Redwood felt beautiful as she sauntered up to the traveling bluesmen.

"Milton, they got to be paying us cash money," a handsome man with hazel eyes and a side part in his thick hair whispered over the washtub bass, a northerner from the sound of him. "Not just—"

"Do you know who you be and where you are, Eddie?" Milton replied, strumming his guitar. Couldn't tell where he was from, but Milton had a city mustache and a breath of hair like black mist, cloaking his deep brown skull. "Backcountry, nowhere Georgia. And you think you're good enough for cash—ha!"

"On a piano, I'm so good, can't nobody touch me. My fingers're so fast can't nobody even see me. That's worth . . ." Eddie shook his head, marveling at his music. "Not just food, not just a lady for the night."

"Excuse me, sir," Redwood said, right in Milton's face. He jumped back as if she'd materialized out of the cooking smoke. "You the one played music for Mr. Bert Williams in *The Lucky Coon* like they say?"

"I did indeed, pretty lady." Milton smelled of moonshine, fried chicken, and hot coffee. "On stages clear 'cross this US of A."

"How you get started doing shows and whatnot?" Redwood asked.

"Me and ole Bert be thick as thieves." He looked like a fancy liar if ever she'd seen one.

"Is that a fact?"

Milton grinned at her earnest face. "You want to go on the stage, little miss woman?"

"It's my dream," Redwood replied.

Eddie looked her up and down. He frowned at her beat-up brogans or maybe it was the size of her big feet as compared to her little tiddies, which hadn't got to half of Mama's fullness and didn't seem like they ever would. "Shouldn't you be at the prayer meeting?" Eddie snickered. "Your mama let you come hear our music?"

"Mama done gone to Glory," Redwood said to Milton. "The angels snatched her up one Christmas night, to be one of their number. But she know, blues ain't devil music."

"You're Garnett Phipps's gal." Milton laughed nervously and plucked at his guitar. Who she was spooked him. Eddie scowled and started singing. He mumbled and slurred so, Redwood couldn't understand a word, but it was good music. The tune went in your head and wouldn't let go, the rhythm got under your skin and took charge. She stepped toward the snarl of young folk dancing in the dirt. They were showing off for each other with swooping bird and bug steps from the Sea Islands, or jumping like rabbits, waddling like pigs, and doing the shimmy-shake from Savannah.

Beatrice and Fanny, who had grown up down the road from Redwood, smiled, swayed their hips, and eyed young men who had yet to find partners. They looked grand with full bosoms already, fluffy hairdos, and red on their lips. The two gals were close friends, always in step, tangled in each other's thoughts, *believing* each other's dreams. Redwood didn't mean to be jealous of them, but she was. Seeing her approach, Beatrice frowned and clutched Fanny's hand. They froze and their smiles drained away. Bubba Jackson grabbed Fanny and a friend of George's snatched Beatrice. With no prodding, they were hopping and swooping like everyone else. No boy ever come up and snatch Redwood's hand like that. She sighed and danced alone. Chasing the beat, she faltered and couldn't find herself for a moment. She stomped on someone's toes.

"Watch what you doing, gal!" Bubba yelled, blood still in his eye where George had punched him on Redwood's account. "I don't want to go lame 'cause you can't dance." He shoved her, hard. "Steer clear or sit yourself down."

Redwood moved toward an empty spot near the food, and though she didn't stop dancing, she'd lost the feeling.

"You looking good to me." Milton winked at her. He was a showman, and everybody knew you couldn't trust what come out a performer's mouth. Actors could say anything and get away with it. Milton and Eddie played the crowd, not the truth. Redwood wanted to believe him though. She took a deep breath.

A powerful stink from sweaty hair, rotten food caught in a decaying tooth, and skin that had never been washed made her dizzy. She turned to a hairy beast pawing a dish of ribs on the table. The claws on the young black bear were filthy yellow. A scar on his cheek was a gray star. The dish crashed to the ground as he stuffed meat in his mouth, crunching bones and gristle and swallowing that too.

Milton halted on an upbeat. Beatrice, Fanny, Bubba, and George's friend hollered, like at church in the grip of the Holy Ghost, only they weren't faking it. Everybody was squealing, and the poor bear was so rattled it stopped chewing. It reared up on its hind legs waving a chicken breast skewered on its right paw and moaned at the mob.

Out of the corner of her eye, Redwood saw a shotgun aimed at the bear. The animal was only half-grown and wetting the ground in terror. Shooting it down dead before it got a chance to live would be a shame, a sin. Redwood jumped between the gun and the bear, close enough for a swipe of its yellow claws to reach her. The chicken breast passed under her nose and smeared 'cross her belly. The bear was hemmed in between a table and a bench, panicking. Redwood fixed her eye on him, felt his great heart thundering in her chest, felt his lungs heaving, felt the mosquitoes burrowing for a soft spot, felt his bowels squeezed tight and his stomach growling. For a moment, there was nothing but the two of them. Calmer, the bear sucked the chicken from its claws and swallowed without much chewing.

"Get on away from here now!" Redwood waved her arms. The bear blew foul breath in her face, grabbed more ribs from the table, and ran off into the cover of the trees. Redwood gaped at him, surprised and relieved. He'd listened to her.

"I'll be damned." Milton's face twisted between a grin and a grimace. "She hoodooed that bear."

Beatrice and Fanny sucked their teeth and rolled their eyes. Eddie just scowled. Everybody gawked at Redwood, whispering and grumbling— Bubba louder than most. She wiped her greasy tummy. The man with the shotgun didn't lower it till there wasn't even a sound of bear. It was big brother George, squinting his eyes, taking aim with a frown, and shaking his head at her, maybe a bit of awe mixed in with the anger. She could never read his mind from his face.

"We're here to have a good time, all right?" Milton picked a rousing tune on his guitar. After several bars he jabbed Eddie. "You plan to leave me hangin'?"

Eddie blew on a stovepipe. "Better put down your nickel and eat that food 'fore more bears come along and beat you to it." Titters flitted through the crowd.

"I'm an ornery cuss and got a mean streak as long and wide as the Mississippi River. My mama tell you, see a bear and me fighting over *my* food, don't worry 'bout me, help the bear!" Milton got everybody laughing. "Yeah, help the poor bear."

Bubba and Fanny danced far away from Redwood; all the other couples did too.

"Please don't tell," she whispered to George. "I didn't mean to. It just happened."

George grunted and rested the gun against his thigh.

Aidan sat up in a hunting perch and enjoyed the blues music drifting in from how far he couldn't say. A second jug was almost empty, and he'd lost sense of distance and time and just 'bout everything else. Couldn't even remember climbing the tree. He still knew May Ellen would worry till he dragged his behind home. She'd want him to eat a big dinner: greasy meat, lumpy biscuits, mealy potatoes, cold okra . . . Well, his stomach wasn't having none of that. And there'd be no loving with him stinking of hooch. Sober, he could get May Ellen singing to sweet Jesus. Drunk, she'd banish him to the shed. At least Princess would let him curl up next to her, 'stead of freeze. He'd better go home and get it over with. No point in waiting for dawn. The sun might not come back for a long while. Moonlight played tricks on him, but ghosts and haints never pestered Aidan with stupid talk 'bout *have mercy* when he was three sheets to the wind.

A young bear trotting through the woods with a rack of ribs in its mouth stopped right under Aidan. The bear gobbled the food and scratched sharp claws on the hard bark. "What you looking at, bear? Go climb your own tree." Aidan threw a stick at him. The bear scarcely flinched. "All right, so I gotta go home. I will. I will. Get on now." The bear licked his lips and cocked his head. Aidan sighed and sang a bit of Princess's twilight song. The bear gurgled and took off into the gloom.

The song petered out. Aidan didn't move like he promised. He would've just drifted off, but *The War of the Worlds* book he'd been planning to read for two days dug into his side. Doc Johnson wouldn't want it back all sweaty and wrinkled. Aidan certainly couldn't afford to buy the man a fresh copy. He reached to pull it from under his hip and fell out of the tree more than climbed down. Miracle he didn't break his neck. Funny too, but he couldn't manage a laugh. He rubbed at bruises on his knuckles that hadn't come from the fall yet looked new. He fingered a dent in his boot and wondered where else he'd been banging 'round this night.

Since he was half out his mind and lost no matter which direction he took, Aidan stayed on a path that led into a peach grove. He recognized a gnarled tree corpse shaped like a gator swimming for the stars. This grove used to be part of the Jessup place, but Jerome Williams owned it now. Jerome aimed to own every direction you looked. Two snowy egrets flew over the orchard. A sharp breeze smelled and tasted of the distant ocean. Storm clouds crossed the moon and chased more birds from the sea to the woods. Stumbling, Aidan followed the path as it climbed up out of the grove. A young colored gal stood above him, her face turned to the sky. She was tall and fierce and beautiful, a bolt of lightning lingering in the grass. Spats of water splashed her face.

"Folk conjure this world, call it forth out of all the possibilities," she shouted at him.

Spooked, Aidan nodded. Hoodoo talk; what Garnett Phipps often said. Ghost clouds swirled above the gal, furiously doing battle over something important. Suddenly these flimsy gray-and-white figures broke apart and silver daggers of rain pelted the hilltop. He and the gal were soaked in an instant. Fists of wind buffeted them this way and that. She grinned and danced as trees in the orchard bent and split. Peaches shot through the air, smashed into trunks, and pummeled Aidan. It was hard to catch a breath or hang on to balance, yet the alcohol fog in his head cleared a bit.

"Damn, you ought to take cover 'bout now," he yelled.

"What 'bout you?" She twirled 'round behind him, a whirlwind herself. "Why're you still out?"

Aidan was a haunted fool, but he couldn't say that.

"I ain't 'fraid of no rain," she said. "I'm rehearsing. I'm goin' do a show, see." She storm-danced right past him again.

Aidan pivoted and should have keeled over, but he didn't. "I know you," he said, staring at his feet still on solid ground. A swollen peach branch sailed by and landed heavily beside them. Twenty ripe peaches busted open. He thought of dashing to cover, but he couldn't leave this crazy child behind. "You Miz Garnett's gal. Redwood?"

"I know you too, Mr. Aidan Cooper."

"You move like a storm brewing."

He wiped his face, flung peach flesh at the sky, and took a long swig from his jug. His stomach rebelled and the hooch came right back up. He turned from her to vomit, and the wind almost tipped him over. The jug flew from his fingers and shattered on an outcropping of rocks. Punishing rain beat the back of his neck. An angry dervish of dirt and debris charged through the orchard. Aidan strode toward Redwood, shouting against the wind. "The full fury of this storm is on us."

"You ain't 'fraid of the storm or me."

"Naw, but ain't no call for us to be out in all this. Let's you and me both go find—"

The wind snatched the final words from his mouth. Smiling, Redwood talk/sang Sea Island Gullah words, working some spell, then darted away from him. Aidan matched her moves and gripped her at the waist. She gasped at his boldness but didn't struggle as he turned her away from the oncoming monster storm. A twister of dust, moss, leaves, and debris blotted the orchard, the hilltop, and the sky from view. Whirling silver specters, a ghost army, a haint battalion battered them with cold, muddy water. Sharp stalks and broken branches pierced Aidan's back. He yelped as hot blood drizzled down his side. This deadly gale hadn't come up out of nowhere—the boneyard baron had been stalking him all day it seemed.

"Spare Garnett's child," he muttered, not sure if anyone was listening, if anyone cared, but he couldn't help hoping. "Spare her child."

Redwood reached a hand 'cross his shoulder back toward the storm.

"You want to touch the fury, huh?" Aidan whispered in her ear. "Well . . ."

The monster squatted on them now. Staggering air pressure slowed Aidan's heart, stopped his lungs, and crushed his muscles into his bones. Just before he would've blacked out, the roar of wind and rain cut to utter silence. He gasped. The storm went absolutely still, suspended, a photograph of twisted fury. At the center of the dark spiral mass, Redwood's palm trembled, and Aidan clutched her wrist, his fingers digging into soft flesh.

After a drunk moment or two, the twister moved again, slowly at first, like a swamp current. Its funnel coiled into tighter and tighter circles above Redwood's palm. Aidan felt the storm racing through her and had to resist an impulse to snatch her hand away. She leaned into his chest; her breath on his cheek was cold as January fog. Going faster now than he could see, the monster gale blew itself to nothing, to a dark swirl 'round a blade of grass in Redwood's hand. She squeezed her fist shut.

In the stillness, in the quiet moonlight that replaced the storm, Aidan let go of her and staggered to the crest of the hill. Two turkey buzzards flew over their heads, disappointed at the lively beating hearts below. Nearby, in a small circle of destruction, battered peach trees leaned into each other, their broken limbs dragging in churned-up muck. A bit farther out, untouched boughs swayed in a gentle breeze. Plump peaches gleamed in moonbeams. Aidan glanced at Redwood's trembling fist and lost his balance finally. He fell to one knee and groaned.

Redwood looked frightened of her ownself. "You goin' run away now?"

"No . . ." Aidan stood up on shaky muscles. "What you do, gal?"

"This is the first one." Redwood took a step toward him.

"Yeah, storm season's just coming on."

"No, the first time I ever catch the wind." Another step. "I ain't never done nothing so grand!"

"What? You a hoodoo conjurer?" He felt light-headed, but the drink had left him. He was sober as a Baptist choir.

"And you *believing* in me. Conjure woman say that's what a hoodoo need to work a powerful spell, folk *believing*."

"Miz Subie ought to know better than to fill your mind with—"

"*Believing*, but not scared." In one swift move, Redwood pulled a sharp stalk out of Aidan's back and tossed it aside. The pain was hot, but whatever she pressed against the wound was cold and soothing and drove the hurt to the dull part of his mind.

"Redwood! This ain't no night to go running off." A woman yelled, not a haint scolding her daughter but Elisa Glover, Garnett Phipps's younger sister. Aidan was glad for that. A light swung in the distance, coming through the dense woods. He heard four feet heading for the orchard.

"We're over here, Aunt Elisa," Redwood shouted and then whispered to Aidan. "This is our secret, all right?"

The light turned and headed toward them now.

"You a magic gal?" Aidan's voice cracked. "Same as Miz Garnett, huh?" He backed away without meaning to.

"Working my way to it. Mama could barter with the boneyard baron. I just—"

"Just? Either I'm drunker than I ever been," Aidan wanted to shout, "or you snatched a hurricane down out the sky."

Redwood reached her storm hand toward him. "This is good for what ails you."

Aidan stepped out of reach. "What you know 'bout what ails me?"

"Take one storm to clear away another."

Gazing in his eyes, she moved toward him. Her palm hovered over his chest. He nodded slowly, and she put that storm hand atop his heart. The cool pressure against his wet skin settled his heart right down. He didn't know what he expected. A hoodoo lightning bolt? Hellfire? They just stood silently, close to one another, breathing each other's breath, tasting each other's spirits—felt like his whole life was with him and all of Redwood's time too, the sorrow, the joy, the thrill . . . He hadn't been so close to anybody for a long time, not even to May Ellen when she was singing to sweet Jesus for him to do her again. Indeed Aidan hadn't been this close to hisself since he was a boy up north in the Blue Ridge Mountains feeling close to everything, lost in everything, his spirit as wide as the sky.

"I hear Miz Garnett on the wind every time the sun go down," he said.

"She talk to you out loud?" Tears brimmed in Redwood's eyes.

Four years now and he hadn't told a soul. Why'd he pick on her? "I'm sorry. I didn't mean to go and make you cry."

"Mama don't *talk* to me since she gone on to Glory." Redwood sniffled against him.

"A blessing, and you should count it so." He patted her back.

"I'm 'fraid I won't remember what she said or who she was or how she looked or . . ."

He spied a postcard in the mud and picked it up. "Miz Garnett's in you. You won't forget that. You the love she had for this world."

"Listen to you." She wiped at tears and left streaks of mud on her cheeks. He pulled a gob of peach from her hair. "Saying just what I want to hear!" She smiled at him.

He smiled back. "Did you drop this?" He held out the card. In the moonlight, the White City on the front glowed.

Redwood grabbed it. "From when Mama and Daddy went to the World's Fair."

"Well, looks like a place you ought to visit too."

"We could go together." She looked thrilled at the prospect. "Couldn't we?"

As Aidan entertained this crazy idea for a second, Ladd and Elisa Glover slogged through underbrush onto the moonlit hilltop, just twenty yards from them. Dry as dust, they wore sturdy Sunday church clothes and working boots. Elisa didn't have her sister Garnett's height, sharp features, or the hoodoo flare. A round woman with pearly teeth and a fierce jaw, Elisa carried a shotgun and a *Maskóki* hunting knife like Aidan's. Ladd was tall and broad and dark as the night sky. His deep-set eyes always twinkled and flashed with emotion. He carried a shotgun too and a lantern.

"Storm come up here and disappear," Ladd said.

"Don't tell," Redwood whispered to Aidan and made a whirlwind gesture. "They 'llowed to skin me alive if they knew."

Ladd and Elisa slipped in the mud and debris and slowed down.

"You want me to lie for you?" Aidan asked, watching them.

"*Believe* in me, the way you did in my Mama."

Aidan wheezed and sputtered. What did she know 'bout him and Miz Garnett?

"Please." She sounded like a young gal and a grown woman too. "*Believe* in me."

"That's the most a person can do for another," Aidan said.

"I *believe* in you too."

"Me?" Aidan choked off a bitter laugh. "Why me?"

"Just between us." Redwood was moving to a safe, proper distance from him. "Everybody already 'fraid of me. They don't need more ammunition. You promise?" She stared in his eyes, like she could see clear through him, back to his ancestors, back to the beginning of everything and up to now. Or maybe that was what he saw looking through her and 'round to hisself. Not a pretty picture.

"All right, I promise." That was the least he could do.

"Friends then." Redwood's face lit up. Her dress was a ruin; wild hair twisted out of once neat plaits; big feet busted out of broke-up brogans—a real sight. What would her aunt and uncle think?

"Friends." Aidan nodded to her.

"Redwood Phipps, you know better than to have us chasing after you," Elisa said. "What is the matter with . . ." She quit scolding when she spied a soggy Aidan shaking mud and peach slime from his mane of thick black hair.

"I'm sorry, Aunt Elisa." Redwood ran to her. "Crazy Coop's been looking out for me though."

Ladd pulled off his cap and stepped forward, his chest caving in, his shoulders hunched. Four or five inches of height got lost to the wide grin masking his face. "Mr. Cooper, don't mind her."

Elisa hugged Redwood to her ample bosom and whispered loud enough for anybody to hear, "Hush your fresh mouth, child."

"She can say whatever the hell she want." Aidan preferred that to Ladd and Elisa acting like he was some fool white man who needed colored folk to act the coon for him. Ever since Miz Garnett passed, since Aidan was a grown married man, it took hours before they let down their guard even a little. The Glovers and the Phippses were his neighbors since he come to Peach Grove from the mountains up in north Georgia, almost family he once thought, yet they acted as if they ain't been knowing him these nine–ten years. Or maybe since he started drinking too much and was a stranger to hisself, Elisa and Ladd weren't sure if they should trust him anymore. Who could blame them? Stumbling away, Aidan got tangled in his feet. Still groveling and grinning, Ladd moved to help.

"I can stand on my own, damn it!" Aidan flailed against Ladd's sturdy arms. Ladd backed off, perfectly happy to let Aidan fall on his ass.

"Thank you for your kindness, Mr. Cooper," Elisa said with warmth in her voice.

"It's still Aidan, and no need to be thanking me."

"I do how I think is right. You too?" She jutted her jaw out, challenging him.

Aidan sucked a deep breath. "Well, ma'am, I do try."

Elisa smiled. "I appreciate you having an eye out."

"No hardship there." Aidan glanced at Redwood. "Good evening."

"Good evening, Mr. Cooper." Redwood smiled.

Feeling better than she had for ages, she watched Aidan tramp toward the woods. Before when she'd tried to catch even a little ole breeze, it'd just blown through her hand. She sighed. A magic man for sure, he was tall and handsome and wild—eyes the color of Spanish moss and hair as dark as coal. He carried a scent of hard work, strong drink, and heavy sorrow. Aunt Elisa and Uncle Ladd watched him too, till he was a streak of light among the dark pines. She had someone to *believe* in her now. And didn't that make all the difference?

Ladd glared at Redwood. "Where you go off to in the middle of the Reverend Washington's sermon?"

"You look like something the cat dragged in," Elisa said.

Redwood glanced down at Mama's ruined dress.

"I tole you don't go traipsing out, dancing with the moon." Elisa shook her head. "Colored Peach Grove don't need more to run they mouths 'bout."

Ladd grunted. "What you been doing up here with that wild man?"

Aidan turned and waved, his pale face glinting in a moonbeam. They all waved and smiled at him till he faded into the gloom.

"You ever see that boy drunk? He a mean drunk," Ladd said.

"I ain't seen it." Redwood could believe it though. "Peach Grove get under his skin."

"This place get under my skin too sometime, but . . ."

Elisa wagged her hand at Ladd and he clamped his mouth shut.

"He ain't goin' do me no harm." Redwood shivered. The fury of the storm had chilled her bones. She missed Aidan Cooper's dizzy warmth. She couldn't catch a breath. Her heart skipped and she almost fainted. Reckless, sticking your hand into all that, Brother George would have said, but she wasn't goin' tell him what she'd done.

"You know it all, huh?" Elisa gripped her. "Men can't always control themselves. Plenty times they don't want to. Aidan Cooper sure ain't no shelter in the storm."

"He brought Mama orchids." Redwood pouted. "I just know what I know."

Aidan reminded Redwood of George, not 'fraid of what he hadn't seen before, not 'fraid to make his own way. And like George, some poison or sickness twisted Aidan's insides. Thank the Lord, George didn't drown his hard head in a jug of hooch. Instead her brother read books, picked fights, and stayed mad at everybody in Peach Grove—colored, white, and Indians too—for being cowards, fools, and nowhere near free men.

Redwood frowned. "How you find me?"

"I didn't believe her, but Iris say you was up here catching peaches," Ladd replied.

"Crazy Coop caught all the flying fruit." Redwood's storm hand tingled where she had touched Aidan's heart. "Is he goin' be all right?" She didn't know how to heal what ailed him or her brother. Not yet.

Elisa sighed, probably so she wouldn't scold. "Subie say he got *Maskóki* Creek or Seminole in his blood, and the spirit of his ancestors be looking out."

"And driving him crazy." Ladd blew his irritation into a tattered handkerchief.

"Indian blood and all, he hear Mama on the wind," Redwood said. She'd ask Miz Subie what to do for him. "He's a friend."

"Friend?" Elisa exchanged glances with Ladd. "How'd you get soaking wet, child?"

"Storm come up here." Redwood grinned and stared up at the moon.

When Aidan finally made it home, he found broken peach branches stuck in muddy wagon wheel ruts. The monster storm had blown through his front yard and chased behind a wagon as it lumbered over May Ellen's herb garden. Aidan fingered battered chives, savory, and St. John's wort. Pungent fragrances screamed at him. Actually, Princess was complaining from the shed. Something didn't set right. Duchess wasn't making a sound, and that ole mare liked nothing better than to sing with Princess. A cold hand gripped Aidan's insides as he tripped up the stairs and through the half-open door. He lit a lamp and lurched into the bedroom. The stench of liquor assaulted his nose, like he was breathing needles and thorns. He snorted blood onto the floor.

"May Ellen, you all right?"

The bed was stripped and cold. He tripped through soggy paper and shards of gray stoneware. Jugs he'd been saving in case of a dry spell had been smashed against Aunt Caitlin's heirloom trunk. Books he'd borrowed from Doc Johnson were scattered on the floor. Walt Whitman's *Leaves of Grass* was ripped in two. Mary Shelley's *Frankenstein* was wedged in a hole under the window. A cracked mirror hung lopsided from the wall. Slimy okra and mealy potatoes were smeared all over its glass face. May Ellen's brush and comb weren't on the bureau. Not a stitch of her clothing hung in the wardrobe he'd carpentered and carved special for her. Not a scent of her anywhere . . .

May Ellen was gone. She'd finally left him.

"What 'bout till death do us part?" Aidan shouted.

He crumpled over Aunt Caitlin's battered trunk. After the first jug, after stowing Princess in the shed, did he and May Ellen fight? Did she weep and scold and smash his jugs 'cause he was drinking too much? Did she say her sister warned her against marrying a drunk Irishman? That's what she always said, but this evening, maybe she couldn't holler at him anymore. Maybe she just watched while Aidan lost his mind and rampaged through the house hunting down *War of the Worlds*.

Closing his eyes, Aidan heard echoes of ragged screams—in his voice all right—'bout haints and *have mercy*. Mystery bruises on his knuckles and arms made sense now. So did the dent in his boot where he'd kicked at the stove before hurling dinner every which way. Had he left May Ellen cowering and wailing in the shed between Duchess and Princess and run off to his hunting perch?

Was that a bad dream, or worse—a memory?

Aidan tumbled off the trunk and dashed from room to room. There were only three, and nowhere for even a mouse to hide. He was chasing shadows. Shattered dishes cut at his boots in the kitchen. Broken chairs sent him sprawling to the floor. May Ellen's braided rug reeked of piss and kerosene. The smell made him retch. Or maybe it was truth churning up his stomach. The house was empty. May Ellen had packed up her things, hitched Duchess to the wagon, and left him. Lurching *again* from room to room, disbelieving his eyes, disbelieving his drunken memory, wouldn't bring her back.

Aidan didn't mean to scare her. He didn't mean to hurt her, and he prayed to any God who was still listening to the likes of him that he hadn't laid a hand to her. Black alcohol fog covered his memory and left him in torment. "Please Lord. Just tell me I didn't hurt her."

The Lord wasn't studying him.

Aidan banged out onto the porch with such force that he almost knocked the flimsy door off its hinges. Blood spurted from his shoulder and soaked his shirt. He staggered in circles. He'd hidden one more jug from hisself under the porch, but would never find it in the dark. He'd save that for sunrise. Princess brayed and kicked against her stall. Nothing else to do, so he tromped into the shed and glowered at her.

"What's a matter with you, hollering in here?"

Princess bared her teeth and wagged her head. The hair on her neck rippled and she stomped her forelegs. Aidan bowed his head as she chastised him. He walked toward her, mumbling what a fool he was and stretching his hand out. Princess nipped his fingers and then licked at peach slime on his shirt.

"What am I goin' do with myself?"

Aidan found his red leather journal tied 'round Princess's neck. Half a page had been ripped out. May Ellen wasn't one for reading or writing. She must've spent an hour scrawling him a note:

Coop
Gone up to Cofee County to my sisters. Jenny warned me. Dont you
dare come after me. Im just tellin you so you wont fret. If you aint died
out in them woods then Im glad for you. My ma watched dady kill
hisself drinkin. I aint her. Dont want to hate you, dont want to die
in your shadow.
May Ellen

Aidan draped his arms over Princess and leaned his face against her neck. She was quiet as he slobbered and moaned on her.

THREE

"What I tell you?" Redwood poked surly Brother George in the ribs. "We goin' reach the swamp a good while 'fore dusk now."

He batted her hand away. "Just 'cause you finally be sixteen, you know it all, huh?"

They stood at a crossroads on a gentle rise of land only an hour or two east of the Okefenokee Swamp. Doc Johnson had carried them in his buggy from Peach Grove to Silver Bluff. Redwood had promised him healing roots from the swamp and jumped onto the comfortable leather seat before George could refuse the ride.

"Much better than walking all that way in this heat," Redwood said.

"So," George muttered. "I still don't have to like it."

She smiled. "You just ornery."

Silvery moss shimmered. Dust from the retreating carriage glinted like gold. Despite the afternoon's enchanted edge, the air was sweaty and the sun mean.

"And you grinning in that cracker's face the whole ride," George muttered.

"Doc's a nice man." Redwood squeezed *Leaves of Grass* and *The Awakening* to her chest. Doc loaned her two books this time. Good thing— she'd run through Miz Subie's stash.

"Nice? Ha! You think everybody's nice. No matter what."

"Naw. You got people fooled, Brother, but I know *you ain't nice*."

"If they pat your head and give you nonsense to read, you'll—"

"You read every page I do."

George knocked the books into the dust and stormed away. He'd been working too many hours in somebody else's field. Redwood scooped the books up, carefully brushed the covers clean, and stowed them in her pack. George veered from the road and charged down a path into snarled vegetation. His legs weren't so long as hers, but when he was in a salty mood, he could march faster through crawling underbrush and domed cypress roots than anybody she knew. Couldn't nobody keep up with George.

"Road's not good enough for you?" Redwood stumbled after him. Thick curtains of Spanish moss tried to swallow her. Hefty oak boughs reached out and almost knocked her down. "Wait," she yelled. Sweat streamed down her belly and under the pack that dug into her shoulder and banged on her hip. Wet tiddies chafed against a rough cotton blouse that seemed to fit fine yesterday, but cut off her breath now. A heat rash bloomed 'cross her chest down to her thighs.

"Since I ain't nice, you better hurry on up." George glared at her, meaner than the afternoon sun. Flinty eyes darted 'round his face. His furry new mustache wiggled like a poor creature caught on his lip, trembling before an impending blast of fire breath. Redwood sniggered at the thought of her handsome brother snorting flames and sprouting scaly wings too. He had all the gals in the county whispering and swooning 'cause they didn't know how he really look.

"Ain't nothing funny." George smacked waxy magnolia leaves and charged on.

Big white flowers dipped down and smeared Redwood with pollen and scent. Satiny petals clung to her hair. She paused in the heavy fragrance. Going too fast to keep up with hisself, George stumbled and then pretended to shift his rucksack.

"I ain't waiting for you," he said.

"Go on then. I didn't want to take this way no how. Road's easier going." She fanned herself in the shade. "I'll do fine in the swamp on my own. I ain't no little child begging you to take me along." At sixteen, a lot of gals were married, bringing babies into the world, and keeping house. Redwood was a grown woman and didn't need a testy big brother to chaperone her. "I don't see why you so mad."

"What?" George halted and turned. "We lost our land. That make me more than mad." He stomped toward her, ready to smack her fresh behind for talking foolish. "In the courthouse, white folk say the deed don't count. They say Daddy and Mama didn't own nothing. Jerome and Caroline Williams can steal our inheritance away. And colored

Peach Grove just laughing at *us poor chillun of uppity Raymond and Gar-nett Phipps*."

"Uncle Ladd treat you better than some men treat they sons. Don't work you to death, and give you earnings."

"Twenty-five cents every now and then ain't goin' buy us a future."

"How much do the future cost?"

"You, me, and Iris got to make our own way." He grabbed her. "How can I do that on nothing? I ain't no sharecropper." He squeezed her shoulders together. She didn't let on how much it hurt. "Raymond Jessup gotta be paying white folk now *so he can work his own damn land.* I ain't hiring out to make some cracker rich. I ain't landing on a chain gang worth nothing to myself even." He spit words in her face and glowered worse than any fire-breathing dragon she could imagine.

"Who's telling you to do all that?" Redwood asked. "Mama and Daddy wanted to sell the land and go on up to Chicago town anyway. When they come back from the World's Fair, they—"

George released her and hit his forehead with the heel of his hand as if she was the dumbest thing living.

"Talk to me if you think I don't know something." She rubbed bruised shoulders.

"What you doing, going to the Okefenokee Swamp to hunt roots for? Why don't you go teach school like Aunt Elisa? They ready to pay you a dollar, dollar fifty a week. You done read every book you can find. You can talk proper when you got a mind to."

"Aunt Elisa say I can't do hoodoo conjuring *and* teach school. It's a Christian school and they don't want no truck with the devil."

"What kind of reason is that?"

"I want to be like Mama was."

"Tell them fools what they want to hear and do how you want behind they backs."

Redwood shook her head. "I hate when you talk this way." Tears filled up the back of her throat. "You scaring me."

"Don't you care 'bout something 'sides yourself? Don't you care 'bout educating colored folk, 'bout Iris, 'bout—" George whirled on his heels and charged away.

Redwood scrambled after him, anger and hurt lending her speed. "I want to go on the stage. Singing and conjuring; that's a good life."

"All your talk of being a grown woman and you still don't know nothing."

"I can help you *and* Iris doing that."

"You living in a dream, gal."

"Better than living a nightmare. That's what Miz Subie say."

"Why Subie got to humor you? Why everybody always humoring you?"

She grabbed his left hand. The knuckles were bruised and caked with blood. "You been in a fight?" His ring finger was twisted and swollen. She caught his darting eye.

He grunted. "Bubba Jackson call Mama out her name, so I—"

"When *Bubba* goin' learn better?" She straightened the bent joint. He yelped and tried to pull away. "Stop!" she hissed. Without letting him go, she got Miz Subie's cure-all from her pack and smeared it over his gashes and bruises. She snapped off a smooth twig and wrapped it against the broken finger. He cussed through gritted teeth. She bandaged the bruised knuckles and pulled as much pain from him as she could. Pulling pain was the first spell Mama taught her. *Use your good heart like a lodestone. Feel the whole Earth pulling on a stormy sky, pulling till lightning strike the hilltop.* "Sorry if it still hurt. I got to practice. Miz Subie say I'll be good as Mama someday." She threw his hurting to the wind.

George stared at the battered fingers like they belonged to somebody else's hand. "We ain't even got a horse or mule to our name." Choking back a sob, he hugged Redwood. "The world ain't full of good folk who want to lend a helping hand. Doc give you a ride, a book, but he don't change anything. He just be feeling good 'bout his cracker self." He sighed, kissed the top of her head, and soldiered on. "We need to get out of this backwater nowhere and go where a man can be a man."

"Where's that?"

George dodged a low hanging branch, but didn't reply.

"Soon, I'll get paid to take away pain." She scrambled after him. "You watch."

Miz Subie trusted Redwood enough to send her off hunting: Culver's root, orangeroot, rattlesnake's master, devil's shoestring, manroot, swamp orchids, floating hearts. A dozen more blurred together in her mind 'cause they was skittish, growing magic that wanted to hide from her and not get plucked, even if she vowed to take only what she needed. Days of hot itchy work, and she might have to come back and do it again, if she got tricked into picking the wrong things or delicate roots gave out and lost the spirit before Miz Subie could get at them. Getting 'round the swamp without a boat would be a trick. Miz Subie say a conjure woman had to make her own way through life. Doc and his buggy was easy, but how was Redwood supposed to conjure a boat? She'd have to know a whole lot more spells to do that.

"... and you could spend your whole life hunting down nothing." George had been going on a while, and she'd missed most of what he was saying.

"I'm goin' do fine."

"Is that a fact or a wish?" He knew her like the back of his breath.

"Hope's better than a mule, a horse, or a canoe even."

"Do tell." He was picking up speed again.

"I'll make good, and then you won't need to go and—"

"What, *you'll* take care of *me*?" He spit at a tree trunk and missed.

"You'll see. Like Mama said. Watching out for each other."

George tried to ball his hands into fists, but the splint and bandages wouldn't let him. A startled bird flew past his face, a screeching blur of red and green feathers. A nest toppled onto hard ground. Speckled eggs cracked and oozed cloudy white fluid flecked with yellow and red. A sign, but George fixed his eyes on the dwindling path in the distance.

"Killing them birds just goin' put you in a worse humor." Redwood toed the shell.

"Hardly none left to kill. Maybe I done already missed my chance."

George come out to hunt snowy egrets and purple swamp hens. A company in England was paying thirty-two dollars an ounce and didn't care 'bout the color of the man doing the selling, long as they got purple jewel feathers and snowy white plumes for high-fashion hats. All over Europe, fancy rich ladies were styling Georgia birds. George didn't want to waste time taking his sister nowhere. He was determined to get rich. Now.

"You got me started in hunting feathers." He wagged a bruised finger at her.

"Birds I found were already dead."

"Folk gotta eat. Folk gotta survive. I don't see you crusading for chickens. Ain't nothing wrong with wringing a bird's neck. I'd rather do that than starve."

"If you was *eating* the birds you catch, I don't think I'd mind."

"Whether I eat 'em or not, ain't no difference in how dead the birds be, but a big difference for our lives. On what I earn, I could get a piece of land, a wife—"

"Just 'cause what you say sound good don't make it right."

"You trying to tell me these birds be more important than your family?" He burped sour breath in her face.

"See, your stomach's turning. Miz Subie say it's bad for your insides to go killing what you don't need."

"That's just her meat pie not sitting right in my belly. Ain't no sign of nothing."

"You a bona fide citizen of the future." Redwood mimicked the principal at the school where Aunt Elisa taught. "Too rational and forward thinking to heed the words of a superstitious ole conjure woman like Subie Edwards, like Mama, huh?"

George swallowed a mouthful of fire breath for sure. She felt it burning in his belly. His deep voice crackled when he spoke. "You won't have to watch me killing nothing, Miz Know-It-Better."

Redwood clamped down on more fighting words. "I'm sorry. I don't mean to pick at you." Fussing wasn't no better than dirt in a wound. George did have a bunch of years on her. What if he actually knew something important that she didn't? She stretched a hand toward him. He stayed just beyond her reach.

"I'll take you far as the swamp. Then you be on your own, just how you want."

That wasn't what Uncle Ladd told him, but Redwood didn't argue.

"Sure I'll marry you." Aidan blew out the lamp.

Darkness cloaked his shabby house in sultry shadows. It was the middle of a hot night. He was half-naked and pleasantly drunk, and trying to get inside Josie Fields for the third time in a month. Josie had thrown down almost as much moonshine as Aidan. He buried his face in Josie's sweet-smelling bosom and held on to her firm buttocks for dear life. He might have promised her anything.

"All right." Josie rode him till the ole bedsprings screeched and quivered. Just when the going was too good to be true, she whispered, "I'm two months pregnant, you see."

"Whoa, no!" Her confession didn't stop the climax, but took Aidan's breath away when he could've used a good mouthful or two. The way he counted, it wasn't his child. Gasping and grunting he managed to add, "That's a good time to be married."

"I thought you'd understand." Josie didn't claim it was his child. Her fields got plowed regularly, two–three times a day. That was the joke 'round Peach Grove. Aidan didn't hold good loving against her—his mother would have been proud—but he felt queasy. They were at it again before he could think straight. He curled his tongue 'round a hard nipple and held off busting loose till she was sucking sharp breaths, till she couldn't stand another second and neither could he. He let hisself go, a torrent of storm water through a gorge. Josie hollered in his ear.

Aidan passed out.

It was hardly morning. Dawn was just a pink slit in velvet dark, and Princess was already fussing in the shed. She was lonely since May Ellen left with Duchess. Aidan was too. His head throbbed so, Princess's hooves could have been pounding his skull. Sunrise hurt, even with a sheet over his eyes. Aidan's legs were wrapped 'round Josie's thighs. His left foot was all pins and needles as he shifted her weight and got his blood flowing. Josie snored and chewed in a dream. He pulled his arm from under her head. Squinting at his dreary room, he blinked sleep out his eyes.

Splotches of sunlight shone through a curtain full of holes as it flapped in a warm breeze. Moths had dined on the thin yellow cotton all winter; spring wind and rain would finish off the remaining tatters. A pink mold was growing on the mirror and dribbled down through decayed okra to the floor. Three books were stacked on Aunt Caitlin's trunk, looking almost smart as new. He'd fastened *Leaves of Grass* together again, carving a red leather spine with swamp birds, bears, and Princess grinning—something Doc Johnson would surely appreciate.

Josie farted. It was air mostly and who knew how bad he smelled, but Aidan just wanted her to go. He wished for a hoodoo spell to make her disappear. Course, Redwood was too good-hearted to do him a *hot-foot* or *drive-away* spell. Josie's eyes popped open as if she could hear his uncharitable thoughts.

"I was dreaming 'bout our wedding." Josie stretched and purred at him. "I bet you could get that colored hoodoo gal to sing something and do us a *good-luck* spell."

"Who, Redwood?" Aidan never expected Josie to hold him to a promise he'd made under duress.

"A wedding is the respectable thing to do. Not just the courthouse." She scowled dark clouds 'cross her rosy complexion.

Aidan scowled back. "I don't deny that, but . . ."

Josie never looked too happy with Aidan in the sober light of day. He didn't much care for her either. She was a handsome woman a lot closer to thirty than he was, with curly hair and curves everywhere else too. A real hard worker, she scratched something from almost nothing without drying up. A plump pink breast flopped in his face, the nipple grazing his nose. Plenty of Josie Fields to make a man feel like a man, even if the man wasn't sure anymore. But marry? Josie was somewhere to hide from haints and ghosts asking him to *have mercy*, somewhere to feel good for a moment. Marriage and love and till death do you part, that was something else. Didn't he regret every time he'd been with her? How would he stand her their whole lives?

Truth be told, May Ellen still had her hands all over his heart.

"You promised." Josie pulled away. Their sweaty skin stuck together. She had to peel herself off him.

"You really want to go through with that?" Aidan scratched his chin at Josie's nodding head and pinched lips. What woman in her right mind would say yes to marrying Crazy Coop? "I'm good for a song and a roll in the hay, but everybody know only my mule, my Princess, can stand me over the long haul." He laughed. Josie didn't. She must be in a real fix, if he was the only one who could get her out. "May Ellen divorced me for *extreme cruelty and drunkenness*. The judge declared her a saint for putting up with me as long as she did."

"I've seen how you are drunk."

"No, you haven't," Aidan snarled. Josie flinched and he gulped down rage. "Judge say, praise the Lord there ain't no children."

Her cow eyes bulged, like she'd seen a haint. "You trying to wheedle out of marrying me?" She looked ready to cry. Splotches of red spread 'cross her face, belly, and thighs. Hot shame flowed over him. Josie dragged strands of her hair into a knot at her neck. "Everybody say you ain't worth a damn to yourself or nobody else."

Aidan couldn't deny this. He just shook his head at her.

"Why you like this?" Josie grabbed at her clothes.

Before he could say *I ain't never marrying again* he remembered the child coming. "You don't know who the daddy is, do you?" He stuck his legs into dirty pants and ripped the seam at the crotch.

Josie held her head high. "Something spooked you last night. I didn't see nothing, but you did. That's when you broke out the jug, so you wouldn't see nothing else." She pulled on her drawers under a stained and tattered skirt.

"They lynched a colored fellow over in Greenville," Aidan said.

"Did you go watch?" She tottered out the bedroom.

"No." Aidan jumped up and followed her. "Harry Evans did. He had a burnt piece of that poor fellow and was showing it 'round."

"Maybe that ole sly darky got what he deserve," Josie said. "You don't know."

"Who deserve that? Huh? HUH?"

She waved her hands for him to stop.

His mouth went dry but he couldn't stop. "You know Harry. Harry usually like him a good lynching. He was in that posse what strung up Garnett Phipps."

"How you know that?" Josie eyed him, her brows wrinkled, her lips trembling. "*Nobody* know who did that."

He grimaced. "After strutting 'round last evening with his souvenir, Harry, he—he wasn't right. Spooked his horse and had to walk five miles home and he come hollering in the door and then he took a knife to his mother-loving eye. He say haints were crawling in his skull and he aimed to dig 'em out. Threatened to stab anybody who come near him. Doc Johnson had to watch him bleed."

"Hush!" Josie shouted and startled Aidan quiet. "Who want to hear all that? You gonna spook yourself. I'm sorry I said anything. I just want to know if you a man of your word, if you a decent man."

Aidan's legs were just as sturdy as butter. *Anybody, please. Somebody do right.* He held on to the stove. *Have mercy.* "So when you want to tie this knot?"

Josie trembled. Tears shimmered at the corner of her eyes as she pulled on her boots. "What you think of a week from tomorrow?"

"So quick?"

"Ma wants me out the house as soon as—"

"What the hell? I can do a week."

"I want to hurry the wedding up so the baby won't be born with a cloud of sin over his innocent head."

"The cloud of sin is over us."

"I don't want to be living up under my mama another minute." She trotted 'round his kitchen, poking and prying like it was hers already. "Is this beat-up ole box what you call a coffee grinder?" Josie filled it with beans. "Won't take long to get the wedding arranged."

Aidan nodded. "Well . . ." Something fluttered from her skirt pocket to the ground. He scooped it up before she could. "What's this?" *AIDAN* had been scrawled in what might have been blood on a scrap of cotton.

"Give it to me." Josie glared at him, eagle eyes now.

"This ain't blood from a wound, is it?" Aidan shuddered. The cloth felt hot. He almost dropped it.

She held out her hand. "I tole you, I ain't seen blood for two months."

He placed the frayed cotton on her palm. "You trying to hoodoo me?"

She stuffed it in her pocket. "If I am"—she moved close, lifted her face, exposing a blotchy throat—"it ain't working. Spell s'posed to drive a man crazy with love."

"Love from a spell ain't love from the heart."

"Uh-huh." Josie quivered but didn't crack.

"Truth sound mean, but . . ." Aidan sighed. It was too late to take anything back. "Well, I can't do much to make ready for a wedding. I gotta be gone for a few days."

Josie hunched her shoulders and turned away. "Fine. I'll take care of the fixings." Grinding the coffee, she threw her whole body into each turn, her head bobbing like a purple swamp hen skipping 'cross lily pads.

"You a strong woman," he muttered.

She grunted at this.

He really did admire her spirit. Maybe he could find love somewhere between them. "You ever seen those swamp birds, underneath all this blue and purple glory, they got big yellow clown feet, so they don't sink when they run on water?"

"What you talking?" The crank moved along smooth. She grabbed a bucket from by the washbasin. "I'll bring in some fresh water." She sauntered past him without meeting his eyes, acting like she didn't want him 'round his own house. "Go where you gotta go, just get on back here on time."

"I will do."

Two hours later, with a banjo slung over his back and a shoulder bag of books banging his side, Aidan set out on Princess for the Oke-fenokee Swamp.

Even with the sun heading down, it was too hot to see straight. George was still going too fast for Redwood to keep track of skittish moss and roots or even how to find her way home. After three hours of them wandering and backtracking she was lost. The smoke from a pork barbecue filled her mouth with a good taste. She wondered if the people doing the roasting were hospitable souls who might set a plate for two strangers. She swallowed a touch of sadness. This was Saturday evening, and most young folk were sneaking out for music and dancing and maybe loving or whatever you wanted to call that burning itch that didn't make you want to scratch but—

"Where are them no-good sons of guns? You see how late it's getting?" Up ahead in a clearing, Iona Richards was stowing jugs of moonshine under a bench and cussing and spitting. She was a big-boned, big-bellied woman in her forties. Everybody said she wore brogans from the Civil War and a rag on her head from Africa. Iona had married Uncle Ladd's second cousin Leroy who hid a still somewhere.

Aidan bought jugs from him. Sheriff had run Iona and Leroy from 'round Peach Grove way. Redwood heard tell they were hiding in the swamp. So this was where George was marching down secret paths to—a good-time gathering before he took off bird hunting.

"Damn guitar-playing con men! I hope they hit Hell hard!" Iona cussed more than anybody Redwood knew, 'cept maybe Aidan.

Lanterns hanging from the pine trees weren't burning yet, just waiting on the dark to do their magic. The ground was mostly needles and very springy. A barbecued hog steamed and smoked from a shallow pit. Iona's twin boys sat at a table eating the first corn on the cob. Sweet potatoes, greens, boiled onions, corn bread, and hoppin' John made Redwood's mouth water. George paused and grinned.

"S'posed to be here an hour ago. When I see those no-good sweet-talking singers"—Iona held up a big knife—"I'm goin' skin 'em, starting in the middle." She went at the hog, slicing off slabs, cutting expertly to the bone. George stood behind her, laughing. Iona slugged him in the chest. "I got a tent if it rains, the best moonshine for miles. Who's goin' resist my chicken, my gravy and biscuits, my black-eyed peas and rice?"

"Nobody." George smirked at Redwood and licked his lips. Hoppin' John was his favorite. A skillet at the edge of the cook fire spit chicken fat at them. "I heard my sister's stomach growling half an hour ago."

"Yeah," Redwood said.

"Them guitar-playing fools best not cross me," Iona said.

"You paid those rascals a little something in advance." George chuckled.

"Not much. Just to sweeten the deal." Iona shook her head. "If I don't have bluesmen to get the fever up . . ."

"You get my fever up every time I'm—"

"Shush. What if Leroy heard you talking nonsense?"

Redwood turned from their teasing. The sun was an ember on the horizon. But dark night doused that so quickly, Redwood gasped. A silver mist hugged the ground. She shrugged off her pack and dropped onto a bench. Sitting, her swollen feet throbbed. The rash on her tiddies flared up, but she didn't want to scratch now. She'd make a poultice if Iona would let her at a cook fire. Hunger churned up her belly and she didn't have a nickel. She munched a dry biscuit from her pack. A crowd of young folk and a few gray hairs strolled in on the fog, smiling, slapping bugs. None of them touched the food, despite their hungry hound-dog looks. Fog curled 'round itchy feet. Redwood smiled as they danced a moment with the rising dew.

Iona shook her head and whispered to George. "Why pay hard-earned money to be eating and drinking if there's no good music to make it go down?"

"You always worry, but they'll get here," George said. "These fancy men got to stroll in late. It makes 'em sound better if everybody's been waiting and waiting."

A chill breeze from the east had Redwood shivering. She drew the air slowly over her tongue and then spit it out quickly. "Something bad happened near here."

"Oh yeah. Ha ha ha!" Iona had a gunfire laugh, shoot you right down if you weren't steady. "You ain't heard?"

"No, ma'am. We been on the road all day, missed the news," Redwood said.

"That's right." George didn't look eager to hear.

"Sheriff took a knife and stab his eye, screaming 'bout spooks and haints chasing after him. Bled to death on the kitchen table in his nightshirt." Iona doubled up in another guffaw. "If ain't no music, I guess we can dance to that." She made a ghoul face and flapped broad arms, doing her best spook imitation. She stomped and cavorted through her reluctant customers and 'round the barbecue pit, laughing herself to tears.

Nobody joined in. Sheriff Harry had never been a friend to colored folk, and him going by his own hand was something to celebrate, but dangerous spirits on the prowl was bad news. Haints didn't mind what color folks' skin was before raising havoc with their lives.

"Haints won't chase you if you stop *believing* in 'em," Redwood said. Twenty heads turned to gawk at her. George groaned.

Iona quit laughing. "What you know 'bout haints, gal?" Everybody stared now.

"Devil at the crossroads teach you what you want to know: dancing, storying. Mama told me—"

"That's my little sister." George sounded proud, but cut her off all the same. "She know something 'bout everything."

"Is that right?" Beatrice, her skirt riding up her hip, made eyes at George and sashayed over to Redwood. When did she show up? "It's what you don't know that'll get you, gal." She talked like she knew the secrets of life or at least something juicy Redwood ought to know.

"So tell me what's what. 'Cause I'd tell you," Redwood said.

Beatrice puffed out her lips, shook her head, and sauntered away. The dust she raised stung Redwood's nostrils.

"Where you get off, bumble Bea?" Iona winked at George. "Switching your behind in front of us that way?"

"How do, Miz Iona. How do, George." Beatrice flounced over to her best friend, Fanny, who was leaning against a dead pine tree, pouting. Fanny was sweet on Bubba Jackson, but he wouldn't look at her no more. He had his cap set for Beatrice. Of course Beatrice was chasing after George. And George didn't really want any gal from 'round Peach Grove. He wasn't in love with nobody but hisself.

Aidan Cooper was Redwood's secret friend. She could slip off to see him anytime, and they could talk everything to each other and not worry. That counted for a lot, but she didn't have somebody *special*, somebody to make her heart dance. She sighed. Didn't Aidan *believe* in her though, like a shooting star streaking through the night *believed* in light? Redwood caught a melody from the wind. She couldn't have told you where the words come from:

> *I got a man say he love me true*
> *He is watery deep like the sea and blue*
> *I got a man sail in with the tide*
> *Ain't looking for a knot let alone a bride*

A fellow she'd never seen before, wispy as a dragonfly and midnight dark, joined her, playing spoons. Another fellow strode up close with hazel eyes, a washbasin chest, and fat melon cheeks as he blew a jug. She remembered him from a year ago, a northerner, name of Eddie who sneered at her little tiddies. A third man with a ragged scar on his jaw and burn marks on his hands pulled a guitar from under his arm and found Redwood's key: Milton, who'd played with Bert Williams and was marked up a bit since last she saw him. Iona's husband, Leroy, stood behind them with a shotgun. His face was twisting and twitching like always, but he nodded at Redwood's singing. Couples were dancing the needles and dirt to a dusty haze. George clapped his hands and winced in pain. He tapped his feet and chortled at Redwood who found another verse. She remembered now. Aidan wrote this song for a gal to sing, but Redwood wouldn't do it with him when he asked her. She'd learned it on the sly though.

> *I got a man say he ride the sky*
> *He do what he do and won't tell you a lie*
> *I got a man say he home on time*
> *He just ain't gonna say if his home be mine*

Singing as if possessed by the Holy Ghost, Redwood squinted through heavy-lidded eyes. Couples doing bird dances floated by her. Feathers sprouted on their necks and down their spines, ending in a flourish of flashy tail plumes. Bubba Jackson was a colossal dragonfly with bulging apple eyes and gauzy wings. He buzzed toward hummingbird Beatrice, but butterfly Fanny snatched him. They flitted off between jackrabbits, waddling pigs, and monster grasshoppers springing up to the treetops. Guitar-playing Milton was a great blackbird warbling sweet nonsense as he plucked a giant harp with crystal strings. Redwood was a flash of lightning, sizzling through the mist. She hadn't done heavy conjuring since before Mama went to Glory—or no, since she caught that storm with Aidan.

"Cut it out." Dragon George was breathing fire and singed Redwood's eyelashes. He grabbed her with scaly claws and shook her till her bones rattled. "What's a matter with you? Mama said don't play with lightning. You 'llowed to burn yourself up." *Now* he was talking 'bout what Mama used to say. "You could do something you can't undo!"

That scared Redwood for sure. She opened her eyes wide and the bird, bug, and animal shapes faded into regular people who were so drunk on the music, they didn't even notice the difference. After a last snort of smoke, George let her go, and Redwood made up a new verse for Aidan's song:

I got a man say he b'lieve in me
Gonna find a way for us both to be free
Hope's a canoe, take us far from here
Where a man can be a man without no fear

George looked at Redwood like his heart would bust, like for once she knew something good. Iona crossed her arms over her chest and glowered at Redwood and the tardy bluesmen as the song ended and the crowd cheered. "You know, I don't pay you for carrying on with tone-deaf drifters who can't tell time, Red. But you and your brother can eat all you want and spend the night in a bed."

"Thank you, ma'am," Redwood said, thrilled not to be sleeping on hard ground. She looked triumphantly to George, but he wasn't paying her no mind.

"You're the gal what hoodooed that bear." Guitar-playing Milton grinned, stomped his foot, and picked out a new melody. "What can you sing to this?"

"Sorry, Miz Iona. You know I don't carry a piece of time 'round with me," said Eddie before whistling in his jug. "Carrying too many tunes." He shot a furtive look at Leroy, who still cradled the shotgun in his arm.

"How you miss the sun going down? Strut in any later, I wouldn't be paying you at all." Iona was smiling though. People flooded in from every direction plunking down dimes, eating and dancing. A nickel only get you one swallow of hooch—Iona's twin boys were so stingy when they poured, you had to spend a dollar to feel good. A man could spend a month's wages and go broke in a heartbeat.

Iona squeezed Redwood's arm. "You sound grand. A voice for Saturday night and to praise the Lord on Sunday."

Everybody nodded at this, including George. The dragon fire was gone from his breath. Beatrice threaded her fingers through George's, and Redwood winced. There was never anybody special for her to dance with. Boys didn't talk to Redwood or even let her catch their eyes—probably 'fraid she'd hoodoo 'em. Nobody at Iona's dared to look Redwood in the face, 'cept one gal who wasn't right in the head. Rebecca was tall, had big feet like Redwood, and stood alone shivering under a tree. Not much of a dancer, she come to hear the blues.

Rebecca grinned a mouth full of crooked, chipped teeth. Her clapping was off the beat. Redwood felt bad for them both and sang on the new melody:

> *How do you miss the ole sun going down*
> *Any later, don't bother coming 'round*

As the music picked up, Beatrice and George were dancing just for each other.

FOUR

Okefenokee Swamp, Georgia, 1903

Bumping along on Princess, more sober than he cared to be, Aidan watched a fire-haint dash through swamp grass, cross black water, and charge between the bulging knees of cypress trees. The haint's feet were flames, burning the ground. Its head was smoke, its heart a red-hot coal, its eyes cold blue light. Gaping at the burning figure, Princess stopped so fast Aidan flew over her ears into decaying water lilies and mushy cypress skeletons. The fall should have broke his neck, but he spit muck from his mouth, wiped slime from his eyes, and stood up slow, not a break or a crack anywhere. His banjo and shoulder bag hung from a tree limb that had reached out to catch his precious possessions. Miracles and demons, everywhere he turned, should've scared him—just made him sad, made him thirsty. He'd resolved not to drag a jug on this journey no matter what might come out to torment him. He regretted that now.

The haint's trail of smoke and fire vanished in the distance. A breeze sighed through the grass. Aidan squinted; Princess cocked her ears. The haint was gone. All he could see was shadows chasing each other between the trees.

"I'll be damned." He grabbed his things from the obliging limb. "Didn't want to stick 'round and spook us, huh?" Dizzy, Aidan wobbled back to Princess. The hummock of land quaking beneath his feet threw his balance off. "Feel the ground shifting under us? A sign." He rubbed Princess's neck; she whinnied a heehaw against his shoulder. "Maybe that was a lonely haint having a look-see, a nosy fellow wondering what we're up to."

Aidan didn't know what else might spook them, but he wasn't heading back home, back to Josie. Not yet. Troubling visions followed him everywhere. No escape, 'cept if he crawled into a jug of hooch. "I got medicine to ward off evil spirits." He clutched his alligator pouch and surveyed the scattering of tree islands, joggling in front of him. "And when a place call to you, you just gotta go."

Aidan closed his eyes and let the ground rock him. A great, great, great *Maskóki* Creek ancestor was born on a floating island of peat in the swamp and took the name, Okefenokee or Trembling Earth, at least that's the tale his daddy told at midsummer harvest, the day of the green corn ceremony. Even far from his first home, way upstate in the Blue Ridge Mountains, Aidan's daddy made sure people took time to celebrate first fruits, light new fires, and forgive what could be forgiven. Aidan's mother made Aidan promise to never forget hisself so much that he couldn't do this too. No surprise wedding, no drunken stupor, no blazing haint would stop him celebrating a new year.

Princess had her nose in Aidan's armpit, nudging and nipping him. She whinnied in his ear, fearful still. "That ghost ain't studying us no more." Aidan rubbed the white feather on her forehead. "See." He led her to the footsteps of the fire-haint. Purple flowers sprouted from the ashes of burnt weeds. Princess nosed a few and sneezed. Aidan shook his head. "Am I driving you crazy too?" Princess licked his hand as he pressed one of the purple fire-flowers between the middle pages of his journal.

The canoe was where Aidan hid it last year and looked in good shape. Cypress wood took a couple lifetimes to rot. Furry critters scurried into the brush when he turned it right side up. A close inspection revealed no damage. He cleaned it out quick and then stripped down to skin. Princess stomped his soggy clothes into the ground.

"You're right. We got to clear out the old time. It's a brand-new year."

He wiped the swamp from his skin and smeared on a bear grease concoction to protect against chiggers, ticks, and mosquitoes. Donning a clean white shirt and a fine pair of pants, he pulled his hair back and wrapped purple and orange cloth 'round his head to hold it down. Princess grinned at his handsome new get-up and lifted her tail high. In a corral he built a few years ago, she had rain-trough water plus feed and grass for two days, maybe three. If she got desperate, wouldn't be much trouble to break out and head home. She'd done that before.

"You'll be all right and I'll be back soon anyhow." He held out a green apple. She shrugged pesky flies off her skin, flicked her velvet ears at him, and snorted. "You know you like apples." She gobbled the fruit from his hand and licked his fingers. He slid the canoe into thick black water and jumped in. The gentle swell of the swampy current rocked him into a good mood before he'd even left the shore. He tuned up his banjo and played. Couldn't remember the last time he'd done that. An hour slipped by with him floating in his music and going nowhere at all. That suited Princess just fine.

Aidan marveled at the sounds his fingers pulled from the banjo. He didn't hear melodies in his head like some folks. He *felt* a song on his tongue or dancing through his hands. Playing a familiar tune was as much a surprise as doing a brand-new one. He recalled being frustrated as a boy, 'cause he could never play anything the same way twice. That didn't bother him anymore. Each moment had its own good music, and when his fingers found the right tune, the right harmony, nothing else mattered—for a while at least. The music coming to him now was whirlwind and storm clouds.

A voice joined in, bold as a lightning strike. Aidan almost pitched out of the canoe. He damped the banjo strings and tracked laughter coming through the trees to the shore.

"Mr. Aidan Cooper, you running off to somewhere grand?"

Redwood Phipps broke through a curtain of Spanish moss. Her braids were coming undone and her cheeks glistened with sweat. She looked to have grown an inch since he saw her two weeks ago. All legs and getting so pretty she was a danger to herself.

"Dressed up in your Sunday best." She beamed at him.

He smiled back at her. "How'd you find me?"

"Playing that banjo is as good as leaving a trail."

"I ain't played for a while, worried I forgot how."

"No, sir! And who could miss your rainbow turban."

"Indeed." Aidan touched his headdress, embarrassed. How did he look to her?

"I got a strand of your hair." Redwood unraveled a long black curl. "I conjured you, a boat, and a song with it."

"Did you now? I got my own magic too, you know."

"Yeah?" Redwood looked stunned.

He flushed with heat. "I got a new year to welcome, my own good story to tell."

"I know that," she said quickly, a child one moment, a grown woman the next. She laid her face against Princess's neck and stroked the mule's nose. "To tell you the truth, I'm lost. My brother run off without me, hunting plumes."

"Egrets getting scarce." Aidan held his temper. "Babies got no parents."

"I found this hair back a ways. Heard the music, so I hoped it was you." She hiked up her skirt and strode through the water toward him, but stopped short of the boat, staring at a silver snake swimming by her feet. "Take me with you."

"I'll be gone a couple days."

"Suits me fine."

Aidan scanned the shore. Redwood was too old to be horsing 'round with a grown man. What if somebody saw them and spilled their secret? George would be thundering mad if he found out—course he did run off and leave her. Miz Elisa would be glad Aidan had an eye out for her niece. Miz Garnett might rest easier too.

"Please," Redwood said. "I won't be no trouble."

She was always good company, a candle in the dark, the sweet little sister he never had. This surely was no hardship for Aidan. And didn't he need family to celebrate first corn? He grabbed a low hanging bough and held the boat steady for her.

"Well, get on in, gal, if you coming."

Aidan's canoe cut 'cross dark water, overturning shiny green lily pads to reveal purplish-red underbellies. Redwood let her oar hover over a dense mat of swollen bladderworts. Yellow flowers on long stalks grew out from a wheel of feathery inflated leaves. Inside these air bubbles was a trap for bugs who might wander in but would never break out again.

"Look, over there. Parrot pitcher plants coming out the peat moss." Aidan pointed to bright red flowers hanging like Japanese lanterns over deadly curling leaves—*pitchers* filled with sweet-smelling poison and shaped like the beak of a bird.

"Oh." Redwood watched a green-eyed fly slide down to its death.

"Cut open all that pretty and what you goin' find? Beetle skeletons."

"Bug-eating poison plants make powerful hoodoo healing."

Aidan had promised to help her get every root and herb Miz Subie could possibly want—in the swamp and all the way back to Peach Grove. Redwood chuckled to herself. George would come charging into their soggy camp with a sack of bloody bird plumes on his shoulder and a smirk all over his face, but Redwood would be long gone. He wouldn't be able to track her through water. He wouldn't get to gloat at her returning to Miz Subie's empty-handed. He wouldn't get to say she was cut out for school teaching, not hunting roots for hoodoo spells. Maybe he'd even worry hisself sick for leaving her with an order not to wander far and a promise to return soon.

"This ain't no sightseeing tour. You gotta earn your passage." Aidan splashed water on her neck. He eyed the shore, still nervous that someone might catch them. "Paddle, gal."

"I am." She splashed water back at him.

Two otters playing in the mud at the riverbank stopped to watch the canoe glide by. They nosed the air and barked. Redwood waved, and the sleek creatures dove into the water, chasing after them.

"They're sure happy to see us," she said.

"We're churning up dinner for 'em," Aidan replied.

"They on the menu too." She pointed at gator eyes floating along the far shore.

"Don't fall out, you look right tasty yourself."

"You been saying that to me since forever. I'm a grown woman now. Gator think twice 'fore snapping at me."

Aidan swallowed a laugh. "Grown? And you ain't scared of nothing, huh?"

"No, sir! Not a bobcat, bear, or gator."

"Them bobcats and bears probably listen to reason, but there are other wild critters afoot who ain't so civilized." Aidan sounded ominous. "You better turn 'round and watch where you going."

Redwood ducked as they passed under a funky vine that climbed up a bush and crossed a narrow stretch of water to the limb of a giant tupelo tree on the other side. Muted bronze flowers smelled like something dead for a long while. Confused flies buzzed over the blossoms, hunting for a corpse.

"Greenbrier," Aidan said to her wrinkled-up nose. "I know Miz

Subie want that. And some swamp iris root." He plucked a violet blossom.

They floated through a corridor of tall iris stalks. Most of the flowers had gone by. Only a few flashy trumpets were left.

"The roots be poison if you take too much, but just enough, clean you out real good." He stuck the flower in her hair.

"That's Indian medicine." Redwood turned again and gazed at him. "You certainly look handsome today."

"Not my usual raggedy self."

"I'm not making fun."

Hot blood under his burnished skin made him look even more handsome.

"I'm glad we're friends," she said.

"Are you?" His moss-colored eyes looked more watery than usual, weary and sad.

She touched his knee. He flinched, and she drew her hand away. "Whatever's ailing you is getting worse!" She still didn't know how to take the trick off him or George. Subie say that would require a mighty spell that 'llowed to kill anyone who worked it.

"I'm getting married again," he said. "Next week." The boat wobbled and pitched.

"Really?" She turned away and paddled furiously. "Nobody tells me nothing."

"Just decided. You the first person I tole, besides *her* of course." His paddling barely kept them from ramming a row of tree stumps where a gator lay sunning. "I asked you to celebrate first fruits with me. Never did that with nobody else, 'cept my folks. I'll even tell you the story Daddy used to tell for the new year, when I was a boy, up north in the Blue Ridge Mountains."

"Next week? Who is she? You ain't said a word 'bout somebody *special*."

"Josie Fields." Aidan stammered something else Redwood couldn't understand.

"Josie Fields? That blotchy woman with the orange hair and big tiddies?"

Aidan almost laughed. "Red hair."

Redwood shook her head. "Miz Subie done help that gal out of trouble twice, but say a third time might mess her up inside, so she give her a love potion."

Aidan bristled. "You ought not judge Josie for going with different men."

"You always sticking up for loose women. Why is that?" she asked. Aidan was quiet for a good stretch. Redwood's arms were getting tired. "I don't know where I am anymore. How far we got to go?"

"A ways. Loose women ain't no worse than me. Loving is a good thing."

Redwood thought on this and forgot her aching muscles. She grinned. Crazy Coop wasn't just known for his wild drinking. "All right, still Josie ain't got nothing in her head but . . . she think *darkies bring her good luck.*" That caught Aidan's breath. "How *she* goin' make you happy?" Redwood fought a stab of jealousy. Everybody had somebody, 'cept her. "I want you to find a good woman, not just any ole body."

They passed fields of tall grass speckled with bright splashes of wildflowers. A bear with a star scar on its cheek stood on hind legs scratching its belly and butt. It darted at the water and held up a fish to them. Aidan gurgled at him, doing passable bear talk.

"Don't you have a heart's desire?" she said. "Don't you just want to do something grand? Go out in the world and make a bright destiny?"

Aidan laughed, a bitterroot sound, too much like George. "I don't think that way no more."

"Why not? You a white man. Can't nobody 'round here stop you dreaming, 'cept your own ornery self." She smacked a vine grabbing for her face. "Well, am I lying?"

Aidan jammed his paddle at dark water, thrusting it from side to side so fast his hands blurred. They raced down the winding stream and careened 'round a curve into a sandbar. The boat rocked and pitched, but didn't throw them out. Soaked in funky sweat, Aidan wheezed and licked his lips. "You don't know what you talking 'bout."

"I know you buying too many jugs and marrying a fool," Redwood said.

"Spitting at a fire won't put it out." He shook his body and closed his eyes. "You can't think I like how . . . how . . ."

"Does Josie know 'bout you?"

"What you mean?"

"She ought to know what she's getting into." Redwood smacked the sandbar. "You a magic man, and—"

A cloud of no-see-um blood suckers attacked, buzzing in her nose, ears, and eyes, stinging and chewing at her. She was too mad to ward them off 'cept with flailing arms. The fierce little critters just bit her hands too. If the canoe hadn't been wedged between some rocks, she would've tipped it over fighting and fussing. She glared at Aidan. The no-see-ums weren't bothering him at all.

"Come on," he said calmly to her wild hands and choked screams. "We don't want to be stuck here. Help me."

Aidan back-paddled and despite her ears, eyes, and throat trying to swell shut, Redwood pushed against the crumbly sandbar. The canoe slid into the flow of the current again. As they moved downstream, the bugs abandoned her and returned to their sand heap. She snorted and dug a tenacious varmint from her nose. After dabbing Miz Subie's cure-all on the bites and swelling, she paddled silently with Aidan.

The sun dipped below the trees. Redwood caught sight of two otters still trailing them, then thought they might have been floating branches or fish feeding at the surface. She touched bleary eyes and lips. The burning and itching had faded, 'cept for the inside of one nostril. The bag of roots Miz Subie gave her to ward off no-see-ums and stinging demons hung 'round her neck where it should have been earlier. She squeezed it.

"Miz Subie say I could work out an understanding with chiggers, mosquitoes, and whatnot; then I wouldn't need funky bear grease or nasty herbs," Redwood said.

"I could use such a fine trick too," Aidan said.

"Can't get it to work for myself. Don't know if I could do it for someone else. I think you gotta work out your own understanding."

"I suspect that's true."

"What you thinking back there all this time?"

His steady stroke slowed. "It's a new year." She felt his hot breath against her sweaty neck. "I thought you might could do a spell for me so that tying the knot would go better this time than last." He gulped more air. "Help get me right."

"Oh, did you now?"

Aidan drank too much, and that brought on an evil temper. Not in front of Redwood, but she'd heard wild stories of him cussing, busting up furniture, breaking down doors, and punching men to bloody pulp. Say something out of the way to him, no telling what he might do. No woman wanted to stay married to that.

"Miz Subie the one to go to for miracles," Redwood said.

"That bad, I need a miracle?" Aidan said, mad or hurt or both.

Why was she always throwing dirt in a wound? "I'm just a beginner."

"Ha! You the one snatching storms."

"That one time, which don't mean I can do everything! I caught it *with you.* Don't really know how we did that." She turned 'round. He still looked wounded, despite her offering him credit. She couldn't stand that. "I'll do what I can," she murmured.

"Thank you, ma'am."

Aidan guided the canoe into a side stream that was nothing more than a trickle of mud. She stuck her finger in and touched bottom. Snarled roots scraped at the boat—there was hardly any water to paddle. Aidan had just the right touch though. After half an hour the stream forked into three directions and they came to a hummock that was more sizeable than the mounds of floating grass they'd passed. Perched several feet off the ground in the center of this island was a hut with a cypress log frame and palmetto thatch roof. Guarding the entrance was a tupelo branch strung with colored glass and a stump carved into the head of a bear. All 'cross the island, every color of wildflower greeted them with waves of scent, spicy and sweet. Poles carved in the shape of lightning bolts with tattered flags on top marked the four directions. Two otters barked a welcome and dove in the water.

"They followed us all the way." So much beauty made Redwood's heart pound. Tears clouded her eyes as she turned to Aidan. He navigated the boat into a rickety U-shaped pier that crawled out the mud onto more solid ground.

"You know, I'm glad we're friends too," he said, cheeks pink with embarrassment.

"Did you do all this?" She wiped her eyes quickly.

"Yes, ma'am." He was proud. "Been coming here since I was thirteen. Hauled in all the fixings, a bit here, a little there." He held the boat still, and she stepped ashore, unsteady on her feet.

"Why you hiding such a place in the middle of a dank stream?"

Aidan shrugged, hopped onto the pier, and tied off the canoe. "You hungry? I got a few green apples in my pack." He strode by her, his banjo buzzing against his back.

"I'll eat when you eat." Redwood stopped at the bear head. She touched its nose with her fingers. "Going without food make your spell stronger, right?"

"You don't have to go hungry, too."

"I want to start over with you. I'll do what you do. I'll help you clear out last year's dirt. I'll . . . Watery crossroads is a good place to begin. Who all we got to forgive?"

"Everything apart from rape and murder." Aidan shuddered.

"That's a tall order."

He set down his things and looked her up and down. She held still, staring back at him, trying to see what was what, trying to see who he really was. Powerful spirits were right at his shoulder, but she couldn't make out how they looked, whether they brought good signs or ill ones. She reached her storm hand to his heart and touched him before he could back away.

"Let's not fight no more," she said.

He eased her hand away from his chest, but kept it clutched in his. "The Master of Breath blows fire through your spirit," he said and led her toward the hut.

"Mama used to say, 'You a hoodoo child. You can do a spell to make the world you want.'"

"You sound just like Miz Garnett." His chest heaved saying her mama's name.

"You miss her too, don't you?"

"I got too many people to miss."

The ground rolled under their feet. They teetered and pitched and got all tangled up in one another. With the earth still quaking, they finally lost balance and fell onto springy moss. Redwood giggled. Aidan was so still and solemn underneath her that she tickled his chin, till laughter rolled through their bellies, till tears flooded their faces. Redwood didn't know why she was crying. Aidan looked surprised at his tears too. He shook his head, flinging salty drops this way and that, and then he hugged her close.

"Josie tried to hoodoo me into marrying her. I ain't bound, but I won't run off."

"But if Josie be working a trick on you and you don't really love her—"

"I gotta forgive her and *do right* like the spirits say, so—"

"So, I gotta forgive everybody for being scared of me and George for leaving me and being mad all the time?"

"Yes," Aidan replied soberly.

"I guess if you can *do right* by Josie, well, I'll try." Redwood stood up and offered Aidan a hand. The quizzical expression on his face made her feel foolish, but before she could snatch her hand away, he gripped her palm and she pulled him up.

The broom was just raising dust and not cleaning anything. Redwood wanted a bucket of fresh water, a good brush, and some of Miz Subie's lily of the valley soap. She surveyed the windswept room. Heavy canvas curtains (walls?) were rolled up into the rafters. Wood was arranged like a wheel in a stone fire pit at the center of the hut—a *chickee,* Aidan called it. Bright new banners at the four directions flapped in a stiff breeze. A storm was coming and blowing dirt over everything again.

"I'm not doing no good here," she said.

The colored glass on the tupelo branch tinkled sweet music.

"I need to get new bottles for the bottle tree . . . All the evil spirits they done caught, just busted 'em up." Aidan was on the roof repairing a hole.

"No good a-tall."

"What you say?" He jumped down behind her. "Been all alone here the other times," he said. "It's . . . it's better with you."

"So tell me that tale your daddy used to tell when you was a boy up in the Blue Ridge Mountains." Aidan's stories were almost as good as Uncle Ladd's, but she always had to coax and plead and beg for any little thing. "No more stalling. You promised."

Panic painted his cheeks.

"It's our secret," Redwood whispered in his ear, "and you know I can keep it."

Aidan stared at her again as if trying to look through her skin. "I wrote the story down in my journal, how my daddy used to tell it." He pulled a red leather book from his shoulder bag. "Let me read that to you, so I get it right."

A TIME BEFORE THIS TIME

Trembling Earth was a mighty warrior, tall like the mountains and wise like a river searching from the deepest forest to the sea. Born on a floating island in a southern swamp, he took the name Okefenokee or Trembling Earth as we say nowadays. Beautiful tattoos told of valor and wisdom from bold youth into full manhood. He wrapped his long hair in a topknot. Arrows thrust this way and that through the silky weave called to mind an osprey's nest. Trembling Earth's bow, made from a supple sapling, was taller than most warriors, taller than the pale men who came at him with smoking fire sticks. No warrior, living or in legend, matched his strength or his courage. He shot an arrow up in the mist and it did not return, but flew to the ancestors, proclaiming all was in balance in the world.

For how long?

The day Trembling Earth's dreamtime and lifetime crossed, the day of his destiny, was midsummer like today, the day of the green corn ceremony, the day to celebrate first fruits, the time to light a new fire and forgive what could be forgiven. Dawn was breaking, the sun a violet promise in the mist as Trembling Earth strode through the houses of his village to the temple dome. The sacred fire was cold from last night, its one cold night of the year. Old debts and grudges were put aside as villagers awaited the new flame.

Bright Spear, a War Chief who hated losing games to Trembling Earth, offered him medicine stones filled with the lightning that had shattered a tree. Bright Spear's nostrils flared, his lips trembled. They'd caught him lying about his exploits in battle and warping other warriors' bows before the games. Bright Spear wanted only another chance to fight and defeat real enemies, yet who would ever follow him again in war or even games? Instead of gloating, Trembling Earth gave him healing roots, bitter bark that eased old pain, and his mighty bow. Bright Spear tried not to accept the bow. Trembling Earth insisted. Was it not Bright Spear's cunning that had saved them in battle many times? Would it not be so again?

Women's talk and children's laughter filled the air. Trembling Earth still felt the sting of his rival's arrow in his thigh. He stumbled and limped as old pain flared. Moon Shadow, the woman he loved, loved another—Silver Fish. Who could deny it? Trembling Earth saw the lovers as he approached the temple mound. He offered them deerskin and precious dyes, then tried to smile on their happiness. They nodded as if his jealousy had never been; as if he had never chased Silver Fish into the sea; as if Moon Shadow had not thrust her body between Trembling Earth's knife and Silver Fish's throat. Trembling Earth turned away from the two lovers. That time was gone. No one should let yesterday use up too much of today.

Easy to say, hard to live.

Blue Eagle, the Peace Chief, wore egret feathers, black and blue pearls, and his face was painted ochre and vermilion. Trembling Earth stopped before him. Here was the true challenge of the day, of his life. Peace was the answer to his prayers. To save the people—all that they had been and could become—he must lead them from their beloved land to a new place, far from the pale invaders with their fire sticks and deadly sickness erupting on anyone they touched.

Once, long ago, Blue Eagle sang of finding a new land and making new allies, but these days he feared the War Chiefs who grew stronger with each successful raid on ancient enemies. Blue Eagle had lost his true power. The way of peace was muddy and confused. The people had turned a deaf ear to his song until he changed the tune and sang their fears. Just yesterday, Blue Eagle spoke against joining with foreign villages, against joining with ancient enemies who were not his people and did not speak his tongue, who did not know his dance or remember his ancestors. "A new enemy should not make us forget old ones." He warned against traveling to distant lands filled with spirits no one would know how to appease. Blue Eagle said, "We should not leave the lush land of our sacred fire."

Trembling Earth pulled the long arrows from his top-knot and laid down his jagged stone knife. He asked all for forgiveness for the many wrongs he had done. He offered forgiveness to those who had wronged him. He gave meat and new corn to any who were hungry. He sang to those whose hearts ached with fear of tomorrow and offered the dream that had come to him whenever the moon faded to a ghostly shadow in the night sky. Many gathered to listen to Trembling Earth. He was a mighty warrior unafraid of death, and he loved the people.

"The battle for tomorrow requires cunning and wisdom," he said. "In my dream travels, the people crossed the land and the small waters and they gathered with old enemies to forgive what could be forgiven and then together they made a long walk into the grassy water. There they lived together as one free people, *istî siminolî,* long after the invaders had come and gone."

Blue Eagle said, "We are undefeated. Why should we run away like cowards?"

"Who do we vanquish? Villages who have few warriors left because they have fallen to the pale men with their fire sticks? And these brave few are covered in boils and pus and can barely run or raise a spear or bend a bow! We are not mighty warriors, only lucky fools who prey on weakness and disease that will come to claim us too."

Blue Eagle tried to protest, but no words came to him.

Trembling Earth continued, "I will be a War Chief no more. Any who follow me in the last journey of my life, they follow peace."

Trembling Earth's mother had been a captive three times. A powerful medicine woman, she had escaped from enemy camps in distant worlds and, running through forests and swamps, always returned to the people. She said, "I will follow my son."

Silver Fish, the rival he had tried to kill, and Moon Shadow, the woman he once loved more than life, said, "We will follow Trembling Earth."

Bright Spear turned to the other War Chiefs and said, "We have followed Trembling Earth many times in games and in battles, let us follow him into tomorrow."

In a village house behind them, a newborn sang his first song.

Blue Eagle asked, "And if that place is the land of the dead?"

"We will die free people," Trembling Earth replied and lit the sacred fire anew.

"Istî siminoli," Aidan whispered. The journal trembled in his hands. "Free people."

Night had fallen in the middle of his tale, and now black clouds rolled over the rising moon and stars. It was too dim in the hut to read. Aidan must have spoken the last words from his heart.

"What a beautiful story, like out of a book." Redwood was buzzing and tingling, as if lightning flared under her skin. *"Istî siminoli."* She repeated Trembling Earth's phrase. "Freedom always feels good in your mouth." She could just make out Aidan as he nodded.

"Storying and thinking on the new year is a free feeling," he said.

"When you're spinning a yarn, you sound different, somebody else altogether."

"I get my daddy's voice in me."

"Your daddy knew a lot of Indians up in the mountains?" she asked, hoping he'd tell more of where he come from, who his people were: Creek, Cherokee, Seminole?

"Uh, he sure did." Aidan set the journal down. "Wherever you go in these United States, there are . . . Indian ancestors afoot, and, well, they come sometimes to talk to us who be living here and now." He was holding something back, she could smell it, and here she thought they could tell each other anything.

"Wish I could hear that," she said.

"They talk to everybody." Aidan tweaked her nose, like she was a little bit, still. "Listen hard enough, underneath a sigh, at the end of a breeze, you catch an echo."

"Were they wise and true?"

"No more than you or me."

"But they got that long view."

"Now they do. Cherokee Will says, 'We are the ancestors of generations yet unborn.'"

"Yeah, but who ever listen to what he say?" She felt Aidan bristle, so she quickly added, "Couple generations out, nothing but lost souls."

He snorted. "Do you really believe that?"

"Cherokee Will never let you forget he used to *own* colored folk. Well, his papa did, when Will was a boy, way back before the war."

"Before white people stole the land and marched most of the five tribes to death on the way to Oklahoma. So all Cherokee Will got now is memory holding up his spirit."

Lightning streaked 'cross the sky, and it was suddenly bright as day. Thunder rumbled. Dead stalks rode blasts of wind through the hut. The storm was fixing to roll over them. Aidan quickly unfurled canvas walls from the rafters and tied them off at the floor. He pulled a bedroll from under the rooftop too. The rain could have been a stampede of wild animals charging 'cross the meadow right at them. Redwood bit her fingertip, anticipating the worst. A hefty gust of the storm slammed into the heavy cloth. Buckets of water pounded against the roof, yet not a drip come through onto their heads. After several minutes of ramming in vain, even the wind backed off.

"Dead folk always leave something behind, a trail. They ain't really lost to you," Aidan said.

"I know. Like how Mama still come to talk to you sometimes."

He winced and choked. Took a moment to get his breath in order. When he finally spoke he was hoarse. "Miz Garnett say, Write yourself down, Aidan. Keep good counsel with your ownself. That's a powerful spell, a hoodoo trick for what ails you." Without another word, he raced out the hut, 'cross the shallow stream, and disappeared into the high grass meadow—gone before Redwood could blink the dark clear.

"You ain't goin' tell me where you going," she yelled. "Or when you coming back?"

Rain beat against the roof and ran down the canvas walls in a steady rhythm. After ten minutes, not seeing nor hearing any sign of Aidan, Redwood tore off her itchy clothes and darted out into the downpour. The cool water cleared the last of her rash away. It felt so good she laughed out loud. Shivering in the chilly wind and fearful that Aidan might return any moment and catch her naked, she dashed back into the hut.

The darkness was so deep she almost fell in the fire pit groping for her pack. After rubbing her skin with oil, she searched for the clean blouse and skirt she'd stowed for the journey home. The clothes got all tangled up and inside out—enough to make you give up on getting dressed. She was glad Aidan was taking his sweet time out there.

"What's he goin' see in the dark?"

Aidan didn't have to take forever though. She thought of George worrying on her in the middle of this storm. She was high and dry, and he was probably cold and soaked through and mad as the devil cursing heaven. She tucked the blouse in her skirt.

"Serve him right, but I forgive him."

She oiled and brushed her hair, platting it carefully. After setting the swamp iris in the swirl of a braid, she sat by the stone fire pit to wait for Aidan's return. Lightning flashed every few moments. In between booming thunder, owls hooted. A cat growled right outside the canvas wall, a big ole panther, not a shy bobcat. Redwood stiffened. Fear crept in the small of her back and slid up her spine. Something bigger still on the other side of the stream gurgled and grunted. Heavy footfalls shook the ground. The island rocked worse than a boat on the sea. She held her breath. The panther fussed and then took off. A bear poked his nose then a claw through the entrance. Might have been a gray scar on his cheek, a twinkling star.

"I know you, bear," she said. "Go on now and leave me be." The funky animal stared right at her, waiting on something else. "I thank you for scaring off trouble."

He loped away and the storm died down. Redwood peered outside, but wasn't nothing to see 'cept more darkness. She kept looking anyhow. Yellow eyes sitting above her caught a distant light. She heard somebody running and panting. A bright red jewel broke through rainy gloom heading for her.

"Aidan?"

He raced toward the stream with a burning bough in his hand. The torch smoked and sputtered in a cascade of rain. He looked spooky and glorious, a night demon. Redwood's heart fluttered fast, dragonfly wings in her chest. She swept back the canvas to let him in.

"Is that fire from the sky? From the lightning?"

Aidan nodded and thrust the torch into the wheel of wood in the stone fireplace. After a few moments of sputtering, a blaze for the new year leapt up at him. Redwood dropped down in front of the dancing flames. Aidan sat beside her, soaking wet and shivering. He sang words in a language she didn't understand and put his arm 'round her. She hummed a harmony to keep his music company.

"*Go n-eírí an bóthar leat.* Irish talk," he said. "A prayer my mama used to say."

"What?"

"May the road rise up to meet you. May the wind always be at your back. May the sun shine warm upon your face and rains fall soft upon your fields. And until we meet again, may God hold you in the palm of His hand." The lilt to his speech was something Redwood only heard him do now and again. It was a good sound and she leaned into it.

"You got a lot of fine voices in you," she said.

"The trick is to listen to 'em."

"*Go n-eírí an bóthar leat.*" Redwood tried the Irish talk. "I feel new and free, like in Okefenokee's dream."

"Do you now?" He smiled.

She took a deep breath of him and tasted pain and longing and love. "We should be heading out like the Indian ancestors till we find what we're looking for."

He laughed, bitterroot and sweet. "When you want to go?"

"Right now!" she said. Aidan kept laughing, but here was a chance to take the trick off him, before she scared herself out of it. Didn't she feel power between them? Crossroads power. So for the first time since the family was on the run and Mama went to Glory, Redwood decided to *conjure herself somewhere else.* This was a spell powerful enough to heal any sick body. Mama said, *Time don't go nowhere. What happened before, what might happen, is always with us, hiding between our heart-beats.* Redwood breathed in the fire of a new year—lightning Aidan had snatched from the sky. She leaned her warmth into his chilly fever. He leaned right into her. She hummed a Sea Island melody, crossing their spirits, riding all the roads at once, looking for a place they both might dream of and then they were in—

"Chicago!" a red-bearded white man yelled to a mixed crowd of wide-eyed spectators who stood on a sidewalk that moved on its own. "Where else?"

Aidan blinked in strange light. Strings of electric lightbulbs turned the dark into twilight. A roving searchlight illuminated a dazzling White City. Greek temples, enormous towers, and giant onion-domed castles loomed over him and Redwood. Fountains spit torrents of water into the air. Gondolas glided 'cross a man-made lake ringed by statues of muscular gods, goddesses, and winged fairy creatures. Fireworks exploded 'cross the sky like colorful flowers going to seed. Underneath a rainbow shower of sparks, a colossal plum lightbulb floated in the sky. The flame under its narrow neck was too weak to light the massive bulb head. Watching it sway back and forth, Aidan was dizzy.

"I want to ride the hot-air balloon," a little boy shouted.

"Ahh." Aidan squinted till he could make out a large basket below the flame filled with passengers squealing in fright or delight. Dizzy again, he leaned over the water.

Redwood thumped his back. "You all right?" she asked.

"Getting there."

Gas torches and electric lights glinted in dark, choppy waves, as if thousands of jewels had been tossed in for good luck. Aidan stood up straight and tried to look every which way at once. Redwood was also busy gaping at first one wonder, then the next. Her mouth hung open. She was as surprised as he was.

"I'll be damned," he said for both of them.

"Hush your mouth." A tall, light-skinned colored woman in fancy dress pulled her two daughters close to her.

"Sorry, ma'am." Aidan clamped his lips shut and eyed the gargantuan wheel turning in the distance behind the woman and her children. The wheel was as big as a mountain. He counted thirty-six coaches hung 'round its outer rim. "What you do, gal? Take us into the future?" He thought of H. G. Wells's fantastic novel.

"No, this is 1893, ten years behind us. I can't believe we're really here."

"I can." Aidan was iron certain that he and Redwood were here somewhere and back in his *chickee* too—a bit of ground fog from the swamp clung to her feet. They were now and then and as real as anybody hearing, smelling, and seeing them would believe. Despite a flicker of irritation, he smiled at Redwood, a powerful medicine woman like her mama. His daddy say that some folks have grace and know how to step into a vision, a dream or—"Just, where exactly is here?"

"The Columbian World Exposition in Chicago!" She grabbed him. "Isn't it exciting? Don't be scared."

He didn't know how to be scared of what was happening. "You might've asked me if I wanted to come."

"I didn't leave you in the dark without a word, did I?" She let go of him. "What if you never come back and I was lost in the swamp with panthers and bears afoot?"

"You said nothing scared you. Besides, my bad manners don't excuse yours."

"It's a *get-well* spell."

"So I can't be mad?" Aidan shook his head. "Sweet roots can make bitter medicine."

"We can't stay long out our own time. Let's don't waste the time we got fighting."

A group of very dark colored folk, men and women dressed in the wildest fashion Aidan had ever seen, split in two to walk past him and Redwood. They strolled close enough for him to taste their breath. Colorful woven fabrics draped over their bodies swished and billowed. Pounds of beads and hammered gold jewelry hung on their necks, waists, arms, and ankles. Aidan wasn't sure what their headdresses were made of.

Might've been their own hair done up in geometrical designs. Talking to one another over his head, they passed little songs of meaning back and forth. These fine ladies and gentlemen could've come from out of this world for all he knew. Aidan stifled a gasp, then took a deep breath. They smelled like a field of spices, hot peppers and ginger. He stared at bright eyes and white teeth. Redwood nodded how a civilized person ought to. The foreigners nodded back.

"I bet they're royalty from Africa, Dahomey or Abyssinia," Redwood said when they had passed. "They came from their castles in a great ship 'cross the ocean."

Aidan never imagined royalty in Africa, let alone castles and certainly not ordinary people who looked so grand. "What if they're regular folk just come to the Fair?"

"You mean same as you and me?" Redwood was thrilled by this notion. She strode 'round him, claiming every inch of her tall bones, taking every breath like a free woman. "Can't believe your eyes, huh?"

"Of course I do," Aidan said. Did she think he was just a backwoods cracker with no sense? He spied a bright yellow bead on the ground that must have fallen from a necklace. He scooped it up and stuffed it in his pocket.

"I want to ride the big Ferris Wheel and see from up high what I done heard Mama and Daddy speak of. What do you want to see?"

"Well . . ." When Doc Johnson told Aidan of traveling to the big Chicago Fair, Aidan had been too drunk to pay much attention.

"Chicago's the fastest growing city in the country," a huckster shouted. "A world of tomorrow right here for you today! Step on up to the Hall of Electricity!"

"In there," Aidan said.

He and Redwood marched with a herd of people into a building that looked to be made of light. Millions of electric bulbs flashed at them, each as bright as the lightning in the Georgia swamp. Marvelous contraptions on every surface of the pavilion buzzed and churned. Singers and musicians had been captured in boxes and on discs, and their music was blared back through gleaming brass horns to eager listeners. Stations were set up to watch moving pictures through peepholes. One counter displayed a row of electric fans. Whirring blades chopped the air into energetic gusts and cooled the hot spectators. Aidan lifted his damp arms up to the strong currents.

"So much, and I ain't never seen the like," he said.

She smiled. "I knew if I got you somewhere else."

"Y'all ain't seen nothing yet," a dapper colored man proclaimed, "till you make it to the Midway. Have you been there?"

"Let's hurry." Redwood pulled Aidan back through the dazzling lights, past a statue of Benjamin Franklin, and outside again. "'Fore we have to go home."

"How long is that?" Aidan could have paid Electricity a good long visit.

"Every minute is stolen, a heartbeat snatched from somewhere else."

He didn't like the sound of that, but didn't press her for details. She dashed off, and he followed. They raced through a blur of people from all over the US of A and the whole world, too, sporting fine clothes and cheerful moods. They rushed by pavilions devoted to mines, transportation, and horticulture; past a Women's Building and a Fine Arts Palace; but despite golden arch doorways, beckoning goddesses, and wondrous machines and inventions defying time and space, they didn't take a moment to step inside any of these astounding exhibitions. Redwood was hell-bent on the big wheel.

Out the corner of his eye, a faint shadow dogged his heels. Aidan spied ghostly flames licking at the White City and turning its awe-inspiring beauty first angry red and then black and gray. Ashes and soot obscured his view for a moment.

"This whole place burns down, you know." Redwood read his mind. "We couldn't go see these fairgrounds in our time, even if we wanted to."

"That's a real shame." Aidan groaned. "So we're running through a ghost town." No wonder they couldn't linger.

A hot-air balloon landed gentle as a feather in front of them. The passengers applauded.

"We've reached the Midway Plaisance," Redwood said.

"Ah, my good chap, the attractions here are very expensive." A shady man with a slippery accent leaned close to Aidan. The man's boots were outsize, and his coat was a costume for a minstrel show, one showy patch atop another: stage rags. "Cost two dollars to do a Balloon Ascension.

But for one dollar and ten cents you could let your pretty lady sample all the features of Cairo Street."

"The Ferris Wheel is only fifty cents," Redwood said. "Course, I don't have a nickel, but a walk through Egypt . . ."

"One spin 'round is all you get on the wheel, Cairo's a whole street of thrills and wonders." This man was slimier than a slug. He reached for Redwood.

Aidan pulled her away and dug in his pockets. He had four silver dollars and two dimes. "It's the wheel or Cairo Street. I ain't got enough for both."

"Hold your money," she whispered.

"You goin' hoodoo your way in?" Aidan smiled.

"It works sometimes at the county fair."

The slug-man slithered over to several smart-looking white patrons. Aidan and Redwood approached the high wooden gate to Cairo Street. Two guards taking money were ready to holler something at Aidan, but missed that train of thought when a fancy white man, his wife, and seven kids mobbed them. The guards had to do the addition before accepting the man's ten-dollar gold piece. Redwood caught their roving eyes and fixed them on shiny river-bottom stones called from the mist lurking at her feet. Staring at this wonder, they didn't blink at Redwood or Aidan striding through the gate toward the Egyptian temple.

"What you say!" he gasped.

The street was jammed. A camel belched and hissed at a dark-skinned boy in its way. Between the animal's small humps a plump man sat muttering and chewing. "No more rides today," he said to Aidan's curious look.

"Outrageous." A white woman yelled over strange music that Aidan had never heard before. "No prayers, no wedding, not even a camel ride, what did we pay for?"

Jugglers tossed flaming sticks in the air. Snake charmers serenaded their sleepy charges—creatures so big and thick, they could strangle a full-grown bull. Wranglers corralled camels who spat and pissed as a stout fellow in billowing pants gobbled down fire and blew it behind his back to the delight of several little colored boys.

Redwood danced to the odd music. "I feel like I've been here, from all the stories I heard from Mama and Daddy."

"This your first trip, in the flesh?"

"Mm-hmm, with you, Mr. Aidan Cooper, for good luck. A *tonic* spell."

Aidan was stunned and touched. "You shouldn't have."

Not more than a foot in front of him, three olive-skinned Egyptian gals shook their tiddies and bellies, and scandalized or charmed gawking spectators. The Egyptian ladies wore colorful ballooning skirts and short, flimsy blouses. Strands of beads, coins, and silky rope bounced against their chests. Silver chains clanged below naked belly buttons as they stirred their hips 'round a sultry beat played on hourglass drums. Tambourines and stringed instruments that were close cousins to the banjo filled out the sound and held the mood high. Folks hollered in a dozen languages at rippling bellies and bold behinds. Redwood squealed in delight with 'most everyone else and then mimicked the dance in front of Aidan. He admired her talent in picking up the steps and even more how good she looked shimmy-shaking.

He grinned. "Better watch who you do that for."

Redwood had her hands on her hips. "Why is that?"

"It's indecent," a woman said and stormed away.

Redwood laughed and pulled Aidan closer to the music. The dancers circled them, rippling hand gestures inviting her to join in. She glanced at Aidan, shy for a moment.

"The music's already in you, gal, nothing to do but step on out," he said.

She danced with the Egyptian ladies like she was born to the moves. So fearless and powerful—it was quite a spectacle, enough to make your nature rise.

"Last call," a voice over a loudspeaker proclaimed, and Redwood had Aidan running for the Ferris Wheel. They raced in front of Buffalo Bill's Wild West Pavilion, and Aidan stopped dead in his tracks. He peered in the tent as Redwood dashed on ahead. A trampled feather headdress lay in the dirt, a Lakota war bonnet or some such. An old man swept the feathers away. He looked colored *and* Indian too. Aidan plucked a feather from the dirt.

The old man paused. "The Chief took a nasty spill, chasing down the wagon train."

"Is that the show?" Aidan wondered who the old man's people were, what story he might tell, but he didn't have the nerve to ask none of that.

"Cowboys and *Injuns* are all gone for the night, son. Come back tomorrow."

Aidan didn't move.

The old man waved him on. "Go on before you lose your friend."

Each car of the Ferris Wheel held sixty people, old and young, fat and bony, foreigners and native born. It made six stops before doing a spin without stopping. Aidan was almost beyond taking in another wonder of the world. In the car's close quarters, folks were eyeing him and Redwood. He wasn't sure why. He paid a silver dollar for the ride—no hoodooing. Colored folk in their car sat right next to white. There were several people who could've been anything under the sun. Aidan glowered at a mean-looking Oriental fellow till the man showed all his teeth and turned away.

"Chicago won't ever be the same," a man with a German accent spoke right to Aidan. "She is a world city now."

"Look!" Redwood gripped his arm. "Sitting on top of the world, with fireworks going off."

Aidan could've stuck his hand through the window and touched sparks. White buildings with Greek columns and half-naked gods and goddesses glistened in splashes of color. The crowd below roared, a great beast bragging over a juicy feast.

"This has certainly been a tonic," Aidan declared. "I feel grand."

Redwood smirked triumphantly. "What'd I tell you?"

"Sometimes I get so tangled up in . . . gnarled roots, last year's bad harvest, or haints spooking through stalks and weeds . . . I can't see further than the next row to hoe, and I don't feel a damn thing other than real bad." What possessed him to say this out loud? He certainly hadn't meant to cuss at her.

"I know." Redwood nodded solemnly. "Me too."

"You? Naw. You only saying that to keep company with my misery."

"Well, I know we can get ourselves to the other side of sad." She had a smile to break even an ornery man's heart. "Didn't you say you were feeling grand right now?"

Everybody in the car turned to hear what he would say.

"Can't deny it."

She hugged him close and tight, then whispered, "This is our secret. Magic we make together. You can't tell nobody. Promise."

"Who'd believe me anyhow?"

The Ferris Wheel spun down and just when Aidan thought to wonder how they'd ever get back home from Chicago, Redwood leaned into him and opened her eyes wide as the sky. Silvery fireworks flashed one last time—a bolt of jagged lightning frozen in inky clouds, like a spark caught in a giant lightbulb. And then they were sitting again in his *chickee* in the swamp. Aidan wrinkled his nose at ashes floating on the air. Lightning had set dry underbrush ablaze but left the tall pines standing. He stroked the bead and feather in his pocket, relieved to touch proof.

"What you mean, magic we make together?" Aidan had a mountain of questions, but Redwood was so tuckered out, she fell over into his lap. Looking at her droopy eyes, he didn't have the heart to press her.

"Don't worry," she mumbled. "I just need to rest up."

Despite a rumbling stomach, she only managed a mouthful of beans and a biscuit. She slept through red wolves hollering at each other, a barred owl barking, and a stag crashing in the brush. She slept most of the bumpy canoe ride down creeks swollen from the storm, waking when he stopped to collect the plants she needed for Miz Subie.

"Ain't you sweet," she said as he filled her bag.

"Least I can do after such a powerful *get-well* spell."

"You *believing* made it easy. Never stayed away so long, not even with Mama."

"Now you tell me," he said. "Maybe we stole too many heartbeats."

"I'm fine." She clutched his arm. "And you're well then?"

He didn't know 'bout that. "I do feel better than I have for . . . years. You're a tonic for my spirit, Miz Redwood, like the balm of Gilead. I'll be owing you for a while."

"No. Sing me something good, with that lilt you can do. Then we're even."

A verse from an old Irish song his mother used to sing came to him:

Love is a fever that can't be cured
Woe to him who bears it night and day
For its knot binds tight and it never can be loosed
And my own dear comrade, may you fare well

Redwood's fingers danced in the air. She murmured nonsense, almost in harmony with his melody, then dropped back to dreams.

As they left the fire forest behind, Aidan spit the smoky taste from his mouth. The sun slid down slow, but the heat wasn't going nowhere. Seeing Aidan come downstream, Princess brayed and whinnied so loud, they must've heard her all over the county. Redwood didn't rouse till he shook her shoulders hard for a solid minute. Dream-talking, she stumbled out of the boat and Aidan had to heave her onto Princess's back. He jumped up behind her and Redwood slumped back against his chest. She passed out again, sleeping so deep she barely took a breath. Nothing he did woke her up.

Doc Johnson had gone off to Atlanta. Aidan cussed Doc's empty house. Miz Subie wasn't at home when they stopped at her house. What if Redwood didn't wake up on her own? What if something was really wrong? What if she stole too many heartbeats staying away too long and didn't want to tell him?

Princess turned down the old oak lane toward his place.

"Whoa, sweetheart, not that way. Ain't going home yet." He dismounted and Princess blew her lips at him. "Going to Ladd and Elisa's. I'll walk and give you a rest." Redwood slumped against Princess's neck, but didn't fall off. Aidan brushed soggy hair from her face and wiped cold sweat from her neck. She sighed at his gentle touch, a peaceful smile curling on her lips. "We got to carry Miz Redwood to the front door. Don't think we can trust her sleepwalking on shaky legs."

Princess butted her nose into his ribs. He pulled the last bit of apple from his pocket. She gobbled it up in a flash. They ambled along, not fast, not slow. Reluctant *and* anxious, Aidan didn't relish walking into Ladd and Elisa's yard, didn't relish walking into their questions. George would have a burr under his butt, but Aidan hoped *somebody* would know how to wake Redwood or tell him that sleeping so deep was fine. Course then there was Josie 'round the next bend of his life. Marrying her wouldn't set the world right, wouldn't make nobody happy even. Josie was settling for him, and he was a falling-down drunk fool, playacting the man of honor.

With a quarter mile to go, little Iris come dashing for him. George was a few steps behind. "Crazy Coop," Iris yelled. She turned and slugged her brother. "Didn't I say they was coming this way?" She jumped into Aidan's arms. "I knew it, I knew it."

Aidan swung her high in the air. "You been riding that pig?" he said as she wrapped sticky hands 'round his neck and he got a good whiff of her. The tattered green frock she wore was covered in slop, as if she'd been *rolling* with the pigs.

"Raccoon got in the pigpen, and I had to get her out 'fore she got hurt," Iris said.

"Well, of course." Aidan smiled, despite worry tightening his chest.

"Red!" George tried to rouse his sister to no avail.

"You smell of swamp and sparks in the sky." Iris squeezed Aidan. "I knew it."

George was ready to breathe fire. "What's a matter with her?"

"I don't know." Aidan set Iris down. She held on to his hand. "I wish I did."

George shook Redwood's shoulder roughly. "She was fine when I . . . left her."

"She found me after . . . you went bird hunting, and then . . ." Aidan didn't know what to say. "She just won't wake up."

"That was three days ago," George said.

"What you say?"

"What you been doing all this time?" George shouted, and then the whole family come charging down the road, raising a cloud of dust. Ladd, Elisa, and the five cousins wore sweaty work clothes like they'd just run out the fields. Miz Subie followed at a slower pace, stepping proud with a carved walking staff, like those folks from Africa at the Fair. She wore a green silk head rag, and a blue medicine bag dangled from her waist. Princess brayed at so many strange people rushing for her.

"Whoa, whoa, they're friendly," Aidan said. Princess wasn't convinced. Snatching Redwood from her back, George looked evil as sin.

Princess wanted to kick him. She wasn't the only one. Aidan rubbed her nose to keep them both calm, but it didn't help.

"They was worried," Iris whispered to Aidan. "I knew Sister was fine with you."

"I don't know that." George staggered down the road away from Aidan with Redwood's head bobbing against his shoulder. The five cousins ran after them. Aidan's heart wrenched, parting from her like this after all they'd been through.

"What did Crazy Coop do to her?" one of the cousins asked. Aidan could never keep their names straight. He always mixed up Becky and Ruby and called Jessie, Tom or Bill, and vice versa.

"Lay her down under that tree." Subie pointed to a battered old oak. "She need fresh air."

"So what *have* you been doing all this time?" Elisa planted herself in front of Aidan, her jaw jutting out like a blade. She pulled a resisting Iris away from him as if he was a poison weed.

"Spit it out. It ain't goin' get no easier, the longer you wait." Ladd was toting a shotgun and an evil look too. He stood up straight to Aidan, no jigging and cooning for once. "You ain't gone deaf, man. You hear me talking."

Subie tugged at Ladd's gun arm. "Give him a chance."

Ladd marched back and forth, barely holding his temper. Streaks of salt on his dark skin made his lean face resemble a skeleton mask. Aidan glanced over to the cousins. Even Becky and Ruby were grinding their teeth and spitting anger with each breath. They must have all been thinking the worst.

Subie calmed Princess with a few tugs on her ears. "Tell us what you can, Mr. Cooper." She fixed him in her eye.

"It's Aidan, ma'am, and we uh . . ."

Subie nodded. "Traveled a long way, huh?"

"Yes, ma'am, that's it and uh . . . her heart's barely beating, just a faint thump every now and then, and . . ." Aidan had promised not to tell. The Chicago Fair seemed to be a dream or drunken phantasm, and 'cept for a bead and feathers from a Wild West Show, what did he have to show for their adventure? "Stolen heartbeats, don't you know."

Subie nodded her head. "I see." Nobody else did from the scowls on their faces, 'cept for little Iris. Subie dug through her blue medicine bag and pulled out swamp iris root and something Aidan didn't recognize. "Get me some hot water." She waved at the cousins. Becky or Ruby hurried off to oblige her.

George settled Redwood down carefully. "I ain't done nothing but worry since . . ."

"She ain't bleeding." Iris sat in the dirt beside her and babbled away. "She ain't hurt, I tell you. She goin' wake up when she done resting."

"You don't say." Elisa put a shawl under Redwood's head.

Iris touched Redwood's brow. "She just be tired in her heart spirit. A traveler coming home though." Iris was a hoodoo, like her sister, like her mama, snatching truth out of nowhere. She spooked folks sometimes, saying things a little child shouldn't. They'd be more spooked to hear what trick Redwood played.

Ladd stopped stamping back and forth and set the shotgun in the shade. Princess was in a fine mood, nibbling something from Subie's hand.

George didn't let up though. "You don't have no better tale to tell?"

"Lightning set a fire downstream. Maybe she swallowed too much smoke and—" Aidan wanted to say Redwood hoodooed her ownself. He wanted to ask George why he run off and leave his sister alone in the swamp. But he wasn't feeling his usual Irish temper and couldn't get any mean, fighting talk out. Same as when he and Redwood were trading words over Cherokee Will in the *chickee*. He hadn't mentioned the colored folk who bought and sold each other during slavery times and who were, to this very day, richer than he ever hoped to be on land Indians once roamed. He didn't have a taste for fighting low with anybody over old history and skin. He just wanted to see Redwood through. This was a new year.

"A little smoke done this to her and not you?" George needed one of Redwood's *tonic* spells. Anger was 'bout to bust the veins in his skull. He was powerful built, almost as tall as Aidan and thicker. His muscles looked cut from dark stone. And George wanted to be mad at Aidan or any white man within a hundred miles of his sister. "You just goin' stand there, staring at me like a damn fool, when I'm asking you a civilized question? My sister gone missing for three days!"

"Three days?" Aidan scratched his jaw. "I reckon I lost a day somewhere."

"I reckon you goin' lose some more days if—"

"Hush George," Ladd said. His nephew fumed, but didn't finish the threat.

Subie dug in Redwood's canvas bag. "She found all the roots I asked for and then some. That's more than a week of work in three days." She peered at Aidan with her blind eye.

"You know how she is," Aidan said.

"Redwood got a talent for getting herself into sticky situations," Ladd said.

Subie listened to Redwood's breath. "That's right. She ain't Mr. Cooper's fault."

"The child don't know better," Elisa said.

"Child? Redwood's a grown woman, Aunt." George snorted. "She better start knowing better."

"How? She built how she built, and people just take advantage of her good nature." Elisa glanced sideways at Aidan. "*We* got to look out for her."

"That's what I'm trying to do here," George said.

"Mr. Cooper ain't have to bring her back if he meant any harm," Iris said.

"Red is headstrong and reckless." Everybody nodded at that. "Something real bad is bound to happen to her. Can't y'all see that?" George balled his fists. He was sweating and spitting mad over the principle, over all the bad that could have happened to her.

"I ain't fighting you, George," Aidan said. They'd been friends once, when they were younger and Aidan was sober. He and George would go off hunting or just drifting in a canoe to anywhere. *Before.* "*She* would never forgive either one of us for acting foolish."

"Redwood or Mama?" Iris said.

"What you talking? You don't even remember Mama," George said.

"Yes I do!" Iris stamped her feet. "I do too. Don't say I don't."

Everybody looked awkward and jittery, as if Iris and Aidan too, had called up a haint. Princess walked close to George and licked his fists. George backed away.

"Why you mad at Crazy Coop?" Iris said. "You know he ain't done nothing to Sis."

George cooled a bit. "I'm just mad, I guess."

"You goin' be a rich man now, all the feathers you sold. You don't have to be mad at what you ain't got." Iris turned away from him and chattered in Redwood's ear. "I missed you. I sure would've liked to take a ride on the big wheel too. I found a baby raccoon, and Uncle Ladd said I could feed her and keep her till she big enough to fend for herself. You gotta hurry on and wake up soon and see her."

Redwood shifted in the dirt; her fingers grasped at something, and then her eyes fluttered open. She squeezed Iris's hand. "A raccoon?" she murmured.

"You know the right spell to call a body back, chile," Subie said.

Redwood's eyes darted this way and that, and she smiled at everybody hovering over her. George sniffled and snorted like he was swallowing down something nasty. Elisa pressed her fist against her lips, and Ladd patted his wife's back. The cousins jumped up and down, squealing and cheering till Elisa hushed them.

"Where you been?" Iris asked.

"I was riding a shooting star," Redwood murmured. She sounded hoarse. "Chasing 'round the world through the night sky."

"Were you now?" Subie laid wrinkled hands on Redwood's face and neck.

"Baby Sister talking scared away a haint on my tail." Redwood stared up at Aidan and set his heart to pounding. "Mostly blue smoke and red fire eyes."

He nodded at this, and Subie poured a brew down Redwood's throat before she could say any more. Redwood coughed and sputtered and then closed her eyes again.

"Her heart's coming on real strong." Miz Subie shook her walking stick at the whole family. "Ain't no use y'all standing here wasting daylight. Go on 'bout your business. She goin' come back full on her time."

"You know what's what, Miz Subie." Ladd signaled everybody to go.

"Thank you, Mr. Cooper, for having an eye out." Elisa herded the cousins down the dusty road. She halted and turned back to Aidan. "Come by for a proper visit."

"Thank you, ma'am." His voice cracked, but he sputtered on, "I surely will."

"Come on, please. PLEASE." Iris pulled George toward the shed.

"I've seen that pest how many darn times?" he said, following her inside though.

Alone, Subie eyed Aidan, sucked her teeth, and shook her head. "How far you two go to be needing stolen heartbeats?"

Aidan sighed. "I promised Red not to say."

"Uh-huh," Subie muttered. "I do like a man who can keep his word, but you need to head on home now."

"I can't, not till I know if she—"

"She goin' be doing fine. And that's God's truth."

"I don't doubt you, ma'am." Aidan couldn't move.

"She need all her power for herself right now." Subie patted Aidan's face. "Don't worry. She'll sing at your wedding. Go on now."

Aidan raised an eyebrow at what Subie shouldn't have known, 'less Josie was talking all over town already. He wanted to ask 'bout that and 'bout Red riding shooting stars, but Miz Subie's milky eye was twitching and flashing so he heaved hisself onto Princess's back. He tasted dirt on his tongue; heavy blood pounded against his skull. What desperate future was he riding into? "I'll be seeing you then."

Iris scurried from the shed, holding a baby raccoon up to him. "George gotta say she uglier than sin. What you think?"

Aidan leaned down to get a good look. It was a scrawny, mangy creature with a smashed-in face and delicate, hand-like paws. "George got a good eye," he said, "but she'll look better after awhile, after you take good care."

"I'm goin' call her Cairo, like the street," Iris said, hugging the creature to her face.

Aidan sat up straight, a chill spooking through him. "That's a fine name, but I believe Cairo's a city in Egypt."

Princess tugged him away. She wanted to get home even if he didn't.

BOOK II

The one who tells the stories rules the world.

—Hopi proverb

BOOK II

FIVE

Peach Grove, 1904

Wade in the water
See those children dressed in black
God's gonna trouble the water
They come a long way and they ain't going back

Redwood mouthed the words with the church choir, leaving a hole in the soprano section. Last time she really sang full out was over a year ago at Aidan's wedding. She sang herself hoarse then. Standing next to his bride, listening to this very hymn, the poor man looked ready to cry, or maybe he was just realizing what *doing right* by Josie Fields meant. Redwood wasn't good for nothing for a month afterward.

Wade in the water
Jordan's water is chilly and cold
God's gonna trouble the water
It chills the body, but not the soul

A November chill had taken up residence in Redwood's lungs, and it didn't matter how many coats or scarves she wrapped up in. Since Halloween, her arms and legs had been tingling something terrible, prickly fireworks going off under her skin. Her mind was feverish too, wandering like a creek through a swamp, not settling anywhere long.

Wade in the water
Some say Peter, some say Paul
God's gonna trouble the water
Ain't but one God made us all

The choir director cut them off at the last chorus. The sopranos sank down on their benches, jostling and poking her. Scrubbing his bald head with a red handkerchief, the choir director fretted at the piano over the wrong notes they'd been singing. Redwood sighed. She'd only had one song in her today—"I'll Overcome Someday." The sopranos had to fend for themselves for the rest of the service. Rev. Washington cleared his throat, swallowing the taste of bad music, then he railed against moonshine and lazy, good-for-nothing Negroes who thought the world owed 'em a living.

"Only folk I ever met expecting something for nothing was rich folk," Redwood muttered what George would say. "Poor folk know they got to break their backs taking care of themselves *and* lazy rich folk too!"

Two altos stared at Redwood who was talking loud to herself. She clamped her lips and clutched a scrap of paper that Miz Subie had passed to her in front of the church.

"I wrote a list, if ain't enough time for everything, y'all just find me some man root." Subie had hurried off before Rev. Washington saw her.

Aidan had invited Redwood for a canoe ride to his secret hut, his *chickee*, to fix new bottles in the demon-catching tree. He always took care with hoodoo rituals and helped Redwood hunt down roots for Miz Subie's spells that nobody else could find. Josie didn't know squat 'bout Redwood going in the swamp with her husband. Nobody 'cept Subie did, but that wasn't sinning if Redwood didn't lie. That was keeping a secret.

"I ain't goin' let nobody turn me around!" Rev. Washington declared. Redwood had to agree with him on that.

Wandering through the crisp Sunday morning after church, Redwood stumbled into the ruins of the Hiller plantation. Rock walls, brick chimneys, and stone foundations peeked through silvery grass and orange leaves. Trees, vines, and bushes had claimed the place. Droopy evergreens and dried-out moss looked sad. A hardy ice plant in a sunny spot was still in bloom, purple daisy faces smiling at her.

"Why you come down here? I said meet me up on the road." Aidan offered Redwood a hand up onto his Princess. "Yankee soldiers torched this place. Killed everybody. Slaves were locked up and burned to death too. Haints 'round here still be mad. Don't nobody walk this way." Aidan knew the story of every pile of rocks or stand of weeds for miles around.

"You ain't scared of those haints," Redwood said. "Me neither." She leaned against his back as they rode off. They were quiet, content to be in each other's company, but melancholy. Princess, however, was stepping high all the way to the swamp.

Rusty cypress needles rained down as a strong wind gusted through the trees. Redwood dipped her paddle in the black swamp water, dodging crimson lily pads and wispy orange leaves. Songbirds feasted on purple berries, coppery fruits, and gingery seedpods hanging from vine trellises 'cross the water. Golden grasses whistled in the breezy sunlight. They didn't see or hear another soul. (Aidan knew how to avoid any nosy body.) A sleepy-looking bear gurgled at them from a tree branch. He was munching something good. Aidan gurgled back.

"Does he have a scar on his cheek look like a star?" Redwood asked.

Aidan shrugged. "He say, we got to sing our way home. Bring some cheer to November."

"Did he now?" Redwood laughed.

After stringing up bright-colored bottles at his *chickee,* they paddled the broken glass that had *done the job* to a watery crossroads. Aidan threw the shards in the fast-moving stream and they paddled away without looking back.

On the return trip, Redwood let Aidan do all the singing, Irish ballads, blues, and songs he conjured up in the moment. His music snatched the chill out of her chest. Coming 'round the bend toward Princess's corral, Redwood's arms ached, but her breath was good enough to join in at the refrain. Coughing took over after that.

"You don't sound good," Aidan said. "You taking care of yourself?"

"Of course." Redwood swallowed a cough. "I'm just restless." The gate to the corral was wide open. Princess had gotten out. "Where your mule gone to?"

"Home I guess." Aidan looked worried.

Searching for her, they plowed through Spanish moss that had gone to seed. Tiny orange fruits had split open and spit out hairy filaments. Redwood was covered with the scratchy things and wanted to cuss. She had to blame somebody for the long trek back to Peach Grove. "Walking, we won't get home till after midnight."

"Heya now!" Cherokee Will held out sweetgrass and oats to Princess.

The mule nibbled at his hands, but every time he took hold of her bridle and hoisted hisself toward her back, she kicked her rear legs and pulled away.

"You trying to steal my mule?" Aidan said. "She don't like nobody, hardly."

"She was standing out here by herself." The old man scratched his bowlegs and fanned his white head with a straw hat. "How would I know she belong to you?"

"I see." Aidan laughed good-naturedly. "You were trying to rescue her?"

Princess nuzzled Redwood, but kept a wary eye on Cherokee Will.

"What do I need to steal your mule for?" Cherokee Will slapped the hat on his head. "Who are you calling a thief? Any direction you look, that was my daddy's place. And beyond that, all Indian land."

"We know." Aidan hushed him up before he started in 'bout slavery times and how much land and people he owned once.

"You be telling everybody all the time," Redwood said.

"I am a great elder. I am of this land. You have just arrived."

Irritated, Redwood jumped on Princess. Aidan was 'bout to leap up behind her, but Cherokee Will broke out wailing. Tears poured down his wrinkled cheeks. He tottered, as if at the edge of a cliff.

"Everybody always making fun. You too, just like the rest. Calling me a thief."

"I'm sorry." Aidan grabbed Will so he didn't fall. "What's weighing on you?"

"Jerome and Caroline Williams stole my orchard."

"How'd they do that?" Redwood said.

"I ain't the only one. Look how they done Graham Wright. His ma is Choctaw. He ain't nobody to these white folks."

"They said Graham owed taxes," Aidan said.

"I'm an old fool, but we were a mighty people once! People to be reckoned with, not people you could beat up with a tax." Will reminded her of George. "It was said, *they shall never become blue,* yet now look at me."

"I see a fine man," Aidan said. "A man full of good life."

"Do you think we'll ever be great again?" Cherokee Will gripped him. "Do I live and die to nothing?"

Aidan glanced at Redwood.

"Of course not." She sucked down a coughing fit and stared a hole in the sky. "There's a land of the future with wonders yet to be wrought, and we . . . we just ain't reached it yet, but it's coming."

"Yes," Aidan said. "When I was a boy, you told me, on the path we don't see what's ahead, but every step we take is a prayer."

"What else to say to a child?" Cherokee Will groaned.

"Every step's a spell, conjuring what's to come," Redwood said. "You're painting the next horizon for us."

Cherokee Will let go of Aidan and stumbled a step each direction. "Thank you, Mr. Cooper," he said as if Redwood hadn't spoken. "You're like a bundle carrier from the old days."

"I don't know 'bout that." Aidan leapt up on the mule.

"Wait. Don't go." Cherokee Will tromped about, gathering leaves and hairy little roots and then pulled a red moss from a ratty pouch that hung on a string at his waist. Redwood gazed at Aidan, who shrugged. Will pulled crumpled paper from his pocket and scrawled strange figures on it.

"Cherokee writing." He wrapped the words with the root medicine in a scrap of cloth. "*Sikwayi*, a great man, he invented our letters, the talking leaves. *Sikwayi* is Sequoia, your name in Cherokee." He held it out to Redwood.

"*Sikwayi*?" She hesitated from taking his offering.

"Good for women problems." Will stood up tall, a fierce fellow thrusting a medicine bag at her. "Boil and inhale smoke. You looking poorly. Cold stuck 'round your heart."

Redwood fell back into Aidan's chest. Princess whinny-heehawed and stepped toward Will. Redwood let him put the medicine in her hand. "Thank you, sir."

"You take care of yourself too," Aidan said; then they rode off.

Redwood turned to look at Will standing bent over in the bare cypress trees. "You think he'll keep our secret?" Aunt and Uncle wouldn't let her run off to the swamp with a grown man, a *married, white* man whose wife would pitch a fit if she knew. Who in colored or white Peach Grove would understand what they were to each other?

"Nobody listens to Cherokee Will, right? They don't think he knows anything."

Redwood squirmed at the bitter truth in that. "I'll be listening more from now on." She leaned against Aidan. "He's a sad man sometimes and lonely too I guess."

"Will didn't walk the deadly trail to Oklahoma. His daddy's second wife was an Irish lady."

"Like your mama."

Aidan's chest heaved against her back. "Yes."

"Please, tell me more. If it's a secret I know I can keep it."

"Shouldn't be no secret." Aidan sounded hurt and mad.

"I'm listening and I won't make fun."

On the way home Aidan told her what he knew of the Cherokee, Chickasaw, Creek, Choctaw, and Seminole, and how white men called them *civilized,* but stole their land anyway, demolished their towns and farms, and marched them to hell in Oklahoma on a trail of tears. "*Sagonege,* blue, is Cherokee color for the north, for disappointment and failure. *They shall never become blue* means good fortune always. My daddy say Georgia had a public lottery to steal Indian territory. One-hundred-sixty-acre land lots and forty-acre gold lots were given away to *citizens.* An Indian wasn't a citizen. Still ain't."

"Oh." She never much cared 'bout being a citizen. It didn't seem to do colored folks much good. "Why'd they—"

"For gold in the mountains, for cotton and corn in the fields. They stole the sunrise and the distant sea breeze. They tore the people from the place of their ancestors, leaving spirits to roam and no one to take heed."

"Mm-hmm," Redwood murmured. "I've seen them spirits sometime. Didn't know who they were, so I didn't know how to act."

"I used to think, just seeing the old ones was paying respect, but—"

"The Seminole didn't all get routed," Redwood said. "*They gathered with old enemies to forgive what could be forgiven, and then together they made a long walk into the grassy water. Isti siminoli,* they were free. I remember what you said."

"I guess you do." Aidan sounded pleased at that. "Still in Florida too."

After sneaking through plantation ruins and trotting overgrown roads, they were getting close to home. "I'll walk from here." Redwood slipped off Princess.

"The people got driven from their land only one lifetime ago, and it's all but forgotten." Aidan clutched the reins so tight, she saw ribbons of blood.

She put her hands on his. "We'll carry the story one more lifetime at least."

For the next week, using Cherokee Will's cure, Redwood got a little better. When the medicine was gone, she was coughing up a storm and so hoarse she didn't talk. Uncle Ladd was so frightened by the sound of her, he made her go see Doc Johnson.

"Ladd's mama died of consumption. I don't think you will," Miz Subie said when Doc threw up his hands and sent Redwood back to her. "Don't do nothing *wild* for a while. No stealing heartbeats for a sightseeing trip with Mr. Cooper. You might meet the boneyard baron and never come back. Risk yourself on something that really matters."

"Like what?"

"You'll know." She tied nine devil's shoestrings 'round Redwood's aching ankles and gave her some ole nasty tea to drink. After one swallow, Redwood was gagging and feeling worse. "It's *foot-track* magic," Miz Subie said. "I swear you done crossed your ownself. You the one got to break this spell, 'less you want to stay sick."

"Oh." No denying it, Redwood hadn't been right since *conjuring* herself and Aidan to the Chicago Fair. She come back to Georgia so restless and lonely, so full of daydreams and nightmares, she didn't know what to do. Out in the fields picking winter greens, eyes open or closed, she'd see herself dancing in bright Chicago lights. Stage houses were filled with fancy audiences from the world over. From Abyssinia and China, folks were jumping to their feet, clapping for her. An hour or two could go by with her wandering the rows of vegetables. She might pluck a few weeds, rout a slug or two, but nothing much else. Uncle Ladd tried to scold her, but Elisa would hush him up and pat Redwood's back or make her drink some of Subie's bitter tea.

"How am I ever goin' find my heart's desire in Peach Grove, Georgia?"

Auntie would nod, rub Redwood's belly with a cool cloth, but she didn't understand. Redwood wanted to do something wonderful. Didn't she have stories to tell and powerful spells to conjure? Sick folk were probably the same everywhere, but there were so many other tricks Redwood didn't know yet—like how to call up the world she see or the world she want to see. Didn't everybody say that life was short? She had to get on the road and make a bright destiny. That's what nobody could understand 'cept maybe Aidan. Nasty tea, Indian medicine, wool scarves, and devil's shoestrings wouldn't help her know how to make herself grand as those folks from Dahomey, them dancers on Cairo Street.

And today, Aunt Elisa be inviting Bubba Jackson over for Sunday supper. He'd had a change of heart 'bout Redwood, but she wasn't studying that boy. The Jackson's weren't rich colored people like the Wilsons or the Garretts, but close enough, so Elisa was wringing the necks of the fattest chickens and plucking white feathers. She had kale simmering, beans soaking, and *three* pies baking. Smokehouse bacon was sizzling in a pan. Christmas jam and pickles come up from the cellar early. Elisa made the cousins stay in their Sunday best long after church service, with a whipping promised if they cut the fool and got dirty. Redwood wore one of Mama's old dresses and pouted like she was ten. Her hips and bosom had filled out, and she cut a fine figure. That's all Bubba was after—a gal with big tiddies who didn't want him back.

"Once he gets his paws on me, he won't want me no more," Redwood said.

For once George agreed with her. "Bubba Jackson is the last person she should marry."

"Miz Subie never got a husband and she do just fine," Redwood said, her throat aching something awful.

"Subie a conjure woman. That life ain't for everybody," Elisa said.

"I don't see why I got to marry a fool, 'cause he come sniffing 'round, flashing fast cash and talking big."

"I don't know 'bout that." Elisa waved a bloody knife. "You gotta marry somebody."

Redwood grabbed a box of tools and headed for Aidan's place.

"We be eating at four," Elisa yelled.

"I won't stay away long."

Redwood hadn't seen much of Aidan since the baby started walking. Josie pitched a fit over his *trips* to the swamp, leaving her alone with a feisty toddler. So Aidan didn't take off on her too much. Redwood had so many secrets saved up to tell him, she was starting to forget. On a short visit before supper, wouldn't be enough time for all their stories, even if they talked fast.

Walking at a good pace for an hour and getting close to his place, she was feeling better. Maybe he'd even have a new song to play her. They could stroll down to the creek and get away from everything for a few minutes. Josie claim the banjo plucked at her nerves. Something had to be wrong with that woman she didn't like Aidan singing to her. Course Redwood had never heard somebody's good music she couldn't hear again and again.

Orange-haired Josie busted out Aidan's front door with a bundle of belongings and a crying baby on her hip. Josie's cheeks were red and so were her puffy eyes. She headed for a buckboard. The horse turned to watch Josie and the few satchels she'd loaded up. The baby was shrieking. Josie stopped, trying to rock her son quiet.

"You that hoodoo gal, ain't you?" She looked Redwood up and down, pretending she couldn't remember her.

"My uncle say thank you to Mr. Cooper." Redwood held up the box of tools.

"Aidan ain't here. Mean son of a snake run off somewhere to get drunk." Josie got in the buggy and laid her son in a basket in the back. He had orange hair and red cheeks, same as his mama, and a tight little angry scream. Didn't look nothing like Aidan. Josie rocked his basket. "Watch out. Aidan ain't worth a damn."

"Why you say that?"

"You know how some white men do, running off to colored gals."

"Aidan and me, just friends." Redwood's breath fluttered into a nasty cough. "Don't be jealous."

Josie sniffled, almost satisfied. "You ain't the only colored gal 'round. Plenty dark meat this side of the creek."

"He faithful to you if that's your worry."

"How you know?"

"I'm a hoodoo, ain't I?"

"I s'pose he is faithful." She gave up on quieting the baby. "I could take him laying up with a darky."

"Uh-huh," Redwood said even though Josie was lying to herself.

"He's a man with a biiiggg appetite." She sat up straight, squeezing herself, like she could feel how good doing it with Aidan was. "I can hold my own against—"

"I tell you, he ain't going with no other woman. I did a *good-luck* spell for you two."

Josie guffawed and scared her son quiet. "Aidan brought in two of the best crops ever. We don't have no debts, 'cept Leroy Richards."

"Moonshine?"

Flushing pink at the edges, Josie lifted the reins.

"So you going away 'cause Mr. Cooper be feeling low?"

"I'm leaving him." Josie wiped at sudden tears spilling down her face. "A haint been after Aidan since before we got married. Spooked him last night. Well, then it's one jug after another."

"He *did right* by you when—"

"I know." She snapped at Redwood. "Who you telling?" Her lips trembled.

"He hit you?"

"Not yet." She was hiding something.

"You got a new beau?"

Josie cut her eyes at Redwood. "It just ain't working out how I thought."

"That happens." Redwood set the tools on the porch, huffing coughs.

"You sick, gal? Too busy passing out cures. You ought to take your own medicine."

"I do."

"Medicine don't cure everything."

Redwood wheezed. Aidan should have gone to Miz Subie for a *good-luck* spell. She would have done it right. Redwood couldn't get nothing *hard* to work out. "I'm sorry."

All the bluster and fight drained out of Josie. "If a man come after me with his fists, I'd have a mind to get a gun." She sighed thinking on this. "That ain't no way to live." She drove off with her son shrieking again and left Redwood standing on the porch.

A bush by the door hung with colored glass bottles tinkled in the wind.

———

It was a week since Josie left Aidan for one of her old flames, or was it two weeks? Down to his last jug and he was having a hard time keeping track of time and space. Aidan come into town and couldn't find nothing where it used to be. Turn his back a minute and Peach Grove done grown into a bustling metropolis. Besides the telegraph and post office there were now *two* general stores, a hotel, a doctor *and* a dentist office, a new schoolhouse with a library upside it, a bigger Baptist church, and too many fancy town houses—where did all these rich folk come from they need two feed stores and a dress shop? The new sheriff got hisself spanking new digs too, right 'cross from the bank. No question who he was working for.

"All we need is the railroad and a good cat house to put us on the map. Josie Cooper the one to see for that." Miles Crawford, a burly white man with reddish-brown hair, was making fun, loud so Aidan and every other body in the post office could hear. Miles was sharecropping for Jerome Williams on good soil he once owned. His wife worked herself to death last summer, and Miles took her dying hard to his heart. Josie run to Miles when she left Aidan. That lasted three days. Josie run from him and his three kids too. She went to South Carolina chasing somebody. So much for Aidan *doing right* by her. He didn't miss Josie much, but little Bobby—

"How she get even a bastard son of a whore to marry her?" Miles roared his nasty laugh. With so many joining in, egging Miles on, the business Aidan had come to the post office for flew out his head. He turned to leave, weaving and wobbling, his fists throbbing. Miles blocked his way. Aidan walked 'round him.

"Leave him be," somebody muttered.

Miles shoved Aidan, twice. "Cheaper to pay by the hour. Hear what I say?"

Laughter died when Aidan slugged Miles in the chin, and he fell clear out the door into the street. Though he'd had a few, Miles was not as drunk as Aidan. He stood up swinging and landed punches on Aidan's side and shoulder. Aidan fell back. The pain cleared his muffled head just a bit.

Miles kicked dirt in his face. "Irish fool, can't never hold your liquor." He took a moment to gloat for his audience. A few in the crowd were chuckling till Aidan slugged Miles four or five times in the head and gut and then kicked his legs out from under him. Miles doubled up, yelping and spitting blood. Aidan slammed a bottle of Miz Subie's cure-all at a post. It shattered and spit glass back at him, cutting his hand.

"You the bastard son of a whore, not me," Aidan yelled. Miles crawled 'round to see who might come to his aid. Men shook their heads at Crazy Coop brandishing a broken bottle. Aidan howled and thrust jagged glass in their faces. "A lot of folks who be ready to laugh with you, ain't willing to spill blood for you."

Miles tried to feint one direction and get away the other, but limping on a bruised ankle, he had no speed. Aidan stopped him cold. "Damn you," Miles said.

"Damn you to hell too." Even if Aidan didn't love her or miss her, "Josie's my wife." He grabbed Miles's arm, yanking till it come half out the socket. Miles screamed. Aidan twirled him so they were face-to-face. For all his bulk, Miles wasn't strong. Just the sort of blowhard fool Josie could convince to take her in. Aidan held jagged green glass to his eye. Miles sputtered and banged at Aidan with a useless arm.

"What you got to say now?" Aidan said.

Miles was crying. "Josie just don't want you no more, you crazy drunk! You goin' kill me for that, take my eye?" He whined like Aidan started this fight.

"I guess she don't want you neither," Aidan said.

Redwood sauntered out the old general store with a bag of flour over one shoulder and a basket of notions in the other hand. "What's going on?" she said.

Seeing her, Aidan felt dizzy. The liquor sloshing 'round his belly and rising up to his head was fixing to spew out his eyes and ears. He didn't need to go to jail over Josie. He dropped the shard of glass, backed away from his whimpering victim, and swallowed a string of cuss words. Redwood crossed the muddy street heading right for him.

"That's Garnett's gal!" someone whispered.

Miles pulled hisself together, nodded thanks at her, and stumbled away. Nobody helped him—the crowd went on 'bout their business like nothing had happened.

Just before Redwood reached Aidan, Jerome Williams stepped out the bank, smiling at her long legs and ample hips. Jerome was curly gray handsome, a silver fox at twenty-seven, finely dressed, and one of the richest men in the county. He and his mama, Miz Caroline Williams, stole land right out from under poor folk—white, colored, and Indian: the Crawfords' fields and the Jessup place, Graham Wright's pastures, Cherokee Will's orchard, and Raymond and Garnett Phipps's farm. The Williams clan had their eye on Aidan's land too. Redwood strode by Jerome without so much as a glance. He stepped directly in front of her and they almost collided.

"Oh. How do, Mr. Williams." Redwood smiled at Jerome. She could smile at a rattlesnake and mean it.

"How do yourself." Jerome admired her. Who wouldn't?

Aidan went from demon drunk to near-sober in an instant.

Jerome was notorious with the ladies, breaking hearts and leaving a trail of bastards all 'cross the county. Aidan didn't want him nowhere near Redwood, for her own sake and her brother's too. George would come after the man with a shotgun and end up hanging from a tree. Jerome ate her up with his eyes. Redwood danced past him without noticing.

"How do, Mr. Cooper," she said.

Aidan rubbed bloody palms against filthy clothes. His hair hung over his eyes in sweaty clumps. Blood trickled down his cheek. Redwood stepped close to him. Jerome took note of her light touch on Aidan's forearm. Aidan smelled the last several weeks clinging to him like rot. He wanted to bolt, but he wasn't leaving her alone with Jerome.

"You promised to come by and visit us," Redwood said, not worrying over the stench, dirt, or the bloody streaks his hands left on his pants; not worrying if Jerome or anybody in Peach Grove saw how close they were. Not seeing nobody really, but him. "Why ain't you stopped by?" Aidan recognized the lonely ache in her voice. She missed him the way he missed her. "You too busy letting your crops go to seed?" She teased him in broad daylight.

"Well," he stammered. She waited for more, but he wasn't sober enough to make sense talking. "I'll come, as soon as . . . I will."

"That's something to look forward to." She squeezed his arm, taking some of the hurting off him, and then sauntered away, a queen of Dahomey in Peach Grove. She waved and smiled at folks all down the street.

"Coop, how do you get an invitation?" Jerome said.

"They're my neighbors."

"You ever had a colored gal? One who was willing?"

Aidan grunted.

"Did you see her smile? She takes after her mama. A gal fine as that would be wasted on an ignorant nigger, don't you think?"

If Aidan hadn't left his gun on the porch, Jerome would've been dead meat. The fool was so busy watching Redwood's behind, he didn't notice how close he come to death.

"You been sleeping up a tree, Coop?"

"Better than a bed in this god-forsaken town."

Jerome studied him and then looked back at Redwood. "I never know what you're going to say."

"The boy is a genius in the rough," Doc Johnson said. He slipped up from behind and clapped Aidan on the shoulder.

Aidan jumped. "Don't come up on me that way."

"You been roughhousing?" In a flash, Doc had Aidan in a firm grip, observing every detail of his current condition. There was no hope of escape. Doc's twin brother, Hiram Johnson, was right beside him, shaking his head at Aidan's filthy getup.

"In between drinking and fighting, the *boy* read more than I do," Hiram said.

Doc and Hiram only had ten years on Aidan, but they were well-off, upstanding white citizens—they owned most of Main Street—Peach Grove aristocracy, like Jerome Williams. 'Cept the Johnson twins thought they were better than most rich folk in this backwater county, more intelligent, more civilized. They'd gone off to college; traveled the world. They read the best books money could buy. Doc donated volumes for a public library and stocked the schoolhouse. He gave books to Miz Elisa to teach the colored kids. Rumor had it he paid her wages. But Aidan knew colored folk did the paying themselves.

"What did you do to your hand?" Doc picked glass from Aidan's wound and poured a clear liquid from a silver flask on the ragged flesh. It stung like hell.

"You're lucky, Aidan," Jerome said. "Doc will treat any sick body, whether they can pay or not. He even let colored folk walk in the front door."

"If somebody minds, they can take their sick selves twenty-five miles to the next doctor," Doc said.

"I want to see you carry on this way in Atlanta." Jerome laughed, not hiding his bile.

Doc glowered at Jerome; so did Hiram. The twins were odd-looking, having inherited their father's bulging blue eyes, craggy cheeks, and dagger-sharp chin. They sported the latest men's coats from Atlanta and fancy boots from Europe. Aidan always felt ill-spoken and shabby by comparison, a curio. Doc, in particular, liked to collect curios, while Hiram put out a weekly town journal and liked to spread the news.

"Preacher fell down his own well," Hiram said.

"Indeed. Coop tells me God has forsaken us," Jerome said.

"Preacher was running from a voice on the wind. In the twentieth century!" Doc said.

"Garnett's curse." Hiram shook his head.

Aidan was trembling all over now.

"You think the preacher was in that posse? Nobody knows who rode out after her." Jerome looked pale.

"I suspect there are some who know." Doc wrapped Aidan's hand in a white handkerchief. "People be spooking themselves and call it the voice of a dead colored woman." Doc was a man of science. He didn't believe in haints and spooks. "They feel so bad for what they did or didn't do, they're haunted. Isn't that right, Coop?"

"That's right, Doc. Hoodoo is mostly in your head." Aidan wasn't 'bout to argue with him on this or any point. Doc could argue a man to death. "You get spooked by what you already believe. Haint don't hound you if there's no reason to."

"Most people in Peach Grove sleep fine, even in the trees," Jerome said.

"More restless spirits than you think." Hiram gazed at the good citizens of Peach Grove, coming and going in a warm winter sun. "Things are never what they seem."

"Do you think that's true, Coop? Everyone has a secret up his sleeve?" Jerome sounded like he had something to hide. "You keeping something from us?"

"Coop is up in the tree branches reading the book of life . . . and half my library." Doc inspected a cut on Aidan's cheek.

"You have to watch out for the smart ones." Jerome studied Aidan again, like a boxer assessing an opponent he'd underestimated. "They'll turn on their own kind."

Aidan hated getting caught in the middle of their spat.

"You'll mend." Doc released him as a wagon pulled up to the post office. "Is that the Atlanta newspaper coming in?"

"Hiram, Doc, Mr. Williams, be seeing you." Aidan lurched 'cross the street away from them.

Redwood angrily squeezed cold water from a month of shirts. The wringer was busted. She twisted one thin shirt till it was wet ribbons. A man from a Negro institute in Atlanta come to Ladd and Elisa's door and asked to photograph the family in front of a "typical colored dwelling." Elisa broke out laughing and Ladd waved his axe in the man's face. Redwood would've at least talked to the fellow 'bout this colored institute of higher learning, but Ladd chased him away with tales of bears, gators, and clouds of mosquitoes that suck the blood and juice out your brains and make you stupid. Aunt and Uncle didn't want fancy people sitting somewhere, laughing at their modest four-room cabin, home to nine hardworking people. Ladd made sure the man didn't take any pictures on the sly and then went back to chopping wood. Elisa went to haul water from the well to the house. Hard to shove Aunt and Uncle off their course.

"I bet company coming for supper." Elisa squinted at someone raising dust down the road. Redwood coughed and turned her back. Bubba had just as much sense as a falling rock. She'd have to do a *hotfoot* or *drive-away* spell to get him to leave her be.

Iris and the five cousins chased the two scrawny chickens they'd be eating for dinner. Bill was ten and Ruby nine, yet six-year-old Iris was almost as tall as them, busting out of her favorite green dress, a rag really. All the children's clothes were worn thin, but the young ones didn't notice the chill in the air or how poor and shabby their life would look in a photograph. They were having too much fun. Redwood moved on to hanging sheets.

Iris tumbled over a chair and fell into a battered shovel. The cousins yelped. Iris ran to Redwood through billowing white. Wide-eyed and hopeful, she presented a bloody, sliced knee, but no tears or squeals.

"Shall I make it better?" Redwood said.

Over Iris's shoulder she spied Aidan, not Bubba, loping into the yard for his third visit in two weeks. His clothes were clean; his hair was slicked back and tucked in his collar. He carried his banjo over one shoulder and a deer over the other. He watched Redwood kiss Iris's bloody knee. He was quite a handsome man for all his foolishness.

"Crazy Coop! Crazy Coop! Crazy Coop!" Iris jumped up squealing now with joy.

The five cousins joined her and ran toward Aidan. He had only a second to hand Ladd the deer and Elisa the banjo before he was mobbed. Ladd headed to the smokehouse with the deer. The children talked all at once. "What you bring us? What's in your pockets? Where you been?"

"Out hunting up that deer," he replied.

"Hush all that noise. Mr. Cooper 'llowed to go deaf," Elisa said, smiling.

"It's Aidan, ma'am. I figured I couldn't eat it all by myself. So if you don't mind."

"It's been a lean month. All the men go out and come back with nothing. You put a spell on them deer?" Elisa said.

"He be singing them right into a trap," Redwood said.

Aidan gaped at her.

"Well, ain't you?"

Aidan pulled candy and carved wooden toys from his pockets. He crouched down and hugged each child. "The bear is for little Iris, you hear? Y'all can share the rest."

Iris held up a carved black bear with a half-eaten apple in its paw. A raccoon peered through the bear's leg at the fruit. "Cairo and Star." She hugged them to her chest.

"You named that bear been coming 'round?" Redwood said. "Don't be feeding him."

The cousins ran off playing with/fighting over the carved bobcats, gators, and otters. Aidan took his banjo back from Elisa.

"What you got for me?" Redwood asked.

"Something I just wrote." He played the banjo and sang:

My love is like a falling star
A passing phantom high overhead
You do not see her fall, not far
For oh my lord, she's dark as the dead

Redwood applauded the melancholy melody. Ladd walked toward them, tapping his feet to the rhythm. Aidan's voice and playing were beautiful, but Elisa scowled, muttering 'bout *the* blues.

"You a conjure man with that banjo," Redwood said quickly.

"I play what I feel. Even Josie said that," Aidan said.

"Sorry to hear 'bout your wife leaving," Ladd said.

"Drunk all the time. She couldn't stand me."

"Well, uh . . ." Ladd didn't want to talk on this. "I got a wife who'll put up with anything."

"Almost," Elisa said.

"Ain't nobody should put up with me." Aidan left off strumming and looked down.

"You're right nice when you're sober." Redwood touched his shoulder.

"Woman run off with your little boy . . . make anyone take a drink or two," Elisa said.

"Baby wasn't mine," Aidan said, so matter-of-fact everyone gulped.

Elisa wiped her hands on her apron and snatched winter herbs from the garden. Ladd lifted his axe and grabbed a hunk of wood to split.

"You staying for supper?" Redwood said. "Ain't much, but if you can stomach my cooking, you're welcome."

Aidan looked at Elisa and Ladd.

"You, cook? Listen to her now." Elisa grinned and poked Redwood in the ribs.

"Man bring fresh meat; what you talking 'bout, ain't much?" Ladd almost smiled at him. "Mr. Cooper can help me chop this wood while you women do your magic."

Flames danced and crackled in the fireplace. Aidan sat in Elisa's plain, cozy kitchen, so stuffed with good food, taking a breath interfered with his digestion. The ruins of dinner littered the large wooden table in case anybody wanted to try for more. Ladd was telling a story. Elisa rocked her chair like drum accompaniment. The children sat in grown-up laps fighting sleep. Iris was curled up against Aidan's chest. She tugged his collar and showed him the knee that was bleeding when he arrived. The wound was healed now, just a wiggly purple line. They made funny faces at Redwood who had her eyes closed, hugging Becky and Jessie.

". . . weren't goin' be slaves no more," Ladd said.

The door bust open, startling everybody fully awake. George tramped into the kitchen, his face and shirt bathed in sweat. Mud covered his boots and pants up to the knees. He glared at everyone, but didn't say a word. Redwood opened her eyes and, seeing him, smiled.

"They ran from the Okefenokee Swamp all the way up into the mountains and was free people." Ladd finished his story. "How do the Seminole call it?"

"*Istî siminoli,*" Aidan said.

Holding a bloody right hand behind his back, George grabbed food from the table with his left hand and ate hungrily.

Elisa frowned. "You ain't even give a Christian greeting."

"Good evening, Aunt. Evening to you all." George waved a rib bone with scraps of dangling flesh. There wasn't much meat left. He chewed at the hard gristle. "You bring the deer, Coop? Must be, 'cause ain't nobody else know where they be hiding."

Aidan nodded at George.

"I guess it's 'thank you' then." George smirked. "How's that for Christian?"

"Yes, *istî siminoli.* Free people," Ladd said. "The hounds couldn't track 'em, and the paddy rollers just give up and went on home. And you see, all sorts of free folks were mixing 'round up there in them mountains."

"Yes." Aidan thought back to when he was a boy.

"Colored still ain't free nowhere else." George chomped on a hunk of bread.

"Bet you got a story 'bout them mountain folk, Mr. Cooper," Ladd said.

George grunted. "You must got stories back to when wild *Injuns* roamed the land." He didn't like Indians any better than he liked white people—double the reason to dislike Aidan.

"Did you tell him the Okefenokee story?" Aidan whispered to Redwood.

She sucked her teeth at him, disgusted. "Of course not."

Half asleep, Iris fussed in Aidan's lap. He kissed her head and patted her tummy. She settled down.

"What you know good?" Ladd asked him.

"I heard plenty tall tales from the mountain folk, like how Miss O'Casey met the Thunder Man."

Aidan's mama told him her story before someone else could. She wasn't shamed of who she was or where she come from. His daddy neither. Aidan still couldn't stand up in the world the way they did and be proud of every bit of who he was no matter what anybody thought. But if his journal had been near, he might have read the story out loud and not just to Redwood, but to Ladd, Elisa, Iris, and the cousins, exactly the way his mother told him. He might have wiped the sneer off George's greasy face.

BIG THUNDER AND MISS O'CASEY

Love is always a good thing.

It was the spring of 1876, darling, and smoke curled from the chimney of a backwoods bordello. No streets of milk and honey, no castles of gold, when you stepped off the boat. Pleasuring poor workingmen, that was the work there was.

Glass shattered and shouts and curses erupted from the second floor of this house of ill repute. Aislinn O'Casey—your own dear mother—and her older sister Caitlin squeezed through a window wedged at half-mast and stepped out onto the roof. They took a breath of free, clear air under the sparkling stars. Back then Aislinn and Caitlin both had red hair, moss-green eyes, and more freckles than clear skin. Dressed in flimsy white nightgowns and carrying bundles with all they owned in this world, they raced across the roof and shimmied down a Greek column to the muddy ground. It was the Athens Bordello, you see. A naked man stuck his head out the window, screaming bloody murder.

He'd paid for both girls, thought he owned them for the night, body and soul.

Aislinn and Caitlin stared up at him, laughed to each other, and then ran like the dickens all through the night. They ran with the energy of dreams, dreams for a new life, if not milk and honey running in the streets, a little less sweat from stinking men. Being the foolish young girls that they were, they got all turned around and thoroughly lost.

Dawn broke open the dark. Aislinn and Caitlin slogged through a swamp and stopped at an island of solid ground. They were hungry and desperate and terrified, fighting with each other about who was to blame for the pickle they were in. They had stolen raggedy coats from their poor customers and thrown these rude garments over their nightclothes, which were now filthy. Standing there, scratching at the bugs, they considered going back to the Athens Bordello. Caitlin did anyways, but she hadn't yet persuaded her sister.

Aislinn heard a thunder of grief. Beyond fluttering swamp grass, a Seminole man stood over his dead wife and a newborn child, still wrinkled and red, an umbilical cord twisted around her neck. The man was a strapping fellow, with an alligator pouch hanging at his waist, a big hunting knife riding on his hip, a bright turban on his head. He sank down, shaking with grief.

Caitlin wanted to run away from this wild Indian, but Aislinn felt his grief and sat on the ground in front of him. It wasn't right to be alone with death, and this fellow looked grieved enough to do himself harm. Reluctantly, Caitlin clutched Aislinn and sank down too. They did not make a sound. They did not move, and then the sun sank beyond the tall grass. Lightning crackled in the dark above, and the thunder was so big, it rocked their little island, yet no rain cooled the hot night. It was as though the man had called his ancestors to witness with him, to grieve at the wake for his family.

At sunrise, the Thunder Man still sat silently by his dead wife and child. A breeze plowed through saw grass. Aislinn got up, so stiff and achy she walked like an old crow. Caitlin tried to hold her back, but Aislinn was bold and strong-willed. She strode close to the Thunder Man, and with an Irish lilt to her English asked, "Are you fixing on dying too?"

The Thunder Man stared up at her, hurt and loss all over his face.

"Wasting another life would be a shame, sir," she said.

He jumped up and grabbed her roughly by the shoulders. She did not flinch or wince, but grabbed him back. They stood taking measure of one another with an owl hooting in the distance.

When night came again, the Thunder Man buried his wife and child in a high tree as Aislinn watched. Caitlin huddled on the ground behind them. Aislinn remembered an old Irish prayer and sang it:

She is the queen of every hive
She is the blaze at sunset
She is the grace of every hope
She is the shield protecting your heart
May the blessings of the Earth be on you

Your father, whose name was Big Thunder, of course, finally spoke, with a whisper of a Seminole accent, saying, "I'm not dying in captivity."

"So, where are we going?"

Aidan stroked his red leather journal buried in the bottom of his bag.

"You goin' tell us or just tease us?" Redwood said. "Your stories are like a trip to the Fair, to the *E-LEC-TRI-CI-TY*." She drew out each syllable. "Or like riding a hot-air balloon to places of adventure and wonder." She almost melted his heart. "Tell us something, why don't you?"

"Please! Please!" Becky and Jessie had their eyes open. "A story we haven't heard."

Aidan was tempted, but he didn't want to steal Ladd's thunder. "Just tall tales, you know, how my folks met. You don't want to hear that."

"A regular romantic entertainment, I suspect." George ate the last hunk of apple pie.

Elisa's voice turned sharp. "If you can't be civil, George."

"I don't guess anyone wants to hear *my* tale." George stomped out the room.

After that, Aidan wouldn't let hisself be persuaded into telling a story, not even by Redwood, but playing the banjo was another matter. Without coaxing, he was strumming away. Ladd joined him on the spoons and Elisa sang, as long as it wasn't the blues. Redwood didn't add a harmony, but she danced the sleepy children into their bedroom. "We're not tired," they protested and almost fell asleep washing their grubby hands and faces. Carrying Iris, Aidan followed Redwood to a room with several beds jammed together. The cousins were stuffed between the sheets and already dreaming when he set little Iris's head on a pillow and tucked a blanket to her chin. She still clutched her carved bear and raccoon. Tiptoeing back into the kitchen, Redwood took Aidan's arm. Ladd and Elisa pretended not to notice.

"I'll tell you that story sometime," Aidan said.

"Iris sure loves her some Crazy Coop," Redwood said.

Aidan blushed and reached for his banjo, fixing to go. "Love goes both ways."

"Stay the night," Elisa said.

"I don't want to trouble you, ma'am." Aidan looked from her to Redwood.

"There's frost in the air." Elisa shivered. "Your place is a good walk from here."

"Don't nag the man." Ladd put his arms 'round his wife. "Let him find his own mind."

"I'm just saying."

Aidan stepped out into the night. Bitter cold cut right through him. He didn't relish the idea of walking the hour and a half home. It was pitch dark too. He'd have to borrow a lamp.

"The moon ain't up yet." Redwood stood behind him, radiating warmth.

There was nothing but a jug to go home to. Was he really crazy? Aidan stepped back inside. Elisa was sitting by the fire cleaning her shotgun. Ladd was smoking a pipe.

"If you staying, close the door and keep the heat inside," Ladd said.

Aidan sat by the fire too and pulled out his red leather journal. After a few moments, he was writing away. Redwood sat next to him, close enough for her thigh to graze his. Reading *Of One Blood: Or, The Hidden Self* by Pauline Hopkins, she come to the end of a chapter and sighed.

"Good?" He turned the book title over in his mind.

"Oh yes." Redwood's eyes flashed with real excitement, like when they were going 'round the Ferris Wheel. "There's this colored American medical student who gets crowned emperor of a lost kingdom underneath a pyramid in Ethiopia."

"That's clear 'cross Africa, to the east, to the horn," Aidan said. Doc Johnson had a big map of the world on a wall in his library. Aidan could see it plain in his head. "That book must be quite an adventure. I'll have to read it when you finished."

She displayed the title page. "Pauline Hopkins is an actress and a singer and a playwright. A colored lady doing all that and writing books too."

"You don't say?" Aidan was surprised and impressed. "I ain't been reading so much. Been hard to find time for anything." He'd been drinking moonshine till he blacked out and could wake up with another haunted night behind him, forgotten.

"What you putting in your book?" she said. "I don't mean to interrupt."

"I like to write down what happened on a good day, like this evening with you all, make it last longer that way."

She traced her fingers along his handwriting. "All that happen today?"

Aidan pulled the journal from her. "I write what I remember too."

"You got a hidden self, huh?"

"I reckon so." He glanced at the words.

COMING TO PEACH GROVE

It was 1892 or thereabouts. Big Thunder and Aislinn, jaundiced and sick, rode through the woods, tearing down a mountainside. Aidan was eleven or twelve and riding between them. It was a hot night. Skunk odor filled the air. The horses were skittish and couldn't always find sure footing. Ahead of Aidan, Big Thunder almost fell from his horse. Aidan cried out.

"Don't you worry now," Aislinn said as Big Thunder righted himself. Her voice was thin. "My sister, your Aunt Caitlin, is in Peach Grove. Not far now."

"You don't even know where she lives," Aidan said.

Aislinn and Caitlin had a big falling out over savage Indians and wild mountain folk.

"We're taking you to a conjure woman. Her people come from the Sea Islands. I knew her growing up. She'll find your aunt." Big Thunder gripped his reins and squeezed his knees into the horse's skinny ribs and they rode on.

Aidan thought his parents might drop dead any moment, and he'd be alone in strange woods. When it started to rain and the gloom thickened, he didn't know how his daddy would find the way. After several wet hours, they reached somewhere. Aidan smelled cook fires and cow manure and ripe fruit hanging in trees. Peach Grove. Big Thunder and Aislinn tied their horses to scraggly branches and staggered in the dark a ways with Aidan between them. Icy rain pelted their thin coats. It was hot and cold all at once. They finally came to a house with lights burning in the windows and smoke curling from a chimney.

"I can't go any farther," Aislinn said. "We do it now, or I won't."

At the steps to the porch, Aislinn hugged Aidan, and Big Thunder hugged them both. They pushed Aidan up to the door. He clutched a red leather journal, alligator bag, hunting knife, and an orchid. He refused to move.

"Go on, boy," Big Thunder said, all the rumble gone from his voice.

"Don't forget to give her the flower, Aidan," Aislinn said.

"You all not coming?" Aidan said.

"We'll come for you as soon as . . ." Aislinn faltered.

"As soon as we can . . ." Big Thunder said.

Aislinn backed away, holding on to Big Thunder. "My sister will look after you, for a while."

"Where you all going?" Aidan shouted.

"Cross River," Big Thunder said.

"Why can't I come?"

"Remember what we told you," Aislinn said.

"And if we're gone a long while, just remember who you are, Aidan Wildfire." Big Thunder sounded a moment like his old self, and then they disappeared into the rainy dark.

Aidan would have stood at the doorsill all night in the rain, but Garnett Phipps came and pulled him in out of the wet. She wrapped him in a blanket and stood him by the fire.

"Thank you for the orchid," Miz Garnett said. She was tall and fierce with strong hands and bold features. Her eyes were deep brown with a flash of fire underneath. She let Aidan stare out the window for his parents, even though there was nothing to see. When he started crying, she patted his shoulder and he turned into her, crying full force, and she hugged his sorrow. She smelled of hickory smoke and peach brandy and magnolia.

"What are these tears?" Aunt Caitlin had the same Irish lilt as Aislinn, but it did Aidan no good to hear it. "You're all grown up since I saw you last. A man almost. Can't be no more crying." She was a proper married lady now, Miz Caitlin Cooper. But her life before had messed up her insides, till she couldn't have no children. "You'll be the son I never had, Aidan Cooper. Put that old mountain life behind you, like a bad dream."

Aidan didn't want to let go of Garnett Phipps. He clutched her fiercely.

Miz Garnett smiled at him. "You got a journal, I see. Write yourself down, Aidan. Keep good counsel with your

ownself. That's a powerful spell, a hoodoo trick for whatever ails you."

The fire was thundering up the chimney and hissing at the cold air.
Ladd poked it absentmindedly. Elisa looked up the barrel of her gun.

Aidan closed the journal quickly. "How we came south out the
mountains is nothing fancy like Miz Pauline Hopkins's adventure."

"I don't mean to pry." Redwood bit at her lip. "Don't worry. I didn't
read nothing."

"I just write 'bout my parents, my aunt." Aidan hugged the journal
against his chest. "I write down Ladd's stories too. All the stories I
hear, what happened, and tall tales too."

Redwood seemed pleased with that. She was right under his nose.
He couldn't help but breathe her in. Her skin was lily of the valley soap,
and a sweet nut oil filled her hair. And there was her own scent too.

"You know I'm no good at storying out loud," he whispered.

"That ain't true, but if you fixed on believing it." Redwood shrugged.
"I been writing stories that ain't never happened yet, but it's like I remember them."

"Stories you think up yourself?" Aidan had never considered doing
that.

"Why not?"

"Aunt Caitlin used to say writing foolishness was a waste. God only
give us so many days."

"Foolishness?" Redwood sucked her teeth. "Your Aunt Caitlin ain't
never read my stories."

"You burn 'em up 'fore anybody can read 'em," Elisa said.

"Speaking of your aunt, may she rest in peace, I just know Miz
Caitlin wouldn't want you to lose that farm now," Ladd said. "That's
good property, real good soil."

Aidan had been doing fine with the farm till recently. "Don't see
the point sometimes to bringing in the crop."

"Better than letting it rot on the vine," Redwood said.

"Miz Caitlin and Mr. Cooper worked too hard," Ladd said, "to see
it all go to ruin."

Aidan shook his head. "You think the dead care what we do?"

"What kind of talk is that?" Elisa said.

"You bad as George." Redwood sucked her teeth again, disgusted.

Elisa set down the gun she was cleaning and flicked a cloth at Aidan's sour expression. "We're all that's left of the dead. Of course they care."

"Caroline Williams be eyeing your land," Ladd said, deep anger in his voice.

"Well, she can eye it all she wants," Aidan said. Ladd nodded.

"Daddy sent me this one. I'll give it to you." Redwood dropped a picture postcard in his lap. "Where all the trains meet—the whole world's riding into Chicago. That's a true story for your journal book too."

This postcard of the 1893 Chicago World's Fair featured a lively rendering of Cairo Street. Aidan recognized the temple mosque, market booths, snake charmers, and dancers. He closed his eyes and the Egyptian ladies were doing their belly dance with Redwood. An audience from 'round the world applauded.

"Them grand buildings be long gone. Workingmen set fire to dreams," Ladd said.

Aidan's hand shook as he tucked the card in his journal. "I'll write on that soon."

"Good." Redwood leaned against him. "Sometimes I open my mind so wide, I can feel myself in everything, dead and alive, yesterday and tomorrow."

"She sound just like her mama," Elisa whispered.

Everyone was dazzled. The fire spit out a shower of sparks.

Aidan leaned into Redwood. "Used to feel that way, as a boy, up in the mountains."

Do right, for the sickness cured, for the babies born true, for the evil spirits chased from your gates, have mercy.

Aidan covered his ears.

"What's a matter?" Redwood asked.

Aidan shook his head as riders in black robes tore down a dark road raising dust, right past Elisa's ironing board.

"You sick, boy?" Ladd was standing over him.

"Just sober," Aidan rasped. He was usually stinking drunk at this point in the evening. He tried to speak again, but his voice was caught in another time. *"I hear you, Miz Garnett. I'm trying,"* his other voice said.

"What he say?" Elisa asked.

Aidan lowered Garnett's body through dense foliage to a white cloth on the ground. Wrapping the burnt remains up, he was grim, fighting tears. Running with the body through the woods, he almost fell.

Redwood had her storm hand against his heart. It was cold as snow. He clutched it for a moment and then pushed her away. "You feeling better now?" she asked.

"I'm out of sorts, maybe I should go." Aidan stood up.

She stood up next to him. "Out of sorts is the time for you to stay."

"I . . . ain't right."

"Why you saying that?" Elisa said.

"I run one wife out the county and the other one out the state with my—"

"You'll find a good woman again," Ladd said.

"Yes, you will. A handsome, hardworking man like you." Elisa smiled at Redwood.

"And scare her away too. They don't call me Crazy Coop for nothing." But the worst had passed and without him downing a jug.

"I won't hear you talk yourself down." Redwood stormed out of the kitchen.

Aidan fingered his journal.

Aunt Elisa was so desperate to get Redwood married till she'd see her niece jump the broom with Crazy Coop! Redwood wanted to be furious or laugh, but she stopped in the hallway and tried to imagine Aidan kissing her or touching her secret spots. She imagined touching him, having his manhood inside her. In the drafty hall, she felt warm, hot almost. A sweet ache deep inside caught her breath. She'd never gone so far in her mind with anybody else. This certainly eased the chill in her lungs.

Didn't Aidan say, loving was always a good thing?

And talking with him, saying what was on her mind, the nasty tingle under her skin let up. Aidan didn't run scared when he saw who she was or what she wanted. He *believed* in her and she *believed* in him. Redwood let herself smile. The way he looked at her sometimes was how Ladd looked at Elisa, as if the world would end if something should happen to her. Truth be told, Redwood didn't know what she'd do without Aidan either. Maybe he was somebody to love after all, even in Peach Grove, Georgia. Course George would have a bird. And then there was the law against them. Since Aidan was probably Indian too, Cherokee or Seminole, might be different, or maybe they could run off to Chicago together and be who they wanted.

But Redwood wasn't ready to marry nobody yet.

She walked into the back room feeling better than she had since coming back from the World's Fair. Her voice was full and strong. She could've broke out singing. George was packing clothes in a canvas bag. Redwood snuck up behind him, ready to poke his ribs. Her smile turned to a frown. One of his hands was wrapped in a bloody rag. He glanced at her, shrugged, and then turned back to packing.

"You been in a fight," she said.

"Can't deny it."

Filled with dread, Redwood stepped 'round a bedroll and tripped over a stack of books and papers. "Don't go, Brother."

"I can't be a man in Peach Grove." He stuffed money from selling feathers for over a year into a pouch. He was a rich man now and could go where he wanted. Still—

"You be *you* wherever you go, George Phipps." She didn't want to lose him too.

He packed the books and papers. "It's better up north, in Chicago."

"Chicago? Take me with you. In Chicago I could find a bright destiny."

"No." George grabbed his bedroll and headed for the back door. He was sneaking out, like a thief in the night.

"You just goin' leave us? Not say a word?"

"Look, I don't know what trouble be on this road."

Redwood blocked his exit. "Why you run from here into trouble?" She took hold of his bloody hand. "Tell me what you think's so wrong with Peach Grove."

George winced as she peeled off the makeshift bandage. "You see good wherever you look, Red. That's not worth a damn where I'm going."

"You're lying to me with a bit of truth." Redwood pulled the pain from his hand, but held the hurting a moment 'stead of throwing it away. "I can feel it."

"Uncle Ladd tell them freedom lies, but he don't *live* none of that, too 'fraid to."

"I ain't 'fraid. Miz Subie say—"

"Subie a conjure woman, same as Mama. Death don't scare her none." He tried to push past her. She didn't budge.

"So what scare you so, you sneaking off in the night?" Redwood threw his pain at the ground. It sparked in the air. "Something 'bout Mama, huh?"

He turned to her, hoodooing hisself. It was dragon George now flexing a healed claw. Scaly wings unfurled from his back. He snarled fire breath through dagger-sharp talons.

"You don't scare me." She crossed her arms over her chest. "I can catch a lightning storm. Tell me what's what. I won't let you go till you do."

The air sizzled with fierce energy. George still looked scary, but his regular self again. "Peach Grove crackers, like the crazy one sitting in our kitchen, strung up Mama after god knows what else and set fire to her."

"What?" Redwood backed up, stumbling and swaying. The solid ground gave way under her feet. She was sinking in quicksand. She gripped the doorway.

"That's how Mama went to Glory on Christmas day." His words burned more than dragon's breath.

"I don't believe you." The air was wrong, grainy and hard. She gasped and gasped, but nobody, not even a conjure woman could breathe dirt. "No." Her blood turned thick and heavy, and her chest throbbed. Nobody's heart would pump mud either. She could've died then and there. "Aidan Cooper wouldn't do Mama terrible wrong and sit up in our kitchen after. Aunt and Uncle wouldn't be having none of that."

George considered lying some more. His twitching nose gave him away, but then he sighed. "Okay, not him. Other white men."

"I could fly apart into every direction." She clutched her chest.

"Mama was busy saving colored Peach Grove, and these chicken-livered Negroes act as if she had it coming to her. 'Cause she held her head up. 'Cause she shot a white man who tried to force her."

Redwood's legs gave out and she slid to the floor. "Why I ain't never heard any of this before?"

"Cowards and brutes each got their reasons to hold their tongues. And the family, well, who's goin' tell *you* that? You the spitting image of Mama." He paused, like he was seeing a haint, 'stead of his sister. "Folks be 'fraid . . . I see how everybody look at you. Bubba Jackson only come sniffing 'round to prove he ain't scared."

Redwood felt hollow and so cold, mountain, ice cold. "Mama was wrapped in a white cloth with orchids and bay branches . . . I was the first one in the church. I saw her there with baby Jesus and the wise men. One wise man was broken. I set him upright against an orchid."

"Coop cut her down and brought her to the church. I'll say that for him."

"Aunt Elisa say it was an angel did that."

"You still believing that?" George shook his head. "Time you grew up!"

Redwood covered her face. "Ain't nobody tole me nothing different."

"Folks swear Coop put them orchids on her. What's that? Did he stop 'em from stringing her up, from—"

"Stop who? Who did it?"

George sputtered and shook his head.

"Don't lie. Tell me, so I know what's what."

"I don't know who did it," he snarled. "Believe me."

"Why? All the lying everybody been doing 'round here."

"I don't know who those men were, that's God's truth, 'cause if I did . . ." Fire was on his breath a moment, then he swallowed it down. "You were just a little child."

"Somebody in the family could have tole me something, 'stead of lying."

"You look like Mama. Act like her too. If she coming through you, why we goin' tell you how she's dead?"

"Mr. Cooper was one of them what *believed* in Mama."

"Daddy and Miz Subie believed in her too. What good did it do?"

"Subie say Mama cheat that boneyard baron."

"Yeah, one colored life 'stead of the crackers burning us all out."

"Now you sneaking off?" Her eyes brimmed with tears. "So when were *you* goin' tell me?"

"Get off the floor now." He stood over her.

She couldn't move. He reached down for her. She fought him, but he finally lifted her up and hugged her.

"I'll write from Chicago, when I get settled."

Before Redwood took another breath, George was gone out the back door.

Mama had been lynched and nobody ever told her!

Feeling like a fool and mad enough to spit poison, Redwood marched into the kitchen. Ladd was smoking and staring in the fire. Aidan was reading *Of One Blood: Or, The Hidden Self*. Elisa dozed in her rocker but woke with a start as Redwood charged over to Aidan.

"If you fixing on lying to me with the rest of 'em . . . you best be leaving, Mr. Cooper."

"I don't ever be lying to you." Aidan set down the book and stood up. "What's wrong? You been crying?"

"You tell me every other story 'bout what happened on this land, but not this story!"

Elisa ran over to Redwood and took her arm. "What George go and tell you?"

"He say, this ain't no place to be a man. I reckon it's no place to be a woman either."

The fire went out. Embers settled with a sigh. Outside horse hooves pounded the ground as George rode off to make a new life in Chicago.

SIX

"If a man carry a gun all the time," Miz Subie said, "he will kill some-one. A gun can hoodoo you. Any weapon you carry, any hate you hold, will use you." She sucked her teeth and shook her head. "Being mad at everybody in Peach Grove won't help nothing. Set your mind to healing. We're here."

Redwood swallowed an angry retort and guided the canoe to shore. She'd never gone so far upcreek. Folks said it was dead land, haunted. She didn't know anybody even lived here, till Subie said where they were going. Just beyond the creek, the soil was scalded, barren but for scraggly weeds. This land was once a fire forest, but the flame-resistant woods had laid down to loggers several years ago. A tiny cabin clung to hardscrabble ground. A stiff wind could've carried it away. The creek gurgled outside its lone window, which had no glass panes, just a dirty blanket keeping out the chill.

Subie walked through the rickety door without knocking. Red-wood was close behind, carrying baskets of herbs, roots, ointments, and Subie's special healing implements wrapped in clean cotton. They both wore red *mojo* bags at the waist, but Subie had her healing root bag too and bangles at her ankles, warding off bad spells. Redwood set the tools of their trade on a table. The cabin had one middling-sized room and a loft. Kitchen stove was only giving off a little heat, and the fireplace was cold. A bed was wedged in the corner, and a sick gal sweat blood in filthy sheets and twisted in pain.

"It's goin' be Christmas 'fore you know it, Rebecca," Miz Subie said to her. "I got the shawl you made me last year." She wore a green spi-derwebby thing.

"A year already come and gone, and I missed it," Rebecca said. Red-wood had seen her at Iona's. Rebecca wasn't right in the head, but she loved the blues. Her teeth were yellow, her skin was ashy, and what flesh she had hung from her bones.

"Spring never come fast enough for me." Subie touched Rebecca's head and the gal shuddered. "I'm always waiting on the heat." Subie chattered on, praising steamy summer days when the ground held the heat like a blanket for the night. Rebecca settled into her words and touch.

A middle-aged woman with a riot of nappy hair busting through a tattered head rag stepped out of the shadows by the chimney. She smelled sour and looked anxious. Trembling, she pointed a bony finger at Redwood. "What's she doing here?"

"How do, Dora," Subie said and tucked her *mojo* bag into her skirt. "Redwood's working with me now. Getting old, got to pass it along."

Redwood hid her *mojo* bag as well.

"Don't tell my husband, Miz Subie. He wouldn't want to know"— she looked right at Redwood—"that y'all been here."

"I don't talk to the man," Subie said. "You can tell him what you please."

Subie listened to Rebecca's breath and felt the pulse of her heart. She wiped sweat from her brow, tasted it, and grimaced. Redwood did the same. It was salty and bitter and a few other tastes that Redwood would talk over with Subie later. Rebecca passed in and out, writhing in pain. Redwood reached a hand to her scrunched-up cheeks.

Subie held Redwood back. "Leave her pain be. It'll guide us for now."

Dora twitched and muttered. Redwood wondered if she had all her wits.

"Dora ain't ask us here on her own account." Subie read Redwood's thoughts and pulled back the sheet. Her face hardened as she examined Rebecca's bloody private parts. Redwood was wincing more than Rebecca, till Subie scowled her quiet. "Who cut her up so bad?" Subie said.

"She lost the baby—a sin against God," Dora said. "Can you fix her up?"

Redwood answered quickly. "Sure we can. Don't worry."

Subie narrowed her one good eye. "Stitching her up won't be enough. We got to bring the fever down." She thrust a needle at Redwood and pushed Dora toward a bucket. "She's all dried out, get us some water. We'll do what we can."

Subie didn't say a word all the way back to her house. No hoodoo spells and wisdom, no stories of her wild youth, no catalogue of plants that can heal or poison, no discussing the folks they'd been curing all day. Redwood didn't dare chatter or ask a question. Subie was in a mood. The temperature dropped quickly as the sun left the sky. Redwood's hands got stiff with cold, and even though she did all the paddling for over three hours, Subie looked more tired than her when they dragged into her cozy kitchen. Healing wearied Subie worse than ever these days. The old woman dropped in a rocker by the fireplace and yawned like a bear.

"I'm feeling every minute of my long years," she grumbled.

After the close quarters at Dora's, Subie's two-room cabin was a palace, fragrant and magical. Dried herbs and flowers hung from every beam. Amulets, mandalas, and painted spells decorated the walls. Bottles of her cure-all lined the mantel, ready for sale. Redwood lit a fire in the stove and stowed the roots, potions, powders, candles, dirt, and tools exactly where Subie liked to find them. The orderliness of her stocks was a lesson of its own. Subie knew the magic of setting one thing against another.

"Today seem like a hundred days," Redwood said.

Not certain she put everything in its place, Redwood set the traveling basket by the stove and went out to the well. She hauled in two buckets of fresh water and set a kettle to boil. A bush by the door with colored bottles strung on bare branches tinkled in the wind each time she passed.

"You and Aidan both catching mean spirits," Redwood said. "We tossed his in the stream. What you do with a bottle of badness?"

With great effort, Subie bent over to arrange kindling in the fireplace. "Don't ever say you can do what you can't." The fire caught quickly.

"Sorry, Miz Subie, I just—"

"Don't *sorry* me. A gift such as yours will turn to a curse without wisdom." When flames were dancing to her satisfaction, Subie sank back in her rocker. "Garnett ask me to look out." She watched the fire, as if it had a story to tell.

Redwood brought Subie a basin of hot water to wash up. "I almost can't remember Mama's face." Redwood washed herself from another basin. "I remember how Mama smelled: hickory smoke, magnolia soap, and some ole nasty tea that seemed sweet till after you drank it."

Subie struggled up again. The cold was settling in her joints. She creaked and cracked like an old door. "I know this tea. Give you the runs. Clean out every evil thing in you." She hobbled over to a chest of drawers and riffled through several. "Here." She pulled out a photo wrapped in a violet handkerchief.

It was a black-and-white image of Garnett Phipps with an orchid in her hair, looking how Redwood would at thirty-five. "I didn't know you had a photo of Mama."

"From the Chicago Fair." Subie sat back down. "I got plenty you don't know."

"Mama don't talk to me since she gone to Glory."

Redwood had promised Miz Subie not to do anything *wild* till she was good and strong, but holding a picture of Garnett, Redwood couldn't help herself. She'd been feeling so much better lately, practically her old self. Being mad at everyone for lying to her hadn't dampened her spirit; in fact it was a tonic for what ailed her. So with Subie nodding off to sleep in her rocker, Redwood squinted through heavy-lidded eyes at the black-and-white image till it came to life: Mama's hot breath fogged the air; big brown eyes reflected red firelight, but not at the Chicago Fair like Redwood expected. It was Christmas 1898, and the family was running through the swamp. Crackers were burning colored Peach Grove. Garnett pulled a young Redwood out of the mud and hugged her as she shivered. Baby Iris gurgled on Garnett's back. George stood beside them, his teeth chattering.

"I know you feel the cold," Garnett said. "We got to keep going till I see the way into tomorrow."

Redwood gulped cold swamp air, and the chill startled her eyes wide again. She was on her knees in front of the fireplace soaked in dew. She clasped the photo to her chest and fought tears. Subie was wide awake watching her, fierce and sharp as an osprey fixing to dive for a big, juicy fish.

"You can't control a spell like that. You go where it take you."

"I was running and hiding with her again," Redwood said.

"I found you that night." Subie nodded. "Garnett left a trail that I had to follow."

"If Mama had all that hoodoo power like everybody say, how come she let 'em string her up that way? How come she died swinging in a tree? How come they burned her, till you almost couldn't tell who she was?"

Subie stuffed tobacco in a pipe. "Garnett run you all 'round that swamp hoping to find a spell."

"Why'd she leave us?" Redwood stared at the red-eyed photograph. Flower in Garnett's hair had a spot of purple color too.

"Can't know all what's in a person's heart," Subie said.

"Why didn't she kill 'em 'stead of letting 'em kill her?"

"Killing goes both ways. Dying is your own business."

"Don't we get to defend ourselves without it coming back down on us?"

"She didn't want more blood on her hands."

Redwood shook with so much anger and hurt, her backbones popped and cracked. A mighty pain shot up her neck. "Why didn't nobody tell me?"

"Don't know 'bout all of everybody else," Subie replied.

"Why didn't *you* then?" Pain shot down Redwood's legs. She could pull somebody else's ache and throw it away, but not her own.

Subie drew on her pipe. "So you could grow into yourself, big and strong, without a shadow over your soul. So this heartless world wouldn't snatch your power 'fore it got going good." Subie sighed. "Garnett asked me to see to that. I did the best I could."

Redwood sat down in a rocking chair that had swamp flowers carved 'cross the back and vines twisting into armrests. She rocked hard back and forth till she could stand herself again. "Is this a new chair?" She rubbed the wood.

"Yes, Mr. Cooper come by, bought a spirit spell, and left that chair." Subie sucked her pipe. "He asked after you."

SEVEN

Peach Grove, 1904

"You trying to go lame on me?" Aidan rubbed Princess's swollen right leg. She grumbled and stomped her left front foot, but tolerated the poultice he wrapped on the bad one. She nibbled at his pockets and he gave her a mushy pear. Overcome, he hugged her neck as she chewed. Princess tolerated a gush of emotion now and again.

"I don't know what's wrong with me today. Ain't everything coming my way?"

Money from the winter crop was burning a hole in his pocket. He should buy what he needed, spring seed and feed and such, so he wouldn't have to borrow against the farm, so he didn't lose it all buying drink.

"I'll see to it in the morning," he promised Princess, patting his alligator pouch.

As he walked from the shed, the sun sat low on the horizon, teasing him with a bit of warmth. Fog curled up from the creek. Garnett's voice on the wind was faint; Aidan couldn't hear what she was saying this afternoon. The nightriders were quiet too—or off riding torment somewhere else.

Aidan hoisted the jug he'd just bought from Leroy Richards yesterday. It was still full. He pulled out the stopper and the whiskey sloshed onto his hands, evaporating quickly and leaving a chill on his palm. He closed the jug and 'stead of licking his skin, he set the jug on the steps and walked into the house. He didn't need to get stinking drunk tonight. Wasn't nobody or nothing haunting him.

Redwood's book, *Of One Blood: Or, The Hidden Self* by Pauline Hopkins, was the first thing he saw sitting on the kitchen table. Sober for a week, he'd been reading every night and was almost to the end. He hadn't seen Redwood since she'd loaned him the book. Was this heartache, missing her? What would she think of his hidden self? The gal was quicksilver, one moment giving him a book to read, saying they had to talk as soon as he was done and the next moment mad enough to shoot him.

Why was he supposed to tell her what her own family wouldn't?

She was headstrong and reckless, running 'round the swamp, sashaying through town with all those crackers, and colored men too, wondering what was going on between them long legs and switching hips. She didn't want nobody to tell her nothing—she knew it all! If she did admit to ignorance, she wasn't satisfied 'less she figured it out herself. Same as her brother, Redwood didn't never want to be caught wrong, and she had to stick her nose into anything. Gal dragged him off to Chicago without an invite or a by-your-leave.

His heart was pumping like he'd run uphill, and he was just standing still, thinking.

He didn't need to be loving a wild hoodoo gal, not a gal from the colored side of the creek, not in Peach Grove, not after all the bad water that come tearing his way. She was Garnett's gal to boot. A stitch of pain in his side made him gasp. White Peach Grove wouldn't give a damn if he dragged Redwood out back to a shed and used her like an animal. Colored Peach Grove might be angry behind their hands or think it served Redwood right for strutting 'round, a queen of Dahomey, getting friendly with whoever she pleased. If she loved him back, if he tried to marry her, if he tried to *do right*, upstanding citizens would want to string him up like a colored man. And the likes of Brother George would want to take a shotgun after him and risk getting strung up themselves. He should leave this love alone.

Aidan started outside for the jug.

Big Thunder and Miss O'Casey would've been disappointed by their son's cowardly thoughts. His parents had always lived in their own world, not somebody else's, *isti siminoli*. They steered clear of regular, drylongso folk who balked at any real test of freedom, exactly the kind of folk Aidan Cooper was turning into.

Course, he had plenty of help there.

Aunt Caitlin didn't want anybody in Peach Grove to know squat 'bout Aidan's parents. She never forgave Sister Aislinn for telling her son they'd *both* worked in a house of ill repute. Caitlin's attempts at turning Aidan into a good Catholic failed miserably—mainly 'cause she didn't like Mass any more than he did. She and Charlie Cooper were scared of any lazy *Injun* they saw in Aidan. Charlie Cooper couldn't figure the point of reading books when there was so much work to be done. Whippings made the boy hide in the swamp. Once, after reading a few sentences (she claimed most of his writing was too blurry for her old eyes), Aunt Caitlin tried to set fire to his journal. She burned up her apron instead. When he told her writing in the book was Miz Garnett's hoodoo spell for whatever ailed him, she let it be. Still and all, Aidan got used to living lies, to walking 'round the easy way.

"How can I *do right*, Miz Garnett? I just don't see it."

After washing his hands and face three times with strong soap and scalding water, he pulled out his journal and sat down to write. Aidan made hisself just another character in the tale, like how his mama told a story.

GARNETT'S CURSE

If there was a *curse,* the upstanding citizens of Peach Grove had cursed themselves, not Miz Garnett. From age fifteen, Aidan Cooper hid away from folks in a bottle or a jug. But he didn't start suicide drinking till after Peach Grovers strung up Garnett Phipps.

In 1898, yellow fever took Raymond Phipps, Garnett's husband, and a lot of men couldn't stand a beautiful gal like her going to waste. They say Everett Williams offered her a pile of money, but she wasn't giving up nothing 'cept roots and *get-well* spells. Everett put his hands to her, and Garnett shot him in the throat. When Miz Caroline Williams buried her rogue of a brother-in-law three days later, Garnett was long gone. She'd gathered what family yellow fever had left her—son George, baby Iris, and sweet Redwood—and vanished into the swamps.

Lone deputies hunting down a conjure woman as powerful as Garnett didn't stand a chance, so a few days before Christmas the upstanding white men of the county rode out in a great horde. They shot up and burned colored Peach Grove. A war Aidan Cooper wouldn't join, couldn't do anything about, and sure couldn't bear to see, so he took to hiding out in the woods, supposedly hunting deer. He was on the coward's path.

A lot of folk in Peach Grove, colored, white, and Indian, always thought Garnett was too uppity for her own good, but this time they said she was goin' get her people killed. Some colored folk were even madder at her than at the posse. Two days into the terror, when they gunned down Mr. Phillip Robeson and his two sons, burned the man's house and his babies still in it, Garnett broke into Sheriff Harry's office—locks never fazed her. She waited by the stove till he come back from hunting her. Seeing Garnett sitting at his desk, fool had a heart attack, certain his time had come and gone. Garnett nursed him back to life so she could turn herself in. Sheriff Harry didn't bother to lock her in a cell.

Garnett had conditions. She swore not to turn the evil eye on the posse, and they swore to leave the rest of the colored in peace. Who wanted a conjure woman coming after you from the grave? Certainly not a powerful one like Garnett who come out of hiding to die for her people.

Christmas eve, Aidan Cooper hid from all the trouble up a chestnut tree in a hunting perch. But weren't no deer, raccoons, rabbits, nothing, and he didn't have the heart to sing 'em out of hiding. He was dozing off till twelve hooded nightriders come clomping by, scenting the air with sweat and fear. A barred owl cut the night with its barking cry. The riders stopped below a scorched pine tree. Peering through moss and sweet bay branches, Aidan noted how these men sat their horses, how they sounded all liquored up. He recognized more than a few. Somebody rumbling hell fever and damnation had to be the Baptist preacher. Twisted-hand Sheriff Harry was carrying a torch. The fellow almost falling off his nag was a dead ringer for that peanut farmer with eleven kids and a bad back. Bringing up the rear and ready to skedaddle out of there was a tall, broad figure—

Hiram Johnson or Jerome Williams. Doc never put a horse between his legs. Their voices were low at first, muffled, unsure perhaps, but Aidan heard them all swear an oath to leave colored Peach Grove in peace: the barber, the deputy sheriff, Ken Smith who lost his farm to the Williams clan. Aidan and Ken had been fast friends once. Never thought to see him at a lynching.

Aidan told hisself he wasn't sure, on account of the hoods and black robes. Didn't the oily smoke from their torches ruin his vision till he couldn't tell who was who? Well maybe Aidan didn't want to look too hard. Maybe he didn't want to see what he was seeing. Garnett, Aidan would have recognized anywhere. She was tied and trussed, her long legs dangling bare and raw in the cold mist. Her mouth bled around the gag. They stripped her naked in the cold air.

It took a long time for her to die. Seemed like they had to kill her four, five times. They tried to set her body on fire, but she just wouldn't burn. Tall fellow who hunched over his black horse like Jerome, stayed in the shadows, never got close, didn't ever join in. His horse kept trying to bolt. Garnett looked right at Aidan, red eyes burning, and then she closed her lids and was gone. Aidan swallowed a howl.

The nightriders left what remained of Garnett's body hanging in that pine. Turkey buzzards gathered. The lazy flap of their wings could make Aidan scream, and to this day, the sound could drive him wild. The nightriders were gone an hour or more, and he didn't move. Wasn't sure he'd ever move again. When he finally climbed down from his perch, his legs were rubber and his bowels let loose all down his legs as he took off.

He wanted to run and run till he came to the end of the world and fell off, but he got no further than Aunt Caitlin's front yard. The laundry still hung on the line, stiff and cold. He couldn't leave Miz Garnett alone and tortured in that tree, to be pecked and mauled, to rot in the morning sun and stink to high heaven, with no company but torment and shame.

"What is comfort to a corpse?" The boneyard baron sneered at coward Aidan.

Aidan gathered hisself and ran back. After scaring the carrion eaters away, he cut her down from that tree and wrapped her in a sheet. Carolers in the distance sang at the stroke of twelve. Joy to the World, Merry Christmas. Nobody at the colored church really knew how the body came to lie with baby Jesus on Christmas morning. 'Stead of cursing a coward, folks blessed the angel who covered her in sweet bay branches and violet orchids.

Aidan never thought the living could haunt a body, but those twelve hooded men hounded him day and night, raided his dreams. Some days, every thought he had ended with nightriders blazing through his brain, the horses' hooves stamping on his nerves. He might have learned to bear that, but along the middle of February, as he turned fields for spring planting, Garnett joined the demon posse, pleading with him to do right.

So Aidan sucked down rotgut liquor till white masked faces blurred into the moonlight on moss, till Miz Garnett was a silent whoosh in his ears. May Ellen, Aidan's first wife, wouldn't talk to him about what had happened, what he'd seen, and the Johnson twins, even Doc, thought he ought to let sleeping dogs lie. By Josie, Aidan stayed drunk. He picked fights over nothing, smashed up barrooms, and he cussed out everyone who came in range. He broke Graham Wright's nose when the man was telling tales of glorious Choctaw valor—his ancestors whipping Creek and Seminole and colored folk too. Aidan couldn't stand nobody. Colored, white, and Indian let him be. Josie was ten years older than him and desperate. Suckling a newborn baby boy that wasn't his, she took off after a year, with half his seed money. Served him right.

Now, if Miz Garnett had sent her daughter Redwood to torment him, Redwood didn't know anything about it. That gal was surely the balm of Gilead. She took to walking by his fields to chat, even when he had nothing much to say. She made him come to her house for supper and play with Iris and the cousins. Listening to Ladd's lies and eating Elisa's stews and pies, Aidan almost felt good now and again. After hiding his ways from everybody since he was twelve, after almost forgetting who he could be, he and Redwood celebrated first fruits, did a green corn ceremony like with his folks. And though she didn't stop him drinking altogether, he never managed much lowdown behavior 'round her. Got him up in the morning, to smell the oil in her hair, to hear the E-LEC-TRI-CI-TY in her voice. Redwood was his medicine. With her at his side, the nightriders' hooves and Garnett's voice faded to a whisper. Still, Aidan wished he could go back and break the locks on his spirit, do what was right.

Whoever got to turn time around, though?

Aidan stowed the journal in his shoulder bag. Redwood could read this story for herself. He'd let her read any story of his that took her fancy. He wrapped his banjo in a blanket and slung it over his back. He strode out onto the porch and gathered the birds he'd finished carving last night: eagles, water hens, osprey, and an ibis. He'd been meaning to make a necklace with the yellow bead he brought back from the World's Fair—something fine African women wore—and give it to Redwood. He'd show her the bead and see what she thought. Feeling good, he jumped over the jug of Leroy's finest brew sitting pretty on the steps and headed for Ladd and Elisa's.

Fifteen minutes later, stumbling over loose stones, he dropped the osprey and ibis in the dirt. "They don't need to hear this story, Wildfire. Well, *she* don't." His banjo banged into his back, into his resolve, a dissonant chord. "Ain't goin' make her feel better. And *she* don't want to see you either."

He gathered up the toys but didn't turn back home. He sank down in the dirt.

———

Iona downed several big swallows of moonshine before Redwood set the bone in her arm back in its place. She howled more racket than a wounded hound dog and almost passed out.

"You should see Doc Johnson." Redwood didn't pull too much pain. That spooked some folks, and she wasn't sure 'bout Iona. "He know how to set a bone good."

"'Less you think this little break'll kill me, I'd rather not." Iona gasped and grunted and drank another mouthful from the jug. Her twin boys watched anxiously. "I don't care much for white folk. Suit me fine if I never have to see one again."

"Be a blessing if they all dropped off the Earth," Redwood said.

The twins cocked their heads at her. She wasn't sounding like herself.

"Mm-hmm." Iona was drunk with liquor and pain. She closed her eyes. "Wishing folk ill make you sick your ownself."

"I guess." Redwood finished fitting on a splint.

"Crazy Coop come by last night, sang a few songs, bought a jug. He asked after you."

"Did he now? Well I ain't studying him." Redwood worried that she'd cut off the blood flow, wrapping too tight. "Keep still and don't lift no weight, till it heal—a month, six weeks—or this ain't goin' work."

"A month?" Iona laughed. "Ha."

Redwood turned to the twins. "Don't let her carry nothing or do heavy work, you hear me?"

"I'll keep still." Iona pressed a silver dollar in Redwood's hand. "Leroy'll give you a ride far as the creek. Just don't spook the man. He believe in too much mess as it is."

Leroy left Redwood at the old Jessup peach orchard. Jerome Williams owned it now. Aidan's place was just through the trees a bit and down the road, closer than home.

"Mr. Cooper sounded good last night," Leroy remarked, following her gaze. "He said it was your fault he ain't buying so many jugs. Don't hoodoo all my best customers, gal." Leroy rode off laughing.

Everywhere she turned, Aidan Cooper was asking after her, talking 'bout her. It was not much of a secret anymore that something was going on between them. Even Bubba complained 'bout her having *somebody else*. Redwood hemmed and hawed under the peach trees. Aidan was supposed to be her special friend, somebody she could trust with *anything*, yet in all these years, he never told her what happened that Christmas night in 1898. In his favor, Aidan didn't lie to her. He just didn't say. The man carried all sorts of secrets. His journal was full of things he kept to hisself. She was dying to get a look inside and not really that mad at him. Mad at everybody else.

Truth be told, she felt ashamed for accepting what folks *didn't* say to her, for being a grown woman and still believing angels took Mama to Glory. A trusting fool and a coward too, she never found the nerve to ask Aidan who his people were.

She started toward his place. Two bobcats fussed at each other, making her spine tingle. Bobcats didn't scare her, and now that she'd imagined how it might feel for Aidan to hold and kiss her, for him to touch her, now that she'd imagined touching him, she wanted to do it and see if it felt as good as she hoped. Redwood stopped cold. What if he didn't want her, like he wanted May Ellen or even orange-haired Josie Fields? Aidan barely let Redwood touch him. What if he didn't like colored gals the way he liked white ones? You had to wonder 'bout white folk and all the misery they done in this world—even one that made your heart race. So how could she, with all this sadness hemming her in, still want Aidan to make her feel good *right now*? How come she would gladly do the same for him?

Can't hide from God's truth, just gotta work with it.

Mama hadn't talked to Redwood since she'd gone on to Glory. To hear the wind buzzing with her voice was a blessing. Redwood was walking again. She stepped from the trees and spied somebody sitting in the dirt down the road a piece with what must've been a banjo on his back. She started to wave and shout at Aidan, but Jerome Williams rode his shiny black stallion right in front of her and dismounted. Redwood frowned at first. She didn't want to see anybody but Aidan, yet Jerome looked so happy to see her, she smiled at him too. "How do, Mr. Williams."

Jerome slapped at a bug. "How do yourself."

"Fog coming in, but that don't make the bugs no nevermind." Cool mist tickled her ankles.

"Bugs don't seem to bother you."

"Me and mosquitoes and no-see-ums, we have an understanding."

Jerome shook his head, charmed. "Do tell."

"What you doing 'cross the creek? Coming to see Mr. Cooper too?"

"This is my orchard." Jerome moved close. "Actually, I was hoping to find you. Cherokee Will said he saw you coming this way."

"Me? You sick or something?" Redwood clutched the red *mojo* bag at her hip.

Jerome tilted his head, furrowed his brow. "Would that worry you?"

"Depends on how sick you are." She teased him. "Ain't Doc Johnson still in town?"

"I don't need doctoring." He sounded mad at somebody. "I've come to . . ." He searched for a good line. "I've come to take you away."

"What you say?"

"Before they ruin you."

"Who? No!" Redwood almost laughed, but his face looked too serious.

"Ruin you the way they did your mother." Jerome's gray eyes got misty, looking past now into back then. "You're even prettier than she was."

Redwood wanted to run, but the horse was behind her.

"I forgave her, you know. Uncle Everett was a pig. But I can take you away from all that." Jerome was talking to hisself really, feverish eyes flitting 'round his face.

"I don't need you to take me nowhere. You talking out your head."

Jerome grabbed her wrist, so tight, he could've snapped the bone. "Every time you saunter through town, you got a smile for me." He tried to kiss her.

Redwood shoved him away. "Stop, don't." How was this happening to her?

Jerome ripped at her clothes, tearing easily through her blouse and undershirt. Spooked by their thrashing, the stallion reared up and galloped off down the road.

"Can't get your scent out of my dreams. Walking 'round like Queen Somebody."

Redwood punched his chest with her free hand. He grunted at her blows and then caught her fist. She was strong, but not strong enough to escape him. They crashed to the ground with her fighting fiercely. The weight of him knocked the wind out of her. One of her arms got twisted and pinned under her back. Jerome was wiggling out his pants and pawing her tiddies. She couldn't think straight.

"Don't do me like this," she hissed right in his ear.

Jerome didn't listen. "I see stars in your eyes and a sweet night blooming between your thighs. Your honey ripe breasts and luxurious hips have called to my blood."

"You talking poetry to me?" Redwood gagged as he tried to kiss her. "Stop!"

He bit her tongue. Blood oozed in her mouth.

"You do Crazy Coop, gal, so don't pretend you're all that particular."

This shocked her still. Jerome had caught her in forbidden thoughts. Seizing this lull in her tight-thighed struggle, he thrust his hard member into her body, ripping and tearing delicate flesh. She shrieked: the sound startled the old oak trees all down the lane. They twisted and turned, lifting ancient boughs. Thick mats of roots strained under the fields. Yet they could not come to her aid. Redwood's cry echoed against the rocks. A bear with a star-shaped scar on his cheek, curled in his den for a winter's sleep, awoke in panic. He was far from Oak Lane and could only snort and bellow in Redwood's defense. Jerome stuffed Redwood's mouth with her head rag. As he pumped toward a climax, she was silent, still, her eyes as hard as flint.

A piercing yelp almost knocked Aidan over. The ground shuddered. He felt sighing branches and aching roots. He heard a bear hollering from his cave. He turned and squinted through fog. He could just make out a naked white behind flexing between a tattered skirt and flailing dark legs and the fog closed in again. He froze, praying for a moment that he was caught in a lurid nightmare. Terror gripped him as Jerome's stallion galloped by. Redwood screamed again. Shaking hisself, Aidan dropped the toy birds and ran through the thick mist. Banjo strings twanged against his back as he clambered down the road. He would've thrown the instrument into the bushes, but he didn't want to take the time. He strained and gasped, running so fast he flew through the air, scrambling now and again for solid ground. Still it took forever . . .

"That's not so bad, is it?" Jerome pumped against Redwood's rag doll body.

Flying over the last bit of ground, Aidan heard something crack, a dry wood sound and then Jerome's scream, breaking up before it really started. Aidan grabbed the man's shoulders and hauled him off Redwood. His fist was raised to slug him. Jerome's head lolled back and forth, a rag doll too. Blood poured from his throat and out his lips. Terror had frozen in his eyes.

"He's dead. He's gone." Redwood lay stone still, one arm still twisted underneath her back.

"What?!" Aidan dropped Jerome and backed away. "You break his neck with one hand?" Her hoodoo storm hand.

Redwood struggled up, grasping at her ripped blouse and skirt. Fumbling, Aidan unwrapped the banjo and offered her the blanket. She smacked it away with bruised fingers and hugged the tatters of clothing to her body. Aidan didn't see many bruises or any wounds. But her sweet features were twisted into a ghoul mask. He had never wanted to spy such horror on her face.

"He was on me so fast, I didn't know what . . ."

Aidan had seen this coming. He knew how Jerome was. Everybody did. The man didn't hide his appetites. He was ruthless at any business and undefeated in love, what he called love anyway. Aidan was such a stand-around-and-do-nothing coward. He should have taken his shotgun and—

"You sure he's dead?"

Aidan got down on the ground and inspected Jerome's broken neck, whistled, and shook his head. He closed Jerome's eyes and sprinkled dirt on the lids. Watching this, Redwood spit blood on the ground. Her tongue was bleeding. She flailed at fog licking her cheeks. She rubbed her skin hard, as if to clean something nasty off.

"I came too late, huh?" he murmured.

"He's dead. Ain't no later than that."

"But you alive, gal."

"Felt like he just wanted to burn me up."

"Light a man's passion the way you do, he 'llowed to burn every-thing in sight."

"Never did anything to the man but smile," she yelled. "Ain't my fault what he be doing with my smile, you hear me? His fault."

Nothing coming out Aidan's mouth was right so he didn't say any more.

They stood over the body a long while, just breathing at one another. Sun slid down under the horizon, leaving a purple glow. A trickle of blood ran down her leg and a trickle of white. Jerome's future was cluttering up her insides. Aidan didn't know how to comfort her.

Redwood clutched the tattered blouse over her tiddies. This left her private parts exposed. Aidan just stared at her, mumbling stupid talk, tears in his eyes as if Jerome Williams had rammed into *him* and torn up *his* insides. Redwood suddenly couldn't stand still. Her feet itched, her mouth was sore, and her skin was crawling 'cross itself. Inside, bits of Jerome swam into tomorrow. But Jerome was gone from this world. With her storm hand, she'd broken his neck and dispatched him onto his next journey.

The wind picked up. The fog on her bare skin was driving her mad. She couldn't see straight and tripped into Jerome's cold butt. She gagged and almost fell over. Aidan broke her fall, and for no good reason she could think of, she beat his chest and face with her fists, hollering like a flock of crows. Finally, he took hold of her wrists, and she was just crying and crying and didn't know if she could stop. She wanted him to hold her in his arms, protect her from what happened, but she didn't want him to touch her.

When the heaving and weeping had drained all the madness and her arms were too tired to carry her fists, Aidan let her hands go and threw a blanket at her shoulders so she could cover herself. She clutched it tight. At least she wasn't naked on the road, her shame on parade. She hugged the rough cloth tight against her raw skin. That was better than slimy fog.

"George was right," she said, walking just to be walking.

"'Bout what?" Aidan followed her.

"Me, everything." She quivered. "I ain't got the sense I was born with, trusting a—"

"George might've figured out the likes of Jerome Williams, but that don't make you wrong."

Any other time she would've smiled at Aidan standing up for her. But there weren't no smiles left in her. Every step she took hurt like hellfire and damnation, every jagged gasp of breath tore at her soul.

"This ain't no place to be a woman," she said.

Aidan gaped at her, shame-faced.

"Am I lying?" she asked. "Jerome say he'd take me away, 'fore *they ruined me.*"

"We have to think." He licked a bloody lip. His right eye was swelling up. He was goin' have quite a few bruises—from her hands, hands that killed a man too.

"My soul, what 'bout my soul?" she asked.

"You should go."

"A hoodoo woman can't always control the spell, don't always know what she be conjuring." She balled a fist. "I didn't mean to kill him. But it—it felt good when I did."

"Get you away from here. They'll hang you over this."

She tripped over nothing. He reached for her, but missed and hugged thick fog instead. She stayed out of reach.

"George is gone already," she said. "I got a baby sister counting on me."

"Iris can't count on you dead."

"What am I goin' do?" She stopped.

"Keep walking," he said.

Redwood lurched down the road toward his house. Aidan kept pace beside her, his arm barely touching her back, catching her every once in a while, so she wouldn't fall. She wished he'd go away, but then she'd be alone. Her head was light. She couldn't find the back of her breath. Nasty little gasps weren't doing much for her.

"Come on now, take a good breath," he said, as if she were a baby.

"I can't. I just can't." But she did.

"You have to be long gone 'fore they set a posse on you."

"Miz Subie say, demon posse can hunt you beyond the grave."

"The demons I'm worried 'bout are men. You gotta run."

"Where? Nightriders will hunt me down, same as Mama. Burn colored Peach Grove while they at it."

Aidan looked at something she couldn't see. He listened to sounds that didn't touch her ears, then turned to her, the blood gone from his face. "Foot won't take you far as a mule, but it's safer. Easier to track a mule."

Redwood halted and sank down to the ground, dragging Aidan with her. She jammed her fists in loose gravel. "Jerome deserve to die for what he did. I just don't deserve his blood on my hands."

Aidan pulled her fingers from the dirt, tried to lift her up. She flung his arms back at him. "Come on and get up now," he said.

"What good is power if it can't save you?"

"Don't let Jerome Williams break your heart, scatter your spirit."

"Spirits be too late to undo what I did."

Aidan sighed. Maybe he was goin' give up on her, abandon her, like a man waking from a nightmare can get up and go on 'bout his business. A twister of fog swirled toward them, gathering force. The old oak trees bent and swayed. Twigs and debris mixed with swirling gravel and vines. One enormous branch was ominously close to snapping. Thick Spanish moss lashed Aidan's face and back. He clawed it from his eyes.

"Listen to me," he shouted over howling wind. "Jerome Williams, he try to bust into you and it's like to drive you mad, but—"

"Why he want to do that?" Jerome's baby soft hands were all over her body still; his sour sweet breath filled her nostrils; his manhood swelled against bruised thighs, breaking a hole in the future. "And why you didn't come sooner?" Aidan took hold of her face and looked into her eyes. She wanted to smack his callused fingers away. She didn't want any man to lay a hand on her ever again or else. "What?"

"I'm not too late to say it was me who broke Mr. Williams's neck," Aidan said. The old oaks rocking above them were suddenly still. The wind dropped to a murmur. "It's a clean break. Who'd believe a skinny snap like you got that kinda power?"

"But you can't." Redwood stood up. "Then I'll have you all over my soul too."

"I gotta do something right," he said.

"Ain't nothing right to do."

"You got to quit being stubborn here."

"I don't know."

He put his arm 'round her waist. She flinched, but he got her to walking again. "What's to know?" he whispered. "Crackers will tear up colored Peach Grove if they think you killed Jerome Williams."

She gazed 'cross a field and beyond a stand of Georgia pine to Aunt and Uncle's place. Chimney smoke snaked over the trees. "Aunt Elisa's making supper, laying out a place for me, Iris, my cousins, even a place for you. Uncle Ladd's telling those big fat freedom lies the little ones love, that everybody love, 'cept George."

"Don't worry. Your sister got people to look after her."

"You goin' take care of Iris?" She raised her fist at him. "Like you took care of me?"

Tears welled in his eyes. "Better. I swear to you."

She dropped her fist. "I can't think," she said. "My mind's gone." They trudged on.

Aidan was glad his house was in sight, even though it looked to have been hit by a storm since Josie left. Tools, clothes, bottles, firewood, empty sacks, broken harnesses were scattered in the yard. A window dangled from its casement. Jagged broken glass he hadn't noticed before was looking deadly to him now. The front door hung on its hinges like a loose tooth. The jug of hooch sat in the middle of the steps calling to his parched throat. Aidan wound through the debris, supporting Redwood. She leaned her full weight into him finally. Princess snorted at them from the shed.

"Don't know where to go. Peach Grove is the only home I got," she said.

"Make your home on the road, make your life up as you go," Aidan said. "Fix your soul somewhere far away from Georgia."

"How am I goin' do all that?"

Aidan let go of her and waited a breath to see if she would stand on her own. She was shaky but did not fall. He pulled a billfold from his pocket and thrust the contents at her. If he couldn't turn time 'round, if he couldn't go back and *do* what was *right*, he could offer her a decent chance.

"What's that? More cash money than I ever seen. You rob the bank?"

"My life savings." He stuffed bills and a tiny sack of gold coins in her hand.

"You just carry it 'round with you like that?"

"Had a feeling this morning."

"I can't take all your money."

"I've been waiting for a special moment."

Going up the steps was a challenge for her balance. He caught her twice. The bottle tree tinkled in the breeze. She hesitated at the door, almost breaking into tears.

"Why you do all this for me?" she said, as if she didn't know he ached to do much more, as if his heart wasn't breaking.

"You think I want to see you swinging from a rope? A colored woman ain't 'llowed to defend herself and live to tell the tale."

"Who you telling?"

Aidan's eyes brimmed with tears again.

"I don't want your cheap talk, your tears, or your money." Her words were a whip lashing his face. She shoved the bills and gold pieces at him. He took hold of her arm before she could get down the stairs. She glared at him, but he wouldn't let her go.

"I'll say, you my gal, and Jerome Williams, he try to take you away from me. I'll say, I saw him on you and I went wild and then I snapped his neck. I'm Crazy Coop, ain't I? I'll say what I should've done."

Redwood's lip trembled, but she couldn't speak.

Aidan's kitchen was as chaotic as the yard. Broken dishes and furniture, half-eaten meals, liquor jugs, smashed boxes, and dirty clothes were scattered everywhere. Redwood perched on a chair. Somehow, she'd gotten out of her torn things and was now wearing Aidan's shirt and pants. Her red *mojo* bag hung from a rope cinching the loose waist. Laying her head on the table between *Of One Blood: Or, The Hidden Self* and a pile of money, she bumped into the banjo. It twanged out of tune. Aidan stuffed her feet into his dew-soggy brogans.

"They're cold, wet," she said.

"They're clean. The clothes too . . . You need things that ain't ripped."

He tied the straps tight 'round the ankles. "Good thing you got big feet . . ."

An old joke between them. Redwood shook her head. "All your money and your best working boots."

"When's your aunt expecting you?"

"She too busy to be checking my time. She just leave my food and fall down asleep."

"Every shut-eye ain't sleep. She could worry 'bout you in her dreams, wake up, and then come looking." Aidan riffled through a cupboard till he found a music box. "Can't nobody find your trail, you hear me?"

"Can't say goodbye, not even to Miz Subie?"

He opened the false bottom of the music box and stuffed the bills and coins inside. "I'll say you run off to Florida, so don't go that a way. Your uncle could track a flea."

"This shirt smell like you, musty and wild. And the pants are too short."

He ran his finger along the box. "Your mama give me this."

She didn't want to think on Garnett. "They might hang you over a dead rich man or put you away from the sun, the oak trees, from your swamp stink and cricket racket. Why risk freedom for me?"

"This is freedom." He twisted the screw and sang the old Stephen Foster song:

> *Way down upon the Swanee River*
> *far, far away,*
> *All up and down the whole creation*
> *Sadly I roam*

Redwood sat up out of her slump. "You a conjure man when you sing."

"Garnett Phipps always had a kind word. The two of you, cut from the same cloth." He put the music box in a burlap sack with biscuits, peach pie, slices of cured ham, and a bottle of Miz Subie's cure-all. He thrust a pistol at her. "I know you can take care of yourself, but this'll scare off the fools what ain't got the sense to leave you be . . ."

Redwood stood up from the table, shaking her head at the gun.

He thrust it at her again. Outside, an owl hooted. She jumped and gingerly took the pistol.

"Brother George is up in Chicago," she said.

"Hush. I can't tell what I don't know."

Redwood hugged him suddenly. He was surprised, but hugged her too. Her tears wet the back of his neck. "How can I thank you?"

"Forgive me."

Redwood shook her head, but did not speak. He stroked her cheek once with clumsy, rough hands. She closed her eyes.

"I ain't used to touching soft anymore," he said.

She wiped at tears. He gently pushed her out the door.

"Forgive yourself and live a long, good life, Miz Redwood. That's more than enough for me."

Redwood walked down the steps into the yard. "Come with me," she whispered, so soft she almost couldn't hear her ownself.

Aidan was grabbing his shotgun from the porch. He didn't hear her.

EIGHT

Georgia Countryside, 1904

Aidan and Redwood ran through shadows and moss. Quiet and lithe, they were at home in the night, in the brush. Aidan swept their foot-steps away with a branch broom held behind his back. They ran into a stream. Dark water raced against their feet. They glided over smooth stone, gaining speed on the slick surface. Running faster than she should in the wet, in the dark, felt good. Bathed in sweat, her heart pounding, Redwood let some of Jerome Williams pass from her into the night air and the fast-moving stream. After several miles, they burst onto a road. Fog rippled over their wet boots.

"I'll leave you here," Aidan said, "my *Sikwayi,* my Sequoia."

Redwood reached her storm hand toward him. He backed away, but then held his ground, sucking a foggy breath. She placed her hand over his heart. They stood silently a moment. Yellow eyes watched them from a tree branch. Aidan set his cap on her head and then disappeared into the trees. Redwood watched the dark until his sounds were lost to the night. How could he leave her, with hardly a word or a plan, after all she'd just been through? The moon rose, a bloody orange fiend stalking the road. The fog snaked up to her waist, rising steadily with her fear.

"Aidan! I killed him, Aidan," she shouted. "Couldn't think of noth-ing else. And killing goes both ways. Do you hear me? Come back, don't leave me all alone."

Animal sounds answered her. What might have been a bear ran 'cross the foggy road into the woods. Conjure woman had to make her own way, call up a boat to cross any stream. Redwood touched the pistol tucked in her pants, and wary of every shadow, she walked on without Aidan.

———

Aidan's heart wrenched at Redwood's plea. He watched her from a perch in a pine tree. He wanted to follow her, but had to go back if he was goin' *do right*. He couldn't leave Jerome's half-naked body sprawled in the road for folks to come along and make up their own story. "I'll turn back," he whispered a prayer or a promise to the night, "as soon as I'm sure she's safe."

When would that be?

A black bear, roused from winter sleep, hid behind a bush and watched Redwood too. She passed the animal, glanced in its direction, and then headed toward the moon. Aidan raised his shotgun. The bear reared up on its hind legs, sniffing the air. Aidan was downwind and went unnoticed. He had a clear shot.

"Just leave her be, bear, that's all I'm asking."

The bear scratched at a tree trunk and vanished into the bushes. Aidan lowered the gun. He had no heart for killing this night.

Redwood was a dim figure in the distance, moving fast. Aidan climbed down and followed her, sticking to shadows. Whenever she turned to look behind her, he stood still, another sapling sneaking up among old-growth trees. Smelling a cook fire and horses, Aidan circled ahead of her to a clearing in the woods.

Traveling bluesmen, Milton O'Reilly and Eddie Starks who played Peach Grove from time to time, were camped on soft pine needles. Aidan had played music with them at Iona and Leroy's the other night. They were harmless fellows who put on a good show. Their swank stage costumes, slick mustaches, and fancy man hair looked out of place on the side of this road. An enormous fire smoked—green wood sizzling and popping—and their bean and bacon dinner stank up the night. Milton crawled under a thin blanket, sweating and trembling. Eddie crouched beside him, a panicked look on his handsome face. Two horses and a mule-eyed Aidan without so much as a whinny. He stroked their flanks gratefully. Redwood strode up to the fire and Eddie jumped to his feet.

"What is it, Eddie?" Milton's voice croaked.

"A woman come walking out the fog." Eddie didn't look happy at this.

"What's the matter with your friend?" Redwood asked. Her hand was on the pistol, a gale wind was at her shoulder.

"Snakebite or I don't know. Milton's out his head."

"Boneyard baron's breathing down Milton's neck." Redwood stood over him.

"So do what you can. I'm not ready to go," Milton said.

"Show me the bite." Redwood set down her bag.

Milton trembled as he exposed a swollen, puffy ankle. She examined it carefully with Eddie hovering over her.

"Spider bite. Blood poisoning," she said.

Pulling a knife from Eddie's belt, she cut into Milton before Eddie could react. Aidan sighed as Eddie eyed her with respect. Milton winced at her sucking out his wound. She spit into the fire. As it hissed, she clutched her *mojo* bag. Pulling a burning chunk of wood from the flames, she headed into the trees. Aidan didn't take a breath. She walked right by him—just another shadow in a forest of moon shade.

Eddie sidled up to her burlap bag. He bent over, fixing to poke inside, but Redwood returned from the opposite side of the camp, brandishing a slimy root. Eddie jumped away from her things. The pistol at her waist caught a bit of light as she tossed her torch back in the fire. She crouched down to Milton.

"You could still die, but you might live. This'll hurt like the devil either way."

Milton nodded. She gave him a stick to bite on. He turned from her and ground down on that wood as she dug into his flesh again with the knife. His eyes watered. She slapped the slimy root against his ankle and tied it there with a rag. Eddie jerked at Milton's pain, scowling at Redwood.

"You that hoodoo gal scared the bear away?" Eddie said.

"We played music with her twice, fool," Milton said. "At Iona and Leroy's."

Redwood threw Eddie's knife right at him. He froze and it landed between his feet. "You go messing through my bag again, your hand 'llowed to fall off. Maybe something else too. I ain't putting up with no stuff."

Eddie must've heard the squall in her voice. He backed away, raising his hands high. Redwood sat close to Milton, lifting his head into her lap.

"She's not goin' be trouble," Milton said. "Are you?"

Redwood was a hoodoo and they knew it. Aidan could smell a healthy dose of fear on both of them. That suited him just fine.

"I remember what y'all played that first night. Bear didn't like your blues." She got the melody going. "Just can't find the words no more."

"Words don't matter half as much as the tune." Milton looked like she was pulling his pain.

Redwood sang nonsense syllables—the most powerful blues Aidan had ever heard her do. Jerome hadn't broken her voice. That was such a relief, he almost shouted and gave his hiding place away. Redwood squinted in his direction as it was. When she come back to the refrain, Aidan turned from her and ran for the creek without looking back. Otherwise he would've never gotten away.

Still a ways from home, Aidan sang a melody that was harmony to Redwood's tune. It was good music for soothing spooked nerves and calming a skittish temper. Singing and stroking the air, he ambled through magnolia trees toward a dark shadow at the edge of the road. Before Jerome's black stallion could bolt, he grasped the bridle.

"You've been tracking me." Aidan stroked its sleek neck. Cords of muscle rippled under his touch. "Ain't you pretty." This magnificent animal was worth a fortune, but not good for much 'cept show. "Jerome don't deserve you . . . I guess it's *didn't* deserve now." The horse nuzzled him, happy for company. Aidan pulled an apple from his pocket and offered it. "My Princess goin' be mad at you, eating my pockets clean."

Aidan jumped on the stallion's back and they charged down the road.

It was almost dawn when holding the horse's reins, Aidan stood at the old Jessup orchard contemplating the remains of Jerome Williams. The body was stiff, cold. Something had pecked at the back and butt. A trail of insects was moving into his bloody neck. The stallion shuddered and shied away from his former rider. Aidan surveyed every direction. The road, the fields, the orchards were deserted, peaceful, dusted in the foggy pink of sunrise. Buzzards hadn't smelled dead flesh yet. He checked the ground. No recent human tracks 'cept his, Redwood's, and Jerome's.

No one else knew what had happened last night.

He rifled through Jerome's pockets and found a wallet stuffed with money—ten times his own savings. The horse nosed the greenbacks, hoping for something sweet, another apple perhaps. Instead, Aidan found two train tickets to New York City and tumbled onto his butt. Was it true then? He, Aidan Wildfire was a drunken coward, 'fraid to do anything, but Jerome Williams wanted to take Redwood up to New York City, where he could marry her if he wanted or throw her away when he was done.

Aidan surveyed the empty road again. He stuffed the tickets and money in the alligator pouch on his hip. Spitting the taste in his mouth in the dust, he lifted Jerome, heaved him 'cross the saddle, and secured him with a rope. Unhappy with this operation, the stallion bucked a few times, working up to a kick that almost threw the body off. Aidan held him firmly.

"Whoa, whoa now. We got to find the right spot to lay Mr. Williams to rest." Aidan sang Redwood's tune into the stallion's ears. When its wild eyes grew calm, he leapt up in front of Jerome. The horse reared once, but didn't buck. "I know a good place."

Aidan galloped through trees and bushes, pressing the stallion till he was covered in white lather and the sun was overhead, hammering them with heat. Jerome stank to high heaven. Taking every back road and secret shortcut, they reached the Okefenokee Swamp without crossing paths with another soul. The stallion stared back at Aidan and the stinking corpse with bulging eyes. A cloud of flies buzzed, and a turkey buzzard eyed them from a mossy snag in a dead cypress tree.

"This is where I mean to be, but I don't quite know what we're doing yet."

The horse trotted into the dark current, splashing water and mud against Aidan's legs and Jerome's head and feet. At the sound of an oar, Aidan pulled the horse up sharp and jumped into the mud. Gently rubbing his nose, he led the stallion into a stand of water tupelos. The tree branches swayed in a warm breeze. Burnished red leaves drifted to the water revealing a feast of tupelo blueberries that had escaped hungry birds. Aidan's stomach gurgled. He could've thrown up.

A boat wound through the bulging knees of cypress trees. The hair

and bulk on the boatman looked like Obediah Barber, but he lived at
the northern rim of the swamp. This fellow, whoever he was, passed
without noticing them—not as keen a swamp scout as Obediah.

Aidan stuck to muddy shallows and shadowy backways. Winter
days were short and going overland took longer than going by canoe.
He didn't reach his *chickee* till the sun was going down. The banners
marking the four directions were tatters now. White bird shit covered
the nose of his black bear sculpture. Broken glass littered the ground
'round the bottle tree. Bad spirits had broken free leaving dangerous
shards of color.

"Not here," Aidan murmured.

His leg muscles trembled as he walked the horse a mile or so downstream from his place to a smaller hummock of land. Something wriggled through floating leaves onto sandy ground. A hissing snake puffed
up its neck and struck at the stallion's right foreleg. The horse reared
and pawed the sand—but hadn't been bitten. The harmless hognose
snake rolled over and played dead. The spooked stallion violently
kicked and unseated Jerome, who landed face-first in the sand. More
terrified by this than the snake, the stallion kicked Jerome's back and
broke his dead ribs. Aidan threw the hognose snake a piece down the
shore, and it slinked into the grass.

"Whoa now, you're all right." Aidan took hold of the stallion's
head, clutching its ears, barely escaping a nip from gnashing teeth. He
glanced at Jerome's body crumpled on the shore. "I guess this is the
place we been looking for."

Smoke got tangled in saw grass. Aidan crouched by Jerome's funeral
fire. The moon rose, missing a chunk of its fiendish face. Snowy egrets,
returning early for spring nesting, flew above, white feathers flashing pink in the firelight. A five-foot rainbow snake with an iridescent
black body and multicolored stripes slithered by. It struck at an eel
and disappeared with its catch below the surface—a rare sight indeed,
something for Redwood. She loved the swamp as much as Aidan did.
But he wouldn't be sharing more Okefenokee treasures with her. In a
fury, Aidan heaved sand on Jerome's ashes. Tears stung his cheeks and
busted lips. Flying grit tore into his throat and nose. He coughed and

hollered and sneezed as the fire smoldered. Before the skittish stallion could bolt, he jumped on its back and headed into fog.

What would Aidan do with hisself now? And Redwood, would she be all right?

The sun rose. Aidan had ridden hard, far out the way of most folks. He handed the stallion's reins to a Seminole woman in a patchwork coat, a friend of Subie's living out in nowhere. She patted his cheek and smiled. Too agitated for the meal she offered, he set out in a borrowed canoe for home. Bumping into a sandbar loosed a cloud of blood suckers, but they veered away from his deadly mood.

Paddling furiously, Aidan tried not to think terrible thoughts, strained not to see Jerome busting into Redwood, her face twisted and her tongue bleeding. He should've taken his gun and shot Jerome before he hurt her so bad she had to—

Redwood was gone. Aidan never told her how much of his heart she was holding, never found out if there was a chance she might look on him with love. She was gone. He couldn't go back and change the past, couldn't get there in time to do right. And folks might go buck wild over Jerome, might hunt her down unless—

"I think I know what to tell 'em," Aidan said to the dark current pushing against the canoe. "Miz Garnett say, a good story can save you. We'll see about that."

BOOK III

A people without a history is like the wind over buffalo grass.

—Lakota proverb

NINE

From Georgia to Tennessee, 1904

The night after Jerome Williams busted Redwood's heart and broke up her spirit, no-see-ums dashed through all her *keep-away* spells, chomping flesh and sucking bruised blood. Her thoughts cut and burned too. None of this mess was *her* fault, yet George spoke true. Peach Grove was no place to be a woman. Redwood had never wanted to believe him, but now a man was dead by her hands, and Lord only knew what they'd do to Aidan. Just thinking on him hanging from a tree with a torch to his feet made her storm hand burn and her throat swell up. Maybe they wouldn't do him that way. Maybe the sheriff would just lock Aidan away. Hard to hope for him living in a cold, dark cell, yet she didn't know what else to hope for anymore.

Milton made it through that first awful night thanks to her medicine. He woke up glad to be alive, but too sick from battling poison venom to do much more than eat and fall back asleep. Eddie didn't waste a minute feeling good that the boneyard baron hadn't claimed his friend. Folks had paid them in goods and services the last few weeks, and they were low on cash money. Eddie wondered right off where their next dollar would come from if Milton was out of commission and eating like a hog. Redwood couldn't fault Eddie for worrying, even though it made her mad.

At dawn, Redwood helped Eddie get Milton onto his chestnut geld-ing. Eddie mounted the frisky white mare. Redwood climbed onto the pack mule between costumes, props, and instruments. Burning welts on her thighs protested. Milton almost fell out of his saddle with the horse standing still, so Eddie set a slow pace.

It was easy going in pleasant country. Redwood filled her mind with waving grass, whippoorwill calls, and bay branches dancing against blue sky—till they come up on a chain gang. Dark figures limped through uneven furrows, getting in the crop and clearing a new field. Redwood spied several dull-eyed boys, hardly more than fifteen, scurrying 'round in rags with rusty shackles clanging on raw ankles. White men sitting shotgun watched her, Milton, and Eddie, like cougars tracking deer. Milton sat up out of his stupor then.

"Blue Freeman!" He pointed and gasped. "A guitarman we played with, right?"

"No." Eddie smacked his hand down. "I never know anybody on a chain gang."

Milton shook his head as Eddie hurried them on.

Redwood shuddered at so many battered men and women, lives lost to sweat and stone. She counted mostly colored and a few dirty-faced whites. "Looked like decent folk," she said when they were out of sight. "What you think they did?"

"Being colored and poor is crime enough," Milton muttered.

Eddie snorted. "Didn't your mama teach you nothing, gal?"

She didn't say *Mama's gone to Glory,* 'cause that was no excuse for talking stupid.

"Chain gang messed up my ankle. Ruined me." Milton was shaking. "I'd rather die than have to do that again." He fell off his horse to the dirt and howled.

Redwood jumped down and patted Milton's back. "I know how they get a chain gang. I just wonder who these folks are." She turned to Eddie. "Ain't you goin' help me here?" Eddie stared at the horizon. His mare pranced a few steps down the road. "I can't lift him back on the horse by myself," she said, before Eddie could run off.

"You don't have to yell," Eddie shouted.

After they tied Milton in the saddle, Eddie complained all morning and afternoon. Redwood didn't mind his tale of woe. Listening to him, she didn't have to think on her bruised tongue or the wound between her legs or the screams thundering in her head.

"Entertainers have a hard row to hoe," he said. "Where's the crowd you had singing and dancing till dawn when *you* need help? Where are the folks who looked ready to die and you got 'em laughing so hard they forgot every sad, brutal thing in their lives? Where are they when you hit hard times? When a snake bite your dancing foot? Ain't you the one put 'em in a mood for sweet loving when they thought they'd done lost that feeling for always? Don't nobody want to see a performer if he ain't happy or funny no more, if his voice is broke or his knee is busted. The crowd turn away quicker than . . ." He looked to the horizon again. "I can't think of nothing fast enough. A colored performer got that and Jim Crow too." He sighed. "I'm no flashy guitarman like Milton, and ain't no piano where we going. Might as well shoot me right now."

Redwood suspected Eddie was tempted to run out on Milton again, but maybe she was just seeing evil everywhere and maligning Eddie's good character. She'd never thought of performers having hard times. "I'll sing with you if you want," she said.

He perked up and then tried to hide it. "Well, we'll see 'bout that."

In a no-name colored town, with a general store that at night was a speakeasy, she used Iona's silver dollar and some of Aidan's money to buy food, supplies, and a ready-made skirt and dress. Eddie told the owner he'd rescued a poor gal after her entertainer ma and pa had died from an honorable but deadly disease. Redwood looked sad enough to fit the part, and the good-natured owner let her take Milton's place that very night. He offered to rent her a back room, if she had a mind for other business.

"No, sir," she said. "I'm an entertainer, just singing for my supper."

She learned the music on the spot. Eddie was relieved she sang better than average. The eager crowd didn't notice wrong notes or wayward lyrics. They were as happy as Redwood to forget everything and get carried off in the music. Her wounded tongue bled on the last few songs. She swallowed salty blood and bowed to gleaming faces.

Milton tried to stand up the second day, but fell down in pain. Redwood pulled what hurting she could from him and sang in his place again.

"Onstage, I go by Sequoia," she told everyone when they were done applauding. "Remember me for the next time."

This was how they traveled north. The days were a murky stew of horse sweat, dusty roads, and funky crowds. Redwood was numb and dull 'cept onstage. She couldn't exactly remember what happened, where they'd been, who she was sometimes. Forgetting was comfort for all her hurting and wounds. So she didn't know when or even who decided she was traveling north with Milton and Eddie as part of *The Act*. Forgetting was a blessing. God had mercy on her. God might even forgive her too, 'cause once she was beloved by the spirit in everything. Still, torment came with this mercy. Thrills of terror ambushed her till she didn't have an hour of peace. Any moment, a posse might ride out the ashes of her old life and drag her away. Jerome's ghost-soft hands pawed her skin as blood gurgled in his cracked neck and wind whistled through dead lips. If it hadn't been for healing and singing, she would've lost her mind for sure. Helping somebody get right, losing herself in good music, she could forget almost everything else, for a while anyway.

Milton took his own sweet time healing. Spider got him in his bad ankle. "My Achilles' ankle," he said on a stormy afternoon and laughed. Redwood nodded.

Eddie shrugged rain off his back. "You know what that Achilles is?"

"A famous Greek fellow, who got dipped in the river of the dead, 'cept for his heel," Redwood said. "That's where death come after and get him."

Eddie curled his lip. "I'm in fast company. You know famous Chinamen too?"

"It's mythology," she said. "My aunt give me a book."

Milton grinned at her. "It's nice to have someone to talk to for once."

After this, in the daytime, Milton took pains to teach Redwood not just words and a melody, but how to give each song a character of its own, how to play the spirit of the audience. He made her read music off the page and sing foreign songs. Redwood was a demon student, pestering him to share all his theatre magic, but he didn't have much stamina. At night when she and Eddie put on a show, for food or money, she practiced what she'd learned, supposedly just till Milton got back on his feet.

Weeks slipped by. Redwood read the newspaper whenever she could get her hands on one and listened carefully to folks sharing tales from all over, but in almost a month she never heard mention of Jerome Williams murdered in his peach orchard or Aidan Cooper being hauled off to jail and strung up for snapping a rich man's neck. In Atlanta, a new train station opened, and a lawyer born in Peach Grove lost control of his automobile, crashed into a horse and buggy, and died. That's what they called big news. The Williams clan owned half a county. Whatever happened to one of them would have been even bigger news. Redwood let herself hope that Aidan didn't get caught in her mess, that she didn't have his suffering on her ledger too. It made her smile to think he'd conjured his way out of court and jail or worse.

The local gossip from colored folk everywhere was mostly husbands cheating on their wives, even a few wives running 'round on their men, and too many tales of how white folk were getting meaner than sin. Redwood had never paid much attention to this before, not like George, who'd been complaining since she was little, that *even the Supreme Court is against us now*. White politicians had been steady passing laws to keep colored from living where they pleased or working near white folk, or even strolling in the park. Free colored entertainers, traveling 'round, making their lives up as they went, could be classified as unemployed *vagrants* and end up on the chain gang, men or women—like the guitarman they'd seen that first day. Worse was the gruesome stories of colored folk lynched every week in one town or another. Course, reports of barbarous white folk wreaking havoc never made it into the newspapers.

Redwood tried not to think on her mama, on upstanding Peach Grove men hanging her from a tree, but terror touched her like never before. She clutched Aidan's pistol. Was there any place to be a woman? Thinking on Baby Sister, her eyes crinkled with tears. Iris was hard-headed and wild, like Redwood. Who'd protect her?

Milton steered them clear of the deadliest towns. He knew good spots for colored performers all over Georgia. Folks were always glad to hire him and his *Act*. At each show, Eddie repeated his rescue yarn, elaborating on the details so he was more of a hero every time, and Redwood was a respectable gal who deserved much pity and a decent chance to earn a way home to her grand-kin up in South Carolina. Eddie could act anything and make a body believe. He never asked Redwood how she come stumbling into their camp that night or why she was always looking over her shoulder. Milton neither. Eddie didn't care what she was running from or why she cried through the night sometimes. Milton was too sick and too gentlemanly to pry.

One chilly Friday night, feelings ambushed Redwood up onstage, and she sang real blues for a raucous crowd that stomped and hooted for her harsh, wailing notes. Eddie leered at her tiddies and behind just a moment. Any longer, she'd have pulled Aidan's pistol on him, and he knew it. "See. When you ain't pouting, folk like looking at you and listening to you too. Ain't so many gals traveling 'round, singing the blues." He sniggered. "A crowd come for just that."

Redwood stopped the next song to pull pain from a loud gal groaning with toothache. This got big applause. The next night she took a jinx off a man crossed by a jealous lover and fighting Eddie over a gal he was talking up. Man felt so good, he gave Redwood two bits. Soon she was earning extra coins at every show. She didn't dare do anything *wild*, but when they had a break in music-making to get thirsty dancers to buy drink and food, she'd do sleight-of-hand magic—snatch a feather from nowhere, make words on a page disappear, or write a card that read one way to a fellow and a different way to his gal. The audience tipped her nicely. She saved up to buy a horse, but shared the rest with *The Act*. Eddie was too busy gambling away what they got to notice her generosity. He believed she was giving him his due for all the times he saved her.

Milton was grateful for every coin she offered, for every new song she memorized. "You got an open spirit and an interested heart," he said.

Studying Eddie's antics, she could do any character they threw at her. Milton also taught her entrances and exits, bows and curtseys, how to put on makeup and look like anybody, where the good spots to stand onstage were, how to throw her talking voice 'round, loud as solo singing. He had her quoting Shakespeare, old minstrel stump speeches, and doing fancy dance steps till she was sweating and aching but twisting like she had no bones.

"You're my best pupil. You can do anything and then some," Milton said.

"It was my dream, since I was little . . ." She trailed off.

"Milton showed me all that too, when I was green," Eddie said. "Man think you got to practice all the time. Maybe you, maybe him, but not me. I'm good by nature."

"Yeah, you're a natural-born clown." Milton laughed.

When Redwood wasn't onstage or rehearsing, she felt heartsick for Elisa, Ladd, Miz Subie, knucklehead George, the cousins, Iris, and

Aidan more than anybody, even if she was mad at him. He should've come with her. Sometimes she couldn't stand her own skin and rubbed it raw with a stiff brush and harsh soap. Still it itched, like from bugs feasting. *Keep-away* spells didn't work, 'cause it wasn't no-see-ums chawing her. She longed to run far, far away, but she didn't dare do anything *wild*, like conjure herself somewhere or somewhen else. What if she fell down in a stupor without Miz Subie's cure? What if she got mad enough to break somebody's neck? Looking into people's hearts terrified her too. She kept clear of strong emotions, even her own.

Frost cut into the late harvest and brought folk low. A tent of angry sharecroppers booed Milton's quiet new tune, till Redwood got storm mad and sang thunder in their faces. Why weren't they mad at the rich folk stealing their labor and sweat? Why'd they come pick on entertainers passing through? She expected the crowd to cuss and spit at her, but sullen farmers jumped up on tired feet and danced till the sun was a promise on the horizon. They left two bushels of fruit and vegetables. Redwood almost cried. Eddie wanted cash money. Milton made them give one bushel back, for goodwill.

"You could be a sensation," Milton said, biting into an apple. "A headliner."

"You just saying that," Redwood said. When she stepped out to sing, audiences didn't always warm to her right off, but after a song or two, they were more than happy to dance or drink to her music.

"The only thing holding you back is yourself."

"What you know?" Redwood challenged Milton's twinkling show-man eyes, but he didn't say anything more.

If some enterprising fellow tried to cheat them or pay less than what Milton and Eddie usually got, she threatened the evil eye or *foot-track* magic that would cross the no-good, thieving fool and jinx him and his family with ten years bad luck. While she was cussing somebody out for cheating, the wind picked up, smashing loose branches here and there. Clouds swirled in too, and when she was really mad, thunder rolled. If the cheating fool hadn't been sure before, he could tell then she was a powerful conjure woman not to be trifled with. These fancy parlor tricks kept people honest.

Even so, on a cold winter day, *The Act* got run out of town by good

Christians who didn't want no truck with the devil or his blues music. These stalwart African Methodists reminded Redwood of Reverend Washington. Brandishing shovels and shotguns, they protected their young people from sin, from loose, ungodly women like Redwood, and from no-'count, lazy bluesmen like Milton and Eddie. A storm wind was nothing to these true believers. They had the force of the Lord Jesus at their backs. These good Christians had nothing to fear from Redwood though. She was through with really powerful conjuring— done killed a man doing that.

"Don't play that hoodoo trickery on no white folk," Eddie warned, "they won't just shoo you away. I don't want to be lynched or die on the chain gang."

When Milton finally hobbled onstage again, he added his guitar licks and sang harmony. Dancing was out of the question, and he didn't solo sing much. Still, Redwood and Eddie sounded better than ever with him at their side. Milton played any music that come to his mind, and Redwood had to sing like never before.

Sitting 'round the fire on a cold morning, Milton counted their stash and grinned. They were earning good money. Eddie stared off into the distance. He was no good on his own, and he knew it. Milton did the finances, wrote and arranged the music, knew the good spots to play. Eddie couldn't run out on that, even if he was a restless soul.

"We ought to do longer skits, material to feature our new assets," Milton said.

Eddie grumbled, but didn't deny the stage magic they made together.

"We could get good enough to tour ourselves out of Georgia," Milton said.

"Is that a fact?" Redwood was still eager to put miles between her and Peach Grove.

"He has illusions of grandeur," Eddie said.

"Delusions of grandeur, Eddie. *Folie de grandeur*," Milton said.

"I'd like to go to Chicago myself," Redwood said before Eddie started cussing Milton out. Why did Milton always make him feel bad for what he didn't know?

"Chicago is a city of dreams," Milton said.

"Chicago got plenty hard-luck performers, why they need us?" Eddie spit at the fire.

"I remember you talking 'bout how nobody could touch you on the piano. So fast couldn't nobody even see you," Redwood said. "They got that in Chicago?"

"Well," Eddie mumbled. "I don't know 'bout that."

Milton hooted at him till he choked.

"I ain't been near a piano for a long while." Eddie stared at his hands.

"I'm back on my feet now," Milton said. "We'll see about Chicago. We'll see about a piano and a real nice dress for Miz Redwood."

They skirted Atlanta and crossed the Chattahoochee River.

"Atlanta's a simmering pot." Milton grimaced. "Too much anger brewing, and it's the colored man who will suffer."

"Colored woman too," Redwood said.

"She's right there," Eddie said to Milton's irritable grunt.

They watched water drop nearly eight hundred feet at Amicalola Falls. Redwood didn't mind missing the big city, but she pestered Milton till he took her up into Blue Ridge Mountain land. It was a cold, hard ride past logging camps—acres of trees knocked over and dying, whole forests slaughtered, but when they finally stood at the foot of Enotah, a bald mountain and the highest peak in Georgia, she laughed and danced like a young gal. Snow was falling, quiet and fluffy as goose down. It melted on her outstretched tongue and hot cheeks and rolled down her face like tears.

"I never seen a mountain in winter make a body so happy," Milton said.

"I know someone who lived in these mountains." She closed her eyes and looked for young Aidan running through snow.

"Someone special?" he teased, stopping when he caught her glare. "After they run the *Injuns* off, it was Scottish and Irish immigrants, poor folk taking land nobody else wanted. Mostly pro-union before the war. Real good fiddle playing in these parts too."

"You know some history," Redwood said, back in a good mood.

"I confess, I am an educated man from Oberlin College who ran off to the theatre."

"You are a mystery, Mr. O'Reilly," Redwood said with theatrical flourish.

"Likewise, Miss Phipps." He bowed to her. She dropped a deep curtsey.

"Is Oberlin a colored institute of higher learning?"

"No, ma'am, but they let in colored same as white, women same as men. Still a station on the underground railroad to our freedom." Her face brightened at this. Milton continued. "Alas, look what I have done with this great gift—a theatre vagabond, the very thing my parents hoped to prevent."

"I don't listen to good people talking themselves down."

"I think we better get back before Mr. Starks runs off with all our stock."

"I don't leave nothing with Eddie that I want."

"He's not all bad," Milton said.

"Well, nobody's all bad, I guess." She didn't feel as sure of that as she used to.

Eddie was itching to get from Georgia to Tennessee, so after sightseeing they headed right out again, barely resting the horses. "I was born and raised in Pittsburgh, Pennsylvania. The Deep South ain't my stomping grounds." Eddie refused a detour to Blood Mountain. "How many big rocks do you need to see, gal?"

"It was a site of a great battle between the Cherokee and the Creek back in the 1600s," she said.

"Who won?" Milton asked.

"The Cherokee, and they called it *the Enchanted Land*." Aidan told her how to say it in Cherokee, but she didn't trust her mouth just now.

"You know some history too," Milton declared.

"Don't matter," Eddie said. "White folk own all these mountains now. That's all the history that counts."

He put up a big fuss when Milton had them ride up Lookout Mountain. This time Milton and Redwood didn't give in to him.

"We got money in our pockets and prospects for tomorrow," she said. "It's not that far out the way."

"We're riding history, man," Milton said. "Fill yourself up and take it onstage."

"Ain't smarter than me, college boy. Not richer neither. Horses goin' end up lame."

The view from Lookout Mountain was better than from the Ferris Wheel. The Tennessee River stretched out below them, a gray snake sunning in yellow fields. Chattanooga hugged the river's shores, going on and disappearing into forever at the misty horizon. It was a city on the scale of Chicago. "Oh, my," Redwood said, her heart fluttering. She had never been so far from home 'cept for conjuring herself away. Eddie laughed at her big eyes and breathless sighs.

"In the war, this is where Grant and Sherman fought the Battle Above the Clouds. They took Chattanooga and sent Johnny Reb skedaddling back into Georgia." Milton spoke as if this was his personal victory.

"That war ain't over," Redwood said, "we're still fighting it every day."

Eddie frowned at his partner. "You don't look good."

Milton had been doing better, but Redwood couldn't get him to heal. If he danced more than a minute or two, his ankle ballooned, and he was limping through the same pain all over again. Eddie was always nagging him 'bout it and doubting Redwood.

"Warmer in the valley," Milton said. "And I'll find something stronger than coffee to chase the chill away."

"Don't talk nonsense. Ain't no liquor goin' cure what ails you." Redwood fussed at Milton, but it wasn't him drinking hard spirits that had her worried sick.

Aidan's hands ached. Plucking at banjo strings, he didn't feel any music, just wrong notes and noise coming out his fingers. Nothing worth playing since Redwood had to run off. Aidan almost threw the banjo out the window, but *she* would've sucked her teeth, cut her eyes, and been so upset—he set it down gently. When Aidan was fourteen, a stranger passing through Peach Grove from the Blue Ridge Mountains had given him this banjo for no good reason. Stranger claimed he saw music on Aidan's spirit. Aidan always imagined it was a gift from Big Thunder and Miss O'Casey.

"Foolish, childish notions," he muttered. He gripped a jug and headed for the shed. It was goin' be another long empty day.

Aidan ran the plow into hard rock, wrenched his wrist, and cussed at Princess. "You damn fool mule! What the hell you think you doing?"

Princess turned big eyes at him and twitched her long ears while he shouted hisself hoarse. She looked over to the setting sun and back at Aidan, checking if he'd noticed that they done come to the end of sunlight. She needed to go home, eat a good meal, and rest her bones if he wanted her to get any work done tomorrow. Aidan cussed with a chewed-up throat and slapped the reins on her back. Princess strained against the harness, ready to leave his crazy behind in the field, where he could yell at the stars when they come out—if he wanted to.

"What's got into you, Aidan Cooper?" Cherokee Will stood in a long shaft of light. "Yelling at your Princess like that." He kept his distance from the gnashing mule.

Aidan cleared his throat and spit in the wind. "What you doing here?"

"You ain't been right, since . . ." Cherokee Will smacked a bug sucking his neck. "I come to look see what I could do."

"I don't need your help! So you can just get on now."

"What you mad at me for?"

"I'm mad at everybody."

"Of course you are, living alone out here. You need—"

"Don't tell me I need the company of good people."

"Iona say, you don't even play your banjo no more." Cherokee Will took the fight out of Aidan with this. "Well that don't make no sense."

"Music make it worse." That was a lie. Music called Aidan a coward and left him. He couldn't even play how sad he felt with tone-deaf fingers. He dropped his head. Dirty hair hung in his face so Cherokee Will didn't see the tears streaking down. What kind of man stand 'round blubbering in the dirt? "I'm not fit company for my mule."

Cherokee Will eyed the jug next to Aidan's alligator pouch on the ground. Princess sensed an escape opportunity. She stamped her feet and snorted.

"All right. It is too dark to see." Aidan pulled off the harness. Princess nipped his side and scampered away as he yelped.

Cherokee Will laughed. "That's an ornery critter. Bad as my wife."

Aidan sank down in the newly turned earth. He grabbed his jug.

"I'll sit with you awhile." Cherokee Will squatted in the dirt, still limber for an old fellow. He sat too close.

"Ain't enough to share." Aidan took a long swig. "And I ain't got nothing to say."

"If I need some talking, I'll do it. A man shouldn't be alone on sorrow mountain."

TEN

In Chattanooga, just after January New Year, 1905, Redwood took Milton to a conjure woman, Mirabella Fontaine, who had befriended Miz Subie in her wild youth, back in slavery days. A Sea Island woman, landlocked far from the ocean she loved, Mirabella wore seashells 'round her neck and in her white hair. "You all from Peach Grove, nuh?" She ushered them in. A giant conch seashell presided over her front hall. Fans of dried seaweed hung over the doorways, and fishing nets covered the windows. "Subie send a letter now and again, but I got to pay some young fool to read it. I t'ink I save my money." Her dress and shawl were slippery green and billowy as sea grass. "I got a spell to keep fools from knocking. How'd you find me?"

"I wrote your address for Miz Subie when her eye was too tired," Redwood said.

Miz Mirabella hugged Redwood against bony ribs. She was so happy to have a report of her dear friend from somebody's mouth that she made a big meal and insisted the weary travelers stay the night. Milton wanted to argue.

"Sheets and springs beat a dirt bed any day," Eddie said.

Milton crumpled on the parlor floor. Mirabella examined his puffy ankle and discolored foot. "Maybe you ain't got dancing feet no more." She wrapped a poultice 'round the swelling and gave him sweet tea. "Count your blessings, singerman. You lucky to be alive."

Eddie pulled a face at this, but Milton took the medicine and the news well. After supper, he snored away in a big white bed like a baby. The mist of hair on his dark brown head and face was scattered with gray all of a sudden. Age had come on him hard in the last few weeks. The ragged scar on his jaw had faded to a wrinkle.

Mirabella pulled Redwood from his door, back to the parlor. "Tell me 'bout Subie."

Eddie paced 'round them, picking dinner from his teeth and sipping peach brandy. Redwood didn't dare say much with him listening. Her eyes kept straying toward the sleeping chamber.

"I t'ink Mr. Milton be all right," Miz Mirabella said. "Subie taught you good t'ing." She glanced at Eddie. "Take yourself out to the night air, cool your hot head. Leave us women be." Eddie couldn't stand *any-body* telling him what to do, but bossy women really rankled. "I got to tell you twice? Get on now!"

"I was thinking of a smoke anyhow." Eddie took his time leaving. Miz Mirabella brought out a cigar box. "See what I got here?"

By the hot glow of an electric lamp, Redwood read Subie's letters out loud, a few short paragraphs in tight handwriting, one a year for over thirty years. She even spoke the ones Mirabella done heard before, reciting till her voice was hoarse and it was late in the night.

"You sound like Subie, make me t'ink her in the room." The old conjure woman's sharp jaw and creased forehead relaxed. "Subie always say reading and writing be a powerful trick in your bag. She learn when them whip you to death for less. You young folk don't want to hear all that—tired of our stories 'fore they even got told."

"Sometime, slavery stories be too painful to hear," Redwood said. "We want to forget those bad times and think on what we doing right now."

"When you want to hear, we'll be long gone." Mirabella chortled at this ancient joke on humanity.

Redwood almost cried, reading Subie's last letter:

> We have lived some wild times and I'm feeling every minute in these
>   old joints. But my young ones are coming due, so I ain't worrying
>   over old bones.
> George got an iron spirit. He'll bend anybody to his will.
> Sweet Iris belong to another world altogether and won't nobody beat
>   that out of her.
> Aidan got an open heart, so he ain't scared of the truth. He ain't scared
>   of change.
> Redwood is my hope, my future, just as sure as if I birthed her. A
>   conjurer like I never seen.
> Dreamers all, and ain't this the time we need the magic and the
>   might of our dreams?

"What 'bout you, chile?" Mirabella leaned close and touched Redwood's belly.

"I ain't a dreamer no more." Redwood told as much of her tale as she could stand in her mouth and pleaded for herbs to make one of her mama's nasty brews.

Mirabella sucked her teeth. "Blood's not *that* late. Too soon to be sure. I knew a woman—men took her against her will. She didn't bleed for a year. Put a trick on her own body."

"I won't . . . I can't have his baby."

"You do dangerous t'ing, maybe you won't have nobody's baby, nevermore."

"Can't have no part of him growing inside me." Redwood balled her fist and pressed it against her lips.

Mirabella nodded. "We ole folks ain't the only ones got a hard story to tell." She stroked Redwood's hands. "Find you a good man soon. You a grown woman who need good loving. Your time goin' fly. Rub this bad man out your body as soon as you can. Snatch you some good moments. Hear what I say? Promise me."

Redwood hesitated. She didn't say what she didn't mean.

"For pain and sorrow, ain't no root, ain't no spell like good loving," Mirabella said.

If a good man was a healing spell, Redwood guessed she could do it. "I promise."

Aidan lurched down Main Street between Doc and Hiram Johnson. They looked dapper and smart as usual. A warm spring breeze made Aidan sweat through winter britches and a heavy coat. It was March or maybe April, 1906. He'd lived a quarter of a century! Time always got ahead of him. He tugged at an itchy sleeve and the threadbare fabric ripped. He tore it the rest of the way off and stuffed it in a pocket with *The Jungle* by Upton Sinclair that Doc had just loaned him.

Clarence Edwards, Doc's colored driver, an Atlanta man with a graying mustache and bulging muscles, followed a few steps behind them with his eyes on the ground and his ears perked, a damn hound dog waiting for a bone. Aidan was several drinks beyond drunk, but he knew Clarence was sneering at him. What was Aidan to him but another cracker, poor white trash, a drunken fool?

Doc mocked him too. "How could you let Jerome steal her away from you and the rest of us too?"

"Jerome didn't steal Redwood from me. She always had her heart set on him." Aidan gritted his teeth. Clarence stared him in the eye, two or three seconds.

"She was very good at hiding that," Doc said. Clarence looked down.

"She had to be," Aidan said. "Jerome didn't want that mama of his to know."

"I'm sure that's a burr in Caroline Williams's britches." Hiram laughed. "What I don't understand is Jerome."

"Taking to the swamp like a runaway slave or an *Injun*." Doc shook his head. "Why not a buggy?"

"I tole you, Jerome and Redwood call themselves *sneaking* off north to get married," Aidan said. "She wanted a big wedding in a church and dancing in the street after." The only story he ever got good at telling out loud was a barefaced lie.

Clarence coughed up a good wad and spit.

"Where are your manners, Clarence?" Doc said.

Aidan continued. "They were getting lost in the swamp. Love had 'em all turned 'round. I tried to talk sense to 'em, but they were too hardheaded. *Isti siminoli*. They planned to get on the railroad in Atlanta. At least I pointed 'em in the right direction."

"I do recall Jerome saying, tonight's the night for me and Redwood," Hiram said.

"You thought it meant bumping and grinding, not riding on the railroad to New York City." Doc laughed.

"I thought he'd tell me the truth," Hiram said. "He'd been talking about *me and him* taking a wild trip up north, just getting on the train one afternoon, not telling anybody. Finding us a few obliging lady friends."

Aidan almost fell over his own feet. Clarence caught him. "Watch where you going, Clarence." Aidan shoved him away, panicked. These Johnson boys could make a mess of his lying. "Jerome planned a trip with you?"

"Naw, Jerome talked a lot of stuff he didn't mean," Doc said. "He paid off his debts, cleaned out his account. You should've smelled something else coming, Hiram."

"Cherokee Will said he arranged a rendezvous for Jerome and that gal in the peach orchard," Hiram said. "I don't understand, with all these fine white women to choose from. Why run off with her?"

"Love's a mystery. Can't say today what it'll make you do tomorrow," Aidan said. Clarence exchanged quick glances with Doc, then glared at the ground.

Doc scratched his chin. "Hard to believe Jerome loved anybody."

"And a nigger gal at that," Hiram said.

"Maybe she hoodooed him." Aidan swayed at a street corner, overwhelmed by the directions he could take. Bad idea, lying at the crossroads. He leaned against a post.

"That must be it!" Doc said. "A conjurer, like her mama."

Hiram quaked at talk of Garnett. "They got a moving picture over to the fair." He pointed to distant tents.

"We got a nickelodeon coming to Atlanta," Doc said. He was spending more and more time up in the city.

"It's all better in Atlanta. What you doing in Peach Grove?" Hiram walked ahead.

"Clarence pesters me to come see his Aunt Subie, before the old gal goes blind in both eyes."

"Naw, sir. You wanted to see your brother and go hunting with Mr. Cooper." Clarence looked at Aidan with undisguised hope.

"What do you say, Coop?" Doc had his arms 'round Aidan's shoulders.

"Maybe." Aidan felt sick all of a sudden. Clarence grinned at him. What did this colored fool want from him? What did he know?

"You look green, man," Doc said. "Don't worry. There's a fat bonus."

"I don't need your money"—Aidan pulled away and wiped at his sweaty neck—"to be your friend." Doc nodded and hushed Hiram before he said something smart. Aidan glanced over to Clarence who was contemplating his feet again. Aidan sucked a breath and rubbed bleary eyes. "Maybe on the weekend. Good day to you."

"So take me to this foolish tent show," Doc said as Aidan stumbled away. "Pictures were meant to stay still, you know."

On a sticky Saturday, Redwood turned nineteen years old, a woman of the world. Wearing Aidan's clothes, she hid behind funky curtains in a sweaty third-floor room of the Cherokee Lake Bordello in backcountry Tennessee. She'd been working here a year, singing with *The Act*. A bad man, a dangerous man, paid top dollar for Elaine, a buxom, high yellow lady whose kinky hair was the only giveaway she wasn't white. Elaine took the bad man's crisp bills and pleaded with Redwood to hide in her room and keep a lookout.

"You a hoodoo, ain't you, Sequoia?" she whispered as he drank a whiskey. "He'll feel that and act right! I don't want to have to shoot nobody tonight."

Redwood tingled with pride. Elaine cussed everybody out all the time and had a gun under her pillow, but believed in Redwood to keep her safe. The fellow was middling-sized, didn't *look* evil, and he talked sweet to Elaine. Last week Joe Graham *looked* like a gentleman in fancy clothes, sounded like one too, but slit a woman's belly, laughing and talking love to her. Stinky Wilson favored sick gals, doing 'em till they puked, and Ole Phil liked to leave a souvenir scar, a *love nick*. Big Jarius was supposed to keep the peace. Three floors of nonsense kept him running, and he didn't always make it in time. Redwood wouldn't have believed none of this *before*, but no matter what Rev. Washington and them say, these were brave, hardworking women at Cherokee Lake who never knew what might come at them.

Hearing a gasp, Redwood peeped through a hole in the curtain. What would she do if things turned nasty? Hairy legs and pale brown buttocks untouched by sun wagged in her face. Elaine plied her trade, teasing and kissing, breathing hard and sucking, finally splaying herself wide open for this man. Redwood's stomach threatened to come up. Elaine winked at her and then, acting overcome with passion, squealed, "Mr. Evans, you sure know how to make a gal holler!" Elaine's tongue was everywhere.

Mr. Evans pawed and thrust harder. Redwood couldn't hear what he was saying. Her own breath was ragged, her fists clenched, her flesh itched and burned. She shouldn't have let herself get roped into this. Hoodoo wasn't a weapon or a shield. A real hoodoo woman was beloved by the spirit in everything and had the power to make dreams real, had the power to conjure a bright destiny, a bold future. Mr. Evans reached a peak of pleasure, and Redwood covered her mouth as she gagged.

"I was having hard times before," Mr. Evans said. "I'm better now, see. I just wanted to show you." He kissed Elaine's private, secret places. Elaine squealed again.

Redwood wanted to escape onto the roof, but made herself watch this too.

When Mr. Evans finally left, Elaine pulled a robe 'round irritated, itchy-looking skin. "The smell of fear will egg 'em on to evil doings. The scent of hoodoo power keeps 'em straight. Thanks." She squeezed Redwood's arm. "My goodness. You look shocked by the show." Elaine waved at the bed. "I can do all that, but they don't ever touch me. Trick is, not to be here with 'em. I'm always off somewhere else. Don't feel a thing."

Without realizing what was happening, Redwood had seen when Elaine left herself. "Yeah." An actress was always learning new parts. Eddie told her to be a student of life. "Well, you're safe now, and I got a show." Redwood headed out the door.

"Take your time getting onstage." Elaine winked. "I'm coming down to hear you. I just need a minute. Is that your new costume?"

"Mm-hmm."

"Guess I'll have to watch out for you tonight then." Elaine's eyes sparkled.

Going downstairs, Redwood ran her fingers over Aidan's shirt and tucked it into his pants. After a few washings his smell was gone, but she could still feel him with her as she cinched the waist tight. The Sea Island conjure woman had given her seashell earrings that tinkled ocean music close to her ears and a river scarf for her waist, blue-green fabric like flowing water. She pulled Aidan's cap over her eyes and strode through the sporting house. Most of the men ignored her. They had too many good-looking women in various stages of undress to appreciate.

The Cherokee Lake Bordello was the one regular job Milton could get them. Faded, raggedy curtains decorated drafty windows. Nasty perfume covered the smell of rancid oil and rotgut liquor. Redwood shouldn't complain—they'd played worse joints and slept in funky barns, horse manure and whatnot going up their noses all night. At least Eddie got to hit an upright piano five hours a day. Redwood didn't look down her nose at working ladies no more. She was just restless, aching to move on.

Two well-dressed men cornered Milton at the door to the common room, gamblers with pearly canes and silk top hats. Milton handed them what looked to be a week's worth of their earnings. "Mr. Starks owes us more than this," the stocky one said. He wore black leather riding gloves and poked at Milton with stiff fingers.

"Eddie's a gambling fool," Milton replied. "I can get you more, but we got to play music just now or I won't be able to get anything."

"We ain't folks to be trifled with," the stocky one said. His partner nodded as Milton pushed through them into the common room.

"You work here, boy?" A fellow with a crisscross of scars on his lips stopped Redwood from running behind Milton, and held up a fat purse. "I heard I might find—"

"In the other room." She indicated a door to the side.

He glanced at her tiddies. "Sorry, ma'am, I . . . You're tall for a fellow even."

"Don't go in there looking for love." She warned his earnest eyes and clapped his back like the young fellow he'd thought she was.

Milton was playing a jug. Seeing Redwood approach, he shifted to guitar. Eddie caressed the piano keys, making love to the notes. The raucous crowd wasn't listening. As Redwood stepped up onto the rickety little stage, Eddie gaped at her clothes. Milton grinned. Last month as part of her theatrical education, he took her to the vaudeville, where a colored lady was performing *His Honor: The Barber* in men's clothes and Ma Rainey was singing the blues. Ma had a big voice, deep and harsh, like she was torn up inside but singing anyway, through fire and storm, through all the good love lost or gone bad, through all the evil people do and get away with. Ma Rainey didn't make her hurting pretty, didn't hold nothing back, didn't ask nobody permission for her style. That's how Redwood intended to sing from now on. She belted a single line:

My love is like a falling star

Half-naked, bored women stopped teasing men who were busting out their pants with desire but acting stingy with their cash. Umpteen transactions got interrupted by Redwood's raggedy assault on a country melody and simple lyrics. She paused, uncertain for a second. Elaine shouted, "That's what I call singing, Sequoia!"

Redwood nodded at her and continued:

> *I said, my love is like a falling star*
> *A passing phantom high overhead*

The whole crowd in the Cherokee Lake Bordello stood still a moment, hanging on her every note. Redwood wondered what Aidan would think of how she sang his song:

> *You do not see her fall, not far*
> *For oh my lord, she's dark as the dead*

A dark, handsome fellow at a table in front of Redwood lifted a drink to her and grinned as she sang a second verse right to him.

"There he is again! Big Red done smote the man in his heart. Have mercy!" Milton said as the vocal ended and Eddie went wild on the piano.

The audience cheered. Two haggard men with fistfuls of cash started fighting over Elaine, grabbing at her yellow hair and big tiddies. Blood spurted at the stage as one man fell onto a table and the other smacked Elaine upside her head. Drunken hollers pierced Eddie's solo as Big Jarius come running. The good times fizzled.

In the third-floor room, Redwood stitched up a gash in Elaine's head. She barely flinched, just stared out a dirty little window as Redwood worked. "I thought Mr. Evans was the trouble coming at me tonight." Elaine sighed. "Is there goin' be a scar?"

"You can cover it with your hair."

"You got a lucky charm? So I could do something else, sing, be a free woman same as you?"

"I ain't free yet; heading there, I hope." Redwood put a tiny pouch in her bruised hand. Elaine in turn tried to press cash in her palm. "I ain't taking money from you. You've been kindly to me since I got here." Redwood grinned. "If ever I get me a man, I'll know just what to do."

Elaine sighed. "I'm usually a mean bitch. That's what everybody say."

"I don't know 'bout that."

Redwood poured Elaine a soothing tea and waited till she was settled and sleeping before slipping out the door. On the stairs down to the common room, the handsome man from the front row table blocked the way. He pulled off his hat and took her hand. His palm was wide and rough. She didn't flinch at his touch.

"I know you don't take money, Miz Sequoia." He said her stage name as if she was something sweet to eat. "You being a proper lady and all."

Redwood quoted Mirabella. "'Ain't no root, ain't no spell like good loving.'"

He leaned in to kiss her cheek. It didn't feel half bad.

"I like your moves, big man." She tickled his ear with her tongue and let her breath follow the shiver down his back. Not just Elaine, all the hardworking ladies of the Cherokee Lake Bordello had given her love tricks when she stitched wounds or helped them out of trouble. "You got magic on you," she said in a husky alto.

"How far you want to go?" His hand was on her waist—still good so far.

"It ain't the destination, it's the ride," she replied.

This tickled him but good, and he had a deep laugh that touched her bones. He'd been coming for weeks, staying to the last song and tipping his hat at her, leaving a flower, a few extra coins, a dozen fresh eggs. Redwood admired his persistence, his open face and clear eyes. She was flattered that someone handsome and good wanted her that much, even after seeing what she did onstage, after getting a taste of how wild she was. She wrapped her long legs 'round his thigh. Singing the blues the way she had tonight, seemed as if she'd come to the other side of something.

"You look good enough to make somebody holler," she said, trying to mean it.

"That's a line from a song."

"I'm a singer, ain't I?"

Upstairs in a moonlit room, the handsome farmer lay on top of Redwood. He smelled of chicken and pigs, of rich soil, of fresh hay and new life dropping into the stalls or pressing up out the ground. His smooth skin was sweaty with pleasure. Hers was dry and shiny. She felt far away from his groin pressing against hers, from his chapped lips and callused hands, from his heart banging so fast. He groaned in her ear and squeezed her tight, sucking at her like she was fresh fruit.

"Be my wife. Have my children. I got my own place. I'm doing good in the world."

Redwood covered his mouth with trembling fingertips. He pulled her hand away.

"Don't I make you feel good?" he said.

Her stomach wasn't fixing to come up, but—"I don't feel what you do."

"A woman can grow into that." He looked so hopeful, it hurt.

"The truth has always been a good friend of mine," she said.

"Uh-huh." He nodded.

"So when I tell you I don't feel anything, it mean—"

Her skin didn't crawl, her mouth wasn't bitter ashes, her heart wasn't pounding murder, like with other men she'd tried. *Good-loving* wasn't a spell that worked for her. There wasn't the *E-LEC-TRI-CI-TY* she remembered just thinking on Aidan—they'd never got to touching. Elaine had showed Redwood how to pleasure her ownself. Every once in a long while, touching the right spot and thinking on good times, *before,* she broke through a blank dark ache and felt so good she cried. Actually she'd only felt her back arching up and secret places throbbing between her thighs twice. A trick was on her body that took the pleasure out of lovemaking.

"It mean I don't feel *not a thing,* not with you, not with anybody."

The farmer's face crumbled. "You sure?" He rolled away from her, tracing his finger 'cross her belly, playing through a soft swirl of hair. Now she almost couldn't stand his touch. "Root doctor can help with that," he said.

Redwood eased her body away from his gentle fingers and pulled on Aidan's shirt and pants. "What's a root doctor know that I don't?"

"You love somebody else?"

"You don't have to be jealous." She closed her eyes. "He ain't real. Met him in the eye of a storm, he held on to me, and then he was gone."

Outside Redwood pushed through the good-time crowd milling on the porch to reach Milton and Eddie, tears standing in her eyes.

"We gotta get moving," she said. "Can't stay in this town forever."

Eddie smirked. "You hoodooed some poor fellow. Now he don't know what to do."

"I ain't conjuring," she shouted. "Just roots and herbs for healing."

"We'll be in Chicago soon enough," Milton said.

"You been saying that over a year, and we're still in Tennessee," Redwood said. "I mean to get to Chicago with or without you." She tromped toward their horses.

Eddie chased after her. "What about *The Act*?"

Milton brought up the rear, favoring his left leg. "We're making good money, steady. What's wrong with that?"

"No. She's right. Can't make no kinda money entertaining niggers and whores." Eddie didn't have a good word for nobody but hisself.

"We could do a real show in Chicago," Redwood said. "I got a brother there."

"A real show? Where you get that idea from? This fool?" Milton said.

"It's the truth." Eddie slapped his thigh.

"You've changed your tune about Chicago, Eddie," Milton said. "Too many gambling debts and jealous husbands after you?"

Eddie hopped on his mare.

"I gave those sporting gents everything, but they'll come gunning for more," Milton said. "I won't save your behind this time."

"So we better leave while we still can," Eddie said.

Milton threw up his hands. "Okay, we play a few more spots I know north of here, then see if we get ourselves into a traveling troupe, take us right to Chicago town. White folk there pay good money to see niggers jig and cut the fool." Milton heaved his butt into the saddle.

Redwood jumped on her horse, leaned over to Milton, and pecked his stubbly cheek.

"Why don't I get none of that when I take your side?" Eddie said. "When I say what you want to hear?"

"'Cause you never mean what you say, you just trying to get something out of me." Redwood spurred her horse. Even if the road turned west out of town 'stead of north, finally Chicago was in her sights.

Aidan's ripped laundry, stained with splashes of mud from last night's rain, fluttered in the breeze. Princess wandered through piles of debris in the yard and strolled to the back of the house. Ladd banged against the door. Elisa clutched a basket of food.

"Mr. Cooper, are you in there?" Elisa said.

"Crazy fool is off somewhere in the swamp, sitting up a tree," Ladd said.

As Elisa pushed the door open, it fell off its hinges. Ladd cussed and grabbed it. She stepped 'round him and into the house. Ladd sighed, set the door against the wall, and followed her. She bumped into a cracked jug that rolled 'cross the floor till it hit a smashed-up chair.

"I tole you he wasn't home," Ladd said.

Behind the house, huddled in the shadows, Aidan watched them through a broken window. The last bit of food he'd tried to eat a few days ago had come right back up and still covered his shirt and pants. He couldn't get his hand through the knotted hair hanging in his face. It took the whole wall to keep him from falling flat.

Elisa shouted, "Ain't nobody but him put that deer in our smokehouse."

"If he wanted a thank-you, he'd've stuck 'round to get it." Ladd shuddered at something on the floor.

Elisa set the food basket on the table. "Where's he going without this?" She picked up the banjo.

"Iona say he ain't been playing, say he lost his touch," Ladd said.

"He ain't been right since Redwood took off."

"I don't think we should be poking through—"

Elisa held up her hand and listened intently. Ladd looked 'round and shrugged his shoulders in a question mark. Aidan buried his face in filthy hands.

"I expect Mr. Cooper to bring me this basket back and say thank you to my face."

"Of course he will," Ladd said.

Elisa strummed the banjo—it was still in tune. "My mama brought this sweetgrass basket over from Sapelo Island. Damp don't matter none to this old swamp grass."

"Why you bring your mama's basket to leave?"

"Iris lost her sister and Mr. Cooper too." She strummed a few melancholy notes.

"Leave off the banjo."

Elisa set the banjo down. Ladd walked her out the kitchen.

"It's still in tune. How far could he be?" she said, going out the front door.

Aidan prayed that they wouldn't come 'round back looking for him. He quivered as footsteps headed away from his house. Princess nudged an aching shoulder till Aidan searched in his pocket and pulled out some smashed fruit. Princess eagerly bit into sweet mush and also chomped Aidan's hand. He jumped up, shaking his fingers, cursing the pain silently.

"Nobody need to be living this way." Elisa's voice carried on the wind.

"It's a wonder the Williams clan ain't stole this place out from under him," Ladd said.

"He got a ancestor spirit watching over him."

"Or haunting him."

Aidan peered 'round the side of the house. Ladd and Elisa were hurrying down the road.

"Mr. Cooper act like it's his fault Redwood run off north with Jerome Williams," Elisa said.

"Ha! Ain't no taming that gal." Ladd chortled. "Mr. Williams bite off more than he can chew."

"Serve him right, for stealing her away." Elisa got choked up, and Ladd put his arm on her shoulder.

Aidan watched them disappear into afternoon haze. Princess nibbled his wounded fingers, and jerking away, he fell into the dust.

"Do right!" Garnett's voice, a dead voice called to him.

As if missing Redwood wasn't enough torment, he had to have her mama on him too. Leaning against the house to stand up, he blubbered all over hisself.

"You know how they sit a horse." Garnett's *sssss* went on like a snake hiss. Princess's ears perked up too. "Have mercy!"

"Who goin' have mercy on me?" Aidan stumbled to his last jug and lifted it to his lips, spilling some liquor as he guzzled till it was empty. He dropped the jug and almost blacked out, but he still wasn't drunk enough to blot out the dead voice.

"How they sound all liquored up! Do right!" Garnett was louder than ever in fact.

All his jugs were empty. Giving his money to Ladd and Elisa to hold was sensible, but why'd he go and tell Leroy to refuse him a jug or two on credit?

"Evil don't take a rest," Garnett hollered.

Aidan covered his ears and crept in the back door. A cross breeze set the bottle tree to tinkling up front. He stumbled over a kettle into the kitchen table and almost knocked his banjo onto the floor. He swung it above his head, batting the air.

"*Hell fever and damnation had to be the Baptist preacher.*" A haint quoting what he wrote in his journal—if that didn't beat all, she seemed to be carrying on right outside his front door. The spirit-catching bottles tinkled with her breath.

Aidan tottered onto the porch. "Preacher fell down his own well." He banged his banjo into the colored glass. He was 'bout to smash it against a post, but Princess was braying like a banshee. Him acting a fool never spooked the mule like that before.

"*Twisted-hand Sheriff Harry was carrying a torch,*" Garnett said. She couldn't have been more than a few feet behind him.

Aidan's heart pounded, and blood banged at his temples. He swirled at the creaky sound of rotten floorboards fixing to give way. In broad daylight, Garnett Phipps was sitting in the busted rocker on his porch, swaying back and forth in a broken rhythm. She was shades of black, white, and gray, like a photograph 'cept for a purple orchid in her swamp-grass hair and sparkly red flecks in dark eyes. Her skin was little more than mist. The dress she wore was a muddy river, flowing from her neck to her bare feet and back up again. A *mojo* bag dangled at her waist, burning fiery red, same as her eyes. She showed him a mouth of pearly teeth and held a misty hand toward him. Aidan lowered the banjo. He wanted to hug her. He wanted to hightail it out of there.

"You didn't need to see their faces, Aidan. You know who they are." She gestured for him to come closer.

He couldn't move. "Peanut farmer shot hisself in the head."

"Bringing up the rear and ready to skedaddle out of there was a tall, broad figure—Hiram Johnson or Jerome Williams." Her voice got softer. She broke off rocking. "Am I lying?" She sounded a moment like Redwood.

Riders in dark robes tore through flames, racing by Garnett and off into the fields. A black stallion reared, almost throwing its pale-faced rider, who turned toward Garnett. The orchid in her swamp-grass hair caught fire.

"Hiram's just a stand-around-and-do-nothing coward, like me." Aidan took a step closer. "Must've been Jerome, hanging in the back."

"They all swore an oath." Garnett stood up. Her breath was swamp stink, greenbrier, dead breath. "You heard it too, didn't you, up in your hunting perch? They swore to leave the colored in peace, leave my family in peace. Else the boneyard baron would claim each one of their sorry souls long 'fore their time. Look at Jerome."

"What you want? Me to be a murderer too?" Aidan shouted.

Garnett drew her mouth to a thin bloody line.

Aidan looked down. "I came too late to stop Jerome, to save your gal, or save myself."

"The dead be counting on the living. You're all we got left."

The rocker moved back and forth. Garnett had vanished, but a purple orchid was on the seat. The fire hadn't made it no nevermind. Aidan gingerly picked the flower up, sat in the rocker, and hugged his banjo.

ELEVEN

Redwood clambered up narrow stairs from the smelly little dressing room to a dim backstage corridor. Her feet barely touched the ground. Over two years on the run, but here she was with *The Act*, performing a few spots from the headliners at the Prince Vaudeville Theatre in Chicago. Out front, an excited crowd poured in. Milton always watched the buck dancers and pantomime as the audience took their seats. Eddie was hiding somewhere from a jealous musician who caught Eddie kissing his gal and feeling her behind. Redwood sucked her teeth, disgusted. Eddie had no sense of time and almost missed their call last night. He was probably up to nothing good again.

She dashed by jugglers and fire-eaters fixing to go on. A young novice blew flames into the flies and got scolded in Greek by seasoned members of his troupe. They wiped ashes from their white shirts and shook their fists. Redwood dodged Chinese acrobats tumbling and racing up the walls. A Chinese dragon puppet with ten legs and a long red silk tongue licked her feet. A scaly tail curled 'round her waist. The Chinese act was on next, so escaping the dragon was easy.

"Eddie?" she whispered at them, stepping away from the tail.

The dragon shook its enormous head. White-faced clowns in raggedy harlequin costumes peered at her, arms and shoulders drooping in exaggerated shrugs. Two dogs from the animal act paced with Molly the trained mule, as if they had stage fright too.

The Prince Theatre offered a collection of entertainment acts from 'round the world. A tenor who'd sung for the president of these United States sat in the wings with eyes closed, lost in music. Theodore Jordan and Sarah Nelson practiced the entrance for a romantic sketch they'd performed for royalty in Europe. Redwood almost couldn't believe she was running backstage with such a fast crowd. Every which way you turn, thrills and razzle-dazzle, and Eddie was fixing to mess up their golden opportunity.

"I've lost a rabbit. You've lost Sambo," the magician said. Was he making fun of her? "The audience will boo."

"I don't plan on cooning forever," she said to him.

"It's an unlucky Friday, the thirteenth of the month." He reached in his hat and his hand came up empty. "Watch yourself, gal."

Not bothering to ask after Eddie, Redwood plowed through the Irish dance troupe—they never talked before going on, just worked their feet. The green room had been commandeered by a French equestrienne and her skittish white horse. Redwood poked her head in and out quickly. The lady was whispering French in the horse's ear and stroking his neck like they were lovers. Eddie wouldn't have lasted a minute in there. Redwood was covered in a light sweat. Behind all the flats and a mountain of props a young white man leaned out the stage door and declaimed Hamlet, Macbeth, and Lear. He shouted his final speech with a gray wig, a gnarled staff, and a mouth full of cotton. Was he supposed to be funny or not?

Eddie was nowhere in sight.

The Wild West pageant had assembled—horses, wagons, and blackface savages brandishing tomahawks. Redwood searched the actors' faces. Blackface could turn you into anybody, even your own Chinaman or Negro self. Saeed, a Persian acrobat playing Chief Blood Curdle, smeared war paint on his bare chest. Seeing Redwood, he smiled.

She tugged long black braids till they were straight on his head. "Ain't you a sight?"

"Not for long." He shrugged. "I get killed first thing."

"Have you seen Eddie?"

"He was hiding in the stagecoach, but I told him you all were about to go on."

"Thanks." She squeezed his hand. "You goin' watch me?"

"Wouldn't miss it." He made a bow to her. The other savages poked each other, certain that Saeed was sweet on Redwood. Saeed tugged her waist and whispered in her ear, playing romance to the hilt. "Perhaps tomorrow we could—"

"Sure." Redwood raced downstage to Milton shaking out tension beside Eddie.

"Where have you been?" Eddie hissed at her. "You 'bout to miss the call."

"He just got here too," Milton said dryly.

Redwood shrugged and peeked through the heavy red velvet curtain. The theatre was jammed, 'cept for expensive box seats set off from either side of the stage. Nobody sat under the painted cherubs that flapped tiny wings and strummed harps. Sightlines at that angle were terrible. Redwood burped up a bubble of tension. With all the rehearsing they'd done, she'd do fine, but who was there to see her shine?

"Remember, you have to love whoever comes out and pays their dime." Milton read her like a favorite poem. "Do your best, give 'em the time of their lives."

"Don't worry," Eddie said. "Chicago is just people, no different than anywhere."

"We're two spots from the headliners tonight," Redwood said. "We got their undivided attention."

The dusty curtain parted, and the bright electric chandelier went out quickly, a fountain of jewels, melting away to nothing. The theatre's leaky roof, ratty seats, and rickety balcony came into sharp relief. A sea of scowling white faces floated in the darkness as the stage lights washed away distant details. The last act had left them sour.

Redwood, costumed as a dapper young city man, danced to lively music between Milton, dressed as a uniformed railroad porter, and Eddie playing a good-for-nothing Sambo—colorful patches, comical shoes, and a floppy hat with a hole in it. Both men were done up in blackface—sooty dark skin, juicy red grins from ear to ear, wide eyes bugging out in fright or glee. Redwood wore regular makeup that highlighted her handsome features under the intense stage lights. Her dress coat, cane, and hat gleamed—not *His Honor: The Barber,* but close.

Less than a minute into their routine, the front rows grew restless and bored, 'fraid they were in for just another coon show. They cussed and spewed insults in Polish, German, Italian, Russian . . . Chicago was a town of immigrants, onstage and off. People had run to the windy city from everywhere in the world. Redwood tried to listen underneath the alien words to catch their spirit, how Mama taught her. That was the best way to work a spell on folk who were foreign or even homegrown.

The music got carried away. Tripping over a luggage cart, Eddie got tangled in a mountain of tumbling suitcases and carpetbags. A demon of disorder, he cartwheeled and somersaulted 'cross the stage. Everything he touched went flying, and Milton ran 'round catching one heavy thing after the other. Redwood sang a sweet nonsense ballad. Milton prevented mishap from befalling her ten times including a big chest landing on her head. Finally, he got snagged by a twirl of her cane and went soaring through the air. Eddie scratched his chin at Milton's sudden disappearance and handed Redwood the last bag. Oblivious to Milton's labors and the dangers she'd escaped, Redwood gave Eddie a big tip. He did a jig, tapping his feet on the stage floor like it was a drum. Milton crashed on the overturned suitcases to an explosion of applause.

Milton stood up and fell down 'cross the stage as the audience laughed and cheered. Redwood observed him with undisguised panic. Finally offstage, Milton crumpled, obviously in real pain. Unconcerned, the musicians played the intro for their next song.

Eddie gaped at Milton in the wings, but quickly recovered his grin. He grabbed Redwood who was 'bout to run offstage. They struggled till she flung his arm away with such force he landed on the ground—on the down beat. The audience howled.

Saeed backflipped onstage between Redwood and Eddie. Barechested, covered with stripes of war paint, and sporting a loincloth, a feather headdress, and beaded moccasins, he threatened them with his tomahawk. The musicians took their cue from him and played *Injun* music. Saeed cavorted upstage and down, screeching as he patted his mouth. This supposed war cry was echoed by *Injun* enthusiasts in the audience. Eddie acted as if Saeed's entrance and his fight with Redwood were part of the show. The musicians played the song intro again, while Saeed and Eddie circled Redwood, *Injuns* riding 'round a wagon of white settlers. A white rabbit hopped across scattered suitcases, and the audience hooted. Redwood finally gave in to the improvisation and, with Eddie and Saeed adding harmony, sang a popular favorite:

> *Come right in, sit right down*
> *and make yourself at home.*
> *You've found the place you're looking for,*

there's no more need to roam.
The sign reads "smallpox" on the door
but a welcome mat lies on the floor
So come right in, sit right down
and make yourself at home.

Saeed improvised an acrobatic dance, more Persian than wild *Injun*. He leapt into the air, twisting and tumbling in an elegant, exotic ballet. Redwood's dapper young man, not to be outdone by a savage, set down her cane and cartwheeled and backflipped 'cross the stage. Eddie did bumbling antics and fell on his behind, trying to upstage them. No one paid him any mind.

Saeed dashed 'cross the floor, ran up Eddie's bent back, jumped from his shoulders, and swung from a prop streetlight down into the balcony box seats stage right. Eddie saw Redwood running for him and turned to escape her. Too slow. She jumped on his back and using their combined momentum leapt for Saeed. He caught her at the waist and swung her into the seat next to him. Sweat made his blackface glisten as he grinned and whispered, "Don't ever scare me that way again." They posed like elegant dignitaries enjoying the show.

The stunned audience didn't take a breath for almost a minute.

Eddie broke the mood shouting, "If any y'all good patrons think you can run up my back too, y'all better have another thought coming."

In a storm of applause, Redwood rushed out the box door. Saeed jumped down to the stage and bowed with Eddie as the curtain dropped in front of them.

Aidan, his ratty hair pulled into a pigtail, his clothes rumpled but not filthy, stood in Ladd and Elisa's doorway. He was close to sober, yet standing up straight without trembling and weaving still took considerable effort. Ladd opened the door. Aidan would've run away, but he spied Elisa hovering behind her husband.

"Evening, Mr. Cooper," Ladd said.

Without saying a word, Aidan held the sweetgrass basket out to Elisa. His hand shook, but he managed not to drop it. Elisa pushed past Ladd and took it, touching his fingers and then squeezing them.

Inside the basket was a carved wooden box stained deep burgundy. She held it up to the light.

"Thank you, Mr. Cooper, that's fine work," she said. Ladd nodded agreement. "We haven't seen you for weeks." She took his arm. "Don't you want to come in?"

"No, ma'am." He slipped away from her. "I just come by to say thank you. *To your face.*"

"You're skinny as a will-o'-wisp. Ain't you been eating, Aidan?"

Hearing her say his name he could have wept. "My appetite's not what it used to be." He turned to leave, but was mobbed by Iris and her cousins Jessie, Tom, Bill, Becky, and Ruby. He got who went with what name on the first round.

"Where's your banjo?" Iris said as they dragged him inside. "You should leave it here for us to keep safe."

Elisa closed the door.

"Can't you get that darn window open? It's a sweatshop in here," Milton said.

In the cramped dressing room they all shared—the only one for colored at the Prince Theatre—Milton fell out on a divan. His left arm was stuck in his jacket sleeve. The rest dragged on the floor. His shirt was half out his pants and unbuttoned to the waist. Sweat streaked his blackface makeup. Redwood, dressed in Aidan's clothes and her face clear of makeup, sat down on a stool next to him to wrap his swollen ankle.

"Hold still," she snapped, not angry at him, but at the healing she couldn't do.

Eddie, out of makeup and costume and in handsome evening attire, struggled with a tiny window. The glass cracked when he finally shoved it open. He brushed his hands together, clearing off the dust. "We were awful tonight. They goin' fire us," he said.

"Audience didn't notice a thing," Milton replied.

"You only did the one number."

"Didn't you hear 'em cheer?"

"For Saeed, wild *Injun* to the rescue, not . . . the air is worse outside than in."

"That's Chicago for you." Milton sighed. "Eating rotten pigs with every breath."

Eddie slammed the window shut. Dust flew up his nose. He sneezed in Redwood's direction. "Milton's got a bum Achilles' ankle, what's your excuse?"

"I don't know." She started the bandage again. What would Aidan think of their *Injun* shenanigans? What'd she think? "And you putting on the good face every night, no matter what . . ."

"That's the show," Milton said. "Didn't I warn you?"

"Why you taking Eddie's side?" Redwood grumbled.

"You want to lose the audience? Go back to Tennessee?" Eddie snorted.

"Doing shows in Chicago is not what I imagined." She set Milton's ankle on a stool.

He flinched. "Not feeling like a feisty blues singer, huh? Maybe you're not suited for nigger shows."

Redwood cut him a sharp glance. "I am disappointed," she admitted.

"Persian skunk was dying to show off," Eddie said. "You can't break Saeed's heart, Red, he don't go with women."

"So? You done tole me that a dozen times at least." Redwood didn't want to fool with love anyhow. "A man could do a lot worse."

"You want to be one of them whores, laying down for whoever can pay?" Eddie picked his way through open suitcases, oversized shoes, several Sambo costumes, and a stack of fright wigs. He stood over Redwood, fuming. "Or do you want to wash nasty floors and dirty drawers like all them other sad Negroes? Or marry some poor colored fool on his knees, blinded by love, ignorant as all get out, smelling of dirt and praying to a fire-and-brimstone god, so Miz Sequoia will love him till doomsday? Cooning ain't no worse than that." He loomed over her, half-truths and spit on his lips. "What you got to complain 'bout?"

Redwood stood up, eye to eye with Eddie, so mad she could catch fire. Milton gripped her, but she shook loose. "Eddie, you don't know what I want, what I dream."

A tap on the door startled them. Saeed stuck his head in. "Are you all decent?"

Before anyone answered, he came in. Without blackface, Saeed was a few shades lighter than Redwood. His angular features and haughty expression were far from the savage buffoon he played. Tonight he was dressed as a fine Persian gentleman. His voluminous blue-and-gold pants came in at the ankles and turned a walk into a strut. A blue-and-purple embroidered belt rode high on his waist, accentuating his muscular chest and broad shoulders. Embroidery accented the flowing sleeves of his short jacket and the blue-and-gold turban on his head. He cut a fine figure. Redwood determined to have a costume such as this very soon.

"Everything all right with you, Mr. O'Reilly?" Saeed said.

"Yes, thank you, Mr. Saeed. Where you going, a Persian gent, dressed to the nines?"

"Attire from my homeland works a spell." Saeed gestured dramatically at Eddie who didn't disguise his disgust. "I am Ali Baba and can *open sesame* all your heart's desires." He kissed Redwood's hand.

She almost smiled. "Thank you."

"No. I thank you, lovely lady, for giving me a chance tonight. But say no more. I am late. I am glad you are well, Mr. O'Reilly. A good evening to you all." He bowed and exited as if from a stage.

"Did you plan this with Saeed?" Eddie said.

"Of course she didn't," Milton said. "They don't have a crystal ball to see my ankle giving out."

"The manager's goin' cheat us tonight. Don't need a crystal ball to see that."

"You so worried about money, take my share," Milton shouted.

"Hell, we be lucky if he pay me and Redwood."

Milton squealed in pain. "Can't put off that boneyard baron for too much longer."

"You ought to see a real doctor," Eddie said.

"I did. White doctor, here in Chicago. He said I oughta be dead already and nothing he could do for me neither."

"I don't say I can do what I can't," Redwood mumbled. "Maybe it's too tight." Her hands trembled as she retied the bandage yet again. Spider bite wouldn't have caused her all this trouble back home in Peach Grove.

The gaslights flickered as the door flung open. Eddie jumped. "Bad news never knocks."

Brother George, a little older, a little thicker, and very fashionable in city attire, strode into the dressing room with a fistful of roses. On his arm was a fair-skinned, striking lady in proper, clubwoman attire. A corset gave her a tiny wasp waist and pigeon chest. Lace poured from her sleeves and almost covered her hands. A fountain of lace flowed up her neck too and bubbled under her chin. She looked a bit older than George and was an honest-to-god upper-class Negro woman, George's woman at that. The cramped, sweaty dressing room seemed to offend her delicate senses. She sneezed and shuddered several times. Redwood didn't take the time to worry over her just yet. Handsome, fire-breathing, big brother George was grinning in her dressing room. She leapt into his arms.

"George, you found me. You did indeed."

"*Sequoia* threw me off a bit."

He swung her in the air. Roses scattered 'round the room. After knocking over a costume rack, hatboxes, and the Chinese screen Redwood dressed behind, George set her on the ground in front of his woman, who murmured "my goodness gracious."

"Baby sister, you were grand," George said.

"Iris is the baby. I'm grown up now," Redwood replied.

"Who you telling? This is my wife, Clarissa, clearing her throat in case I forget my manners. This is Redwood, my grown-up sister."

Redwood bowed to her. Taken aback, Clarissa covered her shock with a curtsey.

"How did hardheaded George ever get somebody so nice to marry him?" Redwood squeezed Clarissa's hands.

After a moment of hesitation, Clarissa squeezed back and looked Redwood up and down. "He said you were a girl, but I . . . I didn't believe it. You were dressed so convincingly and your voice was so . . . rough. And now this outfit too."

Redwood hugged Aidan's shirt close to her skin. "This is Mr. Eddie Starks and Mr. Milton O'Reilly."

"Mr. Starks." Clarissa smiled at Eddie and then looked at Milton with concern and disapproval. "Mr. O'Reilly."

"Forgive me if I don't get up, ma'am." Milton nodded to her as if tipping a hat. He tucked his shirt in and pulled his jacket back on. "My father took an Irish name for the stage, as if he were a white man in blackface. The name stuck to the whole family."

Milton had never told Redwood that. He had secrets too. "We come up from Georgia together," she said. "Singing and dancing and whatnot."

"Whatnot?" Clarissa raised her eyebrows.

"Singing and dancing don't always pay, ma'am." Milton smeared cold cream on his face and wiped the black away with a white towel.

"I did root medicine too, but no conjuring," Redwood said.

"That's the truth, so don't worry, Mrs. Phipps." Milton had cleaned one cheek and his forehead. He looked like a haint or a ghoul for sure. "Miz Redwood won't let any man get next to her, not for long." He wiped away his juicy red grin. He was sweating again. "They're afraid to mess with her."

Eddie groaned and rolled his eyes. Clarissa looked stunned.

George let loose a big laugh. "Whole family's wild. You know who you married."

Milton crossed his arms and shook his head. "Redwood's a real hoodoo, beloved by the spirit in everything. I tell you one night, I saw a bear—"

"Mrs. Phipps might not have much truck with backcountry hoodoo," Eddie said.

"That's true, Mr. Starks." Clarissa tried to smile. "I am a good Christian."

"I won't apologize, ma'am, for us show people." Milton finished cleaning his face and looked human again. "For us doing the best we can."

Clarissa took a breath and her angular features softened. "I expect it's difficult without a family, on the road, without setting down roots."

"Most colored entertainers come from good, respectable families, ma'am, just like yours." Milton didn't hide his irritation.

"Redwood was always talking 'bout her brother up in Chicago town," Eddie said quickly. "Kept us going."

George's eyes widened. "You all played Peach Grove, the night the bear—"

The theatre manager stumbled over a loose board in the dark hall. A skinny white man with a red face in a dull brown suit, he backed right into Clarissa, cussing. She smiled graciously at him as he sputtered and stepped away from her. He stood in the doorway and looked at all the fancy colored people crammed into the tiny room.

"What happened?" He toed the fallen screen and costume rack. "Oh. Admirers."

Eddie shrank several inches. George snorted. Milton tried to sit up, but pain defeated him.

"You know we's wild!" Redwood spoke in darky dialect.

The theatre manager pretended not to hear her and without uttering a greeting, launched into business. "The box office receipts were down."

Redwood frowned. "I thought it was—"

"We're just grateful for you putting cash money in our pockets." Eddie talked over Redwood and hunched his shoulders.

"Looked to be a full house to me," George said.

The theatre manager considered him. "Poor sightlines up in the balcony," he said.

"Sir, excuse my husband." Clarissa spoke sweeter than Redwood could imagine anyone being. The theatre manager nodded at her reasonable, honey tone. "But I know," she continued, "you don't plan to cheat these hardworking colored performers out of their rightful due. Why, the audience loved them."

The theatre manager was so taken aback, he stepped out of the room.

"Don't worry," Redwood said. "They cheat all the performers."

George chortled. "My sister always see the good in everybody."

The theatre manager deposited a small pile of money on a dressing table. "Well, she'll be finding somewhere else to sing." He disappeared down the hall.

"We were two spots from the headliners!" Eddie darted for the cash and began counting it. "What'd y'all go talk that way to him for?"

Redwood was disgusted. "I could do your dialogue, but I'd sound like a fool."

"Now don't you two start," Milton said.

"I'm sorry," Clarissa said. "It's my fault."

George grabbed Clarissa by the waist. "My wife think women

should get the vote and then go agitate for colored people's rights. She believe in speaking up."

Clarissa looked flustered at George.

"That's grand," Redwood said. "Eddie don't believe in nothing 'cept Eddie."

"You'd be begging on the side of the road without me. I rescued you." Eddie had been telling these lies so long he'd convinced hisself. "I taught you everything you know. I made you a star performer. Otherwise you'd still be picking cotton in Georgia!"

Milton groaned and passed out on the divan. Redwood pushed Eddie aside and stumbled through boxes to the divan. Eddie was hot on her heels.

Redwood touched Milton's damp cheeks. "He's burning up." She tasted his sweat. It was metallic and bitter. "He might not make it through the night."

"This is the end of us." Eddie brandished the money in her face. "Even if we split his share, it's not enough. He won't be good for nothing for weeks, maybe not ever."

Redwood turned on him. "Milton's your best friend in the world. He picked *you* off the side of the road!"

"He tole you that? Well, I've been doing the picking up here of late."

Redwood wanted to smack him. "He always found a piano for you! He give you the biggest share and even paid your gambling debts. Now he could die. Are you goin' leave him high and dry like that fickle audience you always talking down?"

"Fickle is it? You been reading the encyclopedia for that one."

"Hush." Redwood put a rag on Milton's brow.

"Milton wasn't nothing till I come along. I don't owe him. He owe me."

"What?!" Redwood hissed. Clarissa flinched. George looked up at the ceiling.

"I can't let him ride on my coattails forever, drag me down." Eddie was loud enough for the back row. "I've been carrying you both for too long." He stuffed all the money in his pocket. "This ship is sinking. You planned your escape with Saeed, well, I gotta save Eddie Starks. I ain't drowning out here with a broke-down dancer fixing to croak while you sail off with a faggot *Injun*!"

Redwood reached her storm hand to an inch from Eddie's throat. She didn't touch him, but he was choking and gagging all the same. He couldn't move a muscle. In an instant, his hazel eyes were shot with blood. George took a step toward her. One violent shake of her head and George halted.

"Who's talking about dying?" Clarissa glided up close to Redwood, clasped her hand, and drew her away from Eddie. He gasped and staggered. "George says you're the best healer he's ever seen." Clarissa spoke so quietly, Redwood had to calm down to listen, had to ask herself what the hell she was doing. "I hear tell, you pull away pain, like magic," Clarissa said.

Milton's eyes fluttered open. "Yes, you're too modest, Red, I'm not dead yet. Melodrama Eddie likes to play the scene at the edge of a cliff."

"Ain't my fault if truth is nasty medicine," Eddie said. "You tried to kill me."

"Ha! If I wanted you dead," Redwood said, "the boneyard baron would be singing your last hymn." She shouldn't get so angry. She had to watch herself better.

"Is that so?" Eddie clutched his throat. "That's a comfort."

"Let's not go on about all that." Clarissa fingered Aidan's worn pants. "Look at these old clothes. We have to get you something to make you feel nice inside, a woman again." Redwood stroked Aidan's shirt and shook her head, not so violent this time. Clarissa slipped her arm through Redwood's, fearless for all her delicate sensibility. "George was hoping you'd come live with us."

"That's right," George said. "I've done well. Chicago is a dream factory. Anything you can think of."

"I used to could feel into everything, dead, alive, yesterday, and tomorrow," Redwood said. "I don't know how to act now."

Clarissa looked baffled, but patted her shoulder. "You were a sensation onstage."

"I'm not talking 'bout that," Redwood said. "I . . . ain't been myself since I left home."

"Time to write a new song," Milton said. With a mighty effort he stood up. "See, I'm okay, Big Red. And let him fire us, Eddie. I still got a trick or two in my bag."

"Another job ain't goin' be easy to find." Eddie moved in on George and Clarissa. "Theatres are hitting hard times. Maybe these good people—"

"Will come and hear us play again sometime," Milton said. Eddie sighed.

"Why didn't you write me?" Redwood meant to tease George, but it came out hard. "Not one word . . ."

"You're home now." George squeezed her shoulders.

Redwood hadn't been able to heal Milton, and she'd almost choked the life out of Eddie. That didn't feel like home or anywhere she wanted to be. "Am I?"

"What a question," Clarissa said. "Of course you are."

Redwood stared out the window to the stars.

TWELVE

The night was too deep, dark, and sweaty; even the haints didn't bother to come out. The stars overhead looked out of place. Aidan hugged an old oak tree, moaning in the moss, so drunk he was lost close to home. A jug rolled away from his feet to a bear with a star-shaped scar on his cheek.

"Firewater. Not good for you. Don't you get started with that."

The bear nosed the blue stoneware. He licked the jug's lip, grunted, and spit.

"I keep trying to give it up. I promise myself. I promise everybody. Then I'm at it again." Aidan snatched his shotgun from the ground and pointed it at the bear. "My word's not worth a damn. Can't trust me. A miracle anybody can stand me."

The animal reared up on his hind legs.

"What do you know? Seminole *and* Irish blood driving me to the drink. I can't help myself."

The bear gurgled.

"Miz Subie say Peach Grove broke my heart, and I need to find something to do with all the love I got for this world that's curdling in my chest. Now I'm talking to a bear." Aidan shot in the air. The startled animal took off into the woods. A turkey buzzard flew up into the dawn light, circling above him. "I ain't dead yet," he yelled at the bird. "So you can just go on."

Somebody 'cross the creek played an out-of-tune banjo. The song was familiar. It was one of his. Aidan sang along, as hoarse and out of key as the broke-fingered player:

> *Running won't set you free*
> *Yeah, a man could still be a slave*
> *On the loose and–a acting brave*

In shackles he just don't see
No—Running won't make you free

Aidan's voice splintered on the last note. He almost fell down. The banjo twanged on, a screechy sound crawling up his back. He reached for the jug, hoping for one last swallow. It was empty. He let it tumble away. A crow hollered at him. This close to sober, out of hooch and ammunition, wasn't nothing to do but head into town and buy a drink; still a few coins in his pocket. He'd sworn not to bother with near-beer. After guzzling half a barrel you were burping and pissing and sober as a Sunday service. But what good were his promises? The bad banjo-playing made him itch. He scratched and squirmed and finally headed for a road he hoped led into town.

After almost losing faith in this direction twice, Aidan reeled down Peach Grove's muddy main street just before dawn. Feeble shadows, otherworldly moans, and a sickly sweet stench greeted him. He sniffed his pits, down at his crotch, and then the air. It was the air that was most foul. Ten minutes and he didn't see anybody upright but Doc Johnson and Hiram. They stood in white pinstriped suits by a wagon in front of Doc's office, calming a gray nag. Aidan stumbled over to them, gesturing wildly.

"Peach Grove look like a ghost town," he yelled.

"Folks are too sick to riot. Makes our job easy," Doc said.

"What you mean?" Aidan looked 'round. "What job?"

"Where have you been?" Hiram poked at Aidan's ripped shirt.

"Ah . . . hunting," Aidan said.

Hiram and Doc exchanged identical looks. Aidan lifted the cloth covering the back of the wagon. Dead eyes stared up at him. He recognized a few. Ed Crawford's blue eyes looked black as Mark Jessup's. Fellows he'd known most his life, friends he never had, starting to swell and stink. Aidan dropped the cloth and stumbled back. Doc held him as he leaned forward, vomit-dizzy. Nothing in his stomach to come up though.

"What the hell?"

"We could use a hand. Unless you're afraid of getting sick and dying."

Doc slapped his back. The blood rushing to his head turned back to where it belonged.

"Yellow fever snatched my folks." Aidan righted hisself. "Didn't want me."

"Hiram and I haven't gotten *whatever* is plaguing Peach Grove, not yet."

"Feels like a curse." Hiram surveyed the empty street.

"No such thing," Doc said coolly.

"If it's not *Garnett's curse* or yellow fever what killed half of Peach Grove in a week and laid up the other half . . . What do you think, Coop?"

Aidan shuddered at the mention of *Garnett's curse*. "I'm sure I don't know."

Doc shrugged. "Maybe we've discovered a new pathogen."

"Patho-what?" Aidan asked. "Half of Peach Grove?"

"A new agent of disease," Doc said. "Hiram exaggerates. He writes news."

"It's true." Hiram grunted at his brother's highfalutin, know-it-all airs and led the horse down the street.

Aidan couldn't imagine plagues or curses bringing down the whole town.

"I guess God has forsaken us, like you've been saying, Coop," Doc said. He and Aidan followed Hiram to a pretty white townhouse that looked brand-new. Doc knocked on the door, several times.

Hiram talked loudly at Doc's back. "Yellow skin, sticking to shadows 'cause of what you call photophobia, light paining the eyes and making the skin ache. What's that?"

Doc pushed the door open. "Hasn't been any yellow fever since 1905 on account of some Cuban gent and Dr. Walter Reed going after mosquitoes."

"Must have missed the grubs in Peach Grove," Aidan said as they went inside.

Doc chuckled at the gallows humor and gave Aidan a look that he'd been giving him for years that Aidan could never figure out. His eyes were high-spirited and sad, as if he and Aidan were buddies who shared a hard secret or faced hard times without running away. Maybe if Doc wasn't a rich man, they'd have really been friends.

The parlor smelled like the inside of a piss pot. Aidan tied a hand-kerchief over his nose and mouth as his eyes adjusted to dim light. The rotting death smell didn't seem to bother Doc and Hiram who just went on 'bout their grim business. Blinking the room clear, all Aidan could make out was chaos: overturned furniture, broken dishes, flies, and a fat rat scampering into the corner. Doc shook his head over the remains of a woman who must have been dead for several days. Hiram hauled an old man with sallow eyes and skin in from another room. The man vomited rust-brown blood.

Aidan followed the sound of whimpering to the kitchen. A tow-headed little gal was huddled under the table in her own filth. Aidan scanned the shadowy room. These were rich folk, and the kitchen was equipped with running water and modern plumbing. He picked the gal up and she moaned and trembled, from fear or pain or both. Setting her in his lap, he pumped water onto a clean cloth and dripped a few drops into her mouth. She sucked it down greedily.

"Whoa, whoa, go slowly now," he said. He pumped more water, peeled off her clothes, and washed her clean in between getting her to drink.

Doc stood in the kitchen door, watching him. "You're a good man, Coop."

"You hardly know me," Aidan replied. "Nobody know who I am." He wrapped the gal in a clean towel since he wasn't goin' go hunting up a dress for her. She clutched him and muttered against his chest. A miracle she was still breathing.

"Looks to be more than just yellow fever," Doc said.

"Don't care what you call it, long as it ain't *Garnett's curse.*" Hiram spit in the hallway. "Peach Grove citizens are dropping like leaves. Even the lice must be hungry, no good blood to suck."

"You always talk down everybody in town. What do you care?" Doc glared at his brother, but it was Aidan who'd wished these folks dead in Hell for what they stood around and let happen, not Hiram. Aidan scooped the child up.

"She might make it, with a little help." He carried her into the parlor.

Doc covered her kin with a dirty blanket. She was an orphan now, 'cept maybe for the old man who didn't look related to her.

"Fever might not kill her, but dehydration and neglect will," Doc said.

The girl trembled in Aidan's arms. "What are we goin' do with them?" The old man leaned into Hiram muttering gibberish.

"We can take 'em up the hill," Hiram said. "Miz Caroline Williams opened her house for the live ones."

"Did she now?" Aidan said.

The Williams place sat at the top of the only hill in Peach Grove—a gentle rise more than a hill—covered in grass and flower plantings, always something blooming, even in January. The mansion had been built before the war, when the Williams clan owned everything and everybody for miles. Patrick Williams had been determined to take back the birthright that got stolen from his family in the hard years after the war. His wife, Caroline, had continued this project after his death from apoplexy. The old house was a big white rambling thing with Greek columns, a red tile roof, elaborate porches, and second-story balconies. Six chimneys puffed smoke into the blue.

Aidan swallowed down the shakes. Scared he was 'bout to be completely sober and delirious, he hurried the sick gal through the Williamses' fancy gate, a curlicue forest wrought in iron by slave craftsmen long dead and almost forgotten. The gate swinging shut clanged loudly behind him. The latch raked 'cross his back and drew blood. Those old black artisans were reaching through the years to challenge him. Aidan answered them with a groan.

Colored servants were tending sick white people on the porches and too busy to take note of Aidan standing with the gal on the bright green lawn. A fierce, gray-haired, gray-eyed woman tugged his weary arm. Miz Caroline Williams took the gal from him without a how-you-do or nothing. She was flat and square for a woman, so bony and sharp, not a sweet ounce of fat on her. Her fine dress was filthy. Sweat dripped down her nose. The gal clutched her. Miz Williams left Aidan stammering thanks in the mud.

Hiram drove the wagon to the undertaker. Doc and Aidan walked beside it. Raccoons scampered through rubble in the stores on Main Street. The curse meant a string of feast days for them.

"I'm surprised she's taking folks in," Hiram said. "She tell you why?"

"That woman doesn't talk much anymore," Doc said.

Aidan shrugged. He didn't have much to say either since Redwood left. His hands shook. He'd kill for a drink.

"Caroline Williams ain't been worth much since Jerome run north with that nigger gal." Hiram was still mad over that.

"Mothers cleave to their eldest sons." Doc rubbed his eyes.

"What was that gal's name? A tree or some wild thing. They say she hoodooed Jerome." Hiram scowled at Aidan.

"Pretty as she was, didn't need magic." Doc grinned, appreciating his Redwood memory.

"She'd need mighty *mojo* to make Jerome take her black ass all the way to New York. Love only go so far." Hiram spit in the dirt.

"Maybe they stopped in Baltimore. Love might take you that far," Aidan said.

Doc and Hiram laughed grimly. "You miss her more than all of us, I bet," Doc said.

Aidan trembled, naked for a second. They had reached the undertakers. "What's he goin' do with all these bodies?" Aidan stared at the caskets piled in the front yard.

"Why these good people? Why smite down Peach Grove?" Hiram said.

"Life's a crapshoot." Doc went in to find the undertaker.

"We're right neighborly for rich boys, isn't that what you're thinking?" Hiram poked Aidan's ribs. Aidan shook his head. He was thinking on a drink. "Well, isn't it?"

"My head's full of moss." Aidan clutched his sides to hold down the shakes. "And I done lost my daddy's knife." He fingered the empty scabbard, trying to remember where it could be. Ladd and Elisa's? "That's a *Maskóki* hunting knife, a hundred years old at least. A Creek warrior gave it to my grandfather. A shame to lose that."

Hiram wasn't listening to him. "I wouldn't be out here. But you know how my brother is."

"Ain't you twins?"

"Not identical, as he is fond of telling me." Hiram punched Aidan's chest. "You look thirsty. Oh! Postcard from Chicago came for you, a month, five weeks ago now."

Aidan jumped at this. "And you ain't give it to me yet?"

"You keep going off on your *hunting trips*. Fancy minstrel show on the card. Who do you know in Chicago working for Mr. Selig?"

"Nobody."

"I saw Selig's traveling show once with Bert Williams. Funniest nigger I've ever seen." Hiram chattered on 'bout this Williams fellow but Aidan wasn't listening.

Maybe Redwood made it to Chicago, and she was up there doing the show she always wanted. That thought tasted good as a drink for a moment.

Several acts from the headliners at Chicago's Magic Lantern Theatre, a blackfaced Redwood was costumed as a yellow-and-white chicken. She pecked and strutted across the stage farmyard, shaking her tail feathers, spreading her wings. Saeed also in blackface was a back-country sharecropper. He had a red patch on his pants as if a giant with rouged lips kissed his bum. Looking over his shoulder, he crept through a hole in the fence, jumping and falling at every little noise, a clown, while Redwood was an elegant bird, preening and singing sweet nonsense to herself.

Saeed drooled at chicken Redwood. Seeing him pull out a giant knife and fork, she screeched and ran. They danced a chase scene 'round the barnyard: over buckets, rakes, fences, feed boxes, and black-faced little children playing chicks. This offered Saeed a splendid op-portunity for acrobatic pratfalls, somersaults, backflips, and balletic cartwheels. Throughout, Redwood did a splendid chicken mime. The white audience was unmoved till Saeed grabbed Redwood's white tail feathers and plucked several large ones, exposing frilly red underwear.

Saeed turned to the audience and shouted in darky dialect. "Lord a mercy. You musta been in dat school for chickens."

Redwood also spoke darky dialect. "Yassir, I'se got dat degree in barnyard philosophity."

"Better dan dat ole coon academy. Ain't no diploma for a spook chicken thief."

"Gimme my tail feathers back." Chicken Redwood roared like a lion, turned, and chased a terrified Saeed who dropped his knife and fork and scrambled through the hole in the fence. The red patch got snagged on a loose wire and pulled off as he shimmied through, exposing his sooty behind. The crowd applauded.

"You read the card, Hiram, who's it from?" Aidan kept breathing through panic. Redwood wouldn't have signed her own name and risked getting caught.

"I tried to read it." Hiram grinned sheepishly. "Something 'bout *working here now, you promised me,* and then a lot of wiggly lines. A woman's hand."

Doc dragged out of the undertaker's. He was shaken by whatever he and the undertaker had discussed. Dark circles of sweat and dust discolored his white pinstripe. He wiped his face. A tight squint turned to a devilish wink as he caught Aidan's eye. "You got a sweetheart in the windy city you been making promises to?"

Too nervous to trust his mouth, Aidan shook his head.

"Come by the office, I'll give the card to you," Hiram said.

"We got several more houses to check." Doc stretched aching muscles and tried to shake the gloom creeping over his face. "Good Samaritans, I could use nourishment before carrying on."

Hiram spun 'round and looked toward the edge of town. "You got land across the creek, don't you, Coop?" His jowls drooped like a lost hound dog. Doc stood behind him with an identical hangdog face as if he knew what his twin thought instantly.

Aidan rubbed his nose. "I been trying to run that farm into the ground."

"We don't know what you be finding over there." They spoke in unison.

"What you mean?" Aidan could have peed hisself.

Doc gripped his shoulder. "Clarence went to see his Aunt Subie, that conjure woman, two days ago. He didn't come back yet, and well—"

The horse spooked at nothing Aidan could see. He gripped the bridle.

"Nobody's been over to the colored houses or the poor white trash living there." Hiram stroked the horse's neck, but she didn't get calm.

"Yellow fever mosquitoes would be biting there too," Doc said.

"Damn! The hell you say!" Aidan couldn't help cussing. Why didn't he think of that? Drinking too much made a man stupid, even when he was almost sober.

"Oh, so now it's yellow fever." Hiram punched Doc. "But when I say it—"

"Hey!" Aidan interrupted their spat. "You boys can finish up here."

Hiram and Doc nodded and spoke in unison. "They're your neighbors."

Doc clapped Aidan's shoulder. "I'll meet you over that way later."

"You're going across the creek by yourself?" Hiram said.

"I promised her." Aidan careened down the street.

"What's wrong with you?" Doc chastised his brother when he thought Aidan couldn't hear. "You got to call him trash to his face?"

"He isn't one of them, not one of nobody," Hiram replied.

"If I gotta do a bird, at least it could be something that flew! A snowy egret."

Wearing Aidan's clothes, her hair stuffed under his cap, the brogans tied tight, Redwood pranced with Saeed, dressed in Persian finery, down a drab cobblestone avenue. Hundreds of horse carriages and automobiles jammed narrow lanes on both sides of the central trolley tracks and raised a thick haze of dust, manure, and engine smoke. Tall buildings pressed tightly against one another and stretched for miles in every direction. With endlessly repeating windows, archways, and columns—undecorated, smoke stained, and monotonous—these streets were a stone honeycomb, home for worker bees, not people. Chicago was not the elegant White City Redwood had glimpsed at the World's Fair.

"I've never been on this street," she shouted to Saeed over the hubbub. "Too many streets in Chicago to collect them, I guess."

Storefronts and stalls spilled onto the cluttered sidewalk, tempting the hordes hurrying every direction to spend a week's wages on trifles. She drew Saeed out of the flow of foot traffic to a patch of stained pavement between a barrel of pickles and a rack of smoked sausages. Boxes of ready-to-wear dresses, skirts, and blouses were shoved in a dirty corner. A grisly merchant looked at her expectantly.

"Where are we going?" She pulled Saeed toward the pickles. "Tell me now."

Saeed touched a patch on a frayed elbow of Aidan's shirt. "Why do you hide in this man's clothes?"

Redwood gazed at him, her head shaking, her tongue thick.

"Do you not say we are friends?" Saeed said. "Tell me."

"His clothes make me feel safe."

"*What* scares you?"

"Myself sometimes."

"Really?" He raised an eyebrow, theatrical but sincere. "Who was he?"

"Nobody."

Saeed shook his head. "You leave a trail of broken hearts. What about your own heart?"

"I miss him. I do. He *believed* in me."

"Do you love him?"

"Never got a chance to"—she winced—"to love anybody."

"Time's not up yet."

"Exactly. Ever think of doing some other kind of show? Ain't you sick of *da coon academy*?"

"I know a colored hotel in the Black Belt looking for good acts."

The Black Belt was the tight little hole on the South Side where they tried to shove all the Negroes pouring into Chicago, hundreds coming each day. Poor families of five and six were squeezed into two-room apartments and renting out closets to lodgers. No space, so little air, and hardly no prospects turned people into less than themselves. Was this where Mama and Daddy had hoped to find a bright destiny?

"Nothing's the way I thought it would be." She glanced at a red-faced woman skewering fat green pickles. The woman's sweat dripped in the barrel.

"We might get a spot after hours"—Saeed turned her face toward him—"doing the kind of show you fancy. It's a mixed crowd, very mixed. I thought we might audition this afternoon."

"I had pictures like this in my head." Redwood showed him a post-card of the 1893 Chicago World's Fair.

"Ahh. I came to the Fair too." Saeed smiled. "And fell in love with your country. Never went back home. Here I am, still in Chicago."

She was enchanted. "Did you perform on Cairo Street for your country?"

"Cairo is in Egypt, not Persia."

"I've been studying the map," Redwood said quickly, embarrassed.

"Someday perhaps, I could take you to Tehran."

She remembered Persia crouched between Arabia and India on Aunt Elisa's map, but couldn't think of one city. "Is Tehran big as Chicago?"

"It is the capital, a jewel, nestled in the southern slopes of the Elburz Mountains, not far from the Caspian Sea. A place for one who loves mountains. And the Caspian Sea is five times your Lake Michigan. We could visit the Golestan Palace and see the peacock throne."

He ran his fingers over the card. A painter had rendered a colorful view of the Midway Plaisance at night: a city of lights, of iron and steel archways and glittery arcades. It exploded into life for a moment, fountains spraying, fireworks going off, but Redwood caught herself before getting carried away and shoved the postcard in her pocket. Saeed flexed his fingers as if they tingled or ached.

"When I first arrived, I was young, foolish," Saeed said. "Chicago almost broke my heart, but are we not in America?" He danced 'round her and the pickle lady. "A land of tomorrow, not yesterday, a land where—" He was twirling and tapping and making a spectacle of hisself. Passersby smiled. "—a magic lady rehearses into the night so a lost young man from faraway Persia is ready for a big chance when it steams to shore." He took her hand and tugged her into his dance. People gathered to watch.

"You play the genie, not me." She broke off midstep. The crowd groaned, disappointed. "If they want entertainment, they have to pay me."

"Genie? It was *your* magic that saved me. Where would I be, what would I do without you?"

"Milton couldn't last on that ankle, and Eddie can't even count on his ownself. I wasn't planning to leave *The Act*. Rehearsing with you was an insurance policy."

"I was in the *Injun* chorus, now—"

"You're a darky headliner!" She laughed so hard her sides ached. "You can act colored, wild *Injun*, or the fine white gentleman."

Saeed didn't laugh. "Why does this make you so sad?"

"I thought Chicago was where I could be who I am inside," Redwood said softly. "What'd I know?"

After a moment of silence, Saeed laid his arm on her shoulder. "In my country, you and I, we couldn't be friends and discuss such weighty matters or even wander the streets of Tehran carefree." He observed the bustling street, a wistful look crossing his sharp features. "I miss home all the same."

"Do you think home misses you?" she said.

Saeed laughed at her serious face. "Look! That one is ours. Hurry!" They ran through screeching automobiles and rearing horses to a trolley pulling up to the stop.

Somebody plucked out-of-tune notes on an ornery banjo, or a cheeky squirrel ran over abandoned strings. Aidan had visions of bloated, yellow-eyed corpses as he staggered 'cross the creek to Elisa and Ladd's place. He fell twice, gashing his head on a rake in the front yard. Chickens pecked at the dirt by his nose, skewering kernels of corn. Happy pigs waddled from behind the shed to stare at him. Coffee brewing scented the air and made his stomach holler. Chaos had yet to come calling here. It was a regular Wednesday morning or Thursday; Aidan had lost track of the days.

As he stood up, the world tilted. In vain he reached his hand out to steady the horizon. "Iris?" he shouted and lurched toward the house.

Iris stepped onto the porch with his banjo. Eleven now, tall and beautiful in a Sunday dress, she looked like Redwood did at this age: proud cheekbones, stormy eyes, and dandelion hair puffing out from a hundred curling braids. Turning into a woman, and he hadn't noticed. Aidan clutched his heart.

"You didn't come and you didn't come and you didn't come," Iris said. "Uncle Ladd thought you died of the fever or left without a word, same as my sister."

"Why would I leave and not take you with me?" He scooped her up and squeezed till they both could barely breathe.

"You hurting me," Iris gasped.

"Sorry, honey bun." Aidan let her go.

"I can usually see folks wherever they are." She sniffled. "I couldn't see you no more, nowhere, just mist and smoke."

"I was lost, and I almost forgot 'bout you, I won't lie, but ain't goin' be no more of that." And then he was hugging her again.

"She say"—Iris pointed into the gloom of the house—"if I played your banjo, your song, you'd come. Back from the dead even."

"Your music called to me, but who tell you that?" Aidan squinted into the dark.

"Did you die? Is this your second chance?"

"Yes, ma'am, my second life."

"Does everybody get one of them?" Iris almost dropped the banjo.

Aidan grabbed the neck and set it down. He wiped her runny nose. "Where's your Aunt Elisa, Uncle Ladd? Them hardheaded cousins of yours are real quiet." He took a step into the gloom of the house, but then stepped back.

Iris's eyes blurred, her lips trembled, and she leaned into him. "We was doing okay. Some folks falling down sick, but everybody helping out, getting better."

"Well, sure." Aidan gathered her in his arms. "Elisa and Ladd be out there with food, water, medicine, easing the way for those 'bout to cross over. They could show the white folk a thing or two."

"Miz Jackson lost her baby boy, but it wasn't yellow fever, a coughing sickness."

"Doc Johnson say something else going 'round."

"Uncle and Aunt brought it home to us kids. Took the whole family. Left me alone. We did the burying last evening. I threw the first dirt on their faces."

Aidan felt that dirt in his eyes. He slid down onto the steps, so stunned his heart skipped a few beats. He almost couldn't believe what she said. Elisa, Ladd, and the cousins, dead and gone, and he didn't get to say goodbye, thank-you-ma'am, nothing. Iris leaned against his chest and broke into tears. Aidan had never seen her cry before.

"What you talking 'bout alone? You and me. We're a family." He rocked her, terrified.

Iris grabbed the banjo and thrust it at him. He'd taken to leaving precious things here, in case a mishap befell him when he went hunting or so he wouldn't just lose something, like his daddy's knife, like the shotgun he left behind in the woods this morning. He took the banjo from her and held it against his chest.

"They didn't leave you here by yourself," he said. "I know that."

Iris pointed into the house again. "She say, play that banjo and he'll come, but I didn't hurt it, did I?"

"Naw." Aidan got the tuning in order. The strings hurt and nothing sounded right.

"I kept your banjo safe. Always do, when you go off." She wiped at tears streaking down the side. "Play, please."

His fingers were clumsy, tone deaf still, and he would've set the banjo back down, but for Iris's tears splashing him. The fingers of his right hand stumbled on a lover's lament where the left hand didn't have much to do. Iris and the cousins would pester him to play this song whenever butter went rancid, hogs took sick, or the crop was scant, whenever somebody was just mad at creation. The whole tune didn't budge off A minor seventh. Iris leaned against Aidan's back and watched his fingers trip along the strings. Pain eased up off her bony little shoulders. When he played it a second time, a little better, she fell asleep against him and snored. Aidan set his banjo down quietly and laid her in the swing on the porch. Elisa's chair rocked beside him. As tears flooded his face, a gnarled hand damped the motion.

"Boneyard baron rock an empty chair," Subie said. Aidan wiped his face quickly. Subie come out the house dressed in indigo blue, a red *mojo* bag hanging from her belt. Silver bangles at her wrists and ankles banged together, making sparks of light but no sound. She smelled bitter and sweet, like the mug of steaming coffee she sipped. Her gnarled fingers made Aidan think of spider legs. He shivered and itched. Seemed Subie was spidering through his mind. "Past time you left Peach Grove, Aidan Wildfire."

He jumped. He never told anybody his Seminole name, not two wives, not Cherokee Will or Doc Johnson, not even Redwood, the only real friend he ever had.

"Iris need to find her sister." Subie touched a finger to his chest. "You too. I figure y'all can do that together."

"Redwood and Mr. Williams could be anywhere."

"Jerome's light don't shine no more." Subie waved at Aidan's mouth forming a tall tale. "Hush, I got a postcard from Chicago. Redwood tell me the whole story. Well, not the whole thing, but I read between the lines." Subie thrust a red leather journal at him. "Ladd say you wrote all his lies into this book. Mice chewed the cover a little."

Aidan wouldn't take it. "You don't wanna keep them stories?"

Subie made a sign from her heart to her head. "I got 'em already." She put his alligator bag on top of the journal.

"What I need an ole Indian pouch for?"

"You give Elisa money in here to hold for Iris." Subie winked her milky eye. "You holding Iris now, ain't you?"

"Sure I am, but—"

"But nothing. Elisa and Ladd wanted you to have these things, if you come back from the dead. You back yet?" Subie sighed. "Ladd wasn't sure you'd make it, but Elisa never stopped believing in you. She just couldn't wait, had to move on up."

Aidan closed his eyes on more hot tears. A blubbering drunk, what good was he goin' be to Iris or anybody?

"Don't go feeling sorry for yourself. No more time for that. Is this Jerome's money?"

"Why can't we just stay here?"

"Iris and Redwood need each other."

"So why I gotta take her?"

"My teeth 'bout to drop out, I lean to one side, fall asleep frying eggs and 'llowed to burn down the house. Besides, you promised." Subie slapped the book and bag against his chest. He grabbed them before she whacked his head.

"Going's one thing. Getting there is another."

Subie picked up his banjo. "You done lost the touch with your music."

Aidan hung his head. He couldn't play or sing worth a damn no more.

"You wanna play again, make Elisa proud, get you some dirt from the boneyard, good goober dust and take it to a crossing of roads. Iron roads be the best for you and Iris. Big black steeds charging every direction. Nine times, the sun'll watch you race by. Drop goober dust where tracks crisscross. Blow it to the four directions. By the ninth horizon, you'll be playing whatever music you want."

"You trust me to do all that?"

"Chicago's a mighty crossroads. Folk from everywhere, calling down powerful juju."

"What I look like messing in powerful juju?" Aidan shook so bad, he spilled coins and bills from the bag. He caught the money before it hit the ground though.

"You goin' make it, Aidan Wildfire."

"You read my journal?"

"Naw, my eye be so tired these days, Luella got to read to me."

"How you know my Seminole name? My true name."

"You speak it sometime without meaning to."

"Oh. So a conjure woman don't hear underneath things, how everybody say?"

"You be turning into a ghost, you don't feed your spirit."

"You asking a lot of a hard-drinking man."

"I see plenty whiskey bottles lined up in your mind. Amber sunset be playing tricks on you though. Every one of them bottles is empty!"

Subie chortled at her joke and sat down with him on the stairs. The sun sank under the creek. Iris sleepwalked from the swing to Aidan's lap, snuggling up to him like when she was little. Holding her close was sweet comfort.

"Iris tole me you wanted to come back, to look for her," Subie patted the gal's head, "but you was lost somewhere in the dark. She played the banjo to call you home."

A shooting star fell from the sky.

"That must be hitting ground in the boneyard," Aidan said.

"A spirit come home." She touched his bruised forehead. "You 'fraid Redwood might love you back and then what, huh?"

Aidan opened his mouth and then closed it. Under Subie's gnarled fingers, most of the aches and pains drained out of him, but how could Redwood ever love him back? Subie struggled up and walked off into dusky fields, her ankles sparking. A second light fell out of the sky.

"Two down." Aidan sighed. "So for sure I'm getting signs."

THIRTEEN

Halley's Comet blazed 'cross the last of the night sky, a fiery snowball flashing its tail in the light from the coming sun. Redwood marveled at the journeywork of stars. Everywhere, miracles and blessings and challenges—Mr. Walt Whitman and Dr. W. E. B. Dubois were whistling in her ears today, chastising her for feeling sorry and sad, when she had such a grand life, doing what she'd always dreamed of.

A *Chicago Defender* article on Dr. Dubois flew out the dressing room window before she could catch it. Redwood had gotten in the habit of reading newspapers and collecting headlines. It was an early morning ritual. She liked knowing what the world was up to first thing. She listened to the gossip at the butcher shop and to the workers coming home from the graveyard shifts in the town that never slept. At the laundry, she listened to women complain while bringing in dirty sheets, breeches, and the secrets of their customers. On the trolley she soaked in the chitchat between the stops. People held on to each other for a few seconds with their humble, breathless reports. She wasn't searching for news of Jerome Williams anymore, but searching all the same, 'cause when she found it, she would know. This morning she only had time to flip through her recent collection of headlines:

1910—MARK TWAIN BLAZED IN AND OUT WITH HALLEY'S COMET!

GOVERNOR OF GEORGIA DECREES: NO NEGRO TO WEAR A UNIFORM.

GIRL GOES TO HUNGARY TO BE WITH FATHER WHEN COMET COMES.

MORRIS WINS COLOR-LINE SUIT. NEGROES TO HAVE
SEATS IN ANY PART OF THEATRES IN ILLINOIS!

MEXICAN ELECTIONS—FRANCISCO MADERO HOPES TO
OUST PRESIDENT DIAZ.

WOMAN DECLARES: "THAT NEGRO BEAT ME, SAID HE'D
KILL ME, SO I SHOT HIM, AND THEN I SHOT HIM SOME
MORE!"

Redwood sighed. The theatre was dark on Mondays, and her day off would be long, waiting to get back onstage, waiting to be somebody other than herself, waiting for the audience to set her free. At least she was going out bright and early with Clarissa to do good work, healing at the settlement house. Putting on her *mojo* bag, she thought of Subie, Aidan, and the wild child she'd been back in Georgia. She reached her hand toward the fading comet and felt an icy burn as she traced the tail. She drew her hand back quickly. The fingertips were an angry red.

"I don't know who I am anymore."

The halls of the settlement house echoed with squeals, groans, and heated conversation. Fearless Clarissa strode ahead of Redwood into a chamber so jammed there was barely room to walk. Hundreds of colored men, women, and children, recent arrivals from all over the South, had come for help in making a home in the windy city.

"They all get here today?" Redwood stepped over smelly bundles and raggedy children.

"More coming all the time. Looking for the promised land." Clarissa scanned the bustling horde.

"In Chicago? Just like me."

"To hear George talk, anything's better than where they've been."

"George talk all kind of stuff, you know."

"I know who I married." Clarissa found her direction and marched on.

Folks frowned as the two women plowed through the room. These backcountry farmers were 'fraid of their own shadows and even more hostile to what they'd never seen before. Redwood knew them like the back of her breath. They whispered disapproval of Clarissa's upper-class corset, lace, and starch, and of Redwood's bohemian, theatrical flair. Babies gurgled and cried. Children ripped through the crowd, dashing between the sour chat and grunts. Redwood caught a few sly eyes sizing her up and offered them a sparkling smile. She did a little turn to show off her Oriental silk dress and jacket.

"I'm an adventure out of the *Arabian Nights*." She stroked a turban borrowed from Saeed to seal the Persian magic.

"Don't start." Clarissa gritted her teeth at such a shameless display. Redwood wore the dress for Clarissa's sake, but sister-in-law didn't approve of foreign fashion or so much free-moving flesh, even if it was all the rage. Well, Clarissa's high-boned collar didn't make skittish farm folk warm to her, and Redwood had 'em smiling!

In a room with sick and wounded people, Redwood donned a white smock over her silk, sucked a deep breath, and set a broken bone. Her patient passed out. Clarissa, also in a white smock, hugged a scared little boy as Redwood finished the job. She pulled as much pain as she dared, but didn't want to spook anybody and didn't want to get tired out before the day was half over. Folk always held on to their hurting. Pulling pain was like wrassling a juicy bone from a bear. Back in Peach Grove, Redwood only had to persuade a few patients at a time to let their hurting go, not hundreds of people.

Redwood drew Clarissa aside. "It's a shame people got to suffer so when I know doctors have drugs for the pain, so you don't feel so bad while you're getting healed."

"We've run out of aspirin and laudanum. Too many people flooding in, wounded and sick," Clarissa said. "Colored aren't welcome everywhere, and Provident Hospital's overflowing. Not enough colored doctors or nurses to go 'round. We make do except for the worst cases." She dropped her voice. "Do you know how much they charge?"

"Don't tell me." Redwood groaned.

"These are poor people." Clarissa smiled at a skinny toddler tugging on her. "Barely can afford the air they breathe."

"Hush." Redwood raised her hand. "I don't want to get mad while I work."

"Colored doctors have a right to earn a living."

"Don't everybody?"

"White doctors charge even more."

"So? I'm doing this for free. These folks work hard and don't earn nothing."

"It's 'doesn't everybody have a right.'" Clarissa corrected Redwood's grammar and avoided the argument. She did that all day. "We have to be a model for the less educated, for the less fortunate."

"I know your grammar," Redwood said. "I just don't feel it. Everything you got in you to say, you can't always say it right. Proper ain't the only talk there is."

Clarissa nodded as if she understood this for once. "The rest of the world can't always see or doesn't even care what you have in you. You can't give them ammunition against you. Besides, women are naturally more generous than men."

Redwood snorted at this, but for her sister-in-law's sake, she decided to apply herself to this role of model colored woman uplifting the race. "Okay. It just seem—*seems* wrong somewhere."

Why put all this effort into being like the white people, like the rich people, when they the ones raining down misery and pain? If she thought too much on that, she got storm mad. Fortunately, when working the roots and healing somebody, time went almost as fast as onstage. She could forget 'bout the evil things people took for granted. Model Negro woman; that was just another role.

Redwood inspected a newborn while the anxious mother watched. "She's only a child her ownself," she whispered to Clarissa.

"The wages of sin," Clarissa said, "snatches your innocence from you."

Redwood didn't know what to say to that.

She stitched a bloody gash on a young mother's neck and shoulder. Clarissa held her toddler till Redwood finished. The gal tried not to wince or flinch too much with her little boy looking on and ready to cry hisself. "I'm called Belle."

"My daughter's name is Belle too," Clarissa said.

"I'm called Sequoia. It's a Cherokee name for a great wise man of their tribe." Clarissa and Belle gaped at Redwood. "Did I say something out the way?"

"Belle means pretty in French," Clarissa said quickly.

"My man done left me anyhow." Belle tugged Redwood's arm. "They say you a hoodoo. You got a spell to bring him back?"

"I got a spell to take away lovesickness. You want that?"

Belle nodded. Clarissa watched, horrified, as Redwood handed her a small pouch. Belle stuffed it down her bosom.

"If you get a powerful urge for him, put that on your tongue. Nasty taste does the job."

"Gal in the corner got a man who thrashed her something awful. She probably on her last heartbeat." Belle pointed. "She asked for you."

Redwood turned. The flap of turkey buzzard wings obscured her view, a lazy shadow crossing the room. The boneyard baron's cold breath slithered down her neck.

"What is it?" Clarissa hesitated, feeling something too.

"We'll see." Redwood wasn't 'fraid of the baron. She respected him, so he wouldn't call her up before her time, but there wasn't no use worrying when death was coming for you. She kept on walking. The woman on the mat was all beat up, inside and out. Her skin was so thin, barely holding her spirit. Her eyes had almost gone dark. She didn't want to look on this world no more.

"Why ain't—isn't she with the doctor?" Redwood said.

"Doctor isn't coming till Thursday." Clarissa kept her distance.

"Be too late then." Redwood took the woman's hands. They were cold as snow and didn't weigh nothing. "What's your name?" Redwood pulled all the pain she could.

"Sarah," the woman whispered. "It's my time, isn't it?"

The baron stood beside her, an icy wind in a black top hat. Diamond teeth caught a glint of sunlight and froze in a grin. Redwood shuddered—she'd never seen him this plain before. Death wasn't a stranger to her no more. Clarissa quavered.

"You want to go, Sarah, or you want to stay?" Redwood whispered.

"I don't know," Sarah said. "Can you help me stay?"

Bartering with the baron for more time was a powerful spell. Redwood had seen Garnett do it when she was a young gal, had even helped her one time. That was before, and truly seemed more a story or a dream than a real-life event. And she hadn't seen the baron, just felt him. Miz Subie didn't dare try a *death-defying* spell but once in her whole long life. Who was Redwood to help this Sarah wrassle with death? Baron might take both their lives for spite, for Redwood thinking herself too big.

"I don't never say I can do what I can't." Redwood tried to look the baron in the eye. His cold countenance burned so, she cast her glance down. His laughter almost cracked her skull open. Her storm hand throbbed, as if it was fixing to bust apart.

"Help me go then," Sarah said.

"I—I don't dare do that either," Redwood mumbled.

"That's right. God sets the time of our coming and going," Clarissa declared and then whispered in Redwood's ear. "Make her comfortable as you can. Sometimes there's just nothing else we can do. And this is also a blessing."

The sun was gone from the sky, not even a taste of pink lingering in the clouds. Clarissa and Redwood hurried down a hall in the settlement house carrying their dirty white smocks. Streaky green walls and scuffed floors looked weary from holding so many hard-luck cases, from catching so many dreamers who got lost in Chicago nightmares, who got beaten to death by someone who should've loved them. Redwood passed her hand in front of her eyes. Gloomy thoughts were tainting her vision. Plenty of colored dreamers be riding high in Chicago. Look at George making money hand over fist, look at her and Saeed stepping onstage six nights a week and soon to be in a moving picture, look at Morris winning the Color-Line Suit and Negroes sitting where they please all 'cross Illinois.

Settlement Negroes weren't the only Negroes in this world, and conjuring wasn't the only good life.

"Sister Redwood, you look weary." Clarissa eyed Redwood's *mojo* bag. Just before the door at the end of the hall, she pulled Redwood aside. "Clubwomen do good work, for our people coming up."

"Yes, sound like Georgia back in there." Redwood sighed, almost homesick.

"We're bringing the colored woman and the colored man into the twentieth century, trying to shake off backcountry ways."

"Don't worry." Redwood tucked her *mojo* bag in her skirt. "I ain't dare do no real hoodoo conjure since—"

"Since what? I've seen plenty today."

"No, you haven't." A powerful spell 'llowed to work a heavy trick on a great conjurer, leave a mark on her soul, even if she take good care. Clarissa didn't know much 'bout hoodoo. "How can I explain what you don't believe?"

"We got to trust each other." Clarissa stood tall, stood close. "I want the truth."

They stared into each other. "All right. *Hot-foot* spell and such is just snagging folk with what they're already 'fraid of. To do more, a conjure woman has to be wild, risk big. You can't know everything beforehand. Hoodoo is an improvisation, like onstage, making up the next moments as you go. If you're touched by the spirit in everything, no telling what miracles and blessings you can do . . . or what tragedy. You can't control a powerful spell, so, I hold myself back—setting bones, stitching wounds."

"That's good discipline, and we're grateful. We're saving up to afford a proper doctor more than once a week." Clarissa cleared her throat. "What sort of improvisation is giving out bags of hoodoo tricks?"

"You think that gal don't—doesn't need help steering clear of a man who cut her up?"

"Yes, but superstition won't uplift the race."

"Who care what you call the help I give?"

"We do good Christian work, no truck with the devil."

"If you think the devil be in my hands, in my heart, what you bring me here for?"

"You're a good woman, but you're wild, like George. You should get married and settle down with a good man." Felt like Clarissa smacked her upside the head.

Redwood slid down the wall to the scuffed floor.

"Get up! Somebody will see you." Clarissa fanned her as if she were feverish.

"Sarah still had a spark in her. I should have wrassled the baron with her."

"Who?" Clarissa scanned the empty halls. "What's the matter with you?"

"I'm a coward." Redwood hugged her legs to her chest. "And I feel so lonely sometimes, like I'm lost in a swamp with gators for my only company."

"Don't be so dramatic. The floor is filthy. You'll ruin your nice dress."

"You and George and plenty folks coming and going in Chicago, the promised land, and I'm stuck in mud."

Clarissa tried to pull her up. "Children and a husband change everything."

"Turkey buzzards just waiting till I drop down and don't get up."

Clarissa shook Redwood's shoulders. "A wife can't just worry on herself. You know what each minute is worth when you're managing a family."

"I don't try to change you." Redwood grasped Clarissa's arms.

"No, you don't."

Redwood stood up. "I got a broken heart. Men touch me and nothing happens."

"Oh." Clarissa was embarrassed by this confession. "You do say anything, don't you?" She fussed over Redwood's dress and jacket as if the floor had done worse to it than stitching up bloody wounds. "Don't go 'round talking that to everybody."

"Ain't—aren't you my sister now, my friend?"

Clarissa's high-boned collar squeezed her neck so tight, it was hard to swallow or breathe, yet she made herself do both before she spoke. "You know, I've seen almost forty summers, not thirty-five. George thinks we married because of his ambition."

"George don't want less than any rich man got."

Clarissa spit on a handkerchief and wiped Redwood's cheek. "He doesn't mess in what I want to do."

"And any ruthless thing George do, he can blame on love for you. Yeah, kill every last egret for feathers to keep his wife in style."

"I don't know what you mean." Clarissa rubbed at something on Redwood's nose.

"Killing birds is how George got his stake to come north." Redwood clutched her hand. "Sometimes I want to be ruthless too and just twist everything my way."

"And do what?"

A group of clubwomen in clean smocks descended on them, all chattering at once.

"Have you read in the news?" one very black woman said. Even though sleek, straight hair was piled in dark clouds on her head and the lace on her dress cost a fortune, she wasn't the right color for this crowd. "Murder! If laziness, superstition, and voodooism weren't bad enough."

"Voodooism?" Redwood said. "Isn't that what white folk call—"

"Those hoodoo colored fools going around tricking and conjuring, yes," she replied. Glint in her eye said she knew Redwood was a hoo-doo. "Spreading goober dust, taking your money, not doing any real harm, I guess. But now these Georgia and Mississippi Negroes are cutting and shooting and killing each other." She gossiped on to eager ears, a fire catching in dry weeds. "Over nothing too. Stick you in the heart, shoot you down dead, just because they don't fancy how you say, 'How do'! The Negro women almost as wild as the men. Pulling out a shotgun and blasting your head off."

"Worse than the Italians even," a pale companion chimed in.

"You don't say." Redwood recalled the headline: WOMAN DECLARES: THAT NEGRO BEAT ME, SAID HE'D KILL ME, SO I SHOT HIM, AND THEN I SHOT HIM SOME MORE. "If a man push you too far, he get what he deserve."

"It's a shame," a wiry little woman said behind the others.

"Colored killing each other more than everybody else in Chicago combined." The pale one quaked.

"Didn't we have Georgia coming in today?" the dark lady said. Georgia was still in her country mouth and in her bold ways despite the hinkty Chicago overlay.

"Georgia coming in every day," Redwood said, using her stage voice. "Strong stock, they'll make it through whatever Chicago throw at 'em!"

They drew away from her. She shook her head. Clarissa and this crew were model Negro women doing good for the race, but frightened of raw colored folk, just up from the South. They didn't believe in their own people. They were ashamed of Redwood.

"Do you have a report, Clarissa? Where do we begin?" The wiry woman chewed the side of her lip. "Mrs. Powell didn't write down anything from last night."

"We just have to find you the right man," Clarissa whispered to Redwood and then turned to the women and their questions.

Aidan, looking clean and handsome and respectable, twisted a final screw and swung the front door back and forth. It worked good as new. Iris, in dusty coveralls, was picking up the last bit of a broken box in the yard. Otherwise everything was very orderly. Princess wandered toward the porch, her tail flicking at flies. Aidan pulled an apple from his pocket and tossed it to Iris. Princess headed for her.

Inside, the kitchen was clean and cozy. Aidan and Iris sat at a new table eating peach pie. Luella, Subie's grandniece, had stopped by. She couldn't stay, but left the pie. In between large bites, Iris balanced a spoon on her nose. Aidan laughed and tweaked her nose and the spoon clattered on the floor.

"I'm glad we're staying here," Iris said as Aidan lifted a hunk of pie to his face. "Aunt Elisa and Uncle Ladd's was so full of good times gone by, everywhere you look, a shadow of somebody I miss." She hunched her shoulders up and stared at him. "I didn't want to be there no more. It was too sad."

Aidan shoved the pie in his mouth and chewed slowly. "It's a good thing to miss somebody you love." He patted her hand.

"You miss Redwood too, don't you? She ain't even dead."

"You feel her, do you?"

Iris nodded.

He grabbed his banjo and strummed. His fingers were stiff, but he didn't stumble so bad 'round the neck. "I think 'bout your sister every day."

Actually, he tried not to think on her, but that didn't work.

Redwood stood in the back of the jammed ballroom of the Ace of Spades Hotel, stretching her tight calf muscles. She had persuaded Saeed to give her a set of clothes that a Persian nobleman might wear. With slight alterations the voluminous tapered pants and embroidered robes fit her long body well. Saeed was dressed in a similar outfit and danced from one foot to another trying to prevent muscles from going cold.

The Spades ballroom was more than a mere café saloon. The large square room had a thirty-foot-high ceiling, a sixteen-by-sixteen-foot raised stage, and a hundred tables with four or five patrons sitting at each. A balcony held more audience and creaked and groaned under the good time they were having. The musicians huddled against the rostrum. There were no wings, backstage, or dressing rooms, but Redwood didn't care.

She scanned the folks enjoying the comedian act that she and Saeed would follow. She spied mostly colored folk, but everyone else too, and heard a welter of languages. This was a real Chicago Fair audience, just how she'd imagined. Several colored performers had come to see after-hours entertainment. Young working folk were out for a thrill or chasing a night of sweet loving. Out-of-town travelers were hunting down exotica, and so were a few nervous but rich-looking white men. Redwood could just see Doc Johnson at a place like this, on one of his travels somewhere.

Saeed grabbed her hand, and before she realized this was the moment, they danced through the tables and jumped onto the cramped stage. The musicians were Saeed's friends and knew the tempo and tone to hit. Onstage Saeed and Redwood dashed over invisible barriers. They got tripped up and trapped, broke free, and ran again. The audience didn't know what to make of this dance at first, but talk died down, drinks lingered at lips, and sweet cakes hovered in the air.

Redwood and Saeed rode a horn solo up into air. Twisting and twirling, bending and bowing, they finally landed with a whisper on the creaky wooden floor to stunned applause. A banjo player with simple jug accompaniment took over. Banjo player was clumsy, but that didn't matter. Saeed chanted softly in Farsi as Redwood, feeling right as rain, sang one of Aidan's songs:

> *Running won't set you free*
> *Yeah, a man could still be a slave*
> *On the loose and-a acting brave*
> *In shackles he just don't see*
> *Noooo, running won't make you free*

In the bedroom, Aidan sang "Running Won't Set You Free" and strummed his banjo rather poorly till Iris fell asleep. He set his banjo on Aunt Caitlin's heirloom trunk, tucked the sheet under Iris's chin, and stood a moment listening to her breathing. He kissed her forehead and slipped out the room into the kitchen.

Sitting at the table, Aidan pulled out his journal. It'd been a while since he kept good counsel with hisself. The orchid Garnett had left on his rocking chair was pressed in the center. In four years, the flower hadn't dried out. After scratching one word on a blank page, his head ached. His skin burned and itched. He stopped writing and stared into the dancing fire. The cavorting flickers and shadows jumped him—fire imps, jabbing his body with red-hot pokers, laughing and hissing. One big fellow with a boar's head and stubby gator legs took to clubbing Aidan with a burning birch log. Setting down the pen, Aidan pushed away from the table. Pain blasted his body. He closed his eyes, hugged his chest, and shuddered. The stabs of pain weren't so bad if he didn't also have to watch the fire imps.

"Jesus." He groaned out loud and then bit his tongue so as not to wake Iris.

If some god could spare Iris from two deadly afflictions, Aidan had figured he could put down the jugs for good. He just hadn't figured how hard it would be. After the fever and cough epidemic, he'd stuck to colored Peach Grove where the neighbors smiling in his face hadn't set torches to Garnett's feet. In fact Aidan thought of settling down with a good colored woman, Subie's grandniece, Luella, if she'd have him. Luella was a handsome, strong gal he could respect. Whenever he checked in on Subie, Luella was there checking on her too. Luella could make a man nervous, eyeing him with a crooked smile and devilish hips.

Could such a fine woman want a busted-up drunk? The imps laughed in his ears. Aidan opened his eyes. The big guy with the boar's head just kept clubbing him with the burning birch.

"Luella be trying to make me fat with her pies and jars of jam!" Aidan told them. Luella had lost her husband, Bubba Jackson, to the coughing sickness. Seeing her dragging 'round, so sad, tugged at his heart. Singing at Iona and Leroy's one night, Aidan did a song 'bout losing the one you love, just for her. Ever since, Luella looked back at him with hope. She was nothing like Redwood of course, but they could raise Iris, have a few sweet babies of their own, and turn a profit with his farm. That would make a good second life. Yes, sober in Peach Grove would be all right once he fought through the delirium tremens. Sweat streamed from his head, stinging his eyes. Demons didn't look tired of tormenting him.

Shaking and wheezing, he stumbled to the door and stood in a cool night wind. The fire imps got blown back by a stiff gust. A shower of falling stars lit up the dark. Such a beautiful sight, and they'd been racing through the sky every night this week, 'less his eyes were playing tricks on him. Watching celestial fireworks calmed him a bit.

Iris shrieked from the bedroom. Aidan ran back in to her. Still half in dreamland, she stood at the window, banging and hollering and pulling at the new curtains.

"Wake up now, honey, wake up." He drew her from the cool draft and hugged away the screams. When she looked him in the eye from this world, not dreamland, he set her back on the bed. "Tell me what's wrong, sugar. So I can help."

She clutched her feet.

"Breaks my heart, you suffering and me not doing anything." When she still said nothing, he resorted to threats. "You don't want me going back to the drink, do you?"

She shook her head. "A demon posse be hounding me out of my dreams."

Felt just like a bottle upside his head. "Who is it?"

"Bad men . . ."

He finished for her. "Men of ash and smoke, burning the backs of horses, chasing behind a haint."

"Every night. They don't scare you none?" She gripped him.

"Makes me mad is all."

"A tall lady with swamp-grass hair. She wear a gush of muddy river water for a dress, face is all shadows and smoke. A turkey buzzard be sitting on her shoulder smacking some bloody lips." Iris was a baby when they lynched her mama, too young to remember her face, but

Garnett Phipps still haunted the little one. "A purple orchid be burning in her hair."

"I seen her too," Aidan said slowly. "Don't need to be 'fraid of her. She's a good spirit."

"How you know? Ain't she chase that preacher down his own well?" Iris was a spooky child. Everybody say, she know things nobody should know.

"Preacher drove his ownself down that well," Aidan said. "Couldn't stand what he see in the mirror every day."

Outside branches rustled and snapped.

Aidan glanced at the window. "Probably just the wind."

"Uh-huh." Iris looked up at him, no more convinced by this explanation than he was.

"All right."

Iris wasn't going back to sleep till he scouted 'round the house for danger. He hurried through the kitchen, grabbing a shotgun as he went. His fingers kept slipping on and off the trigger. No whiskey drowned his bloodlust—he wanted to kill somebody. He wanted to go hunt down the rest of Garnett's posse and shoot 'em in their beds, only three out of twelve were left. He could do it in one night. A branch snapped, and whirling toward the sound, he almost sent a load of buckshot through Miz Caroline Williams standing a few feet in front of him, holding her gray horse. Her face was moonlight and fog, her hair, a knotted spider web. She looked like a ghost.

"Good evening," Aidan sputtered.

"Middle of the night, actually," Miz Williams replied. "I saw your light."

Aidan grunted, still eyeing her through his shotgun sight. Her kin took part in every misery that plagued colored, Indian, or poor white Peach Grove for a couple hundred years. Shooting her might feel good.

"That sick gal you carry up to my house a while back, dry as death then, be doing fine now." She stared down both his barrels. "She asked after you."

She threw him off guard mentioning a good deed. He glanced 'round for other nightriders. Wind scattered dry leaves, and shooting stars cascaded 'cross the sky. They were alone in the night. Aidan lowered the gun.

"Why you riding so late? All alone?" he asked.

"Folks say, you be leaving here. Taking Iris Phipps up north, into winter."

"It's spring all over, even in New York City, and I ain't selling you my land in the middle of the night any more than I would in daylight."

She thrust an envelope toward him. "For Jerome and . . . and his wife, for my grandchildren. You're a good man. I trust you'll do right." Miz Williams hadn't talked this much in years. Not to Aidan.

"Everybody calling me a good man all of a sudden, and it used to be Crazy Coop."

"They say you put the jug down and take in Iris Phipps. I call that good." She talked like a normal, decent person.

"Why you steal all them people's farms from them?"

Caroline bristled. The hand holding the envelope shook. Aidan didn't touch it.

"My husband's land," she said. "I was just taking it back." She looked at him without blinking. "So will you do me this kindness? Since you're leaving anyhow, can you do right by Iris's sister and my Jerome?" She couldn't even say Redwood's name. "This is just between you and me. Nobody else needs to know."

"I'll do what I can." He took the envelope. "Everybody but me know I'm leaving."

"I hope Jerome didn't ruin it by now." She got back on her gray mare. "Nothing like the yellow fever to make a body glad for any future we been offered."

Aidan should have said her son was dust. No use her carrying false hope 'round like that. But she galloped 'cross the creek, stirring up murky water—gone before he could form the words. Maybe that was better. He went back into the house and threw cold water at his face. He was so steamed up, it didn't make much difference.

Iris slept sound, curled in his arms. Aidan was wide awake the rest of the night, wrassling with hisself till finally he couldn't fight no more. The time to leave had come.

BOOK IV

In all the ten years that I have appeared and helped to produce a great many plays of a musical nature there has never been even the remotest suspicion of a love story in any of them.

During the same ten years I do not think there has ever been a single white company which has produced any kind of a musical play in which a love story was not the central notion.

Now why is this? It is not an accident or because we do not want to put on plays as beautiful and artistic in every way as do white actors, but because there is a popular prejudice against love scenes enacted by Negroes.

—Aida Overton Walker in the *Indianapolis Freeman,*
Oct. 6, 1906

FOURTEEN

Chicago and Peach Grove, 1910

Redwood slipped behind a bush and jumped from the bicycle to catch her breath. Her light cotton bicycle pants clung to damp thighs. The evening air was warm, and she'd been pedaling hard. She mopped her forehead and took stock of her environs. What show could Milton be doing 'round here? This modest residential neighborhood featured comfortable two-and three-family structures, all with running water, no doubt, and indoor plumbing. Robust trees, planted on an esplanade in the 1890s, provided a canopy of shade. Skilled white craftsmen—printers, machinists, master carpenters, electricians—and their families enjoyed a good life on these streets. Garden plots were in flower, and an occasional automobile rumbled down the cobblestones. The residents weren't factory workers or from a slaughterhouse floor, but they also weren't wealthy.

Redwood left the bike in thick bushes and strode down the street. Spying Milton and Eddie lugging furniture and boxes from a horse-drawn wagon into an empty house, she hid behind a tree.

"It's gwine be hebben living here!" Eddie shouted. Milton grinned.

They wore loud colors and patterns and sang nonsense as they struggled with a large table. A white couple and three children observed from their next-door porch. An elderly white man stopped as Milton and Eddie disappeared into the house. Leaning on his cane, he twitched and gasped till Milton and Eddie come back out the house, laughing too loud. Nothing was that funny 'cept onstage.

"Who's moving in?" the elderly man demanded, his face purple, his breath choked.

Milton and Eddie exchanged glances; Eddie was doing his best Sambo, darky act. "Why, we is, sir," he replied.

"Yes, uh, thass the uh plum truth." Milton had never been good at cooning. These folks didn't notice his bad acting though. "Da gall darned truff."

The old fellow was downright apoplectic. "That's outrageous."

Milton and Eddie grabbed a stuffed chair and headed into the house again. George crept behind Redwood and grabbed her 'round the waist. She turned quickly and held a knife to his throat.

"I don't like men sneaking up on me," she hissed, harsher than she intended.

"I don't like my sister spying," George said.

"I ain't goin' stand in the dark no more. What you got Milton and Eddie doing?"

"Blockbusting."

Redwood had been studying all kinds of words to uplift herself, but hadn't come 'cross that one. "What's that? Something shady I'm sure."

"You goin' put down the knife?"

"After you tell me what you doing."

George laughed. "Fair enough."

"And if I don't like what I hear . . ." She didn't know what, so she got quiet.

"When I buy my house two years back, panic peddlers try to cheat me like some ignorant Negro, but I offer to cut the fool and scare more white folk out, so blockbusters charge me a third of what other Negroes got to pay."

Another white couple on a second-floor balcony watched Milton and Eddie wrangle an upright piano into the house. It banged Eddie's toes. He dropped the heavy instrument, which clanged something awful. He hopped 'round, squealing louder than the grumbling piano. Milton hooted.

"You must've got yo' porter diplomie from da coon academy," Eddie said. "My toe 'llowed to fall off after dis."

"Ain't my fault if you got budder fingers."

"You saying I'se done dropped it on meself?"

"How is you gwine play piano wid broken toes?"

George laughed quietly. The white people were not amused.

"You scaring these people into selling their homes dirt cheap?" Redwood said.

"They 'fraid of living next to colored, not me."

"After you scare out these fool white folk, how much colored goin' have to pay to live here?" Redwood still held the knife to his throat. "Three times as much?"

"A landlord gets the best rent he can, to make a profit. I'm not in this for my health."

"Clarissa know 'bout this?"

"Clarissa married me for my money, my business sense, not my Georgia family pedigree."

"What you marry her for?"

The white folk grimaced as Milton and Eddie carried on with a sofa now. Redwood marched away from George, disgusted.

He ran in front of her. "We all jigging and cooning for white folk."

Redwood pushed past him to her bicycle in the bushes. "Corking your face and cutting the fool is one thing." She hoisted herself onto the saddle. "But this."

"Same difference." He blocked her.

"Are you goin' get out of my way?"

George didn't move.

She drove the bicycle 'round him, yelling. "Gotta be something better to do than steal money from ignorant poor people."

"When you think of it, let me know."

Aidan jumped from Miz Subie's roof and brushed his hands. Dawn had yet to scatter the dark. Cold fog rising from the creek puckered his skin. Princess snorted at him, her hot breath turning white. She was packed down with traveling bags, shotgun, and banjo. Iris stroked her neck, chattering softly to her. Miz Subie surveyed Aidan's efforts. She looked so small wrapped against the morning chill in a Seminole patchwork coat, so fragile, like she could tip over.

"That leak shouldn't bother you no more," he said.

"Thank you kindly," Subie said, teeth chattering in the cold.

"I'm not used to feeling the weather." Drunk all the time, Aidan had lost touch with the seasons. He handed Subie a packet of papers.

She tucked them into the folds of the coat. "You in a hurry to leave all of a sudden."

"You hold on to that deed, now." It struck Aidan hard that he might never see her again. He clasped her hand. "I just 'bout run that farm into the ground. A miracle if it's worth anything at all."

"I'll hold these papers till y'all decide where home is," Subie said.

"Thank you for looking after my Princess." He hugged the mule who nosed his pocket till he pulled out sweet corn and a sour apple and watched her eat. "She's getting old, can't do much heavy work. She's good company though."

"I know how that is. Here." Subie had a *get-there* spell ready for him: a map she drew to Redwood, powder to fight alcohol demons, and his *Maskóki* hunting knife.

The back of his throat clutched. "I thought I lost that." He thrust the knife in the empty scabbard still at his waist.

"Luella found it. She say, put the blade under your pillow when you sleep, to cut pain."

"Thank her for me," Aidan said. He'd been willing to *settle* for Luella, for an easy life, but not the life he wanted. Luella was a warm bosom and a feisty spirit. She wasn't adventure or love or forgiveness. "And tell her—"

"Luella understand already." Subie thrust the tin of powder at him. He tasted it and grimaced as he swallowed. Subie shrugged. "Gotta be nasty to fight firewater demons."

"Your map have us going every which way."

"You know a better route to Redwood, take it."

"Sorry, ma'am, I—"

"Don't forget dirt from Garnett's grave. Spread the last bit with Redwood."

"I won't forgot none of your *good-music* spell." Aidan kissed Subie's cheek quickly. "I'm goin' miss you."

Subie ran her hand over the sharp ridge of his chin. "Don't never wish I was young again, but every once in a while, I do wish I was still wild."

"I don't know if I could take all that heat." He hugged her hard. "Thank you, for everything."

"Keep your heart open. Snatch the change on the wind."

Iris ran up and hugged them both.

"Remember, a good name is powerful juju."

Subie held Princess who whinnied and brayed as Iris and Aidan, laden with baggage, staggered down the road.

They wound down an overgrown path to the colored cemetery. Even knowing where the boneyard was, you couldn't always find it. Aidan was glad to have Iris leading the way through the dark. He figured Subie's *good-music* spell wasn't just so he'd be a good banjo player again, but he didn't try to guess what she really had in mind. He'd just collect the dirt and *do right*.

"Nine is a hoodoo charm, a crossroads number," Iris said.

Elisa and Ladd's resting place was in the shelter of a massive grandmother oak. Gnarled branches trailing silvery Spanish moss leaned on the ground, scraggly elbows holding up a lopsided trunk. A pipe, Ladd's music spoons, and a carved wooden box stained deep burgundy adorned their graves. The hardheaded cousins were buried in a circle 'round their parents. Wooden birds and animals sat on each little plot. Aidan brushed his fingers against the favored possessions of his friends, his *family* actually. Had they clutched these things before their spirits flew?

Aidan shivered thinking on what he still had to do.

Iris hugged him with her warm arms. Her little-girl sweat smelled sweet. "I'll wait here. I don't like going up there," she said.

"Me neither." Aidan grabbed his red leather journal.

Some folk didn't rest in peace.

He climbed a slight rise until he saw an ellipse of white marking Garnett's grave, shells from a Sea Island—she was a Gullah woman in life and death. Star magnolias at the end of a bloom sprinkled petals and scented the air. Aidan's legs felt rubbery, his mouth was dry and ashy, and blood was heavy in his heart. The headstone sparkled with its own light. It read:

Garnett Phipps 186?—1898
You can't set the spirit on fire except with love.

Tiny rocks had rained down on the hilltop, singeing the grass and flower petals on the grave. Meteorites, from the lights falling out of the sky last night?

"Has your soul come home, Miz Phipps? A falling star . . ."

Aidan poured whiskey from a bottle he'd found under his porch and placed a silver dime near the headstone.

"Miz Subie say, I got to buy some dirt from you to work this trick." He patted hisself, cussed under his breath, and looked 'round anxiously—nothing to put the dirt in. He took the train tickets and money from the alligator pouch and stuffed these in his shoulder bag. The rain of rocks had left the seashells unblemished. He fingered several quickly, almost expecting to feel an echo of Garnett's spirit ringing in their chambers. The shells were quiet under his touch. Then he noted a single broken shell. He scooped it up along with the goober dust and glassy meteorites, and digging from the head, the heart, and the feet, he filled the pouch.

Suddenly overcome, he sat down by the bright headstone and wrote quickly in his journal for the first time in several years. A story spell was better payment for Miz Garnett than one thin dime.

A NAME IS POWERFUL JUJU

Aislinn laughed as Aidan and Big Thunder chased her up through the last stunted trees and scraggly bushes to the edge of a cliff. The early morning sky was misty. Blue-green mountains rolled across the horizon like waves of an ancient slow-moving sea. Aislinn tottered on an outcropping of rocks, as if falling, and scared Aidan, but Big Thunder put his arms about her.

"Don't fall," he said. "This is Enotah, a high place. One of the highest in all the Enchanted Land. It would take you a long time to reach the bottom."

"I knew you'd catch me," she said.

"This place is so high, it can save you." Big Thunder said. "A long time ago when a flood raged and killed all the people in the valley below, a few families escaped in a great canoe. But where could they grow corn? Where could they hunt? The Master of Breath filled them with hope until they reached Enotah. Here, above the floodwaters, where the trees gave way, they planted crops, fed their babies, and grew old, content to watch the stars shooting by."

"A sacred place then?" Aislinn said.

Aidan came and stood close to his parents, feeling their warmth as the wind whistled through the bare rocks. They gazed out on the forests below. The deep green seemed to go on forever, even though Big Thunder complained of the loggers who toppled mighty trees and left the land naked.

"Why is this an Enchanted Land?" Aidan asked. "Are there fairies and leprechauns here, like in Ireland?"

"It's what the Cherokee called these lands," Big Thunder said. "Many peoples have come and gone, fought and died over this ground. The Cherokee say the *Nunnehi,* invisible spirit people, lived inside the mountain and also the tiny *Yunwi Tsunsdi.* Perhaps the fairies of Ireland too."

Aislinn pulled away from them and dropped down to the ground at the edge of the cliff. She found a cracked white shell and put it to Aidan's ear.

"That shell swallowed the ocean a long time ago. You can hear it inside still," she said. "It will never forget this song."

Aidan listened and heard waves crashing against the tiny walls.

"Your daddy swallowed the lightning," Aislinn said. "That's why they call him Big Thunder."

"You are Wildfire, like your mother, a spark that takes hold in someone's heart."

"And we too have seen the Enchanted Land." Aislinn kissed Big Thunder.

Aidan knew he should look away from their passion, but he felt like a seashell catching an ocean wave.

"Big Thunder and Miss O'Casey would smile on this medicine work." Aidan tied the alligator bag to his waist. "Even the gator must be grinning at what its ole dried skin be holding. Goober dust for the whole trip." He stood up and passed his hand over the headstone. "Sorry won't do, I know, Miz Garnett, but the rest of my life could be a prayer to you."

When Aidan came down the hill, Iris didn't ask him what took so long. She grabbed his arm and hurried him out of the boneyard. Lugging heavy bags, they were soon sweating in the heat. They passed

Leroy Richards and Cherokee Will sitting under an oak and sharing a jug. Iris waved. Aidan paused and licked his lips. The two men lifted the jug toward Aidan.

"How 'bout one for the road?" Leroy shouted.

"This is his special brew, too good to sell." Will swallowed a good gulp.

For the first time since he watched the stars fall with Subie, Aidan actually wanted a drink. Not on account of a demon posse or some other good reason. He had passed through delirium tremens and cleared his system. Doc Johnson said he'd turned the corner. Yet right now, the thought of bourbon, gin, whiskey, or any ole rotgut made him itch and ache, like an awful hankering for no lady in particular. Enough to drive a man wild, and so soon after pledging his life.

Iris pulled Aidan away. "We're in a hurry," she yelled.

"When you were born, you cried and the world rejoiced," Cherokee Will said. "Live your life so that when you die, the world cries and you rejoice."

"Amen. Blessings on you both," Leroy said.

"Thank you, sirs," Iris said. Aidan only nodded.

If Iris noticed Aidan stumbling and weaving, she didn't let on, just bounced along, keeping him upright and on track. It probably never occurred to the child that he might drag her down too.

"Come on," she said. "Doc Johnson say it's better not to ride off in the heat."

George and Clarissa's house was a well-appointed mansion with Oriental rugs, modern art, fine pottery, and beautiful furniture. Something you could've read 'bout in a book. From down the block, Redwood saw an electric light burning on the second floor. As late as it was, Clarissa was looking in on her four sleeping children. By the time Redwood pushed the heavy front door open, as quietly as she could, Clarissa, in a luxurious dressing gown, was sitting at a table in the front parlor, crying. The large clock next to her read ten minutes after four. Above her, portraits of stern, high-yellow Negro patriarchs glared disapprovingly at the heiress to their beleaguered good fortune.

Redwood didn't want to hear nothing sad tonight. Dressed as a Persian nobleman and tipsy from a glass of champagne, she braced herself for the set-to with Clarissa, who insisted on treating Redwood as if she were one of the children of the house 'stead of a grown woman. Hoping Clarissa hadn't heard her come through the front door, Redwood tiptoed toward the back parlor—her sleeping chamber now. Clarissa could hear a mouse pissing on cotton, in her sleep. Redwood tripped on the Oriental rug and trying to get her balance, made more noise than an elephant running 'round the jungle.

"Oh." Clarissa dabbed swollen eyes. "I thought you were George. I've been worried."

Redwood halted two steps short of her room. "Ain't he got a phone at the Dry Cleaning?"

"Yes, but he has to use it, doesn't he?"

Redwood turned to her. "You look tired."

"What keeps you out so late?" She pulled a sour face at Redwood's Persian attire.

"Let's not fight."

"You were out with Mr. Saeed, weren't you? And I've introduced you to several eligible colored gentlemen."

"I don't want somebody . . . who is 'fraid of . . . of who I am."

"Seems you don't want anybody decent at all."

"Some women may be better off alone."

"There is no such woman." Clarissa's face went pasty yellow. Her stomach heaved as she choked down something trying to come up. "Excuse me, I think I'm going to—"

Redwood caught her before she fell and hurried her down the long hallway to the kitchen. Clarissa threw up several times in a large basin. Redwood held onto her until the sickness passed.

"You better now?" Redwood covered the heavings and then wiped Clarissa's sweaty face with a cold cloth.

"You can tell what's wrong, can't you?" Clarissa said. Redwood swallowed and nodded. "This is a terrible thing." Clarissa pushed back a wave of weeping.

"How can you say that?"

"The twins almost killed me." Clarissa sat down at the table. "I shouldn't have another baby. Dr. Harris said I should do what I have to, not to get in a family way."

"Kick George out your bed? Ha!" Redwood sat down next to her.

"He has another woman as it is." She looked ready to cry again.

"Some folk ain't satisfied with just one person to love."

"Are you taking his side against me?"

"What do you want me to do?"

Clarissa took hold of Redwood's hands. "I don't want to know what you can do. Because then I'd lose my soul, asking you to do it."

Redwood snatched her hands away, and they sat quiet for several minutes. Neither could look at the other.

"You 'bout to fall over," Redwood said. "Let me . . . help you upstairs."

Clarissa leaned into Redwood as they climbed the stairs, weeping a little at any bump in the rug. Redwood helped her out her robe and into the world's best bed from the Sears catalogue. The silky sheets were a comfort to her feverish skin.

"I haven't told him. Do you think I should?" Clarissa's eyes were foggy gray.

Redwood squeezed her. "Wait till you be absolutely sure."

In the kitchen Redwood stared at a kettle heating up. She drank a cup of tea and twisted the key to Garnett's music box. The drum had gotten warped but she could still hear the melody. Aidan sang "Swanee River" for her the night she had to leave home. His voice was still in her. So was Subie's, even her mama's, dead so long ago. Redwood hadn't come to Chicago empty-handed. These highfalutin Negroes didn't need to be 'shamed of her *mojo*, her hoodoo, and then ask her to get 'em out of trouble on the sly.

The water boiled and the kettle sang. She let it cool a bit and then brewed one of Mama's nasty concoctions.

Redwood stood by Clarissa's bed with a steaming cup. "Thought you might want some of Miz Garnett's tea. Help you calm down and sleep."

Clarissa took the drink with shaky hands.

FIFTEEN

On the Road, 1910

Aidan and Iris left Peach Grove an hour after sunrise on a warm day in May 1910. Doc Johnson was on his way back to Atlanta and gave them a ride in his buggy. Two sturdy horses pounded the dust at a moderate pace. Clarence wore a fancy duster, a stylish hat perched on the side of his head, and fine leather gloves as he gripped the reins. Behind him under a canopy, Doc sat facing Aidan and Iris. The luggage was piled in the space behind them.

Doc was grinning to beat the band. Carrying Aidan and Iris to Atlanta made a grand addition to his collection of intrigue and exotica. Doc wouldn't take any money, but made them listen to his theories, scientific and otherwise, for miles. He marveled at how well colored folk survived yellow fever epidemics in Peach Grove, Memphis, everywhere. He wondered if it was something in African blood, something that made them fierce and neighborly too.

"Not a complicated people—real close to their emotions." Doc patted Iris's head affectionately and winked at Clarence. "That's what I love."

Aidan squirmed. Clarence rolled his eyes, tucked irritation under the collar of his fancy livery, and clucked nonsense at the horses. He glanced back at Aidan, who forced a smile at Doc's foolishness. Iris cocked her head at Aidan, but he was determined to get them all the way to Atlanta in the comfort of the buggy. Clarence spit into the wind.

Doc held forth on a German scientist, Dr. Albert Einstein, and time and space being one. "There's no absolute time, no big clock running the heavens. We're all a piece of time, happening over and over for each new set of eyes." He was full of funny ideas from everywhere.

At sunset, Clarence paused by a crisscross of rail tracks to let Aidan blow goober dust in the four directions. "Miz Subie's spell will have folks buying tickets to your music, sir." Clarence grinned and wasn't a yellow or broken tooth in his mouth. "Miz Subie and me are kin, on my father's side. Nobody conjure or work roots way she do."

"Mr. Cooper already play banjo real good," Iris said. "Miz Subie's spell will make him great."

"*Gris-gris* at a rail crossroads." Doc displayed his voodoo savvy. "Goober dust from whose grave?"

"You don't want to know." Aidan's hands trembled as he tied the pouch to his waist.

Clarence hunched his shoulders and lit the lanterns.

"Powerful juju indeed." Doc squirmed in his plush seat.

Clarence clucked at the horses as if they were the jittery ones, and then they were underway again, the lanterns winking in the dark.

Iris bounced in her seat. "You driving us, Mr. Clarence Edwards, out of all them hundred fifty thousand people in Atlanta, and you being Aunt Subie's kin too, that's what you call a coincidence."

"Not at all, sugar," Clarence said. "I see Miz Subie's sign on you, plain as moonrise. This journey be following her map. Neither you nor your spirits can lose the way."

"Taking this orphan gal to find her sister, that's more than neighborly. You're a good man, Coop. Or crazy." Doc grinned.

"Tell you the truth," Aidan leaned toward him, "the thought of seeing Redwood again has me pissing blood."

Doc leaned into him as well. "You don't say."

Aidan regretted his confession immediately. "She—she was like a sister to me."

"I wouldn't have picked her to fall in love with Jerome Williams. Some things money can't buy, or should I say, some people?"

"That's true." Had Doc seen through his tall-tale lies? Aidan sat back in his seat.

Doc did the same, watching Aidan carefully. "Redwood had quite a job, civilizing Jerome Williams. Even his mama wanted to shoot him, from time to time."

Clarence chuckled at this, and Doc laughed outright. Iris looked puzzled.

"Jerome and Hiram were friends, but I never liked the man, although I didn't wish him ill. I just can't see him with *our* Redwood."

"Redwood's a hoodoo. Jerome have to come to terms with that," Clarence said. "No man goin' rule her."

"Chicago would be where I'd go. Not New York City," Doc said. "Where all the trains meet."

Iris and Aidan gaped at each other. If Doc knew all along that Aidan was lying 'bout Jerome and Redwood, why hadn't he said so before?

"Well, I'm goin' see Chicago someday too," Iris said.

"Doggone it. I thought we'd get a piece farther." Clarence scowled at the road. "Your cousin's place is still two hours, and we got to rest these horses now. All this luggage and books we hauling, Boo's tuckered out and Buttercup be fretting over Boo."

"You call 'em Buttercup and Boo? Mr. Cooper ought to write a song on that," Iris said.

They decided to spend a night sleeping under stars. Nobody wanted to stay in a backcountry inn and put up with Jim Crow foolishness—colored out back in hard dirt maybe and Doc and Aidan laying up in sheets and soft pillows. Aidan certainly didn't want the temptation of even near-beer. Doc was as excited 'bout the camping adventure as Iris. They found a dry spot not too far from the road. Clarence let Aidan collect wood and get a fire going while he fussed over Buttercup and Boo. Iris hauled water from a tiny stream then sat down to warm her naked toes. Doc dropped down beside her and pointed to a smudge just above the horizon.

"Halley's Comet," he said. "These shooting stars we been seeing for days are courtesy of this fiery snowball. Tomorrow the Earth will hurtle through its blazing tail."

"Could a person ride the comet's tail?" Iris asked.

Doc laughed and then scratched under his chin. "Depends on who and what you are, I suppose. Do you know what a comet is?"

Iris shook her head. Aidan and Clarence were listening now too.

"Comet comes from the Greek *komētēs,* literally, long-haired. In ancient times, people thought comets were new stars with flowing tresses. Beautiful women roaming the heavens, free spirits—a bad omen." Iris laughed at this. Doc looked gleeful as he talked on. "Fearing the comet's curse, Nero assassinated successors to his throne. But Edmond Halley had studied Sir Isaac Newton, and well, when the solar system was

born, these comets were flung around the sun in great parabolas . . ."
and then he explained the whole sky. Iris was enchanted, Clarence and
Aidan too, even if Aidan fell asleep after the first few billion years.
Eventually Iris fell asleep too, curled next to Aidan.

Moans and short breaths drawn through clenched teeth startled Aidan's eyes open. It took a moment to figure out what he was
hearing—sounds of lovemaking, quiet, careful, but unmistakable.
'Cross the fire, closer to the gurgling stream, Doc and Clarence
reached a peak of passion. Aidan's stomach threatened to come up as
he listened to them grope and grunt and then growl sweet release. He
glanced at Iris. Thankfully, she was deep in dreamland. Once didn't
seem to be enough for these boys. They were at it again. Aidan ground
his teeth together. The third time, 'stead of jumping up and screaming
at Doc and Clarence, Aidan forced his eyes shut.

Finally, everybody was snoring 'cept for him. He didn't want to
think 'bout what he'd just heard, but it played over and over again in
his mind. He knew men went with men sometimes, and women with
women. Who was he to judge Doc and Clarence? On the road in a
fine buggy, with free people, *isti siminoli,* who loved each other, the
rest of the world be damned; that's all there was to it. He kept talking
to hisself, *if I don't like it, I don't have to do it,* but he didn't get a wink
more of sleep.

Just before dawn, they struck out again through the mist, with
Aidan still feeling sick to his stomach. He could barely look at or talk
to Clarence or Doc. He didn't want Iris to talk to them either, but
she chattered away, telling them the books she'd read and the wild
creatures who were her friends. Aidan sat sullenly in the corner of the
buggy, dozing on and off. He just couldn't get his mind 'round who
Doc and Clarence were anymore. They were strangers suddenly.

In the afternoon, Doc sipped from a medicine bottle and offered
Aidan a swig. "You're in an ill humor, Coop. Perhaps this will help."

Iris pushed the bottle away. "He don't drink no more, sir."

"Medicine, little darling." Doc chuckled.

"We got Miz Subie's medicine," Iris said, fresh as sweet cream.

"New York is an unholy city, hard-going for a sober man," Doc
said.

"We'll survive." Following Subie's map, Aidan had tickets for New

York to throw off suspicion. In Charleston, they'd turn west to Chicago.

"You never traveled so far, have you?" Doc asked.

"Only in dreams." Aidan thought on Cairo Street, the Ferris Wheel, and *E-LEC-TRI-CI-TY*.

Doc emptied the *medicine* down his throat. "Freaks of nature do congregate up north, but I tell you, New York City outdoes 'em all. Chinamen, savage Indian chiefs, devil worshippers drinking virgin's blood. Isn't that right, Clarence?" Clarence hunched his shoulders noncommittally as Doc rambled on. "We saw an elephant-man—head as big as a wagon wheel, skin like boot leather." Tangled in a memory, Doc's face twisted. "Half-naked colored folks ran wild in the streets, hollering to God, calling down angels and demons."

"Is that a fact, sir?" Iris tried to sound grown-up.

Doc gripped her arm. "A lot of mixing of the blood is not so good. I'm a doctor. I know these things."

"Don't be scaring her with tall-tale lies." Aidan pulled her away.

Doc's eyes burned. "Wild folks pouring into America from all over. Revolutions in Mexico, Russia. Men like you shooting down men like me. Yet look at us, Coop, we're friends. Clarence too, since we were boys." Aidan and Clarence both spit in the dirt. Doc gripped Aidan's shoulder. "In Atlanta, we know how to live together. All them Yankees know is riot and chaos."

"Bloody 1906 race riot in Atlanta must have slipped your mind." Aidan shook Doc's hand off him.

A wild cat hollered in the woods. "Whoa now, Buttercup and Boo," Clarence said.

"That ole cat ain't studyin' us." Iris grabbed a book from Doc's lap, *The Goodness of St. Rocque* by Alice Dunbar-Nelson. "You say a colored lady wrote this book?"

"New York does suck up all your magic," Doc said. "But love's always a good thing, however it comes. Remember that when you judge people."

Iris looked over toward Aidan, who spoke with an Irish lilt. "*Love is what you got to do to be free.* My mama used to say." An Irish woman from a house of ill repute on the run, loving a Seminole man—what would Doc think of that?

Clarence smiled. "Love is the best thing."

"Yes." Aidan prayed Doc hadn't bought Clarence the way men bought his mama.

"New York City could turn you away from yourself, Aidan," Doc said.

"The Coopers are a big Manhattan family." Aidan commenced to lying. "They'll take care of me and Iris till we find Redwood and Mr. Williams."

"Such a pretty girl ought to have a pretty life. Miz Subie should have *gris-gris* for that." Doc sank back into his seat, face twitching and fingers jerking. After a moment, his eyes slid shut.

"Don't let ole Doc scare you. New York is more cloud than storm." Clarence winked at Iris's big eyes. "We had us some good times too. City try to bite you, but you can bite back." He clucked at the horses and they picked up speed.

"Love is the best thing," Iris said, nuzzling close to Aidan.

The sun was warm, the air sweet and thick. Everybody 'cept Clarence, Buttercup, and Boo slept the rest of the road to Atlanta.

SIXTEEN

Chicago, 1910

Dressed as an Arabian knight or perhaps a Persian buccaneer, Redwood slinked through shadows following George into the heart of Chicago's Black Belt. She told herself she was a fool, but kept going. She told herself she was following George for Clarissa's sake, but that was only half true and certainly didn't make her feel less a fool. George wasn't goin' keep Redwood in the dark, like back in Peach Grove when nobody told her how Mama died or nothing. She had to meet Saeed at 11 p.m. for the show; that was a good hour away. The Ace of Spades Hotel was nearby, and she was already in costume. She gave this mad scheme ten more minutes—no need to push her luck.

George never looked behind him once. This was too easy or he was too cocky. Nobody with a good conscience looked 'round to see if somebody was tracking 'em, so maybe George didn't have anything to hide.

The colored residents sitting on stoops and porches, catching the last bit of air before suffocating the night away in tiny apartments, were in better spirits than she was. Teasing and laughing, they were on the lookout for the comet or anything interesting passing through the night. One young fellow called out to her.

"Hey! Ain't you that Arab fellow in the show over at the Ace of Spades?"

She put a finger to her lips and gestured quiet. He obliged. George didn't notice. A block away, he was running up the back stairs to June Thomas's place. She was a brown woman with stringy yellow hair who did laundry for Clarissa and all the high-tone colored ladies, washing and pressing all the linens, starching shirts and tablecloths too— the personal touch, not a factory. *Personal touch*, indeed. George was through the door quickly. June scanned the street and looked right through Redwood coming her way. Like everybody else, June mistook her for Saeed and closed the door.

Redwood stood under June's porch worrying the inside of her cheek. She wanted more proof. She could imagine what June and George were up to, but she hadn't witnessed it. Lord knew the stories people told on Redwood and Saeed, so she climbed up to the second floor and out on a railing, to peer into the window.

George was making love to June. They looked to be enjoying each other more than Redwood could ever imagine enjoying anyone again. She felt jealous and foolish and tore her eyes away to another room where three children slept in one bed. She wondered if any of them were George's.

What now that she had seen for herself?

She climbed down the railing, tumbling through a somersault to land upright in front of her admirer from a block down the street.

"Ain't the Arab fellow, it's Sequoia! *Running won't set you free?*" He sang out of tune.

She hurried by him. Did he see what she'd been doing? "We're playing tonight," she called back over her shoulder. "Come see us again."

Dawn was done. Morning was in full swing. Redwood crouched under a sign proclaiming PHIPPS DRY CLEANING: CLEANER THAN NEW. She was half asleep. Her cummerbund waist was coming undone. Her robe and pants were wrinkled and sweat-soiled. She'd stayed out all night dancing at one of Saeed's wild parties. Show people, writers, and folks trying to change the world for the workingman. Hardly nobody was talking 'bout the working *woman*. Redwood ought to bring Clarissa next time so she could say her piece. Course this sort of party might be too racy for her sister-in-law, with those two ladies necking in the corner and Saeed hanging on a suave impresario. In fact, it might've been too racy for Redwood. She had heartburn and a mighty headache, and she hadn't drunk anything.

George opened the window in his office and almost closed it again 'cause the wind threatened the stacks of orders and receipts, five rows deep on his desk. He settled on just cracking it at the bottom. His telephone chimed. All the well-off colored folk, and some Italians and

Greeks too, came to Phipps Dry Cleaning 'cause the price was right and the workmanship very good. Business was excellent.

Redwood wanted to talk over June with him here, not at home, but she didn't like to interrupt him on the telephone. Actually, she didn't know what to say. Spying was nasty business. The truth you got felt dirty on your tongue. She ought to be on the lookout for her own good life, 'stead of sneaking 'round somebody else's.

"I was here all night keeping the machines running, Clarissa," George lied and paused while Clarissa said something on the other end. "Of course I'm coming home tonight." He paused again. "I don't know what my sister does with herself at night. I'm too busy earning a living. I can't chase after her."

A rock whistled over Redwood's head and smashed through the window, shattering the glass. She threw up her arms and ducked down as George dropped the phone and raced for the door. Redwood picked her way through the broken window pieces, taking pains not to slice her fancy boots but quickly blending into the curious onlookers. She dug a splinter of glass from her eyebrow. George bust through the front door of the Dry Cleaning, hollering. He scanned the street for any sign of the culprit. No one.

"Did anybody see what happened?" George shouted, throwing the rock up in the air and catching it. Everybody hurried away from his question.

Redwood's heart was racing. Who would do such a thing?

The end of the late-afternoon shift swelled the crowds in the streets with dirty, tired workers. Redwood had cleaned up and changed into Aidan's clothes. She even mimicked his loping gait. With the cap pulled down low, she plowed through the jammed avenues and people said, "'Scuse me, mister," when she bumped by.

Stockyard stink clung to everything. Redwood shuddered at gutter streams of horse piss, blazing coal furnaces, and heavy-metal spew. She got blasted several times with greasy automobile exhaust and wanted to take a bath all over again. In these neighborhoods near the stockyard, she heard Polish, Italian, and the Irish lilt that Aidan did sometime, which sent a quiver up her spine. She smiled at an Irish woman talking to her children. A little girl smiled back at Redwood as the mama hurried the family toward a church for evening Mass.

"None of you can stand to see a colored man doing well with his own business!"

Redwood flattened herself behind a corner wall. Holding the *rock,* George argued with a brawny white man in dirty work clothes. This fellow had Aidan's lilt on his tongue too, but she couldn't quite make out what he said. *I'd have done more than smash a window* or some such. George had several colored workingmen at his back, covered in soot and blood and oil. The brawny Irishman kept eyeing these dark, silent men as he measured out his words.

George was practically breathing fire. He slammed the *rock* in the Irishman's chest and marched away, shouting, "You do that, Seamus."

George's colored gang followed, bumping and jostling brawny Seamus till his hat fell off. Humiliated, he snatched it off the filthy street and jammed it on his head. He stood still, huffing and puffing in anger, like a bull ready to charge. George may have won this battle, but the war surely wasn't over. Redwood's heart fluttered as she dashed by Seamus. The *rock* was a gentle warning for what was to come. Seamus stomped down the street, snarling and grinning to hisself.

George and crew hopped on a trolley. Redwood ran full-out to catch the same one. She hid in the back. George peeled greenbacks from a stack in his billfold and paid each of his fellows as they got off at the next stop. George sat down in the front of the trolley and pressed a balled-up fist into his chin. Unlike Atlanta, Negroes could sit anywhere they wanted on Chicago trams. Since coming north, George always sat up front. He eyed white men defiantly. Bored or lost in their thoughts, they didn't notice his insolent stance. He nearly missed his stop impressing white folk with his high-toned cooning.

Redwood barely made it off after him. The trolley charged away before her feet hit the ground good. George hustled the half-mile walk home so fast—she was panting to keep up, so like when they were young, and despite longer legs, she could never go as fast as he did.

Clarissa brushed soot from George's coat as Redwood climbed in a kitchen window.

"When I open the second cleaners, we'll buy us an automobile," George said.

"The children are already in bed. Supper's ruined and your sister's still not back yet," Clarissa said.

They didn't hear Redwood slipping and sliding on the hard floor. They were too busy kissing and stumbling up the stairs.

"Redwood always do what *she* want; don't matter what nobody else say," George said.

"You're the older brother."

Redwood crept to the second floor, listening hard.

George grunted. "Redwood's a hoodoo, like Mama, working the conqueror root. Only a fool mess in that."

"You sound like a Georgia sharecropper."

George usually spit fire at somebody calling him a sharecropper, but he talked soft to Clarissa. "That's what you married, woman. Too late to complain."

"No, after a day's work, you smell clean and fresh, a businessman, not a field hand."

"You still smell sweeter than me." George picked her up and carried her to their bed. Redwood started downstairs but froze as Clarissa spoke.

"You're no backward fool running to the conjure woman for hoodoo nonsense—rabbit-foot and cat-piss spells. Colored have moved on, and you're leading the way."

Furious, Redwood huddled under a hall table, thinking of what to say back to Clarissa. She could bust in on their lovemaking and ask if some irate white carpenter or electrician that George blockbusted out of a house was throwing rocks through the Dry Cleaning window. Or she could ask how many of June's children were George's or just wonder out loud what else he did with his gang of colored strongmen. And sister Clarissa wasn't too good for "hoodoo nonsense" when she was backed in a corner with her belly 'bout to swell up.

Several high-pitched moans and a few low grunts startled Redwood and made her blush with shame. Here she was listening in on another good time—the sweet sounds just made her want to cry. The bed stopped its rhythmic rocking. Their voices were quiet at first and Redwood couldn't hear. But then George shouted. "Shaking her fanny onstage. That's the way of performing folk. Half of 'em hoodoo too."

"She's living under your roof. She's a scandal," Clarissa said. "Running the streets with wild Indians."

"Saeed's from Persia, 'cross the ocean, and I don't think he like womenfolk much. He got hisself a fellow."

"That puts your mind at ease?"

"Redwood can hoodoo an audience and make more money than I do." George sounded mad at that.

"I'm not saying she isn't generous."

"She's helping buy the new shop and a motorcar and ain't lying on her back to do it."

"George, don't be vulgar." Clarissa's voice wavered. Tears were coming.

"What you think I can do to change her ways?" A loud thump on the mattress punctuated his question. "Huh?"

"I'd rather light a candle than curse the darkness, husband, that's all I'm saying."

"You be quoting the Bible next. Don't know if I can take that."

"Hoodoo is the devil's workshop."

"I can't hear you speak ill of Mama."

"God rest her soul, but the minister says—"

"Or of my sister. They do hoodoo to help folk, to take the trick off wayward souls."

Sniffling swallowed Clarissa's next words. Mortified, Redwood started to slip away and banged the table. "What's that?" Clarissa said.

Redwood froze and decided then and there against spying ever again.

"This old house groaning," George said. "What you got to cry so for?"

"Who'll take the trick off Redwood's soul?"

"What?" The bed creaked as he stood up.

"I've seen how she's hurting. You stand next to her, you can feel the pain."

George stomped 'cross the room. "No. Big Red is tough."

"She needs a husband. I've invited Arthur—"

"Arthur Robinson?" George shoved the door open, and it blocked Redwood's hiding place. "She'd as soon shoot that crook of a banker as marry him. I don't blame her. He's a jackass." He sauntered out of the bedroom, scratching his balls. Redwood focused her eyes on his bare feet. He stopped at the stairs. "I can't believe you thought of Arthur Robinson for my sister."

"Come back to bed, you'll wake the children."

"They could sleep through Judgment Day."

"That's what you think."

"I'm hungry."

"What if your sister comes home and you're walking around in your birthday suit?" Clarissa came out in a gown. She tried to hand George one, but he wouldn't take it. They headed down the stairs. "I don't know how to help her." She had a tearful catch in her voice. "If she doesn't believe in anything I believe in . . . Hoodoo and conjure and—"

"What's come over you, woman? You don't even sound like yourself."

"Nothing. Nothing. I'm just worried."

As they went into the kitchen, Redwood slipped from under the table. She squeezed her *mojo* bag and headed down the back stairs. Clarissa had some nerve thinking she could cure Redwood with a mean rich man who hated colored folks even more than white folks did. Arthur Robinson got wealthy cheating Negroes and was proud of it. George knew Redwood didn't want a high-toned scoundrel, but he never noticed she was hurting. Nobody ever cared to find out what she really felt, what she really needed.

Back in her room, 'stead of crying herself to sleep, she tried to pleasure herself. She used everything she'd learned from Elaine and the gals at the Cherokee Lake Bordello. But the sweet feelings slipped through her fingers.

SEVENTEEN

From Atlanta to Chicago, 1910

Putrid pig and rotten fish, factory spew, and overfull outhouses—the city smell of Atlanta woke Aidan from a sharp nightmare. The stink clung to his tongue as the bad dream dissolved. He cussed, certain there was something he should remember—or somebody—but he couldn't. The dusty brown road had turned to black asphalt, and the buggy wheels were grateful. Buttercup and Boo neighed, and Clarence clucked at them. The bright afternoon had gone to smoky gray. A light mist chilled the evening air. Iris was nestled in his arm, a warm ember against his chilly chest. Doc studied them both and scribbled on an artist's pad. Aidan looked beyond Doc's sandy-haired crooked countenance to the city of Atlanta in twilight.

Awkward, square-boned buildings hunched together. They cluttered up the skyway, blocking Venus and an early moonrise. Lights glimmered in town house windows like ghosts seeking refuge. Motorcars, wagons, and electric trolleys materialized in the twilight and surrounded Doc's modest buggy. Aidan gasped at the sudden crush of noisy vehicles. A horn blared, and Iris woke with a start. She clutched his arm. The winking kerosene lights played over her frightened face. Doc chuckled at his country companions. Bicyclists and pedestrians filled every available space on the broken pavement. Clarence reined the horses in.

"The speed limit is supposedly eight miles per hour," Doc said.

They were trapped in more traffic than Aidan had seen his whole life and going too fast.

"Watch yourself, fool," Clarence shouted.

The comet caught the last of the sunlight as an automobile heading south lurched into the north lane right toward Doc's buggy. Hell broke loose. Iris squealed with more excitement than fear as they swerved from one danger into another. Pedestrians scrambled into storefronts. A bicyclist soared through the air and into a shop display, busting a basket of apples and pears. A picture window fractured along a thousand fault lines, but did not shatter. Chickens ran into the street, trying to fly away. These flightless birds got trampled as Boo and Buttercup charged toward a clanging red streetcar. At the last second, Clarence got them to swerve. The door of Doc's buggy was scraped raw by the trolley. Electric sparks showered down on them. Aidan patted out a fire in Doc's beard. Doc took another sip of his *medicine* and laughed at the curlicues of ash swirling 'round his face.

Boo and Buttercup reared several times, but finally settled down under Clarence's firm hand and soothing voice. The air smelled burnt and shitty too, as horses all down the road voided their bowels. The reckless driver who'd started the accident staggered from his vehicle, a bottle still in hand, unscathed. Drunk as a fish, he stumbled through disaster, raving at his stunned victims.

He grabbed Aidan. "It's Comet Halley. The end of the world is nigh! Tomorrow never comes. Don't wait, don't regret. Do you hear me? Live now!"

Aidan was dumbstruck. Clarence shoved the man away. Crumpled automobiles spouted hot foam, and a horse limped toward the sidewalk dragging a broken buggy. The passengers had tumbled out somewhere. A sooty woman moaned in the gutter, holding a bloody leg and calling to Lord Jesus.

"The heavens are angry and cannot hear you, ma'am," the reckless driver declared and collapsed on the curb beside her. A busted kerosene lamp blazed at their feet. Aidan wondered if he would've driven a mechanical beast, falling down drunk like this fool. It took all his restraint not to leap from the buggy and pummel the man.

"He could have cost us our lives," Clarence said.

"Julius Caesar banned wheeled traffic in Rome. I'm inclined to agree with his wisdom," Doc said.

"Miz Subie's sign brought us luck," Iris said.

Somewhere, a wounded animal cried out. "Do you hear that?" Aidan said.

Clarence lifted his head, listening far into the distance, and shrugged.

Iris opened her eyes wide. She heard what Aidan heard for sure. "Too far away to do us any harm," she said.

Saeed and Redwood, dressed as savage Africans with grass skirts, animal skins, and gator-teeth necklaces, paced the brightly lit studio of Chicago's newest motion picture factory. Large bones from a nearby slaughterhouse—turkey most likely—were stuck through their hair. They squatted in front of a round hut with a thatched roof. Other *natives*, similarly dressed, huddled near them at the edge of a *jungle*, fake palm trees that had been added to local crabapple, dogwood, and sassafras trees. Redwood blew a purple prairie smoke blossom that trailed silvery filaments as it went to seed.

"What part of Africa is this?" Saeed asked.

"Chicago, Abyssinia." Redwood laughed.

Saeed laughed too. "And who are we again?"

"Nobody." Redwood suddenly turned glum and clutched Saeed.

"What is it?"

A lion grumbled. "What're they doing to that old cat?" She looked toward the sound.

"They tease him to look ferocious." Saeed squinted. "He doesn't want to come out of the cage."

"Ahh." She hugged herself. "Well, I got an idea, for a motion picture. A colored romance on a Sea Island."

"No one will make that. White folk are scared of colored romance." Saeed shrugged. "Who'd come to see it?"

"For a nickel, colored folk will. Don't they come to the club after hours to hear us, or head on over to the Pekin Theatre to see all-colored adventures in Darkville? White folk come too. Everybody does."

"I hear rumors, the Pekin's going broke and about to close down. You can't get rich entertaining nig—"

"Don't be quoting Eddie to me."

Histrionic yelling was followed by fevered drums. Saeed pulled her up.

"Time to welcome the great white hunter." He put on his savage face.

Throwing up her hands in exaggerated fright, Redwood ran with

Saeed and a crowd of screaming savages toward a row of cameramen cranking away.

Traffic was jammed up from the automobile accident for quite a ways. The trolley had jumped the track, and setting that to right took forever. Clarence maneuvered 'round one marooned or busted vehicle after another. A lame horse lay in the grass making a pitiful noise. A shot rang out as they passed and the horse shuddered quiet. Doc peered over the side of the buggy and traced his fingers along the door.

"We have suffered only a scratch," he remarked.

"Miz Subie's sign kept us safe," Iris said.

Clarence whistled. "Remind me to bring my aunt that peach brandy she like."

Sober all of a sudden, Doc dug out his medicine bag and jumped into the street.

"We ain't never goin' get out of here now," Clarence mumbled good-naturedly.

A hefty man was threatening damage to his wife. She was only checking how bad he was hurt. Doc walked right up to him, laughing. "Women! What did Cherokee Will used to say—when the white man discovered this country, Indians were running it."

The man cradled a limp arm and scowled at Doc. His woman stepped back.

"No taxes, no debt, and women did all the work," Aidan continued the old Cherokee joke.

"The white man thought he could improve on a system like this." As the man chuckled, Doc yanked his arm back in the shoulder socket. The fellow hollered something fierce, but was soon laughing at the miracle of it.

Doc ministered to every wounded person he found. 'Stead of worrying 'bout missing the train, Aidan, and Iris too, marveled at him.

A young mother with a deep gash in her head was bleeding all over her baby and wouldn't let nobody near. "Myrna," someone pleaded with her. "Be reasonable—"

"Helen and me don't need your help," Myrna yelled. It wasn't a reasonable night.

"Cousin Myrna." Doc smiled. "Helen's getting so big and the spitting image of grandma!" Telling tall tales on grandma, he had Myrna stitched up before she knew it.

A woman was weeping and wailing, fixing to bury a dead husband. Doc brought him back to the living with a foul smell. The man had fainted when the trolley swiped his motor car. His wife's weeping turned to cussing. Doc slipped away.

"You will be fine!" he said over and over, and everyone believed him.

Mostly cuts and scrapes and hearts pounding too fast with fear, but it wasn't long before Doc's bag was empty and his clothes filthy. He looked lost and ready to fall over. Clarence hauled him back in the buggy then. "We don't want to get stuck here."

"Sorry," Doc said. "I know you two got a train to catch—"

"We shouldn't just ride by folks in need." Iris turned to Aidan. "Should we?"

"Of course not," he said quickly. "I first met Doc helping out the Jessups, riding on the poor side of the creek, s'posedly heading out for a hunting trip. Never got there."

Doc nodded. "You told me hunting for sport, for what you didn't need to eat, wasn't good for the soul!"

"Did you now?" Iris poked Aidan.

"No. Actually, he said it would crack my good spirit."

"Aunt Caitlin told me to hush." Aidan grinned at the memory.

"I'd say we've been friends ever since." Doc was grinning too.

There were no more wounded folk, but the traffic was impossible. To sweeten the long wait, Doc read them the title story from *The Goodness of St. Rocque* by Alice Dunbar-Nelson. Iris was all ears for this hoodoo romance.

"Her former husband was that colored poet," Doc said. "Whosy?"

"I won't need a charm like the lady in the story to get my man," Iris said.

Doc squinted, examining her. "No, I don't think you will."

"Paul Laurence Dunbar," Aidan said, pleased he'd remembered the name.

"That's the man!" Clarence nodded. "You read colored books too, Mr. Cooper?"

"Ha, he reads anything. A reading fiend." Doc sounded proud.

"Miz Elisa loaned me his book once. She and Miz Garnett were never done teaching school." Aidan sighed, missing them both. "I guess, I've read plenty colored books." He was carrying *Of One Blood: Or, The Hidden Self* by Pauline Hopkins, which Redwood had loaned to him *before*. He wanted to return it to her and have that discussion, if she still wanted to, after so many years. "I like a good story."

"In that case—" Doc read a second tale. Aidan was now too worried they'd miss their train to listen. He didn't want to spend a night at Doc's and feel more beholden. He didn't want to worry what sort of men Doc and Clarence were. He just wanted to hurry on out of Atlanta and be on their way *north*. Clarence guided Boo and Buttercup through mayhem and congestion with a steady hand. Doc's mellow baritone, Miz Dunbar-Nelson's words, and the twilight streets blurred. Finally they were back up to eight miles per hour.

Atlanta's Terminal Train Station looked to be a castle for dragons and wizards. Comet Halley cut 'cross the sky between the station's golden towers, a magic beacon heralding an auspicious journey. Reaching into the alligator pouch, Aidan cut his finger on the broken seashell. He sprinkled goober dust mixed with his blood where the tracks crisscrossed in the train yard. The dirt exploded like fireworks under the metal wheels.

Aidan didn't want to lose heart. "How am I goin' do a thousand dry miles?" he asked the train spirits.

Black engines, sweaty with steam, roared at him and charged off in every direction. He marveled at these magical fire-breathing beasts busting through the night. Railroad music played up Aidan's spine as he headed inside the terminal. The great hall was so crowded, he could barely snatch a breath, but a new song ached in his throat and on his fingers. Music was coming back to him.

Iris, Doc, and Clarence waited near a train fixing to head out. Passengers climbed aboard behind them. Aidan approached, hat in hand, and looked from Doc to Clarence.

"Tell me," Aidan wheezed, "how I can repay your generosity."

"Me too, kind sirs," Iris said.

"Breaking Garnett's curse. What more?" Doc whispered. Aidan's face burned. He wanted to ask how the hell was he supposed to do that, but Doc turned from him to Iris. "Can you read, little darling?"

"Since I was five, sir." Iris strutted her long-legged stuff. "Education give you the keys to the kingdom."

"I know you like these hoodoo romances." Doc handed her Miz Dunbar-Nelson's book of short stories and a copy of *The Wizard of Oz.*

"You be writing your own stories someday," Clarence said, proud already.

"They do a musical show of *Oz* in New York," Doc said. "But it's also fun to read."

"Thank you, sir." She clutched the volumes to her heart, sliding and kicking her feet in a dance. "I'll read these here twice."

"Man throw his money away, buying all them books, then be giving the books away." Clarence laughed.

Aidan felt the devil for a moment. "I'd like to see your collection."

Doc and Clarence exchanged quick glances. Doc shrugged.

"I got use of the whole library!" Clarence laughed and slapped his thigh.

"Yes, you do." Doc allowed hisself a smile. Aidan wondered how hard their lives in public must be. Men got strung up for doing what they did. What was their story? How did people like them find each other? Who dared the first touch, the first kiss? How did they hold on to each other and trust when the going got rough? Doc and Clarence had to be very brave, even in hiding.

"The *whole* library! That's—that's grand." Aidan wished for something better to say. Maybe they wanted him to know. Maybe they trusted him. He didn't know what to think of that. "Love is the best thing," he finally said, staring in the eyes of his friends.

"Yessir!" Iris tap-danced a rhythm to *love is the best thing.* The three men shifted awkwardly as she strutted 'round them.

"It has been my pleasure to get to know you better, Aidan." Doc turned to him with that odd, intense look, the way he'd done for years. Aidan thought he understood this now. They shook hands and Doc thrust several drawings at Aidan. "You're quite a handsome man. In-triguing physiognomy. Do visit me in Atlanta on your way back to Peach Grove."

"I will do." Aidan gaped at a beautiful drawing of Iris in his arms.

His hair was blowing free in the wind. Another picture caught him tweaking her nose as she giggled.

Clarence beamed at Doc's artwork. "Man's got a good hand, don't he?"

Iris and Aidan both nodded.

"Good luck to you, sir," Clarence said. After an awkward second, he shook Aidan's outstretched hand vigorously. "And you too, Miz Iris." He patted her head. Then he and Doc worked their way through the crazy quilt of humanity, coming and going or standing a moment utterly lost and breathless, like Aidan.

"ALL ABOARD!" Iris chimed in with the conductor. "Let's go!" She spun 'round, more alive than Aidan had seen her in weeks. "Doc give me a five-dollar gold piece." She displayed it. "He say, at the end of the trip, we'll be stepping out in another world."

"You didn't tell him where we was going, did you?"

She blew her lips at him, a fresh colt showing off. "I can story too, good as you."

"Is that so?"

"I think he might know where we're going anyhow." She had her hands on recently curved hips. Button breasts were thrust up toward him. Half child, half woman—and the spitting image of Redwood as a young gal. "I ain't my sister," she said. "Can't help it if I look like her."

Aidan almost fell over.

"You think half-naked colored folk be running wild in Chicago too?" she said, brash and free despite nightmares and throwing grave dirt on the faces of loved ones. "Well, do you?"

"No need to repeat Doc's storytelling. He made all that up to feel good 'bout hisself. We're starting on our own adventure. You can tell that story."

"I'll put it in a book like Miz Dunbar-Nelson."

"Now you're talking." They gathered their things and headed for the railcar door. Aidan staggered under all their baggage. "What we pack, boulders?"

Shotgun and banjo strapped over his back banged against each other and into his ribs. Climbing onto the cramped and musky colored coach, he almost fell down. Iris steadied him and then went ahead scouting seats.

"You in the wrong car, sir." A colored porter grinned at him without meaning it.

Iris dashed back to him. "I found two together."

Standing up straight, Aidan gripped her hand. "I know where I belong," he said to the porter. That was the biggest lie he ever told.

He pushed past the grinning fellow and headed for the empty seats. Evil grunts and cutting eyes greeted him, or maybe people were just tired and sleepy. Liquor smell on a passenger's breath had him sweating. For a moment, he would've given anything, handed over the rest of his life even, for a drink. Luckily, nobody was offering. How would he manage a thousand temperate miles on a promise and a song? He was no damn good at promises.

"Can I sit by the window?" Iris asked, as if Aidan cared where he dropped his body down. "Don't be hangdog. We goin' see my sister and get us to the other side of sad."

"You get the view," Aidan said.

"Is Chicago big as Atlanta, with buildings up into the sky?" Iris squeezed his hand.

"It's Atlanta times ten."

"How you know, if you ain't been there, 'cept in dreams?"

"I . . . I heard tell." He showed her the picture-postcard Redwood sent from Chicago, a playbill for one of her minstrel shows actually. Redwood was dressed as a dragonfly with gossamer wings and big eyes on her head like a hat.

Iris flapped her arms and buzzed at the picture. "We got minstrel shows in Peach Grove too, remember?" She turned the card over and read aloud, proud of all the hard words she knew. *"I'd tell you about this Chicago metropolis, but anything I say now won't be true tomorrow. A colossal city of the future, springing up from yesterday's dreams like magic. Everything's possible, me, my little sister, you too."* Iris wiped his damp face with a rough kerchief. "See? Sister agree with me."

Different message than what he'd read or what Hiram couldn't read, but he didn't get spooked. Magic words on a card was nothing. He'd seen Redwood call down a twister to the palm of her hand. She calmed the storm till it wasn't but a dance of dust and a gentle spray of mist. No telling what kind of future they'd be making up there on Lake Michigan. Nothing Redwood did would surprise him, 'cept if she forgave him.

"I know you 'fraid of my sister, but it'll be all right." Iris patted his hand.

"Not really 'fraid of your sister." Aidan spooked hisself. "When you get older, a big adventure can take your breath away."

"I'll watch over you," Iris declared and just 'bout broke Aidan's heart.

As they pulled out of the station, Aidan's hands were twitching fast as a rattlesnake's tail. He swallowed a mouthful of Subie's nasty powder. He didn't know if her conjure would help or not. One teetotal minute at a time though.

"I don't work with divas anymore!" Mr. Payne looked like the dead president for true this afternoon as he yelled at the idle cast and crew on the back lot of *his* motion picture factory. The light was better outside, but—"Three days wasted!" Payne resented every red cent spent to keep a village of screaming savages on hand for the rampage and the big hunt.

Redwood sucked her teeth. She slouched against a flimsy *African* hut and scratched the itchy grass skirt going to seed 'round her waist.

"Payne's not yelling about you," Saeed teased, scratching too.

The lion was still refusing to act. Redwood wanted to yell at the lazy creature herself.

"They're happy." Saeed pointed at *African Savages* rolling dice.

Of course the Pullman Porter extras weren't complaining. In between grueling trips through wild country with cheapskate passengers, acting *African* put good money in their pockets. But Redwood and Saeed were headliners, real show folk itching to perform. Shooting a moving picture wasn't strutting 'cross the stage to get lost in applause and laughter, in the audience sucking one breath together. It was endless waiting for the sun to escape clouds, for crew to pamper finicky lenses or catch huts blown about by the wind machine.

A turkey bone slid from Saeed's slippery hair. He shouldn't have tossed the kinky fright wig. Redwood sighed. "With this beetle-headed scenario, who can blame that lion for pouting in his dressing room?"

"Get that lazy cat moving!" Payne coughed into his handkerchief and marched off.

A cage door opened to the lion snarling and spitting. Several white cameramen looked anxious as they cranked images of this beast, old and broken-toothed, but still a ferocious sight. A muscular handler with a pockmarked, ruddy complexion and streaks of gray in his black hair smacked the lion in the belly with a big stick and cracked a whip. The lion snarled and swiped, mane bristling with rage. The handler cracked the whip again and caught the lion in the face. The animal drew back as the handler jabbed harder at skinny ribs.

"That ain't a good idea!" Redwood shouted at the handler and then whispered to Saeed. "That must hurt."

Saeed groaned. "Too many people. This animal is frightened and very angry."

With another whip crack from the sunburnt handler and more painful prodding, the lion retreated farther into the cage 'stead of coming forward. The handler shouted, and the lion crouched up against the bars, looking weary and pathetic.

"Damn fool, you want to get us fired?" The handler was cussing the lazy beast, talking 'bout an ole bag of bones, when the lion leapt. Redwood was stunned by the sudden power and grace of the rippling muscles, but something was wrong. With jaws gaping and claws slashing the air, the lion aimed itself at the foul-mouthed handler whose whip now hung limp in his hand. The lion's golden eyes flashed murderous rage. The handler shook his head and turned his back as if he couldn't believe the lion would dare attack him. He moved in slow motion while the lion was a streak of light.

"Where are you going?" Saeed yelled as Redwood ran toward the lion.

A sharp wind from an electric fan tore the mane from the lion's neck to reveal a she-cat in disguise. Cast, crew, and cameramen gasped. The lioness was momentarily distracted by her costume problem. She shook violently till she was free of someone else's ratty old mane. The handler had gotten up to speed and was charging away. Too late. The lioness recovered her momentum and cut the distance between them in two easy bounds. She tore into his behind, ripping through the pants and sinking teeth into soft flesh. The handler howled.

Redwood slowed to a walk, praying for a good spell to come to her. Two cameramen froze above their lenses. One thin, pale man continued to film, while the *African Savages* and the *White Hunter* screeched

and knocked each other over, scurrying away. Redwood recognized
the curly red beard and scraggly eyebrows—Nicolai Minsky. A determined fellow, he shook off his comrades urging him to run and continued to roll. They gripped their cameras and dashed away.

The handler, with the lioness clamped to his butt, struggled toward
Nicolai, begging for help. Nicolai's eyes darted up from his lens. Without a whip or a gun, what could he do? Running was his only *safe* op-
tion. Possessed, a demon driven to capture this deadly spectacle, Nicolai
shifted his camera's vantage point and continued rolling.

Redwood danced in front of the lioness. The wind got caught in her
fierce moves. A train of fog snaked through the dust at her feet. Prairie
smoke seeds, a cloud of silvery purple filaments, spun 'round her head.
As Redwood swirled like a hurricane brewing, the she-cat let go of
butt flesh and raggedy pants and spit her mouth clear. She licked blood
from her broken fangs. Stepping over the whimpering handler, the
lioness crouched low and moved toward Redwood.

Staring out a filthy train window, watching the flat Indiana landscape
skitter by, Aidan's eyes ached. Thirty years of living, and he'd never
been farther north than the Blue Ridge Mountains, never been on a
railway, tearing 'cross these United States of America on iron wheels.
Engineers say, hardly any friction on this ride. So true, here he was
almost a free man, not on the run, not under the shadow of a Peach
Grove lynch mob, *gliding* to his destiny. Chicago was an hour or two
away. Thinking 'bout seeing Redwood again, being worthy of her forgiveness, maybe worthy of her love, and he had an inkling of what the
Seminole meant when they said *isti siminoli.*

The urge to pour a bottle of hooch down his throat came over Aidan
at least five times every day and ten times at night in his sleep. As a
free man now, he ignored the drinking itch, but he couldn't get it to go
away. Iris pretended she didn't notice his infirmity. He was thankful
for this and for the good folks who rode the trains and made him and
Iris feel like family.

Colored people from all over the cotton-picking South, tired of
breaking their backs to make white landowners rich, were coming
north. They hoped to make a better life, a beautiful life. In Pittsburgh,

in Cleveland, Philadelphia, Chicago, and New York, colored men had a vote, and women were agitating to get their say too. Cities sprang up overnight. In Indiana, halfway between beds of iron ore and rich coal mines, US Steel wrangled a river 'round and built a spanking new town with all the modern amenities: waterworks, fancy plumbing, electricity, and indoor toilets for the workingman. They called it Gary after a US Steel bigwig. The first furnace blasted out steel two years ago, in '08. There were decent jobs to be had, rows of fine little houses to raise a family, and education for gals like Iris who wanted to teach school and write books. All along Lake Michigan, colored folk could dare to dream.

Stories of the high life in the bright north sounded like sure enough tall tales to Aidan. But when Iris read reports from the *Chicago Defender*, a colored newspaper, Aidan hoped some of the tales were halfway true. Miz Ida Bell Wells-Barnett had just started a Negro Fellowship League to help people coming up from the South. There was a colored hospital, the Provident, with colored doctors, and colored theatres, like the Pekin. A vote, a say, and a job—every morning would look bright, and after work there'd be a night on the town. No wonder colored were flying west, flying north.

Aidan was more than happy to leave King Cotton, Lord Tobacco, and the lynchmen behind. If Chicago would open its arms to the children and grandchildren of former slaves, maybe there was a place for an Irish-Seminole swamp man. Maybe he could open his heart and forgive his ownself.

Following Subie's map, Aidan dropped the goober dust seven times, twice in Georgia, and then in South Carolina, Tennessee, Kentucky, Ohio, and Indiana. On hot afternoons, he played banjo halfway decent—railroad songs for a new century. Like Miz Subie promised, his music got better. New songs came to him. Fellow travelers pestered him to start a session up or join in. He played anything: Irish ballads, Buddy Bolden's jazz, or Ma Rainey's blues. Not as grand as his playing used to be, but good enough. He led an impromptu jug band, and ladies flirted with him shamelessly. He flirted back. Getting close, touching soft flesh, feeling deep sighs was a delicious, almost forgotten luxury. Aidan had been without a woman's love too long.

Just outside of Indianapolis, Iris declared her passion.

"When I'm grown, I wanna marry you," she said, her cheeks hot, her eyes flashing.

Aidan wanted to tweak her nose, but nodded his head solemnly instead.

"Uncle Ladd was sixteen years older than Aunt Elisa," Iris said. "You ain't got that much more on me."

"I'm waiting on you, sweet pea. So you hurry on up," he said, but winked at a buxom young lady two rows down, who made him feel good to be a man. Her silky hair, courtesy of Madam C. J. Walker's straightening pomade and hot iron, was piled in the shape of a whirlwind. Coy ringlets came undone in the afternoon humidity. She pursed full lips and batted long-lashed eyes. Aidan had to take his next breath slow. Iris punched him in the gut. She wasn't having none of that.

"It ain't a good idea to doubt true love," she said.

"You can do better than me is all."

"I don't want to trick you with a root or spell like in Miz Dunbar-Nelson's stories."

"I appreciate that." What kinda book had Doc given her to read?

"But if I have to, I will." She waved *The Goodness of St. Rocque* at him.

"You don't even know half of who I am, honey bun." Aidan turned deadly serious. "Best to know what you're getting involved in."

"So tell me." Iris folded her arms over button breasts. "I want to love you, not somebody I made up, like a story."

"Is that so?" Aidan smiled at her, charmed.

"And I'll tell you what you don't know 'bout me, and we'll be even."

Aidan studied Iris's wise eyes, so like her sister's, yet somehow hers alone. What dark secrets could she have after her short sweet life? Nothing like the lies he lived, passing for whatever was convenient, hiding from what was difficult, inconvenient. Since Atlanta, most everybody thought he was a light-skinned colored man. A nosy young wrangler from Texas had asked if he was Mexican, running from the revolution. Aidan said he was Georgia born and bred, but didn't mention Big Thunder or Miss O'Casey.

"A white man passing as colored and stealing that child?" A mountainous man with pink scars on his dark face hunched over smelly beans with his bear-sized mama. They whispered 'bout Aidan and Iris behind their hands. Everybody heard anyhow.

"He has to be crazy, an outlaw, or just up to no good," bear mama said.

Aidan took out his banjo and made a song on the spot. Didn't rhyme quite right yet, but it would tomorrow.

> *Some folk look at the world through their behinds*
> *Get it all backwards and turned 'round in their minds*
> *Give 'em salt and they'll think it sweet*
> *Give 'em honey, they'll complain 'bout the meat*

"We can't talk secrets on a train full of people," he whispered in Iris's ear as people laughed and clapped. "I'm only telling *you* my true story, not the whole world."

Iris stuck out her chest mimicking the buxom woman who'd caught Aidan's eye. She threw her arms 'round his neck and pulled him close. Her little-girl smell was sweet peaches and magnolia. "Only me."

Aidan doted on Iris, and she loved him more than he deserved, and that was that.

A stiff wind chased clouds 'cross the sky. Nicolai praised the returning sunlight as he cranked on his camera like a demon. Redwood sprang high in the air, cloaked in a cyclone of fog and prairie smoke. In the middle of a spin, she fixed her eye on the lioness. She felt a great thundering heart, wheezing lungs, and aching joints. Front paws that had bounded through fire were tender. A bruised shoulder ached where the handler had poked too hard. Cheeks and eyes stung from the whiplash. Yet, more than all this, Redwood tasted rage, killing rage, swallowed down too long and coming up strong now—breath become rage, flesh become rage, and fangs and claws the sharp edge of rage. Redwood landed at the lioness's nose. Prairie smoke seeds settled on her grass skirt, and fog evaporated in a whistling hiss over her head. The lioness came to a halt also, fangs bared.

For a good while, there was nothing but the two of them.

Redwood hadn't done any *wild* conjuring since 1903, when she and

Aidan had gone off to the Chicago Fair. That trip seemed like a dream, a story she told on her young self. Who could say if it was true or not? She had known killing rage since then, and it had made her a stranger to herself. She remembered that wild young gal, beloved by the spirit in everything, not 'fraid of bears, gators, hurricanes, or crazy men wandering the night. She just couldn't find her. The lioness snarled. A tall figure in a black hat watched from the shadow of an old oak. If Redwood had lost her hoodoo power too, if this conjure trick called the boneyard baron to her and she died this day, at least Nicolai would get a record of her true spirit on film, and who would be able to deny that?

The lioness circled Redwood, crouching till her belly brushed the ground. She drew her lips back over jagged fangs. The crowd roared and startled them both. Behind the lioness a brave *African Savage* dragged the blubbering handler toward a distant circle of folks who looked ready to run but eager to see the show come to any gruesome end.

The lioness's chest rumbled.

"She's purring." Nicolai reeled in the images, his eyes ablaze, his thin frame shaking. Saeed stood next to him, waving and speaking beautiful words, yet their meaning escaped Redwood. Perhaps Saeed was so desperate, he spoke Farsi.

Behind Saeed, one of the animal wranglers waved a rifle. Where'd he been all this time? "That's a growl, fool," the wrangler said.

The boneyard baron tipped his hat.

"She's all yours." Nicolai urged Redwood on. Saeed gaped at him.

"Move out the way, gal," the wrangler-gunman yelled.

Redwood ignored him and tangoed with the snarling or purring lioness toward the cage.

Chicago had more stink than Atlanta. Aidan smelled it miles before they reached the station. The air was swamp thick and sluggish. Lights jumped and gyrated in the distance; buildings squeezed closer and closer together. The clamor and clang hammered his ears as they joined a rush of trains wheeling into a Chicago railroad depot. Iris couldn't sit still, pointing out the window to hazy wonders yet to behold.

"We're here! Can you believe we're here?" She was jumping up and down.

The heavy brick buildings closed in on Aidan, a mob of giants gathering in the twilight gloom, squatting on his new life. The train finally came to a halt, but so much hullabaloo and racket made his country head spin.

"Chicago is Atlanta times a thousand!" Iris leapt off the train and pulled Aidan behind her. The shotgun wrapped in a Seminole blanket banged into the banjo slung 'cross his back. The strings protested. The coppery smell of fresh blood filled his nostrils. Men, their aprons slick from critter guts, stepped out of a chilly refrigeration car. Farmers with dung and dirt clinging to their breeches jostled the butcher men.

"I never support Zapata, just I—I act like I do," said a young man with a heavy Mexican accent as he banged into Aidan's bags. He clutched a once-colorful sombrero to his dusty poncho. An older man in blood-stained pants and shirt, a butcher or meat packer who looked to have just stepped off the killing floor, backhanded him. Iris flinched. "I swear. I am for your side." The young Mexican wiped blood from his nose. A splotch dripped on Aidan's boots as he pulled Iris away from them.

An older Indian man with feathers in a black felt hat spoke to Aidan in words he did not understand. "Sorry, mister," Aidan said. "I don't talk your talk."

"It is Lakota," a younger Indian man said. No feathers in his hat, and his thick hair was long, like Aidan's, his face broad and calm. His manner commanded attention. "My father says, his nephew's in Buffalo Bill Cody's Wild West Show. Has that train come?"

"I really couldn't tell you." Aidan remembered Buffalo Bill's Wild West Pavilion at the Chicago Fair. "That show is still going after all these years?"

Both men nodded and headed on. Behind them, white women in starched white dresses and fancy white boots paraded through the terminal. They carried banners demanding the right to vote. Marching in sync and looking straight ahead, these ladies walked by Aidan and Iris and surrounded a big-shot politician disembarking from a luxury coach. A clump of colored country folk, smelling of sea breezes, tobacco, and dirt, glanced sideways at the suffragettes. They didn't know what to make of these agitating white ladies neither.

"Danger's dropping from the sky tonight." A seedy-looking huckster shoved a foul-smelling tincture under Aidan's nose. "Two bits buys the protection you need."

A woman hustled children past the snake-oil man. 'Round her neck was a fox biting its own tail. The talk she made was kin to the buzz of an old banjo string. She gave Aidan a warning look.

"What do you say, sir?" The greasy blond huckster leaned in too close.

Aidan caught the fingersmith's hands before he got near the alligator pouch and almost snapped the man's bones. "I say, I don't part with my money for any ole fast talk."

"I ain't a quack." He bounced his voice off the high ceiling. "A bona fide chemist. My emulsion of amyl nitrite, sodium nitrite, and sodium thiosulfate will protect you from cyanogen poisoning as the comet tail engulfs our planet." His coat was lined with brown bottles of brackish fluid. "Guaranteed to halt the dizziness, nausea, muscle spasms, and loss of consciousness. Yes, ma'am, cheat death!"

"We ain't 'fraid of comets, sir. Just a bit of heaven flying by." Iris pulled Aidan away, before any damage was done. "The ceiling in this train station's as high as the sky." She strained her neck. "You see Sis anywhere?"

In Ohio, Aidan telegrammed Redwood at the Magic Lantern Theatre to say they were coming. Who's to say she got word? He stepped up on a bench, looked every direction, certain he couldn't miss her. A grown woman, changed and all, she'd still be a bright star in any constellation. He scanned a mob of faces from the world over. More different kinds of folks than he ever imagined looked right through him.

"I don't see her, sugar."

His vision blurred for a second. Actually it was the air wavering as from high heat. He gasped. The fire-haint had taken the train north too and now crossed the tangle of tracks. Slipping between sweaty black engines, it blazed through the cavernous hall, right toward Aidan and Iris. The haint's feet were flames scorching the pavement; its head strands of smoke like a comet's tail; its heart silver sparks; and its unblinking, merciless eyes were rubies or garnets, peering through lies to truth. Aidan stumbled down from the bench. Iris clutched his hand. Seeing sparks in her eyes, he didn't need to ask if she saw the haint too. He hadn't left misery back home. It was tracking him.

As the haint swooped close, a few men in the politician's party broke into sweat and fanned the air. The bigwig withered in a blast of heat. Drenched suddenly in sweat, he turned pink and tore at his collar and the buttons of his shirt. The huckster fell down coughing and heaving. The cure-bottles that lined his raggedy coat shattered. Volatile vapors soaked him and filled the air. In the wake of the haint, sparks flew like troubling afterthoughts, and the huckster's alcohol-sodden coat caught fire. In a second he was a roar of flames. As the politicians backed away, the huckster wriggled his arms free of burning sleeves and rolled away, dampening the blaze on his shirt and pants. Rivulets of alcohol carried the fire in every direction. Aidan unwrapped his banjo and threw the heavy blanket on the still blazing coat. Iris and the suffragettes ran 'round stamping out the flames before they spread. Their hems were singed yellow and white boots turned sooty brown.

"What the hell was that?" the huckster clutched Aidan's blanket to him.

"You're a fire hazard, man, that's what!" the bigwig politician shouted.

Aidan had to yank the blanket from him. "Sorry, sir, but I'll be needing this."

"You're the one smoking a cigar," a suffragette said to the politician.

Distant doors flew open. Hot ashes floated up to the ceiling as the haint vanished in the Chicago twilight.

"What a welcome to Chicago!" Iris looked pleased as Punch.

Aidan tipped his hat to the suffragettes and pulled her away. "I don't see hide nor hair of Redwood." He scanned the hall, unsure which direction to go or what to do. Getting here was one thing. Finding Redwood was—

"Don't give up yet," Iris said, and then whispered, "The haint, she's a good spirit. You said so, remember?"

"Yes." That *was* the tale Aidan told. The haint's own story was another matter.

Like a sudden waterfall after a storm, three women in silvery dresses, with veils covering their hair and faces, flowed out of a private railcar. A man, taller and wider than Aidan, wearing red silk pants and a long robe, came down after the women and paused in front of Aidan and Iris. Their robes snapped and swirled as a train, trailing a rush of air, charged out of the station.

"I see you are a musician, sir." The robed man had a singer's voice and a foreigner's tongue.

Iris pulled Aidan's ear to her lips. "Are *these* the wild people Doc Johnson was talking 'bout?"

"Hush now," Aidan said.

"Might I ask for your aid?" The foreigner held out a colorful playbill. "You look like a helpful chap."

The women's eyes above their veils were dark and welcoming.

"I'm new in town." Aidan took off his hat. "But I'll gladly give it a shot."

"We're from farther away than you," the foreigner said.

Iris stepped in front of Aidan, bold as a full moon rising. "We come all the way from Georgia. Where you folks come from, sir?"

"Have you heard of Iran—of Persia—down in Georgia?"

Iris nodded. The women smiled with their eyes.

"We have?" Aidan said. "Now don't you be telling tales."

"From the Bible and a book on ancient kingdoms Aunt Elisa gave me," Iris said.

"Persia is ancient *and* modern," the foreigner said. "My younger brother's an acrobat, performing across your great nation. I must find his theatre." He handed Aidan a playbill for the Magic Lantern Theatre.

Aidan grinned. "Well, after I sprinkle some dirt, we're going the same place as you."

"A mighty coincidence like this means good luck, sir, where we come from." Iris beamed at him.

"Where we come from as well, little beauty." The foreigner bowed to her.

Iris blushed and bent down to the ground with Aidan. "Do you think he's a prince?"

Aidan opened the alligator pouch. "I don't know, but the way you eyeing him, makes me think you falling in love again."

"He's a spectacle all right and good luck too, but that ain't in the same county with love," Iris said in her grown-up voice.

"Well, now tell me a thing or two, sweet pea." Aidan scattered the goober dust on the crisscross of rail tracks. As it sparked under the iron wheels of a train, the three women bowed their heads like this was a holy moment for them too.

The sun dipped low, setting wisps of clouds on fire. Payne was out another day's wages. No more filming today. Redwood had danced the lioness almost back to the cage. Their motions blurred into one another, and Redwood felt heartache, for a time before this time, for fierce sisters, babies lounging in the heat, and a great bearded fellow rolling in the grass. Redwood peered with lonely lion eyes through bars at a barren landscape of circus tents and train boxcars. She turned her nose up at rotten meat covered in maggots and flies as each second stretched long and unbearable. Fire singed her whiskers, and she gulped a breath of smoke, coughed, and growled.

The lioness batted a sore paw at Redwood, bringing her back to the smelly cage.

"I can't, damn it! Sequoia's in the way," someone shouted. Nobody dared get close enough for a clear shot.

Redwood gently took hold of the swollen foot. The lioness laid her head against Redwood's hip. Redwood pressed her cheek against a furry ear, drawing the pus and pulling the pain from one paw, then the other. With a rumbling chest, the lioness danced beyond reach to deep inside the cage where bars kept the leering and snarling people out. She sat on her haunches and licked her paws, eyes never leaving Redwood.

A shot rang out. Stunned by the force of an impact, by skin and bone exploding, Redwood's arms flew open. She stumbled and closed her eyes on a punctured lung and fatal heartache. A second shot whined by in the darkness and slammed through downy fur into soft flesh, and then Redwood could hear no more.

Time was undone, bleeding away.

Redwood opened her eyes. The lioness was twisting in the air. The second bullet had hit her belly and ripped her open. Guts poured out with blood. The *White Hunter* and *African Savages* stood behind a gunman, cheering and laughing. With fear standing in his eyes, Saeed ran into the cage.

The dead weight of the big cat fell into Redwood. She hugged the animal to her. Claws dug at her ribs as they tumbled to the ground. Blood spurted onto Redwood: sticky, hot, smelling of copper and bile. The lioness's tongue flapped against Redwood's shoulder. Coarse as sandpaper, it scraped away skin. Puffs of bloody, fetid breath fogged the air. Golden eyes turned glassy and gray.

Grimacing, Saeed rolled the lioness off of Redwood's heaving chest and talked at her, but she couldn't hear him or anything else. He looked concerned at her injured shoulder and the blood dripping down her side. As he checked her wounds, she pushed him aside with such force, he tumbled several feet and hit the ground hard. The wind was knocked from his chest. Saeed scrambled in the dust to regain his senses and came for her again.

Redwood jumped over the lioness and charged at the gunman, running faster than Saeed, running with gale force rage. As she bounded toward them, the *White Hunter* and *African Savages* grew silent, motionless, and then backed away. The gunman lost his grin as he noted their retreat. Panicked, he aimed his weapon at Redwood and shouted something, but she charged on. He fumbled and stumbled and then pulled the trigger, at point-blank range.

His rifle misfired, burning his fingers and dislocating his shoulder.

Redwood smacked the gun from his hands and slammed into him. Terror and pain disfigured his face. She balled her storm hand into a fist. It took great effort not to punch him again. He fell down at her feet and clutched his chest, like an actor miming a broken heart. She turned away from him, walked past a frightened *White Hunter* and stunned *African Savages,* past Saeed even, and back into the cage.

Redwood sat with the lioness's head in her lap, staring through the bars. Saeed shrugged at everyone and sat next to her. Demon Nicolai cranked the last of his film. He nodded at Redwood, pleased it would seem with her bravura performance. Redwood took a choked breath. Sound returned, but she didn't want to listen to the voices babbling at her and wished for the silence again.

It did not come.

EIGHTEEN

After depositing banjo, shotgun, and their heavy bags in the Persian prince's railroad car, Aidan and Iris headed for the Magic Lantern Theatre. The prince joined in this scouting expedition. They rode a horse-drawn trolley since the electric train lines were down. So many people were cutting the fool in the streets on account of Halley's Comet, the prince refused to let his wives come along on public transport. The women offered to watch over Iris while the men did the scouting, but Iris didn't want to stay behind. Aidan didn't want to leave her, so no argument there.

The Magic Lantern Theatre was opening a big production tomorrow night, yet it seemed to Aidan the show needed another week. Actors in half-finished monkey suits dangled from ropes and got tangled in each other. One fellow, a walking tin can more than a knight-errant, limped by them. He was missing a tin shoe and hobbling after a woman who toted a bushel of funny hats. A drawbridge slammed onto the stage floor, nowhere near its green silk moat. A lion-mask in a red union suit dodged tiny people practicing dance steps. A chorus of midgets sang off-key. Nothing but white folk everywhere, and standing in the wings, shouting at riggers and carpenters, the harried manager claimed he'd never heard tell of Redwood Phipps.

"Don't know her, haven't seen her." He darted away from Aidan through flats and props. "How'd you people get back here?"

Aidan licked dry lips. A drink wouldn't help nobody remember, but he wanted one all the same. "Six feet tall, a real pretty colored lady."

"Redwood?" A stocky blond stagehand hung from the flies next to a farmhouse flat and rubbed at dust in his eyes. "You must mean *Sequoia.*"

Aidan brightened at her Cherokee name.

The stagehand scratched his neck. "She hasn't worked the vaudeville revue for several months. I bet she didn't get your telegram."

Iris just 'bout fell over as a circle of dark clouds got hauled up with the farmhouse flat. The prince admired the machinery.

"Don't know where Sequoia's living, but I hear tell she's making moving pictures."

"Why would she do that?" the prince asked.

The stagehand shimmied down a rope. "Colonel Selig and everybody's brother is doing films. That's where the money is, and show people always chase money."

Iris gazed into the flies. Lined up behind the farmhouse flat were castles, cornfields, a big green city lit up in the night, and a sky of flying critters. "Is this all for one show?"

The stagehand leered at her. "You must be Sequoia's kin. Or is that just how they grow 'em in Georgia?"

Aidan bristled and Iris leaned into him. "What show you doing here, sir?" she said.

"*The Wizard of Oz.*"

"I read the book." She grinned. "Twice."

"That acrobat buddy of Sequoia's said I couldn't get a house in a twister to land on the wicked witch. Watch me. HEADS!"

Screeching like polecats in heat, dark clouds spiraled 'round the farmhouse flat as it headed for the stage floor. Iris was enchanted.

"Acrobat?" the prince said.

"Somebody need to oil that contraption." Aidan pointed to the noisy winch.

"He and Sequoia are thick as thieves. Find him, you find her."

"And where might that be?" Aidan didn't want to be jealous of no acrobat.

"Don't really know. Son of a gun still owes me five dollars too."

"My brother's a bit of a rogue," the prince said when Iris told his wives of the debt. Aidan wasn't sure how much English they understood, but they smiled and nodded.

"Coming inside this railway coach is like we done stepped into another world, Mars or maybe Venus." Iris admired the spicy colors, rich fabrics, and plush cushions. Fanciful creatures, cast in bronze and silver, frolicked over every surface. Aidan's fingers itched to carve something after seeing them.

"This place is a palace on wheels," Aidan said.

"Far from home, we have an oasis," the prince said.

One of his wives poured tea into fancy cups and saucers. The second laid a low table with steaming meats, colorful vegetables, and flatbreads. The third held on to Aidan's banjo and stroked the neck, just enough to make the strings buzz.

"We can't trouble you no more." Aidan tried to ease his banjo from her fingers, but she wouldn't let go. "We'll just take our things and—"

"What trouble is that?" the prince said. "Farah loves making tea. Akhtar could cook a man into heaven. Abbaseh wants to know of this instrument you play."

Iris pulled the map from Aidan's bag. "Aunt Subie led us right to you." She danced around, showing off a drawing of colorful folks in fancy dress at the train station. A Persian prince in red balloon pants and an Indian man with a feathered hat were hard to miss.

"On your map, why you do us honor," the prince said. His three women stood behind him, nodding. Even if they didn't talk English, they seemed to get the drift of things.

"Don't worry, Mr. Cooper." Iris squeezed Aidan's hand. "We goin' find my sister. We just get us a good night's sleep and catch her in the morning when we're fresh."

"Listen to the little one. She is wise," the prince said. "You must stay. My wives do not argue with me over strange company. This too is miraculous."

Aidan wanted to turn down the prince or whatever he was back in Persia for no good reason. "I don't know." Maybe he just didn't like trusting a rich man's whim, or maybe he didn't like the odds, three wives to one husband. Abbaseh stroked the belly of the banjo, listening eagerly to faint vibrations, a musician for sure. "You ought not to be so neighborly," Aidan said. "This United States of America is a wild country, and plenty of folk out there as soon rob you blind as look at you."

"I appreciate the warning. More reason for us to join forces. The food cools. We must eat soon." The prince ushered them to cushions 'round the low table. He was a man used to getting his way.

"You offer fine hospitality, sir. I ain't never seen the like." Aidan crouched down and ran his fingers through a thick carpet. The colors had daylight in them. Flowers, branches, birds, and horses wove in and out of one another on a deep sea-blue. The dense pattern got him to thinking on the Okefenokee Swamp—homesick already.

"Six hundred Persian knots to the square inch," the prince boasted.

"Does it fly, sir? Does it have spirit power? Can it take you to your heart's desire?" Iris asked.

The women laughed in three-part harmony.

The prince smiled. "Carpets do not fly for me. Perhaps you will find a way to unleash this talent."

"I can try." Iris was delighted by the enchanted coach and the mysterious beauties who talked only Persian. "Like one of Doc Johnson's storybooks."

"These folks got their own story to tell," Aidan said. "You ain't read that in your book."

"Do tell." Iris would've pestered the prince and his ladies with a thousand questions if she hadn't fallen asleep after the rich meal.

The prince sat on plump pillows; Farah and Akhtar sat behind him. After tucking Iris into soft bedding, Aidan sat on a cushion in front of him.

"My wives wondered if you would grace us with song."

Abbaseh strummed once and placed the banjo in Aidan's lap. His hands trembled over the strings, uncertain. He was playing better, but he wasn't sure he'd gotten good.

"I'm all tuckered out too," Aidan said. "I promise a real show tomorrow."

The wives made a lavish bed on the magic carpet of scented pillows, fine blankets, and cushions, as if Aidan was also a prince. In the dark, when he was sure they were all off sleeping soundly, he got up from the forest of Persian knots and fell asleep on the bare ground next to Iris. Sleeping on the magic carpet seemed a sin and a shame to him.

The back parlor of George and Clarissa's house had been converted to Redwood's room. Framed sheet music covers and theatre posters of colored plays and performers decorated the walls: Bert Williams and George Walker in *Abyssinia* and *In Dahomey*, and Aida Overton Walker in *His Honor: The Barber* and *Salome*. Plays and books covered a writing table. Voluptuous white lilies filled plump vases and scented the air. Redwood was buried in sumptuous bedding, her shoulder and ribs bandaged. She clutched a beat-up music box in her right hand, and as the tinny version of "Swanee River" played, she stared up at the painted ceiling. Mythical figures from a tale she didn't know, drawn with a whimsical hand, chased each other 'round the room, warring, loving, cheating, dying, and saving each other over and over.

Clarissa tiptoed through the doorway as the song wound down. She set a teapot on the nightstand, pulled a chair close to the bed, and took up Redwood's left hand. "That old thing is so warped," she said. "I know a shop where you can get a new one, with lovely music, show music that I know you'd appreciate just as much as that Stephen Foster song. Negroes have other things to sing about, besides missing the old plantation. I can't believe you still listen to that."

"It was Mama's box." Speaking hurt, like Redwood had been screaming for hours.

"Oh . . . I didn't know." Clarissa cleared her throat.

They sat silently. Clarissa shifted as if the fat upholstered chair hurt her bottom. She worried the lace at her neck and peered in the teapot twice. Redwood wheezed and stared at a mythical beast with wings flying through a midnight Milky Way.

"What are you reading?" Clarissa picked up an old *Atlantic Monthly*. "'"Why I am a Pagan" by Zitkala-Sa—a Sioux Indian woman defends her religion.' Oh my." Clarissa set it down quickly and rubbed her hands on a clean handkerchief. "We all missed you at the poetry reading tonight," she said. "The whole club turned out to hear poems by Mr. Paul Laurence Dunbar and our own Anna Warner. Dr. Jeffrey spoke on the advantages of polygamy—that's many wives to one husband. How much more responsible it is in light of the social temperament of women and the *male appetite*—fewer children out of wedlock. He seemed surprised that we ladies all disagreed so vehemently with him. There should be an article in the *Broad Ax* on our discussion, and also a piece on industrial versus academic education for the Negroes coming up from Georgia and Mississippi. Mr. Booker T. Washington is right. So much refined thought is wasted on those poor souls who need work, a vocation so they can get ahead and feed their families. What good is Mr. Dunbar's poetry to them? And all that singing and dancing. How will we uplift the race if they just want to cut the fool? I know you'd disagree, but even Dr. Dubois admits to . . . limits. Maybe you'll come and speak to the club and persuade us to your view." She suddenly ran out of steam.

"What?" Redwood croaked. "I'm listening."

"I'm just bibble-babbling at you, because you're so quiet, it . . . scares me." She looked in the teapot again. "Do you think this is ready?"

Redwood nodded. "They didn't have to shoot her," she whispered. That hurt too.

"Who?" Clarissa gripped the teapot. "The lioness? But you might have been killed."

"Yes, thank the stars that gunman had a lousy aim and a dirty rifle."

"You know what I mean." Clarissa poured a dark brew through a strainer into a cup. "I hope I made this right." She held it out to Redwood. "I followed your recipe. It's amazing what you got growing out back. A pharmacopeia."

Redwood took the cup. "Some things won't grow up north though." She drank the brew and shuddered. It tasted bitter but soothed her insides.

"Do you have a charm in your garden to trip up a wayward man?"

"I don't lay down tricks to cross folks. No good trying to hoodoo somebody into going the way you want if they ain't—if they *aren't* going that way."

"Oh, I wasn't serious." Clarissa laughed. "I'm a God-fearing Christian woman." She sighed. "George loves me in his way, but sometimes—"

"Brother's selfish and—"

"George Phipps charged into Chicago when my first husband's laundry business was going under. My parents had invested in us and were about to lose everything too. If it wasn't for George, I would have been out on the street, like those other poor women and with a baby to feed. My first husband coughed himself to death, and . . . George isn't charming or refined. He's a hard patch of dirt, but I love him for everything he did, for everything he still does."

"George do know how to work hard."

"He gives me a pain right here." Clarissa touched her chest. "Like a hot poker."

"I'd like to help you, but George would require a powerful spell, and . . ." Redwood tried to sit up. "Like I tole you, I ain't hardly done no real conjure magic since I left Peach Grove. I don't dare."

"What about this stunt you pulled with a wild lion?"

"I didn't plan that. I don't know what come over me," Redwood said. "If I do a powerful trick, I get sick or somebody be hurt, or somebody die even, like today. Make me 'fraid of my ownself."

"I've never seen you afraid of anything."

"Mama used to say, *We conjure this world, call it forth out of all the possibilities.* But I've lost my good magic."

"I won't listen to you saying you've lost your goodness." Clarissa was hoarse now too.

"They didn't shoot that she-lion to save me. 'Fraid of us both. Good reason too."

Clarissa's hands shook as she poured a second dose. "Don't be so dramatic."

"I almost stopped that gunman's heart from beating in his chest."

"Of course you didn't. What nonsense."

"You have to hear what I say."

Clarissa searched Redwood's face. "How could anyone *believe* such tales?"

"I can pull somebody's pain," Redwood declared. "Not my own though. And if I'm wild and crazy and feeding on rage, I think maybe I can pull the life right out too. Or maybe not. Anyhow, I didn't." Snapping Jerome's neck was enough killing for her. She swallowed the blood rising in her throat. "I can see times that are over and done or haven't even happened yet. I went to the Chicago Fair after it was long gone, back to 1893 before it burned down. Aidan and me worked that spell together."

"Who is Aidan?"

"He's . . . He's a conjure man with his banjo. Aidan was my friend, *before,* back home."

Clarissa tried to smile. "A sweetheart?"

"My friend. We . . . Sometimes I open my mind so wide, I can feel myself in everything, dead and alive, yesterday and tomorrow. Aidan can too." Redwood didn't have much voice left. She gripped Clarissa. "Do you hear what I say?"

Breathing hard against corset and collar, Clarissa marched away from Redwood. She opened the window, and a night breeze filled the room. She gulped chill air. Down the street, horses whinnied and a child wailed. Maple trees rustled with the wind, and two squirrels teased each other 'round a nearby branch. Nestled under the eaves on the third floor, the twins snored loudly, safe in their dreams.

"I don't tell you a lie," Redwood said, more frightened than when she danced with the lioness. "You're my friend, aren't you? Friends *believe* in each other."

Clarissa whirled to face her. "All right, all right. I believe you. I've been believing you for a while—I just didn't say."

"Thank you." Redwood drained the second dose of medicine and then opened the false bottom of Garnett's music box. It was stuffed with money. "Don't fret. I'm goin' do my own moving picture. They won't gun me down 'fore I get started good."

The next day at breakfast in the luxury railroad car, Aidan and Iris feasted on things Aidan couldn't recognize by sight, taste, or smell. While they ate, the Persian prince, whose name was way beyond Aidan's country mouth, went out and leased a motor hack to hunt his brother acrobat and Redwood. He also hired a chauffeur—a lanky Scotsman with a thick brogue and a sickly freckled face who claimed to know everything 'bout what he called "the movies."

"Slang sure can eat up words, or am I just getting too old?" Aidan shook his head.

"I hope you don't mind if my wives join us," the prince said.

"It'd be a pleasure." Aidan tipped his hat to the ladies as they filled the back seats.

Iris squeezed in next to the women. "This is our first time riding a *motor* vehicle."

As they combed the windy city for colored folk making moving pictures, Iris told the Persian ladies everything they should know 'bout America. She read snatches of Miz Dunbar-Nelson's book, offering hoodoo advice on men and happiness. Aidan only half listened. He scanned the broad streets in the hazy daylight. Chicago was a magic city, crowded with the future, and Aidan was one of them nineteenth-century relics some editor railed against in the morning paper. Modern folk paused in dirty alleyways to stare at the foreign entourage, but it was beauty making them gawk as much as anything. The chauffeur honked and sped up.

"It's a wonder Mr. McGregor can see where we're going." Aidan shivered in the cool wind off Lake Michigan. "With this dirt storm squatting on us."

"Air's not so bad." Iris hugged Aidan from behind. "Worrying's put you in a bad mood."

The prince glanced from Iris to Aidan. "A young wife is good for a man."

"If I had me a prince, wouldn't share him with nobody," Iris said.

"I'm enlightened, as you can see. I do not shut my wives away from the world. When their English is better, I will let them speak to whomever they like, even young girls who spout revolution."

Aidan snorted. "You talking big now, but wait."

"Abbaseh, my third wife, sold her dowry to educate her sister. She agitates for women's rights, similar to your suffragettes, but in a secret society. They say I was a fool to marry her."

"Well, women got as much sense as men do 'bout most things," Aidan said.

"More sense," Iris said.

"If a woman has wise words, why shouldn't a man listen?" The prince plucked *The Goodness of St. Rocque* from Iris's hand and thrust it at one of his wives. "It was Abbaseh's idea to enlist your aid."

Aidan stared at Abbaseh. It was hard to tell who was who when they were all wrapped up. "She's a musician."

"Yes, and a poet." The prince frowned. "How did you know?"

"We're here and arrived in one piece." Mr. McGregor interrupted with a thick Scottish burr. "Let's be quick, sir."

He left the motor roaring in front of a studio on Peck Court in the Levee district. The buildings were run-down and overgrown. A man had fallen asleep in stringy weeds, hugging an empty bottle to his lips.

To the surprise of the Persian ladies, Iris bolted from the auto and chased down seedy strangers. The wives called after her.

"These whores dinna care if you be the king of Egypt," Mr. McGregor said. "If your pockets look rich, they put a hole in your heart and bleed ya."

Iris found a friendly woman, makeup smeared 'cross her face, clothes tumbling off a fleshy figure, who directed them to another studio, on the nearby South Side.

"Redwood's famous." Iris plopped her behind on the leather seat.

The wives spoke harsh words to her, a plain-as-day scolding.

"That gal's hardheaded, won't listen to nobody," Aidan said, proud of her.

Mr. McGregor sped off at fifteen miles per hour, like a thief making a getaway. Aidan sat up out of a slouch as more colored faces stared in the motor hack.

"What're y'all s'posed to be?" A dark face sneered at them.

"This is where most of the colored live," Mr. McGregor said. "A danger zone."

"I shall reward your bravery in driving us here," the prince said.

The streets got narrower and meaner; the buildings crammed into one another; thrown up quick, they were tumbling down quicker. Somber working people dribbled out of factories at the shift change. Tired out and caved in, they resembled sharecroppers back home, the Jessups and the Robesons, who didn't work a lick for themselves—not the dreamers Aidan rolled into the station with last night. Children playing in the street weren't plump, but stick and sinew kids with hard eyes and stone tears. Was Aidan writing his fear all over their faces?

Mr. McGregor drove up to a third motion picture factory. A sign proclaimed:

COLORED PEOPLE ARE FUNNY
If colored people weren't funny,
there would be no plantation melodies, no banjos, no cakewalks,
no buck and wing dancing, no jazz bands, no minstrel shows
and no blackface vaudeville!
And They Are Funny in the Studio.
Real Colored People Caught in the Act!

Above the words, a grinning Redwood in a chicken suit chased a blackface sharecropper. Redwood had a pillow on her belly and another on her rear. Her hair was running wild 'cross her head. Aidan touched her face on the crumbling yellow paper.

"That ain't how I remember her." Iris leaned into Aidan.

He put his arm around her bony shoulders. "You was just a little bit when she left."

Aside from the photo, there was no sign of Redwood or the prince's acrobat brother.

"Colonel Selig's moved to the outskirts of the city, shooting Wild West shows and jungle movies. You should try there," a colored crewman said. "You folks gonna play in his next motion picture?"

"My wives in front of a camera?" The prince pointed to clown Redwood as they drove off for Irving Park Road. "They won't sell themselves to any man's greedy eyes."

"He didn't mean no insult, sir," Iris said. "Back home, working in traveling shows, a colored woman make more money than anything, even—"

"Hush," Aidan said.

The veiled ladies stirred behind the prince like shadows caught between cracks of daylight.

"I'm just saying," Iris said.

"It's none of our business, honey bun," Aidan said.

"Aunt Subie say a hoodoo should always help folk understand what they can't see themselves," Iris whispered.

"You a hoodoo like Miz Subie now? At twelve?"

Iris blushed and didn't say any more. Mr. McGregor picked up speed.

"Sequoia's around here somewhere," a white production manager at the fifth studio said. "And we got Jap acrobats—they're playing the Eskimos, but I don't know about a Persian one. What's that look like? Another colored fellow?"

Aidan exchanged glances with the prince, who shrugged. "Yeah, but light-skinned," Aidan replied.

The production manager leaned close to Aidan. "One colored fellow look pretty much like another to me: dark hair, dark eyes sitting on top of a grin." Aidan didn't know what to say. The manager chuckled and patted his shoulder. "But colored women, now that's a different story. Go on in and see for yourself."

The studio was a big ole barn, the ceiling several stories high. Hanging from the rafters, banks of electric lights loomed out of shadows. A painted drop covered one wall, a nature scene done so real, Aidan might have walked through it if he wasn't paying attention. A few backless buildings were set off from the painted prairie, and cowboys on horses milled around, waiting on the cameramen.

"They're doing a moving picture about the Wild West." The prince pointed to half-naked actors in dark face paint and buckskins crouching in dirt. "The Indians are waiting to attack."

Aidan winced as Iris cornered a colored man with a camera.

"Sequoia? In there." He pointed. "Booma went wild, attacking everybody, tore the place apart. Mad Nicolai kept rolling and Sequoia, well, you gotta see her dancing for yourself." He directed them to a screening room.

Nobody noticed Aidan, Iris, the prince, his three wives, or Mr. McGregor push into the back of the crowded room. Spears of dusty sunlight streaked the dark as a breeze lifted black curtains from the windows. Moving pictures flashed against a white sheet hanging on a wall. Aidan saw a lion spring in the air and lose a fake mane. Redwood exploded into view, and she and this lioness danced toward a cage. Even in a silly grass skirt costume, she had him breathing hard.

"What did I tell them? I had her going back in," Redwood said. Her voice came from no more than ten feet away.

The spit in Aidan's mouth dried up. His heart stopped. Iris clutched his elbow. "She's somewhere close," he whispered.

Aidan scanned the dim room until he spied Redwood standing between a skinny fellow with a curly red beard and a muscular man who must have been the prince's brother. As a spark of jealousy was 'bout to burst into a bushfire, he noted that she was wearing his old shirt and pants. His cap was stuck in the back pocket. That had to be a good sign. Of course, she'd changed too. Her brown hair was shiny and sleek, in the Madam Walker style now. Her long neck sloped into graceful shoulders. Her hips were fuller than he remembered, round mounds dropping from a delicate waist. A sparkly blue scarf circled her belly, a cool creek that flowed almost to the ground.

"You see Sis?" Iris said.

"Yes, ma'am. She done come into herself." Aidan struggled through the crowd.

He fought tears as onscreen the lioness was shot in the chest and belly.

Turning away from the lioness dying in her arms, Redwood came face-to-face with Aidan. She gasped and tried to blink her vision clear, expecting him to vanish, like a haint you refused to believe in anymore. But he was flesh and blood torment, not a ghost. Tears stood in his moss-colored eyes, and his chest was heaving. Her chest was fixing to burst too. He was tall and straight and strong, just as she remembered him. Shiny black hair hung free, and a song was on the tip of his tongue, whistling across his lips with each breath.

Onscreen the gunman crumpled at Redwood's feet, not dead dust like Jerome, but close. She was a danger to herself and fools who made her blood boil. Quiet fell in the screening room like a heavy stage curtain. A few folk slipped out the side door. The projector sputtered and smoked. White curlicues spun 'round her and Aidan, gathering into a pale gray twister before surging out the open window. Aidan knew who and what she was, but stepped so close, she could taste the grin on his lips. Nicolai observed this, wishing for a camera no doubt. Redwood didn't care what he or anybody saw. She reached her storm hand toward Aidan, then balled it to a fist.

Behind Aidan, a gangly colored gal, with scraggly braids sticking out a rat's nest tangle of hair jumped from foot to foot—Iris, all grown up but still wild and spooky, light coming from her eyes. She and Aidan wore dusty rough coats, muddy brogans, and lopsided grins, resembling what Clarissa's set would call backcountry fools. Saeed turned to see what had caught Redwood's attention. Stunned, he spoke in Farsi and moved to greet a man dressed in Persian finery.

"You came all this way to find me?" Saeed said or something close. Redwood's Farsi was spotty.

"You are my brother, always," the stranger replied.

Applause skittered like wildfire through the crowd as onscreen Redwood placed the lioness's head in her lap. The business manager for

the whole picture factory lingered at the back door as the black curtains in the windows were opened and light flooded the room.

"Dancing with lions, I see," Aidan said, "my brave *Sikwayi*."

Redwood blushed at her Cherokee name and made herself turn
from him. "That can't be my baby sister, grown up now." She opened
her arms. Iris glanced at Aidan.

"Don't look at me." He pushed her toward Redwood.

Redwood scooped Iris up and swung her as if she were a child
again. Iris tried to say something 'bout, "I'm too big," but squealed
instead as her feet lifted high in the air. Redwood set her down by one
of the Persian women.

"This is Abbaseh," Saeed said. "This is my Redwood."

Abbaseh nodded/bowed slightly to her. Redwood matched the gesture, but felt too shy to try any of the Farsi words Saeed had been
teaching her.

"This is my brother, Anoushiravan and his other two wives, Farah
and Akhtar."

Redwood bowed and gestured at Aidan. "Saeed, this is Mr. Aidan
Cooper, a . . . neighbor from back home, and this is my baby sister, Iris."

"Are you the prince's rogue of a brother?" Iris said.

"Prince?" Saeed smiled. "Well, I am indeed the rogue."

"I didn't know if I'd ever see you again," Redwood said to Aidan.
"Either one of you. Kept your promise, I see, Mr. Cooper."

"My pleasure, ma'am. But if it wasn't for Iris, I'd have been lost."

"Coughing plague took the whole family 'cept me and Mr. Cooper."
Iris blinked tears. "So we come to find you."

"I felt the dying, wasn't no good for days." Redwood's voice cracked.
"Miz Subie sent word, but I didn't want to believe her." She hugged
Iris close.

"Everybody said you run off to New York City to marry Mr. Williams. I saw that wasn't true." Iris's eyes flickered, like candlelight in a
breeze. "Mr. Williams was smoke rising to the stars. You were a tree
pulled loose in the storm, walking off, then taking root in hard soil and
sprouting a new name too, Sequoia."

The business manager applauded Iris's hoodoo speech. "Family
reunions warm the heart." He sidled up to Saeed without looking
Redwood in the eye. He whispered and gestured and passed Saeed

an envelope. Dodging Saeed's brother, his three wives, and a white man in chauffeur livery, the business manager headed for the door. He spoke to Aidan like he must be in charge of them all. "A miracle that she-lion didn't rip out Sequoia's throat. Our business is pleasing the crowd, not scaring 'em to death. I'm sure you understand." He hurried off as the last words settled in.

"Understand? The mullahs everywhere claim righteous wisdom." Saeed handed Redwood the envelope. "He gave us a bonus *before* firing us."

"He fired you too?" Redwood didn't know what to do with all the feelings storming her. She let the crisp paper money spill from the envelope. The bills swirled around her several times and landed crumpled and frayed at her feet.

Aidan grasped her empty palm in his. "Does my heart good to look on you."

BOOK V

It is not light that we need, but fire; it is not the gentle shower, but thunder. We need the storm, the whirlwind, and the earthquake.

—Frederick Douglass

NINETEEN

Chicago, 1910

Aidan sat up in George Phipps's fancy house, hat in hand, sweating in the stove heat. Iris clung to his knees and twittered. George hadn't looked happy when he set eyes on his baby sister with Aidan standing next to her. Redwood dragged her brother out of the kitchen to a front parlor. Aidan patted Iris's back. He hadn't managed a moment alone with Redwood to see how she was, to see who she'd become, to see if he really had a chance. He'd go on back to Georgia if he wasn't wanted, and take Iris with him.

George and Redwood commenced to arguing before the door was shut.

"I don't need no lazy crackers or overgrown *country* heifers to feed," George said.

"Heifer? Iris is our sister, not a stranger! Mama said to watch over each other," Redwood said. "Aidan come all this way, carrying her to us, I don't care what he is."

"So we can help him back home. We can—"

"This old house is so drafty." Clarissa, George's elegant wife, closed the parlor door on more ugly words. "And this cold snap is a surprise."

"Yes, ma'am." Aidan thought it was sweltering hot inside the house. He wiped his damp forehead.

"In Chicago, if you don't like the weather, just wait." Clarissa said. She knit her brow at Iris shuffling her feet and scratching up a nice wooden chair.

"Iris, honey, quit horsing 'round." Aidan wiped dust off her cheek.

He could make a better chair than this in a day. He'd make Miz Clarissa a new one as soon as someone showed him the tools. He knew just the wood to use and a good stain. Iris fidgeted against his shins. Clarissa shook disapproval from her head.

"We're used to a spring chill. I guess you Georgia folks aren't."

"No, ma'am." Iris hunched her bony shoulders.

Her coat was covered in dust and soot. The grime must have been an inch thick on Aidan's rough coat too, but he couldn't brush it off, not against these spanking clean floors. He scratched the patchy beard itching up his neck. Riding all day in the motorcar looking for Redwood, they never had time to clean up and look decent for these swank city folks. He wouldn't look or smell so bad after a spell in a tub.

Clarissa turned on the electric lights. "What're you sitting in the dark for?"

Aidan shrugged. Wasn't nothing to say. It didn't seem that dark to him, so why waste electricity? He couldn't contradict her, couldn't look at her.

"Or don't you know how to do it?" She had a laugh like bottles tinkling in the breeze and a sultry sway to her hips, enough to break the hardest heart. Her slender waist and curving neck made him nervous. She smelled like apple butter, and he knew from the handshake she was soft and springy like wet moss. Her skin was olive brown and so smooth. Who wouldn't want to run his hand up and down her back, touch the sweet skin inside those thighs? It was too long since he felt love in the palm of his hand, tingling on his fingertips. Just a thought though and not really 'bout Miz Clarissa but 'bout Redwood. Hers were the thighs he wanted to kiss; hers was the heart he wanted to hold. Falling in love with a memory, with a hoodoo gal who shouldn't forgive him for what he didn't do, that was enough to send the soberest man to hard drinking. He fumbled open Miz Subie's nasty medicine and swallowed a good mouthful. The tin was half-empty.

Clarissa watched him like a curio at an exhibition and reminded him of Doc. "Redwood speaks so fondly of you both. You're not exactly who I imagined though." Aidan and Iris exchanged furtive looks. "I'm sorry. That sounds worse than I meant."

Iris stood tall. "The Persian prince and his wives got magic lanterns and carpets that you might talk into flying. His brother's an acrobat and can jump and fly on his own. They say we be welcome anytime."

"You can write them nice folks a thank-you." Aidan pulled out his journal and hunted up a loose piece of paper.

"I don't know what's taking them so long." Clarissa smiled at Iris. "Would you like some lemonade, some biscuits?"

Iris looked at Aidan, and he nodded approval. Clarissa retrieved a pitcher from an icebox. She poured the drink, dropped in a lemon wedge and three spoons of sugar. The glass fogged up. Northerners were strange. Drinking an ice drink on a chilly day. "Lemons all the way from Florida, and a pink glass with flowers on it for you."

Iris took the glass and said, "Thank you, ma'am."

"You're welcome. Nice to have a grown-up little lady in the house with such good manners."

Four children dressed in their Sunday best peered at them from the kitchen stairwell like little buzzards waiting for somebody to drop dead.

"The big one is Frank from my first marriage," Clarissa said, "and then George Jr. The twins are Ellie and Belle. Belle means pretty in French." Iris waved and the children ran back upstairs. "I bet you like it sweet, Mr. Cooper?" Clarissa scooped sugar.

"It's Wildfire, not Cooper, ma'am."

Why he offered his Indian name to a complete stranger, he couldn't say. Iris stared as if seeing him for the first time. Clarissa poured his lemonade, pretending not to notice. "Mr. Wildfire then." She looked sweet as her lemonade. She went through the parlor door before he had to take a sip.

"I won't have both of you ganging up on me," George roared. Clarissa's reply was too soft to catch the words, and then the door swung shut.

Aidan wiped another smudge from Iris's chin. "Your brother's just surprised to see you with me."

"Uh-huh." Iris downed her drink in two gulps. "You not goin' drink yours?"

"An ice drink on a chilly day? You go ahead, honey. I'm not thirsty."

"It's too hot in here." She downed the second glass. "Wildfire?"

"We be stepping out in a brand-new world."

Iris puffed her cheeks and blew out cold fog. "Uh-huh."

"A good name is powerful juju."

"I know."

Iris was asleep before her head hit the pillow. Too nervous to linger inside, Redwood pulled Aidan down the creaky steps from the attic, through the kitchen, and into the garden.

"Miz Subie's map took you and Iris right to Saeed's brother!" Redwood smiled. "Goober dust exploding at the crossroads. A *real* conjure woman, Subie be calling us to the thunder, to the whirlwind, 'cause ain't no gentle breeze goin' change this world."

She stormed past a row of purple irises in the backyard. Aidan crouched in the dust she raised, watching her, his eyes shining. George had vegetables growing every which way between her flowers and herbs. He leaned out the kitchen door and yelled. "Don't trample the harvest. I got a fortune planted out there."

Redwood wasn't studying him. "Fire me for dancing with a she-lion? And Saeed too? That ain't right." She stopped in front of Aidan. His hair hung loose on his shoulders. His face, clean-shaven now, was handsome as all get-out. Only his clothes were grubby. "What you thinking, grinning like a monkey?"

"If he own the motion picture plant, I suspect the man can do what he want."

"I'm goin' show up in Mr. Payne's office, and he have to tell me that nonsense to my face. Don't send no flunky with a bonus to throw me away."

"You looked so pretty on that screen. He'll come to his senses."

"Man ain't got no sense to come to." Redwood couldn't shake her anger.

A few stars twinkled in navy-blue twilight. A red-orange comet rode the horizon.

"You got him spooked." Aidan seemed pleased as Punch at this. "Payne be too scared to come hisself."

"Coughing his chest away, Payne is half dead and whole scared. What 'bout you?" Feeling bold as a shooting star, she drew Aidan up next to her. "You 'fraid of me?"

He took her storm hand and pressed it to his heart. "I've lived through mad mama bears, nightriders, rattlesnakes, yellow fever, demon posses. Hoodoo women don't scare me."

"Since I was little, folks have been 'fraid to get next to me, but maybe not you."

He grimaced. "No, ma'am."

"Big men wanna wrassle me to the ground, steal my fire, stomp my heart spirit." She ran storm fingers over his face. Touching his frown turned it to a smile. "But you said, *Make your life up as you go*."

"You did that all right."

"Clarissa say I'm a spectacle and a scandal, dressing like a man, singing the blues in honky-tonks, running the streets with wild Indians, walking the treacherous path."

"Miz Clarissa is a real upstanding lady. That's all that is. She—"

"She want me to burn my backcountry clothes, but shoot"—Redwood ran a finger down a threadbare seam—"I put on a bit of you and I can walk through anything." Aidan winced. His big eyes looked ready to spill over—some secret pain still hounded him. "Iris say you be family now." She touched his shoulder. "Can't tell you how I been missing home."

"Peach Grove . . . ain't a place to call home no more. How people act make home."

"Yes, gotta forgive yourself to go home."

Watching her eyes, he kissed her fingers. She trembled a bit at the touch of his lips. A sweet ache caught her by surprise. Behind Aidan's back, George glared, a dark storm cloud in the kitchen window. Clarissa pulled him away.

"Don't know where to begin with all the sinning I done," Aidan said. "God's showering down the miracles, and I don't feel no ways worthy."

"Get out." She slipped away from him through tomatoes and kale, dancing good feelings before they turned sour or vanished. "What you think of all-colored motion pictures? Not just cutting the fool, but adventure and romance."

"Folks be lining up, pay a nickel, see *you* over and over." He pulled her close again. "They won't be able to get enough of you."

She liked the feel of his hand on her hip. "Clarissa is a clubwoman. She think I oughta act the proper lady, be an example for backward colored women coming up, and show white folk too. How refined and civilized we are."

"What do you want?"

"Nobody goin' pay me to act the lady. And George already be counting the money I'm s'posed to make." She tapped his chest. "And more family showing up."

"I got a stake, and I can work. Me and Iris won't be a burden on George."

Redwood laughed. "What you know how to do in Chicago?"

"I can make a house crash on a wicked witch without screeching like a polecat, make a winch just whisper while it work."

She laid her head on his chest. "Think you could do theatre magic, huh?"

"I can try." He kissed her neck and made her tremble again. He put his arms 'round her. "I'm ready to try all kind of magic."

"I bet you are." Redwood kept waiting for calamity to hit, for her skin to crawl away from him, for her mouth to turn bitter. But this was Aidan doing what she'd imagined a long, long time ago.

"I'm goin' make Miz Clarissa a fine chair." He stroked her back, rough banjo fingers making her want to sing.

"Clarissa is on your side, after you bring Iris all this way."

"I'll get a house of my own, as soon as . . ."

"Ain't a lot of places for colored folk to live in Chicago. They're squeezing us into nowhere. But I guess *you* can live where you want."

"You know where that'll be."

"You ain't Crazy Coop no more. So what, you sober now?"

"As the stars up in the sky."

"What kind of answer is that?" Redwood sniffed him. "What you smell like?"

"Hard work and a long road. Clothes need a good scrubbing."

"Six years. I'm a grown woman now."

"I've changed too."

"From Crazy Coop to Aidan Wildfire? You have to tell me 'bout all that."

"Aunt Caitlin didn't want nobody to know. I think she was 'fraid I'd turn into some kinda savage . . ." He trailed off, lost in painful thoughts.

"When you get to it. We got six years of storytelling to do."

"Yeah. How'd you get to be such a fancy show lady?"

"Fancy?" She cringed. 'Cept for an occasional Ace of Spades show, she was cooning—nothing grand or beautiful like she imagined back in Peach Grove, nothing like those ladies on Cairo Street or *His Honor: the Barber;* just smart-aleck chickens or mumble mouth savages.

"Maybe there's a carpenter job for you at the motion picture factory, since you looking to stay."

"Tell Mr. Payne to shoot that all-colored romance. I'd build what you want for that."

"Payne? Do a colored picture? In this lifetime? Ha!" She wanted to holler and cuss and smack the stars out the sky. "I'm saving up money to make my own—" Overwhelmed, she dropped down on a bench under a maple tree, breathing hard. She shouldn't let herself get so crazy angry. Did she want to kill somebody and end up swinging from a tree? Aidan sat beside her, so close she felt heat rising in his body.

"Doc Johnson explained the sky to us," he whispered at the comet on the horizon.

"How long to tell it's moving?"

"As long as it takes. Comets are free women roaming the night."

She smiled in spite of herself. He was always taking her part. "You don't say?"

Aidan traced the comet tail. "Ow!" His fingertips turned red. "What the—?"

"Reaching up, touching the sky, s'posed to hurt I guess."

"Doc ain't say nothing 'bout that."

"He don't know everything." She kissed his fingers, then drew away.

"What?"

"I hope you ain't a story I made up in my head, is all."

"Iris said the same thing."

"Baby Sister is sweet on you." Redwood jabbed his ribs, and they laughed. "Sober as the stars." She turned his face to hers. "I never knew why you was drinking yourself away. Uncle Ladd said I was right 'bout you putting a spell on them deer. With all that liquor in you, couldn't keep the side of a barn still long enough to hit it close range."

"Hard drinking burn a hole in your memory. Let you forget anything."

"What you want to forget so bad?"

Aidan grimaced.

"After Mama died whenever I dragged by your place, you was singing. You'd take the crook out my back, soothe the ache in my heart. One of your songs, and I knew I could make it to the other side."

"Really?" Aidan scratched his jaw. "I thought you come 'round to cheer *me* up."

"You laid Mama in the church with baby Jesus on Christmas morning, didn't you?"

"Naw, I was out hunting when—"

"Folk said it was hoodoo or an angel."

"A coward more like."

Redwood put her finger on his lips. "I didn't know how she died, but I knew you had a hand in bringing her in 'cause of the flowers, even 'fore George tole me everything." She leaned into him. "You was always bringing Mama purple orchids. Nobody but you could find the ones she liked."

Terrible emotions crawled 'cross his face. "I wish I could have done more."

"Don't we all?"

"I'd give anything to see Miz Garnett rocking on a porch in Chicago town. Anything . . ."

They sat a moment in silence. And then Aidan sang.

> *On the other side of the sky, riding through the dark*
> *my true love's a smoky light, a million miles away.*
> *If you ask, I can't say why, but in my heart*
> *she still be bright, bright as a brand-new day.*

"You just make that up?" Redwood meant to tell him he could turn the worst thing into a pretty love song, but started crying instead.

"Don't you weep." He squeezed her close. "I'll get the rhyme right tomorrow."

"Sound just fine to me."

"Thank you, ma'am."

"Why'd they do her that way?" A storm of tears came.

"Fear drive a man insane."

Redwood hadn't really cried since she left Peach Grove. She had six seasons of tears dammed up. Aidan stroked her back and hummed his song till she ran dry. He was still her *special* friend. A magic man full of good voices, good stories, he made her heart race. He wasn't 'fraid of her or things he didn't understand. And she loved him for all that.

A chill breeze off Lake Michigan cut through the dark and goosed the flesh on her arm.

"You ain't got used to winter in May yet?" Aidan teased.

She shook her head. An icy wind from inside set her to shivering. What if it was too late for a *good-loving* spell? Redwood wanted to get up and run, but the comet looked to have moved. She gasped at this, and then truth dropped from her lips like a falling star.

"I'm damaged goods."

"Ain't we all."

'Stead of heading to the guest room Clarissa made up for him behind the kitchen, Aidan followed Redwood into a back parlor that had been transformed into her bedchamber. Posters of fancy theatre artists grinned at him from the walls. Somebody's gods, fairies, or *Yunwi Tsunsdi*—tiny people—flew 'cross the ceiling, waving from fanciful drawings. A bay window with a generous seat brought the garden right into the room. Cherry blossoms scented the air. The bed had a breezy canopy hanging over it and looked like a ship fixing to set sail. Must have been a hundred books scattered over everything. He tripped on a copy of *Leaves of Grass*.

"You still be loving books, I see." He set the volume onto her crowded desk.

"'I believe a leaf of grass is no less than the journey-work of the stars,'" Redwood quoted Mr. Whitman and blew out the candle. She rustled somewhere behind him, slipping off clothes by the sound of it. His eyes took their time adjusting to the darkness.

"Where are you?" he whispered.

"Find me." Her voice echoed off the ceiling. She seemed to be everywhere.

Neither time nor distance had dulled their connection. She was still the beautiful, headstrong, wonderful, aggravating, enchanting Redwood he'd known in Peach Grove. And this was Chicago, a city of tomorrow where they could be who they wanted.

"A hoodoo gal what can conjure herself here and there got an unfair edge," he said.

"You a conjure man, ain't you? Tracking haints, catching demons in bottles, talking to the ancestors, and I done heard you sing, so you can't lie."

In his wild youth, Aidan had pleasured many a woman, even loved a few. He usually got as good as he gave. He'd only really been 'fraid the first time. Even then he forgot fear quickly, or perhaps named fear passion. This night in a bedroom fit for a king, in a noisy, smelly city on the other side of the world from his home, with a woman that was swamp fire, a queen of Dahomey, a hoodoo wonder dancing with lions and bears, all his backcountry passion terrified him. He had never loved anyone this much.

"I ain't goin' stand still and make it easy for you," she said.

"So get going." On the move she'd be easier to find, but he wasn't telling her that.

Tracking her breath, her warmth, her sweet scent, he headed toward the sound of bare feet on the carpet. He slipped his hands around her belly. She was tense as a banjo string. Her heart pounded as if she'd been running.

"You smell of railroads and motorcars." She shied away from him, but not too far. "Making me itch."

He wiggled out of his scratchy shirt and pants, and she came close again. The cool touch of her skin made him ache and burn, as did the softness of her tiddies, pressing against his chest with each breath. His leg slipped between her thighs. Her hair was soft as peach fuzz, the skin buttery, and as she moved/danced slowly against him, his manhood swelled against her hips. She was suddenly still, breathless.

"Are we going too fast?" he said. "Six years between us, and—"

"I don't know how long I been wanting you and so 'fraid you didn't want me."

"I been loving you since probably before I should have."

She grunted at this confession. "Given the *male appetite*," she sounded like Clarissa, "you've shown great restraint." She flinched. Her words hung in the air.

He touched a soft cloth on her shoulder and another at her waist. "What's this?"

"Bandages. That she-lion got a tongue like sandpaper. She licked a bit of my shoulder off and clawed my ribs." Her voice cracked. "She-cat didn't mean no harm, dying and couldn't help herself."

"You must have been a great comfort to her in the end."

She took a step back.

"Where you going? Don't . . ."

His daddy told him, *a woman who wants you isn't waiting for you to fall down and fail. She wants to make the world new again, with you. It's nothing you can know* till *you do it together*. Standing in the dark, the house shifting and sighing 'round them, he didn't know what Redwood wanted.

A wild-eyed black stallion galloped down the empty night street, pausing at Redwood's window to rear and neigh. Aidan worried it was a haint 'bout to bust in the room, till a man grabbed the loose reins. Redwood took a ragged breath. She was lost somewhere and standing right next to him.

"What's wrong?" He stepped close.

She grunted at his foolish question. He didn't need an answer. Jerome was riding her in the dirt, breaking a hole in her heart. She wanted to conjure herself far from that.

"Don't go," he whispered, "don't go where I can't follow." He kissed her neck, and she trembled like before.

"You remember the World's Fair?" she said.

"How could I forget? They tamed lightning into *E-LEC-TRI-CI-TY*. We danced to the music of Cairo Street—or you did, shimmy-shaking like a snake charmer, then we looked out on the whole world from atop the Ferris Wheel."

"We had us a time, didn't we? From the swamp to the White City."

He kissed the tip of her nose. "Bugs tried to eat you alive."

"Wasn't so bad. You read me the story of Okefenokee."

"Walking down the Midway Plaisance, you was as pretty as them royal ladies from Abyssinia."

"Dahomey. You said they were regular folks, like us." Redwood's storm hand was against his chest. "Sometimes, I don't *believe* we were really at the Fair."

"I got proof." He kissed the cleft of her collarbone. "We can do that together again."

"What?" She lifted his face to hers.

"Dream up what we want to do with ourselves and *believe* in it."

"I don't know." Her voice was a trickle of water in a streambed going dry. "I just don't know anymore."

"We can make that all-colored romance, with you the leading lady," he said. "Sounds grand."

"Ain't it close to first fruits? Who we got to forgive? When can we light the sacred fire anew?"

"Don't." His voice shook. "Don't make fun."

"I'm not." Her fingertips traced the blood flowing from his heart, down 'cross his stomach, to his groin. She wiggled her fingers through curly hair and soft skin, holding the weighty stones of his manhood, and then she kissed him. He was startled by her boldness and fell back on to the bed with her landing on top of him. The bed rocked and swayed with the weight of them.

"I know a thing or two," she said. "Sang in a bordello and learned all sorts of tunes."

"I guess you did."

He reached down and kissed her mouth, his tongue tangling up her next words, his hands searching 'cross her skin, following blood and shivers to the source of pleasure, but when he found his way inside her, she was vanishing again.

How did they hold onto each other and trust when the going got rough?

He stopped abruptly. "You still with me?"

"I wish." She mumbled something he couldn't hear, close as he was.

He wanted light. He wanted to see her face. "Is it me? Something I'm doing?"

"No. I thought, I hoped for . . ."

"What?" He slid out of her.

"You goin' run away from me now?"

He smacked the wall with the palm of his hand. "What you say?"

She flinched away from him. He pressed his forehead into the headboard 'stead of cussing out loud. It took a whole lot of breathing to pull the desire back. Hot and feverish, he bumped into her ice-cold foot. She was trembling.

"The bed ain't big enough for us to be so far apart," he said. "I'm your friend, remember, since that day you caught the storm."

Hearing that didn't seem to help. She curled up in the pillows and moaned. Aidan sucked air in and out till he had enough to hum the melody he sang earlier. Calmer, he kissed her shoulder, then gathered her in his arms and rocked her.

"I'm no baby like Iris."

"I know. A grown woman need tender too."

He sang to her, wondering if she might cry again or what, but she didn't do anything. She was so quiet and still, he just 'bout couldn't stand it. Then, when his throat went dry and his voice was ready to give out, she added a harmony. Singing, they drifted into sleep.

Banging on the door startled Aidan awake. He looked into Redwood's sleepy eyes as in strode Clarissa without a by-your-leave. She wore a knee-length skirt over loose pantaloons and no corset under a colorful jacket—bicycle clothes.

"Mr. Wildfire . . . I . . . uh . . . Well now." Clarissa swallowed shock as Aidan clutched the blanket to his neck. She'd only expected to find Redwood.

"A woman needs your help, baby won't come," Clarissa said. "I've arranged an automobile from Mr. Wildfire's Persian friends."

On a raggedy bed in a tenement in Chicago's Black Belt, George's other woman, June, sweated and groaned, her stringy yellow hair a knotted mess. She clutched a *mojo* pouch of good-luck charms that Redwood had given her: nine strands of devil's shoestring and a lodestone from a lightning strike. Clarissa and Abbaseh, the Persian woman Aidan said was a musician, stood at the head of the bed, holding June's arms, breathing with her. Redwood was crouched between her legs. The room was smaller than it looked from on the railing. The ceiling was low; the dirty walls leaned in too close. June's three children, two boys and a gal, watched anxiously but quietly from a doorway. Iris hovered over them, stroking the youngest gal who was 'bout to break out in tears. She looked at Redwood with naked hope.

Redwood hung her head. June's baby didn't *want* to come. Redwood couldn't argue with that tonight. Why be born to lies and misery? You could be beloved by the spirit in everything; you could pull pain, snatch lightning out the sky, ride comets through the night, even hear the ancestors telling their stories to the wind, and still, it wouldn't be enough to *save* you. With all her hoodoo power, could Garnett Phipps really change anything, make anything better? Acting, singing her heart out, healing folks, Redwood had been running. *Running won't set you free.* What about her soul?

Aidan Cooper had walked back into her life with Baby Sister, both of them grinning at who she used to be. Lying in bed, Aidan hugged and squeezed a memory; he kissed the gal who rode the Ferris Wheel, had fireworks in her eyes, and conjured a bright destiny. Redwood wasn't that gal anymore. She'd snapped a man's neck and turned into a haint. She didn't dare feel herself, didn't dare feel Aidan. *Running won't set you free. On the loose and-a acting brave, in shackles you just don't see.*

"Don't worry," Clarissa said to June. "Redwood Phipps is a powerful midwife. She knows just what to do."

"Well . . ." Redwood had too much on her mind to be bringing a new life into the world. And this baby was turned the wrong direction, kicking with fat feet against being born to misery. Redwood wiped at sweat dripping into her eyes. "I don't know. Maybe you should get a doctor. Dr. Harris—"

"Naw," June said. "Doctor kill my last baby. I ain't having him kill another one."

"Dr. Harris is not a murderer. Don't talk like that," Clarissa said.

"Ain't his fault. Somebody jinx me."

Redwood glanced at Clarissa and then back to June's frightened eyes.

"I found cross marks, wavy snake lines of salt and red pepper, hemp rope, and sulfur, buried at the bottom of my steps. I don't know how long me and everybody who come here been walking over that mess."

The struggling baby kicked Redwood's searching fingers, and June groaned at a painful contraction. By the time Dr. Harris got here, this child would be dead, maybe June too. Redwood had to clear her mind and focus, like for a show with a difficult audience, or else . . . "From what I feel, this baby's coming in by the foot. That ain't no jinx. It just happens." She cracked an egg into a glass half-full of water, careful to keep the yolk intact. She dropped a needle in it. "We need you on your hands and knees."

"You doing a good spell for me?" June said.

"What you holding in your hand?" June waved the *mojo* charm at her. "See what I'm putting under the bed? If someone want to do you wrong, this'll take away their anger." Redwood set the glass along with Aidan's *Maskókî* hunting knife under June's belly. "Can't pull the pain, you got to feel what you're doing, but cutting through it. Ain't no evil spirits goin' touch your child."

"They say you a witch, but sometimes that's what a good woman need," June said.

"I guess so." While Redwood washed her hands in hot soapy water, Clarissa and Abbaseh wrangled June into the new position.

"What y'all doing? I ain't a cow dropping my calf in the barn."

"Ain't nobody thinking that," Redwood said. "Better for the baby."

"Robert if it's a boy. Violet if it's a girl," June said. "Oh sweet Jesus. I gotta push."

"Then go on. You feel wide open," Redwood said.

June's water broke and the baby's toes appeared. After twenty hours of hard labor, the baby's legs and buttocks came so easily. "I'm pushing," June said.

"Yes you are." Redwood supported the baby's bottom as she spiraled out of her mama.

"It's a girl," Clarissa said. "God has blessed you with a baby girl."

"That's my Violet coming," June shouted.

Redwood let Violet find her way, gently untangling her arms and guiding them out before her head. With a final push from June, Violet's wrinkled face emerged. June turned over and sank into the bed. Redwood held up the newborn, and June cried a gush of tears and snot. Violet's sister and brothers cheered and then hugged each other. Iris beamed at them. Clarissa cut the umbilical cord, and with a final contraction the afterbirth came. Redwood tapped the baby's back. Nothing happened.

Abbaseh spoke in Farsi. "This baby is not breathing."

Redwood cleared the gal's mouth, listened to her heart.

"What you saying?" June gripped Abbaseh. "Is my Violet dead?" She grabbed Clarissa. "What she say?"

With a breech birth, a baby could get tangled in the cord and suffocate. A woman labored a child into the world only to bury it. Redwood had seen this happen too many times. She didn't have the heart to say this to June.

"I don't want my baby to die," June shouted. "Don't let my Violet die. You said no evil spirits could touch her. Didn't she say that?"

Redwood squirmed. Subie always told her, *don't ever say you can do what you can't.*

"Who want to cross a little baby like that?" June repeated this over and over as Clarissa and Abbaseh held on to her.

Wrinkled little Violet looked so peaceful, so beautiful. Why mess in that? Why—

"Violet ain't gone yet," Iris said. "She just not quite here. You gotta call her."

"Call her?" Redwood sputtered. How was she supposed to do that? "Well, Mama say, blow breath into 'em if they don't wanna take it themselves."

"Do it then! Blow! Do something!" Everybody jumped at Clarissa's harsh tone. "You can't let bad spirits have this child."

Abbaseh nodded. The children stood silently in the doorway. Iris had her arms 'round the little one. Through the window Redwood spied the boneyard baron, ambling down the street, tapping a diamond-tipped cane on cobblestone.

"You gotta hurry," Iris said. She saw the baron too.

June cried and thrashed. "Please."

You can act, can't you? Subie's voice made the baron waver. *Act like you believe what you're doing and you will.*

Redwood blew in Violet's mouth several times. "Violet, if you swinging between life and death, trying to make up your mind, this place be ready for you. This place is your home. This place got good people who been waiting on you, who love you, your mama, your sister, your brothers, all of us, and that sure do make life beautiful. Don't go on your way till you know love." Redwood's throat clenched. She'd been talking to herself as much as to Violet. She blew again.

A distraught June slapped Clarissa in the mouth trying to struggle out the bed. Abbaseh managed to hold both of June's arms while Clarissa stumbled away from her. Redwood was ready to blow one more time, but Violet opened her eyes and gurgled.

"She's alive," Clarissa said.

Violet's powerful voice filled the room.

"What I tell you?" Iris said.

Trembling, Redwood placed Violet on her mama's belly.

Chattering away, Clarissa, Iris, and Abbaseh raced down the steps into the alley outside June's place. Redwood was moving slow. She paused in the doorway, feeling heavy, exposed, all inside out. The boneyard baron pushed an empty swing on the porch. It banged her hip and went still. "No one for you to claim this time."

Clarissa came back for her. "What a pretty speech you used to call Violet. Poetry. What do you mean, you've lost your good magic?"

Redwood grabbed Clarissa's arm. "What you do against June?" Clarissa squirmed but Redwood wouldn't let her go. "Tell me."

"I asked you for a charm to hold George. You wouldn't give me one," Clarissa said.

"I won't help you cross nobody."

"Mambo Dupree said it was just to keep George in *my* bed instead of June's."

"That woman ought to be ashamed of herself. Shame on you too."

"I know it's not Christian, and I would never, *never* buy a charm to hurt that woman or her baby, but I was desperate."

Redwood sighed. "Violet coming that way wasn't your fault."

"Really?" Clarissa sniffled. "It could have been."

"You have to talk to George. Work this out. You can't conjure nobody into loving you the way you want."

"Is that so? Mr. Wildfire was in your bed the first night."

Redwood's face stung. Clarissa might as well have slapped her.

"Oh my goodness." Clarissa covered her mouth. "He didn't change anything for you, did he? You still can't—" She waved her hand.

"You should have knocked." Redwood stormed away.

"I did, but, I'm sorry. I . . . don't know how to be anymore."

They hurried to catch up with Iris and Abbaseh who were already in the motorcar.

"Why you carting colored folk 'round?" Iris said as Mr. McGregor opened the door for Clarissa.

"No one else would hire me. I have a dark past," he replied.

Iris looked enchanted. "Will you tell me 'bout it sometime?"

"You certainly shall not, Mr. McGregor." Clarissa put on a face for everybody's questioning eyes. "You must thank your husband for loaning us his automobile in the middle of the night," she said to Abbaseh, who smiled in reply.

"Is the wee one all right then?" Mr. McGregor asked.

"Why yes, she is." Clarissa stepped inside. "My sister-in-law is the best midwife I have ever seen."

Redwood fell to her knees. She shoved her fingers in the gravel. A sudden wind blew dirt through her hair as she clawed the ground and split her skin on stone. Stunned, Mr. McGregor offered her a hand, but she smacked him away. Iris squealed. Abbaseh jumped up, speaking Farsi too fast for sense. Redwood rubbed dirt against her chest. She couldn't stop herself—felt like a demon had taken her over.

"What's wrong?" Mr. McGregor kept his distance.

"She's always dramatic." Clarissa stepped with Abbaseh back out of the car.

"That's how show people are," Iris said to Mr. McGregor, leaping by him too.

"What are you carrying on for?" Clarissa hissed in Redwood's ears. "Your power has come back to you." It took her, Abbaseh, and Iris to get Redwood standing back up. Mumbling something strong, Abbaseh brushed off the dirt and plucked tiny stones out of Redwood's skin.

"We best be going on." Mr. McGregor glanced 'round the dark alley. "People here have a hungry eye."

"I'm fine." Redwood pulled away from them. "I said I'm all right."

Abbaseh and Clarissa reluctantly took their seats.

"Come on," Iris said, slipping her arm through Redwood's. "I know you can get to the other side of sad."

"Show people?" Redwood hissed at her. "How could you talk such foolishness?"

Iris whispered too. "I was just trying to help."

"Well, don't. Not that way."

"*They* don't know what it mean to have the baron challenge you," Iris replied, her lips trembling. "Miz Subie say, a conjure woman risk everything doing a *death-defying* spell."

"No denying that." Besting the baron should've put Redwood in a better mood. "Sorry, I don't mean to scold you." Iris got her onto the leather seat while Mr. McGregor cranked the motor. Without mentioning the blood she was dripping on the fancy interior, he sped away.

After several blocks of silence Clarissa said, "Speak your mind. You've given everybody a terrible fright, and they would sorely like to help you."

"I'm sorry," Redwood said. "I don't know what to tell you." There was a trick on her body, and she didn't know how to get it off.

"Sister has a dark past, like Mr. McGregor." Iris kissed Redwood's bloody palm. "I wish I could do like you, heal with a kiss, but I can't."

"What good is power if you can't save your ownself?" Redwood said.

Chicago swallowed time up. Everything in the city went too fast. A week gone, and what did Aidan have to show for it? A thousand miles from Georgia, and nightriders were still haunting him and Redwood both. Mountainous dark clouds rolled over the sun and turned daylight dull gray. Aidan didn't usually read fortune from nature, but rumbling thunder and sharp wind set him on edge as he and Redwood marched through the gate of the motion picture factory.

"Hold up." He set down a raw wood rocking chair and a painted altar and worked the circulation back into his hand. He had a bad feeling 'bout coming to see Mr. Payne. Rich white folks always thought he was trash—so what good would it do Redwood to have him along?

A tent blew over, and soldier-actors ran from their open-air battle scene to take cover. Enemies no more, they huddled together against the coming downpour.

"That storm come up out of nowhere," Aidan said.

People stared at him and Red all 'cross Chicago town, and now they gawked here too. Aidan laughed in the pinched face of a young white actor made up like a wounded Union cavalryman. What could this fellow possibly be imagining that was so awful he had to scowl and mutter at them? Aidan had expected more from northerners.

Redwood didn't pay the cavalryman—or any of them—no mind. She marched on like a queen of Dahomey. She had on blue satin and silks that surged 'round her hips. A blue lace blouse rustled with each breath. Her hair was done up like a bouquet of flowers; her face was painted with the hues of sunset. Aidan wore a suit Clarissa had *borrowed* from George. It was the latest fashion for rich gents, fine cloth and a clean line. George had more bulk than Aidan, but Clarissa tailored it to fit him with a few stitches here and there. Fancy new shoes were light on his feet, giving a real bounce to his step.

"I guess we are a spectacle," Aidan said.

Redwood stopped midstride and turned to him. He almost ran her over. "You sure you not mad at me?" She sounded mad herself.

"Your third time asking," Aidan replied. "You want me to be mad? Would it help?"

"No. No. I just—"

"I'm a mean drunk with an awful temper. I can get so mad I don't remember what I've done." He pulled out Subie's medicine tin and put a pinch of powder in his mouth. "You just ain't seen it."

"You don't scare me."

"Good. It's mutual."

"Besides, all that Crazy Coop nonsense is behind you, right?"

"Yes, ma'am." He grimaced. The nasty medicine took the taste out his tongue.

"Really?" She grabbed the hand holding the tin. "I bet you want a drink right now."

"Big difference between wanting something real bad and doing it."

She let go of his hand. "Yes. Yes, there is."

"I ain't goin' fight with you, Miz Redwood. Fighting won't do us no good. Believe me, 'cause I done plenty of fighting."

Drops of rain splashed her eyes. "I couldn't bear *his* child growing in me." She spoke in his ear. "Now maybe I can't have nobody's baby. Is that the woman you want?"

"No children?" Aidan shuddered in spite of hisself. "You certain?"

"No, but only thing certain in this world is death."

"I only been here a week and you trying to drive me away?"

"I ain't trying to drive you nowhere."

"Yes, you are. Why?"

Her breath sparked. She looked angry enough to catch fire.

"It's that business with Jerome. 'Cause I didn't get there in time, 'cause I didn't—"

"Shame on you. How could you think I blame you for what he did? Or for what they did to Mama?"

Despite feeling shamed of this very thought, Aidan kept staring her in the eye.

"Don't be using me to feel bad 'bout what you ain't done in this world."

"I tole everybody you run north with Jerome to get married in New York City."

"I know you a conjure man to get 'em to believe that lie."

"It was easier than you think."

A tiny white ball whizzed over their heads and startled them apart. Behind Redwood, two Sioux men in war bonnets and battle regalia used round wooden paddles to bat a ball back and forth on a tabletop. Unconcerned with the weather, several other Sioux warriors watched the game with cavalrymen and two Russian Cossacks in dress uniform. An older Indian man in street clothes nodded at Aidan. It was the fellow he'd met at the train station coming into Chicago. Aidan nodded back.

"Walter Jumping Bear and them are shooting a stagecoach raid and a massacre," Redwood said. "They gotta wait till the sun come back."

"Who wanna see all that?" Aidan muttered.

Redwood balled up her storm hand. "What if I'm bad for you, Aidan?"

"Let's go on in." He couldn't hear such talk. He'd rather fight with her. "Payne's waiting for us."

Inside a crammed office, reels of film, jars of chemicals, and broken cameras looked ready to fall on Mr. Payne, a tall, gangly white man with fierce Abraham Lincoln features. "An all-colored romance? Well, a pirate picture could be good." Payne dodged Redwood to reach Aidan, who stood between the raw wood rocking chair and painted altar. Payne inspected his handiwork. "You're a fine carpenter and fast, Mr. . . . ?"

"Cooper," Redwood said. "Mr. Aidan Cooper."

Aidan eyed Redwood. "Pirate loves the schoolteacher. It's a grand idea."

"Irish? Irish do good stage work." Payne talked on top of Aidan. "The wood was knotty and warped, but you got around that."

"Colored pay their nickel same as everyone else," Aidan said.

"Don't you think colored people are funny, Mr. Cooper?" Payne laughed till a cough racked him. "You have to admit though, it is hard to take 'em in a serious story."

"Well, sir, I think that's just what you're used to. I read a lot of serious colored stories, and—"

"You're a sharp fellow. I didn't think you'd get it done on time." Payne ran his finger along the altar. "What part of Georgia are you from?"

"I come up from Peach Grove. It's kinda out of the way."

"I'll bet." Payne chuckled. "Up here in Chicago and back East, folks got a taste for chicken coop comedies, for cowboys and *Injuns*, just like in Georgia."

"Folks got a taste for a lot of things," Redwood said, as if spitting out poison.

Payne sat heavily in the rocker. "What the hell can I do about that?"

"William Foster is going after all the colored vaudevillians. They're happy to work with a colored director, but his picture ain't 'bout adventure or romance or something grand."

Payne snapped at her. "If that Negro Foster doesn't want you, I hear Selig's moving his operation to California, chasing sunny days where he can shoot all year long. He might have you."

"Why fire me *and* Saeed? I had that she-lion in her cage, no call to shoot her dead."

"Who said anything about that darned lion?"

Payne and Redwood glared at one another. Her silk and satin skirt turned to a torrent of blue-green water, streaming from her waist to the floor. Stunned, Payne reached for the flowing fabric. Aidan strode between them.

"Miz Redwood couldn't just stand there and let that she-cat run rampage."

"Exactly!" Payne said. "The lioness was a rogue even back in the cage. A rogue is no use to us. Better off dead." With no warning, he hurled the rocker out the window. It landed one story below in front of two cowboys, unbroken.

"Damn," Aidan said. Redwood claimed Payne didn't have no sense, but—

"Damn indeed!" Payne hoisted the altar over his head.

The cowboys below shouted and cussed, then hushed when they saw Payne fuming in the window. They dodged the furiously rocking chair like it might bite 'em. Even after such harsh treatment, not a screw was loose. Take more than a short fall to bust something Aidan made.

"See. I can do pretty and sturdy." Aidan gritted his teeth.

"We don't need sturdy, Mr. Cooper." Payne dumped the altar. It fell on its side intact. "We need things that look good and break easy."

Redwood rolled her eyes and sucked her teeth, but she did settle down. Her skirt was satin again, yet still cold as storm water when it brushed against Aidan's fists. She put a cool hand on his clenched shoulders. Aidan wanted to slug Payne, wanted to feel his face break under his knuckles, wanted to slam into his gut and take his last stinking breath. Fighting would sure *feel* good, even if it wouldn't *do* no good.

"Mr. Cooper can build it any way you want." She slipped her arm through Aidan's, cozier than she'd gotten in days.

"Is that so?" Payne lifted an eyebrow.

"Yes, sir." Aidan wasn't flying off the handle like a broken axe head over this fool.

"I've hired more woodsmiths than I know what to do with." Payne had the nerve to sit down behind his desk and grin at them. "I'm jealous, Mr. Cooper."

Aidan scowled, ready to hurt him for sure if he thought of laying a finger on—

"Sequoia says you're an actor too." Payne grinned. "You've got a bushel of talent."

"I've—I've done some time singing for folks, and I guess I could act if I had to."

"You've got the right look, wild, dark, handsome. You got a lot of spirit too, I can see that. A moment ago you were ready to slit my throat with that knife on your hip. It was all over your face, don't deny it. I guess I got Sequoia to thank for the blood still in my veins." He laughed. "That's a bit of an exaggeration."

Aidan didn't deny wanting to murder him. "I heard tell you were coughing yourself to death, till *Sikwayi* pulled the chill out your lungs."

Payne sighed. "You have a face for the camera, Mr. Cooper. You could play a half-breed *Injun* or a robber who ain't so bad. *Robin Hood*'s a story I'd like to make. Have you heard of *Robin Hood*?"

"Stealing from rich lords to give to the poor," Aidan said.

"I never believed that story," Redwood muttered.

Payne ignored her. "How are you with a sword, Mr. Cooper?"

"I can handle a shotgun and a knife. I never had cause to pick up a sword."

"Are you good on a horse?"

"He can ride anything," Redwood said.

"Real Wild West *Injuns* can't do a character. Got to have an actor for that." Payne chortled. "Give the audience a handsome rogue dashing about."

"I guess they don't want a Seminole farmer riding the rail to his ladylove." Aidan stared at Redwood.

"Is that another harebrained story idea?" Payne looked confused. "I thought you wanted to do pirates."

"It doesn't matter," Redwood said. "You know what folks want to see."

"I do." Payne winced. "The way of the world is against us, Sequoia," he said softly.

"Us?" Redwood let go of Aidan and strode close to Payne. "What us?"

"People are running shy from working here. I'm in a bad fix. I lost two actors last night in a brawl. Both shot and killed, over a . . . woman." He escaped Redwood and sidled up to Aidan. "I pay thirty-five dollars a week," he said and then whispered, "forty if you can get Sequoia to call the hoodoo spell off. That's generous."

Aidan turned to Redwood. "I could get us a piece of land and farm. You could heal folks. We don't need to do this."

"A man could take care of a family in high style with that money. Tell Mr. Cooper he won't find a better deal." Payne laid a week's salary in a clear space on his desk. "That's forty-five dollars I'll give you in advance. Fifty a week if you work out."

Aidan never had anybody try to bribe him out of his good sense. "I don't know."

Redwood circled Payne. "I can't tell you what to do, Aidan, but, save enough and we can make our own picture. White folk got adventure and romance. Why're we stuck in the coon academy?"

She turned to Aidan, looking like a young fearless gal on a rainy hilltop, reaching out her hand to grab the lightning. Hadn't he promised to *believe* in her? Even with her heart torn up, even hurting bad, wasn't she holding on to him?

"If it mean that much to you," Aidan mumbled.

"Don't you just love her?" Payne shook Aidan's hand. "I need you to start today." Sunlight streamed through the window. "Storm's over. We got several good shooting hours left. I'd appreciate you getting us back on schedule, Mr. Cooper."

Before Aidan knew what he was doing, before he could register how bad it'd make him feel, he was half-naked, sitting on a horse with a painted face and feather headdress 'bout to ambush a wagon train of white settlers. Behind him was Walter Jumping Bear and a band of similarly ferocious savages. Nicolai nodded from above his camera. Aidan whooped, raised a spear, and charged.

TWENTY

Stumbling out the back door of George's house, Aidan snorted bad air. The Chicago night stank, even after smelling it for a year. A lot of bluster and too many factories farting poison, too much meat rotting on the hoof—Aidan wished he could close his nose with a lid against the stench.

"We're not really related." Thirteen-year-old Frank sneered at Iris. Wearing long breeches, a fancy hat, and Sunday-going-to-meeting shoes on Tuesday, he swaggered through lilacs, smacking plump blossoms.

Iris tugged an ill-fitting dress. "Everybody's related!" She stomped her feet, splattering him with dirt and worms. "That's what it means to be alive. Master of Breath give everybody a piece of spirit . . ."

"Good grief! My *real* father would have a proper lady for a sister, not some backcountry fool full of superstition and lies!" Frank shoved her.

Iris shoved back. "Biology ain't lies. Mr. Darwin say everybody be in the human race together."

"What do you know? You can't even speak properly." Frank took off at Aidan's approach.

Aidan squeezed her shoulders. "How 'bout a story or a song tonight?"

"I'm too tuckered out from school."

"I'll only be a minute in the shed." He banged it open. "You too tired to listen?"

"They make fun of you too." Iris bounded over George's vegetables and slammed the kitchen door.

"Damn it!" Aidan hoisted the chair he'd made for Clarissa. Hurrying out the shed, he stumbled over boxes, tools, and a rolled-up Persian rug—a present from Prince Anoushiravan who was riding the rail to California and everywhere else. Thinking of all that open country, Aidan was jealous. "Good for him."

Aidan rubbed a bruised thigh. Never enough room to move in

Chicago. Always so many stacks of this and that; so many shopkeepers, factory workers, hucksters, and day laborers; too many trolleys and autos coming and going, speeding to nowhere. Funny languages shouted at you, weird faces screwed up in disgust or god knows what. Folk pressed together too tight, but nobody touching. Aidan couldn't hardly stand it. Walter Jumping Bear told him he'd get used to it soon enough. That was several months ago. Soon didn't seem to be coming.

"Watch where you're going, Chief!" George shouted.

Aidan halted by a patch of kale. "You the one tramping in the flowers."

George snorted and stalked from the lily of the valley on into the street. He was working late tonight, again.

Aidan set the new chair in the kitchen. Clarissa broke into a smile. "Why, you shouldn't have gone to so much trouble." She squeezed Aidan's hand. "I'm surprising George with a late supper. Man won't stop to eat otherwise." She dashed off.

Aidan trudged toward Redwood's back parlor room. After making a fool of hisself in front the camera all day, he was stiff and aching, like he'd been behind a plow, breaking rock-hard soil. Redwood was in Clarissa's modern bathroom, soaking in a tub after finally hunting down a show that would have her. Months of begging, and it was just more darky wench and chicken foolishness—made Aidan want to spit and cuss. Redwood had Iris laughing at Saeed playing an ornery mule and even got a harmony out of her on a show tune. Aidan was jealous. Cooning didn't tarnish Red's spirit and Iris was too shy, too something to sing with him anymore.

He switched on the electric light and caught hisself grinning, hair blowing in the wind. Doc's drawings hung over Redwood's writing desk now. She insisted Aidan looked every bit a dashing moving picture star. Indeed, Mr. Payne was so pleased with his work onscreen, he'd lined up a string of wild *Injun* projects. "A handsome savage is better than an ugly one," Payne declared. "Women are swooning for you. A secret, naughty thrill in a dark theatre."

Aidan's stomach churned. He wished the pay was as good for real life as it was for fantasy. He slumped on the floor by the bed, his head empty and his heart heavy. No denying the money in his pockets, and surely he wouldn't be doing naughty *Injun* thrills forever. Doing it at all, though, and living in George's house was worse than taking nasty medicine ten times a day. George hadn't said more than three civil words to Aidan since he arrived last year, and that was only due to Clarissa's prodding. Good thing the man was always out making deals and hardly home, or he and Aidan might have come to blows and killed each other by now.

"Yes, God is very good, but never dance in a small boat." Aidan spoke Aislinn's warning out loud, enjoying his mama's Irish wit, even as worry hit him. All the mess he and Redwood had to put up with, Iris too, and still he didn't see how they'd ever make a motion picture play. And how would they break the curses trailing them from Georgia? Batting these doubts away, Aidan banged into Redwood's newspaper collection stacked by the bed. A *New York Times* article tumbled into his lap:

MARTIANS BUILD TWO IMMENSE CANALS IN TWO YEARS
Vast Engineering Works Accomplished in an Incredibly Short Time by Our Planetary Neighbors
Wonders of the September Sky.

Staring at photos of a balding Professor Percival Lowell, his Flagstaff Observatory, and Martian canal drawings, Aidan wondered what Doc would make of Martians and their engineering genius. Aidan's nerves tingled thinking on some stringy body grown tall in shallow gravity walking on the red soil of the evening star, looking over to Earth, and maybe wondering 'bout the folks living 'cross the sky. Did Earth look blue like the sky? Or green like the forests? Or maybe you couldn't see none of that when you were so far away? Maybe it was just a sparkly grey pebble in the sky.

He leaned into the pillows and caught a whiff of lily of the valley, rosemary oil, and Redwood's sweet scent. He spied his old pistol next to Garnett's music box on the nightstand. The gun was clean, but empty. He smiled. Redwood said it brought her good luck, long as there weren't bullets to tempt her. Aidan picked up the music box. The false bottom came undone and money fell onto the bed. Aidan whistled, fingering tight bundles of bills. All they'd been doing for the past year was chasing a paycheck; he'd hardly found time to think, to keep counsel with hisself. The Martians tickled his fancy. He dug up a fountain pen and his red leather journal to ponder visitors from another world. Flipping to blank pages, he came upon the envelope from Caroline Williams to Jerome and his wife.

"Oh hell!" Aidan dropped it and bolted up. He'd forgotten this damned letter.

He peered down the hall. Nobody in sight and the house was still. The nanny had gone home early to call on her ailing grandmama. The children were asleep. Redwood was still singing in the tub with Iris, sounding good too. Satisfied he had a few moments alone, Aidan tore the envelope open. Unfolding the letter, ten one-hundred-dollar gold certificates drifted to the bed. A fortune!

"Blood money." Miz Williams truly trusted Aidan to be a good man, to *do right*. "That's harder than you think, ma'am." He glanced at her stiff handwriting:

> *Dear Jerome,*
> *I'm sure you must have a family by now and need money but you're just too proud to say. I don't want to know where you are, but Mr. Cooper has been good enough to deliver this to you and your wife. Of course I don't approve of what you're doing, and frankly I don't know why any woman in her right mind would have you, even a colored one. But I am your mother. You are my eldest son and I love you.*

Aidan crumpled the paper before reading the last lines. Promising to deliver this was a kindness to an old woman grieving her son. But he didn't need more of the past to come spooking him like an angry haint. He grabbed a match from the mantel and set the letter on fire.

"What you doing?" Redwood said from the doorway as flames flared up. She cinched one of Clarissa's elegant robes tight. Curls of hair hanging 'round her face got tighter in the moist air.

He tossed the burning paper into the fireplace. "I need to fix the hinge on your mama's box," he said. "Thought I'd add some money to what you got saved."

"Quite a stake you handing over." She inspected a gold certificate. "I ain't for sale, you know."

"Why you say something like that to me?"

"I don't know. I feel mean." She dropped the money. "I done lost my magic. I used to be—"

"You still are. Think on baby Violet."

"Don't tell me who I am."

"I can't say nothing right to you."

"Power ain't magic." She put the money back in the bottom of the box. "We got to raise five times what's here, even with your gold." She sounded weary. "You so cold you need a fire? Close the window. I like the air is all, don't need it open."

"Air is fine by me."

"George say I ought to put my money in a bank and get interest."

"George always know how to make the most out of whatever you got."

"Chicago's hardly a Midway Fair of dreams."

"A dream ain't a place to go to; it's what you do."

Redwood had lightning in her eyes and tears, yet half a smile curved her lips. "Ain't that the truth?" Shimmy-shaking, she grabbed Aidan's hand.

"What you up to?"

She danced him 'cross the room, bumping into furniture and books. The silky white robe billowed against her damp thighs like clouds passing in the night. Suddenly the walls fell away and the ceiling was gone. A dark new moon loomed above them, a dusky gray disk in inky black. Beyond that was more stars than Aidan had ever imagined. Not just shiny white specks, but spirals of brilliant color too. He and Redwood spun 'round, and a bright blue ball with swirls of white and splotches of brown filled up the dark. Aidan laughed, but there was no sound, just cold filling his lungs, turning his eyes to ice. Redwood stomped against the floor. Aidan looked down at her feet and then up. A flying serpent dashed through the Milky Way, fluttered its wings and settled into the painted ceiling over their heads.

"What you do?" Aidan gasped warm air.

"Ain't just me." Redwood poked him. "It's what we do together. I don't even know how."

"Better than a hot-air balloon." He gathered his magic, wild woman in his arms.

She leaned into him, damp and soft and smooth from the bath. Her heart was racing. Her breath was cold. "It's only a ride though." She pulled away and sat down, a heavy weight, sinking into the mattress. He sat next to her and stroked her face. She closed her eyes on his hand. "Where we goin' find five, six thousand dollars, 'less we both keep cooning?"

He bowed his head, shamed of his own doubt and worry. "It ain't no easy spell conjuring this moving picture, but you ain't thinking 'bout giving up, are you?"

"Now why would I be doing that?" Redwood eased her face from his hand. "Sometimes, I feel far away from myself is all."

He clenched his jaw. Jerome's dead eyes flickered in the fire. Aidan walked to the window seat, closed the shutters, and curled up in the cushions there.

"Ain't just what Jerome done to me, you know." Redwood read his thoughts. "It's also what I did—"

"What kind of foolishness is that? I won't listen to you talk yourself down!" He threw what she used to tell him back at her. "You did what you had to do!"

"You don't understand."

"Naw, I don't agree with you! That's different."

She shook her head and said no more. He was bone tired, too weary to fight with her. The deep breath of sleep claimed him quickly.

Redwood snuck out the back door; her skin was itchy, her blood heavy, her heart raw and achy. *The lioness clawed her side and golden eyes went dark.* Redwood groaned and dashed 'cross slippery cobblestones. She passed some fool humming *Running won't set you free.* "Well damn it," she tried cussing like Aidan. "What the hell will?" Foul language just made her feel worse. She ran faster.

Clarissa would've said Redwood was being too dramatic, too histrionic, but this was no vaudeville act. Since the lioness died in her arms, since Aidan, and Iris too, hit Chicago town, she couldn't pretend she was fine when she wasn't. Redwood needed to find someone to take the trick off her body. Even a powerful conjure woman couldn't pull her own pain. But from a little girl, Redwood hated asking anybody for help. When she was beloved by the spirit in everything, help just came to her. Now she'd have to pay for it . . .

Redwood hurried through a dark alley in Chicago's Black Belt. She stopped at the sound of gravel crunching under boot heels and turned. Nobody. Shadows wavered in the wind. Curtains blew through tight little windows. Scraggly trees swept crooked branches against the brick backs of tenement buildings. Whoever was following her could disappear in the middle of an empty street.

"Show yourself," she shouted.

Pigeons cooed in a chorus and swooped to a tangle of wires above her.

It was late. Aidan was sleeping like the dead, Iris and the other children too. Redwood had left George and Clarissa rocking their springs and groaning 'bout how much they love one another. If it wasn't any of them on her tail, she didn't know who it could be. Everybody else usually know better than to chase after her. Even bad men didn't bother Redwood Phipps, with thunder and storm on her heels.

"What you after?" she asked the darkness. "Man touch me against my will, end up dead." Perhaps she heard a startled breath. "I don't want to go where I'm going. You shouldn't either." She pulled her Persian robe tight against her ribs and sped on.

Winona Dupree claim she was a New Orleans mambo—a *Vodou* priestess bringing good fortune and health to those who come to her with harsh troubles and a heavy purse. Rich colored women who secretly held to the old ways were happy to buy *gris-gris* charms from Mambo Dupree. She had fair skin and straight white hair and made sure everyone knew she was a quadroon: colored, Indian, French, and Spanish. Clarissa had bought charms from her to hold George and cross his other women. How could Redwood be running to her?

The Dupree house was rude-looking on the outside—peeling paint, rotten wood, and tipping to the right, but inside the front gate, altars to the *Loa*, the *Vodou* spirit-deities, made everybody tremble with fear and respect. Sacred charms were etched on the walls and ground: skulls and bones; fire, water, and lightning shapes; crossroad signs; and serpents circling the tree of life. Miz Subie called these *vèvés*—spells to call down *Vodou* spirits.

Redwood lifted the brass knocker but hesitated. She set it down softly and backed away. Too late to escape. The door screeched as rusty hinges protested a late-night visit. Mambo Dupree thrust a candle in her eyes.

"As I live and breathe, Redwood Phipps at my door."

Mambo Dupree wore white robes and carried a bowl of bright-colored flowers. Spicy incense and heavy perfume made Redwood woozy. In the hallway behind her, paintings of the *Loa*, of sweet Haitian saints and dark-tempered tricksters, danced in the flickering candlelight. These figures, with swords through their hearts and skulls on their hats, laughed in Redwood's startled face. Snakes wiggled at the *Loa*'s feet and 'round their necks. A crown of fire sat on a woman's head and did not burn her.

"What you want of this *Vodou* queen?" Mambo Dupree didn't invite Redwood in. Who could blame her? It was no secret that Redwood spoke against selling charms to cross an enemy or a rival.

"I gotta talk to somebody." Redwood had written Miz Subie ten letters since Aidan and Iris come up, telling all her troubles and woe. She was too ashamed to send even one.

"Sneaking here late, ain't even a moon to see you by."

"That was the idea." No use denying truth.

"A man murdered three women yesterday at the end of this street." As Mambo Dupree spoke, the spirits settled back into the walls. "You must be desperate to walk danger. Has the baron been chasing you, or just a spirit of the dead?"

"I got a trick on my body won't let me find love."

Mambo Dupree looked her up and down. "I ain't surprised at that."

"Can you do a body healing? Or are you just a flimflam snake-oil woman?"

"Rude gal! Why you at my door, if you don't *believe*?"

Redwood had swallowed her pride, not her good sense. "I—"

"You hate asking for help, don't you?" Mambo Dupree sniffed her flowers as Redwood squirmed. "You have plenty magic, me only a little bit."

"What you mean?"

"You a busy conjure woman, up onstage every night, telling one lie after the other, and people pay you plenty." Mambo Dupree waved the candle 'round Redwood's face. "You mad over the dimes I earn?" Clarissa's friends complained of the price they had to pay, but they always seemed eager to keep going back.

"Dimes? Not what I heard." Redwood had come with a sack of money, stolen from their motion picture stash.

"Rich ladies like to exaggerate." Mambo Dupree smiled purple-stained teeth. "Make bitter medicine taste better."

"What proof that you won't take my money and give me foolishness, but no cure?"

"All right, for proof, I'll give you the cure for free."

"Free?" Redwood grunted. "Okay."

Mambo Dupree roared a good laugh. "What you can't respect ain't goin' help you, gal. Don't let your life be ruled by what you fear." She slammed the door in Redwood's face. On the ground was a doll with pins stuck in its wooly head. Redwood snatched it up. Mambo Dupree sold these to fools who wanted to hurt their enemies.

"Give 'em dolls to prick," Miz Subie said once 'bout *Vodou gris-gris,* *"better than sticking knives in somebody's gut."*

As Redwood put the doll in her bag, a shadow slipped into a doorway beside the Dupree house. Bright eyes flashed. "Who is that? Iris?" No answer came but Redwood could feel Baby Sister. She was spooky like Mama, there and not there at the same time. "Searching for a cure like a thief in the night, what do I expect?" She shoved a few bills under Mambo Dupree's door and headed home.

Redwood tiptoed into the back parlor. Aidan was still on the window seat, snoring. She was cold and damp and felt ridiculous holding the bedraggled *Vodou* doll. Its hair was falling out and a button eye was missing. *Vodou* was close kin to hoodoo, but it was a religion she didn't practice. So, what *did* she believe?

Aidan shivered and fussed as if a chill had entered his dream. Redwood threw a blanket over him. Startled, he opened his eyes. "What?" he said sleepily.

"Maybe we could work up a show for the Ace of Spades Hotel," she said. "Find routines for your new songs."

"Sure." He yawned and rubbed his eyes. "When I ain't dead tired and half asleep."

"And I can show you and Iris the Chicago sights, like I promised."

"I know you been busy . . ." He was snoring again.

Redwood sat over him through the night.

It was weeks before Aidan would agree to play music at Saeed's. Then the trolley was on the blink and that was just the excuse he needed to back out. Iris raced into the front hall as he was hemming and hawing with Redwood.

"I don't want to go!" She gripped Aidan's arm, hanging on to him like a child.

"We're not having this argument," Redwood said.

Iris whispered in Aidan's ear. "I've read more than any of them teachers, but since I don't agree with 'em, they say I'm stupid."

"They're jealous," Aidan muttered. "You just gotta go and stick up for yourself."

"Georgia's in my mouth. Nothing else matters." Her dress had a rip at the hem.

"You been fighting too?" he said.

"The other kids started it." Iris pouted. "I hate going there."

Redwood lifted an eyebrow at Aidan like this was all his fault. "What you got to say?"

"You don't have to like everything that's good for you," he said. "And you don't have to fit in with fools. Just learn what you can."

Iris thrust his banjo at him. "You play better than anybody in Chicago. I'll go if you go." No arguing with that. Iris grinned at Redwood.

The elevated train was ripping and roaring right through Chicago town, going twenty miles an hour at least, streaking between brick and stone and sounding like the end of the world.

Redwood pressed her lips to Aidan's ear. "Is this really your first time?"

"Yes, indeed." Aidan held on to his hat even though inside the train, the air was still and heavy. Outside, giant skyscrapers loomed above storefronts and apartment dwellings, blotted the sun for a moment, and then faded quickly from view. Chicago's two-million-plus inhabitants bustled through morning streets in a colorful, blurry knot.

Maybe the train was doing thirty miles an hour.

"Whizzing along up high, we're flying, getting the birds' view." Aidan had to shout at Redwood to be heard. "Ain't the same as tracks on the ground."

Redwood smoothed her silky pants and shouted too. "I'm glad the trolley cables were all knotted up today. The El is quite a ride. We're not goin' be late after all."

Passengers gawked at her long legs and masculine attire, at the Persian turban on her head, the *mojo* bag at her waist, and the African fabric 'round her neck. Aidan was used to her style. He wouldn't have her any other way, but he couldn't stand the evil looks or the hungry eyes crawling over her bosom and behind.

"This old thing rattles like it's ready to fall down." An older white woman in a smart gray jacket and skirt spoke to Redwood. "A train jumped the track yesterday and fell into the middle of the road. Two people almost died."

"That is too bad." Redwood waved the image away. "This one's got a bit more life."

The El pulled into a rickety station perched among old brick houses. Aidan spied rotten wood and rusty joints. Clean white sheets flapped on a taut laundry line. A man in thin long johns ate his breakfast on a third-floor porch. He chomped a fat sausage, washed it down with a steaming mug, and scratched his rear end. Aidan grinned.

"It's so dirty in here." The old woman squirmed on a brown paper sack. "Do you know what you're sitting in?"

"Just as well that I don't." Redwood waved at big-eyed children staring in their compartment.

As the train pulled out, Aidan inspected splintery walls and grimy windows. Wet filth on the floor had dried into a crust. Most of the seats were coming undone. 'Cross the aisle, some critter had crawled in the stuffing and—

"You have to get off and pay again just to get anywhere." The woman sighed. "They treat upstanding *paying* passengers as if we were poor riffraff. It's criminal."

"Yes, a rich man's dime is usually worth more than a poor man's." Aidan chuckled.

"Excuse me, sir?" The lady looked puzzled.

"The El's carrying me to where I'm going. You too." Redwood beamed at her. "What you complaining for? Are you scared?" She patted the lady's freckled hand. "The moon could tumble out the sky and crash into everything. But it does look pretty rising early, like a white pearl in the morning sky. That's what I want to think on."

"You're in a good mood, girl." The woman looked from her to Aidan. "I guess you have a rich sweetheart showing you the town? That's the way to do it."

The passengers were mostly white folk, and they were all staring now, blue-and green-eyed strangers waiting for Redwood to answer.

"We're going to a rehearsal." Aidan waved the banjo case—a present from Redwood—in their faces. "And then my sweetheart's goin' take me to the sights."

"Show people." The woman nodded as if everything made sense, as if she knew who they were now. "Happy-go-lucky, footloose."

"This is our stop." Redwood pulled Aidan up. "Good day to you, ma'am."

"And to you." The lady smiled at them both. "I'll be looking out for your music."

Redwood jumped to the platform and hurried down the stairs.

"Was she trying to make us feel bad?" Aidan asked.

"She's lonely." Redwood watched the train rush off. "I bet her sweetheart's passed on. Bet he showed her Chicago town once."

On the ground, the street went too slow. Aidan stumbled over the stillness. His eyes wouldn't settle; the background kept hurtling along in a blur. He shifted his banjo case to the other shoulder and kept pace with Redwood's brisk walk.

"Why does Saeed want to live way out here in the suburbs? Take you half a day to walk to anywhere. He has to ride the train all the time and that cost a fortune." She stopped at a row of houses. One ancient maple tree was hanging on, boughs clipped here and there to accommodate cables and wires. Its scraggly leaves were already yellow, and it was only August. No other green growing things, the rest of the street was under asphalt. "Can't smell the lake from here. When the sun goes down there's diddly to do." She fanned her hot face. "I mean no singing and dancing, and Saeed can't get enough of city nightlife. You all right?" She stepped into the sparse shade of the tree. "You haven't said but a couple words all morning."

"I'm happy listening to you," he said as they climbed a few stairs to number 291, Saeed's place. He was too jittery 'bout music-making for good conversation.

"You like it here?" She tilted her head and licked her lips. "In Chicago I mean, up north, away from your swamp stink and starry nights."

He couldn't tell what kind of answer she hoped for. "You teasing me?"

"It's a question." She banged the knocker. When nobody came she rang the doorbell.

"I don't know if I like it yet," he said. "Getting used to the city take time."

"The air's so humid, don't need clouds, just wring it out and it could rain."

"You complaining?" The wet heat made him feel at home. "You like it in Chicago?"

"I don't know either." Redwood looked almost forlorn.

Saeed opened the door. "Welcome." He ushered them in. "I wasn't sure you'd come, Mr. Wildfire."

"That makes two of us," Aidan replied.

"It is a surprise and a pleasure," Saeed said.

"Nothing against you, sir, just—" Aidan hung his hat on a rack shaped like a briar. It looked to have snatched coats and caps from folks running by.

"Iris persuaded him," Redwood said. "He thought he didn't play good enough."

"We can always get better," Saeed said.

Redwood frowned. "That's what I tell you, and you argue with me."

"I am found out—to believe what you say on occasion." Saeed bowed. "I've heard Mr. Wildfire perform and need not take your word for how good he is." The prince's rogue of a brother was certainly a charming fellow. "Follow me. We're in back."

"The trolley was down. Lightning struck the lines last night. We rode the El." Redwood took Saeed's arm and breezed ahead. Aidan hugged his banjo and followed.

Saeed's apartment wasn't at all like his brother's train car. Heavy drapes kept out bright light and hot air. High-ceilinged rooms were cool and dry. Aidan smelled coffee brewing. Fruit, bread, and cheese were on a table at the parlor door. 'Cept for a piano, there was hardly a stick of furniture. No Oriental rug covered the parquet floor. The wood was worn shiny-smooth in the center. How much dancing did Mr. Saeed do? Seeing Aidan and Redwood, a colored man sat down to the keyboard; another one jumped up strumming a guitar; a compatriot of Saeed's set the bow to his fiddle. They were familiar fellows from shows Aidan had seen, but he'd lost their names. They nodded at him and the banjo. His fingers itched and ached. Hoodoo magic is one thing, but spells don't work without practice!

"Are we late?" Redwood asked.

"Everybody else was early," Saeed said.

"Let's get going." Aidan released the banjo from its case and strode to the piano.

"What do we want to do?" Saeed said.

"Start, I guess, and see what happens." Redwood dipped down to the ground and sprang back, warming up for real dancing. Saeed got busy, stretching too.

Aidan played a few licks on the banjo and the fiddle sailed in underneath him. They were lost several moments in the music. "Like on the elevated train, rushing 'round all over the place." Aidan smiled. "But we got to tune." The piano player hit a couple notes, and when Aidan tightened his strings to the right pitch, the fiddle started up fast. The guitar and piano jumped right in. Aidan took his time, taking each player in before his fingers found a few phrases to add.

One song slid into another. Saeed and Redwood danced 'round the room as Aidan traded tunes with the musicians. "Too long since I played." His fingers were tender. Nobody complained of bad notes though. Turn a mistake 'round right; it was bound to sound decent. "This beats raiding a wagon train of settlers any day."

Hours slipped by, and he played his fingers raw. Spots of blood dotted his banjo strings. His neck was stiff and his back muscles cramped. While the other musicians drank coffee laced with strong spirits,

Aidan sipped pomegranate juice—a Persian specialty. Redwood and Saeed guzzled a pitcher of icy lemonade. Everyone gobbled the fruit.

"You sound good, Aidan Wildfire." Redwood slurred her words as if she were drunk. She swayed back and forth on unsteady legs. "How you doing?"

"Playing this music with you all," he said, "well, it feels like coming home."

"Home. Yes." Redwood stood close enough for him to feel the heat from her skin, to have a taste of her in his mouth. Was she trying to drive him crazy?

The doorbell rang. "My guests are arriving early." Saeed disappeared down the hall.

"Is it evening already?" Aidan took a step away from Redwood.

"It's night," the piano player said. "The sun's been down."

The guitarman grunted. "Time ain't nothing in here."

Elegant strangers flooded the room. Aidan recognized their manners and gestures if not particular faces: actors, producers, poets, and dancers dressed in bohemian fashions, puffing on cigarettes, and drinking from flasks. Flashy folk talking loud and fast, certain they'd seen everything worth seeing and knew everything worth knowing.

Redwood leaned her damp face into Aidan's neck. "I gotta sing, 'fore too many people come. What you got for me?"

Aidan sang without thinking too much. Saeed danced behind Redwood, showing off for a handsome fellow slouched against the wall:

Talk to me, sugar
Talk to me, walk with me
Tell me what you know good
'Fore the moon fall out the sky
Don't you cry for me
'Fore the train jump off the track
Don't you lie for me
Stole my heart, now bring it back
Treat me like a good woman
Treat me like a good woman
Treat me like a good woman should

Saeed rolled hisself through the air, like a barrel rumbling 'cross the floor. "I can dance the lyrics you sing."

"You sure can." Aidan's throat throbbed. His fingers tingled. "You had the moon falling and the train jumping."

Redwood had sobered up from whatever made her tipsy. She snorted and cut her eyes at Aidan. Maybe she was mad at the lyrics, maybe she was sad. "I think I got it." She joined him with a high harmony on a second time through. The fancy guests were enchanted. The fellow leaning on the wall stood up straight as Saeed vaulted in the air. He was a workingman with soot on his knees, rough cap and gloves stuck in a back pocket, and a union flyer in the front. He didn't mingle with the crowd, just watched Saeed's every move. It looked like love if ever Aidan saw it. The union man caught Aidan staring and lifted his chin defiantly. Aidan shrugged. Chicago didn't shock him the way everyone thought it should.

"What does the good woman say in reply?" Saeed did a flourish at Redwood.

"Sing something, Sequoia," the union man urged.

"I stole this song from Aidan." She hummed it. The musicians knew just what to do. "He wrote this a long time ago back home in Georgia, but I would never sing it for him. Well, I'm singing it now with a few of my own lines."

> *I got a man say he b'lieve in me*
> *Gonna find a way for us both to be free*

"You remember that?" Aidan was touched.

Redwood was in fine spirits. As she sang, Aidan would've sworn the elegant crowd turned into giant hummingbirds and butterflies buzzing between monster jackrabbits, waddling pigs, and grasshoppers springing into treetops. Redwood was a bolt of lightning lingering on a hilltop. He smelled ripe peaches and burnt air from the lightning.

> *Hope's a canoe, take us far from here*
> *Where a man can be a man without no fear*

She opened her storm hand and pulled the bird, bug, and animal forms into her palm, leaving regular dancing folks behind. Saeed's guests were so drunk on good music, they didn't mind the strange magic.

"That's one for the show." Saeed smiled at Redwood and then at his union man. "I'm sure I can think of something to go with that."

Whizzing through the night, sparks flew under the train and tiny lights winked in the buildings, but hardly made a dent in the darkness. Redwood put her arm through Aidan's. "I felt my old self again, rehearsing up a show with you." She pressed against him. "More and more myself, since you hit town."

"That's grand." His face twisted up in a grimace.

"What's a matter?" She touched his frown.

He drew away from her. The seat cracked open and stuffing poked his behind. "I ought to play more music."

"Making moving pictures can take all you got."

"We ain't young anymore."

"Speak for yourself." She tried to laugh. "You didn't like the magic we did tonight?"

"We?" He glanced at the other passengers. Nobody paid them any mind. "No. I feel grand making music with you. Best I ever feel."

"What ain't you saying?"

"You asked me once if I had a heart's desire, if I wanted to go out in the world and make a bright destiny."

"I used to say all kinds of nonsense."

"Nonsense?" Aidan sighed. "I don't want us to settle for anything less."

A few weeks into rehearsing for the Ace of Spades, Aidan woke up on the wrong side of a nightmare, spoke words with nothing behind them, and said, "don't touch me," when Redwood reached to hug him. He offered no explanation, just took off for the motion picture factory in the dark. Dumbstruck, she sat on the window seat, dust balls swirling at her feet. With the rehearsals to look forward to, she'd been feeling hopeful, and thought Aidan was doing good too, but—

"Can you fault him?" She scolded herself, like Miz Subie might. "He a lusty man who always liked the good company of women. Got an Irish temper, and no telling how Seminole spirit be firing his nature up."

She opened the window and watched him stride away. He paused, feeling her eyes on him no doubt. Crickets sang in the trees; a milk wagon clattered down the cobblestones. Aidan waved a hand over his head to her and raced 'cross the road, looking handsome and mad as all get-out.

Redwood was mad at him too, half the time, and then she wanted to kiss and squeeze him tight the other half. She just didn't know how far they could go, before something bad happened, before her skin tightened like a shield 'round her heart, and she couldn't feel pleasure or pain. Aidan got prickly or furious or guilty whenever she touched him. How could she find anything out without torturing him? They were goin' lose each other this way, picking at old wounds, but seem like they didn't know what else to do.

Redwood climbed onto the ledge and jumped over a hydrangea bush. Heavy blue/violet blossoms bobbed in her face. Dew and pollen tickled her nose. The streetlight near the garden burned out with a hiss. The moon had set and the sky was a carpet of stars, yet none of them were shooting 'round making a show.

Distant footsteps and a sinister laugh sent a charge up Redwood's spine. Somebody out there was up to no good. Chicago was a dangerous town with folk doing each other in over pennies, and if she wasn't goin' let fear rule her life, she had to figure out what scared her so till she hid it from her ownself.

"Conjure woman s'posed to call up a boat if she need to cross the water," Iris said. She stood in the herb garden with a bloody gash on her leg. "But nobody 'round here like me enough to *believe*."

"What you doing up?" Redwood pretended not to be startled out her skin and hugged Baby Sister, who was tall and skinny as a sapling racing for the light.

"They hate me mostly," Iris said solemnly. She was thirteen going on a hundred.

"Who? Little Frank and that roughhouse crew he run with? The boy's jealous of Clarissa's other kids and you too. He want his mama all for him." Redwood pumped water on a handkerchief. "You so beautiful, folks just don't know what to do."

"Uh-huh." Iris rolled her eyes.

"Was Frank picking on George Jr. and the twins? Are you sticking up for your nieces and nephew?" Redwood sat down with her under the maple tree. "What you doing roving dangerous streets in the night?"

"You do it too," Iris said. "And not just to go heal folks. I ain't 'fraid of—"

"You ought to be. I been ambushed and hurt so bad, till I still ain't healed." She gripped Iris. "Spying is poison. It curdles your spirit. I'm speaking from experience."

Iris shuddered and looked away.

Redwood plucked a bottle of cure-all from her waist bag. "This might sting." She dabbed the long wound. Iris was never one to squeal or cry. She didn't even flinch. "You got something special," Redwood said, "a bright light shining through the night." She pointed to the stars.

"Shoot, everybody got that." Iris blew her lips, like a disgusted filly. "I can see folks shining even in daytime, even the dim ones. You goin' kiss it and make it better?"

Redwood hesitated. Clarissa said colored folks didn't need backcountry healers with all the modern medicine available.

"Yeah, Aunt Clarissa say, why eat pig knuckles or pig innards if you can have a ham steak." Iris held up her leg. "But everything we did back home ain't like making do with the worst parts of the pig."

Redwood touched her lips to the wound, drawing the hurt away, and then hugged Iris again. "We been neglecting you. I'm sorry. Don't let your light go dim 'cause some folks don't want to see you—or nobody else—shining."

"Fire-haint come up from Georgia with me and Aidan. I follow her sometimes. She don't let me catch her though."

"Haint? I never hear 'bout this before."

"Can I help?" Iris said.

"Help what?"

"You and—" Iris changed her mind midstream. "To make a scenario for the moving picture. Aidan said I had to ask you too."

Redwood sputtered. "If you want to. Of course."

"I've been reading stories and spending all my nickels seeing picture shows. Teacher said I was good at letters and *making things up*. She think I'm a liar."

Redwood laughed. "What you been telling her?"

"Not much anymore." Iris pouted.

"Write your true life, write what you fancy for stories or the moving picture, and show me or Aidan, all right?"

"Can I show George too?"

"He don't have time for stories right now. Maybe Clarissa."

Iris shook her head.

"Give her another try. I think sister-in-law can hear what you got to say."

"Sun's coming." Iris pointed to pink on the windowpanes. "I'm fine. You better hurry if you want to catch him."

Clarissa caught Redwood crawling back in the window. "I thought you were a cat burglar, sneaking in from the garden." Stead of scolding Redwood, she offered a hand. The ledge was slippery. "Mr. Wildfire left already?"

Redwood grunted and peeled off her dew-damp nightclothes.

"You know he loves you like a fool." Clarissa touched Doc's drawings of him on the wall. "You've ruined him for other women."

"Well, we haven't, we don't . . ." Redwood gestured over her half-naked body.

Embarrassed, Clarissa pulled her silky robe tight. "At least you're not living in sin."

Redwood groaned and sponged the night sweat from her skin. "When Iris tell you a story, just listen to her, all right? Don't try to set her straight or tell her it can't be so."

Clarissa pursed her lips. "George says Iris is living in her own universe."

"You won't change her, fussing at her." Redwood combed the knots from her hair. "You'll just make it harder for her."

"All right." Clarissa nodded. "But you, what about a wedding? Colored marry who they want in Chicago. Indians too."

Redwood laughed. "You think that'll take the trick off my body?" She wiggled into an undershirt.

"Don't smirk at the blessings of the Lord."

"I'm not."

"Wedding doesn't have to be in a church, if you're . . . pagan. And I'll say a prayer."

"You're the best friend I prayed for since I was little." Redwood hugged Clarissa suddenly. "Ready to go before Lord Jesus and plead my case."

Clarissa was startled, but suffered the embrace. "I've been reading. Even pagans talk to God or a great spirit." She headed for the door. "Cook's going to be here any moment." She paused. "I know you could get Mr. Wildfire to propose. That's a simple conjuration." Clarissa closed the door behind her.

"Gotta get him to talk to me first."

Redwood dressed up in swamp colors. She tied a gurgling stream to her waist, dangled Indian beads from her neck, and went down to collect Aidan from the motion picture factory. They were shooting a sunrise scene to get the shadows just so. Nicolai was a crazy man with light. Over a year of Aidan working in the "movies," and she hadn't seen him in full *Injun* regalia till now. He never let her see his pictures. Aidan strutting in buckskin pants, beaded moccasins, breastplate of bones, and feather headdress made her smile, till she caught his expression. He and Walter Jumping Bear looked splendid, of course, but Aidan was mad enough to take his spear and run someone through. He didn't have to playact *wild and ferocious* for the camera.

"Was biiiig fight," Nicolai explained to Redwood while his crew set up. "Aidan say *nyet* to tomahawk. Say he got piece of this tribe, piece of that one. Walter say Buffalo Bill never do such a mix-up, other directors neither. Mr. Payne say, Griffith already make *The Red Man's View*, *The Indian Runner's Romance*. Mr. Payne, do *The Last Drop of Blood* for to sell tickets and don't care which savage wield tomahawks." Nicolai eyed her bosom and hips, not like a man who wanted to bed her, though. "You look beautiful. You should be in a picture today."

"Ha! Mr. Payne is scared of putting me on the screen."

"I would not be." He filmed her with his eyes. "Wonderful picture." Redwood wondered what story he imagined. "Come."

She followed behind Nicolai and his camera crew as Aidan played Chief Red Cloud, a drunken scout leading the cavalry to a secret hideout of his people. The white soldiers paid Red Cloud in bottles of cheap whiskey. As night drizzle turned to sunny day, Red Cloud guzzled a bottle and fell off his horse, breaking the rest of his stash for comic relief. Between the horse acting up, the darned costume blowing off in the wind from a giant fan, and clouds covering the sun, it took ten tries to satisfy the director.

"We made this damn story already!" Aidan said. "What shitty drunkard would have such a war bonnet?"

"It was a great hit, so we do it again." Walter shrugged. He was calm water. "Payne wants money to move his studio to California, so next week I am drunken Chief Storm Clown." Walter smiled at Redwood coming toward them. "Good morning."

"You were watching?" Aidan dropped a spear in the dust and threw a blanket over his bare chest. "I didn't know."

"The sun was in your eyes," Redwood said. "You couldn't see me." She strutted in front of him, offering a good view. Aidan hustled by with barely a glance. Why get done up for a man who didn't want to look at you? If he didn't trust her hips, thighs, or secret spots just a bit, how would they get anywhere?

"We have to stow the costumes." Walter cleared his throat. "Play-acting with firewater demons puts him in a very bad humor."

"You're his friend, and it is sweet of you to make excuses."

Finally a day off from the Wild West. Aidan soaked in Clarissa's bathtub for an hour, ruminating on his foul mood. Nothing new occurred to him. Redwood opened the door, and steam hit her face. She looked so pretty fanning herself, it hurt.

"A hot bath on a hot day?" she said.

"Gotta do something." He wanted to sweat and scrub the ornery blues away.

"You still stewing 'bout drunken Chief Red Cloud?" She came all the way into the tiny room. "You've seen me playacting all kind of mess, and I don't like it either." She did her best chicken mime, circling the tub, pecking at his head and scratching her feet in his clothes. She squawked and flapped her arms. He had to smile.

"What are you all doing in there?" Clarissa called from down the hall.

"Nothing." Redwood laughed. Brightness was a habit with her, most of the time. Aidan felt sullen again. "You as bad as Brother George," she said.

Aidan sat up, face burning and nostrils flaring. "George is mad all the time. He don't like nobody 'cept Clarissa, and he don't have to ride 'round in a feather clown suit."

Redwood splashed water in his face. "You ain't just what they got you doing for their picture shows."

"What am I?" he said.

"Iris is cooking up a good character for you in our picture." She backed out. "Hurry up, 'fore this day's all gone and we ain't done nothing good."

Aidan might have sat home, stewing all day, 'cept Redwood had planned a sightseeing tour and picnic. Iris was dying to attend the International Aviation Meet at Grant Park and see women pilots fly. She didn't care a hoot for old monuments, for museums built way before she was born, or parkland squeezed between skyscrapers and stockyards. Aidan only agreed to come out if they went to the fly show too. Spoiling Iris was a habit for him.

"We'll have to hurry then," Redwood said.

They were almost out the door, but Iris went back for her *mojo* bag, so Aidan tried to convince Clarissa to let her kids come out with them, see the aviators or run through grass and trees. Clarissa didn't care what Aidan had managed with Iris and the cousins in a Georgia swamp. Her children were bona fide demons, too much to handle in a big wild city.

"We probably missed two trolleys messing 'round," Redwood said as they got out at the 57th Street stop. Chicago had too many streets to name 'em all. "You can't do nothing when Clarissa has her mind set."

"We're here, ain't we?" Aidan muttered. "You're just as stubborn as her."

"Jackson Park's where the Fair was 'fore it burned," Redwood said.

Aidan's eyes snapped at this. "Really?" Walking on dirt 'stead of stumbling over broken pavement was a relief to his ankles. The path snaked between brambles, late bloomers, and nodding red rosehips. He peered closely at everything, looking for a sign of the time that burned. "Why didn't you tell me where we were going?"

"I like surprising you."

Iris ran ahead down a tree-lined path, over an arched bridge, and onto Wooded Island. The lagoon water was murky green. Geese chased gray clouds 'cross a white sky. Moldy leaves, drowned spiderwebs, and rotten wood added a swamp tang to the lake breeze. A cloud of mosquitoes avoided Redwood. He smacked two bloodsuckers on his arm.

"Aidan, you goin' stay mad at me all day?"

"Why not?"

"Me and Clarissa ain't got nothing to tell you 'bout stubborn." She stopped under an old tree. "This bur oak's seen near two hundred years." The crown was at least six stories high, and its branches stretched to a ninety-foot span, big as a live oak from home. "Imagine a little acorn striking out in the dirt in 1700 and something," she said.

Aidan traced his fingers along the black corky bark and picked up a fat, shaggy acorn bigger than his fist. "Little?"

"I don't mean to torment you." She threw another acorn at him.

He caught it. "Trees are built more patient than people."

They wandered over a moon bridge through the Osaka Garden. Muddy green turtles sunned on a tiny island. Red lanterns hung in the trees, and colorful birds darted through raspy leaves, squabbling and singing. The wooden path zigzagged right over lagoons and streams. Oriental statues stood guard in tall grass and behind bushes. Aidan stopped at a waterfall of gurgling scum. Muddy water every direction he looked—sky even looked muddy.

"With a path twisting and turning this way"—Redwood headed over a stone bridge—"the bad spirits dogging our heels get worn out and fall into the water. Japanese folk say, evil need a straight line, but good find its way in the curves."

"That's why the water's so dirty." He followed her. "Full of bad spirits."

Redwood stopped in his face. "It's torment for me too."

"I know." Aidan wanted to avoid her eyes, but he couldn't.

"Hurry up," Iris yelled from 'cross the water. "We don't want to miss the lady pilots." She dashed off, long legs lending her speed.

Redwood pulled Aidan along. "Look where I brought you—the Palace of Fine Arts from the World's Fair. It's the Field Columbian Museum now."

"This is here and now, huh?" Aidan picked up speed.

The Palace resembled the Parthenon or some other Greek temple. Gods, goddesses, and fat granite scrolls of long-forgotten stories were perched atop tall white columns. The lagoon in front was smooth as green glass, reflecting the hazy day back to itself. Throngs of people tumbled up and down the sprawling marble stairs.

"I thought it all burned down," he said.

"Cairo Street's gone." Iris darted up the steps. "But the Osaka Garden and this Palace is still here, and they'll be here in a hundred years too." She danced between columns, moving her hips like an Egyptian belly dancer charming snakes and tourists. She got mostly grins and full-blown smiles from the flock of museum patrons. Even the frowners were impressed. Aidan applauded. Redwood stopped his hands.

"Clarissa blame us for Iris not knowing how to act in public," she said.

"Gal just showing some spirit," Aidan said.

"Where's that goin' get her?" Bitterness caught in Redwood's throat.

"Swallowing down who you are is no good either." Aidan held out his hand.

Redwood curled her fingers between his, and they climbed the steps to Iris.

Passes from Clarissa's club got them through the entrance free. Inside the majestic foyer, the temperature dropped. The air was dry; footsteps echoed off high ceilings and marble floors. Aidan pulled off his hat. The rowdy crowd metamorphosed to devout supplicants, in awe of what God had wrought, of the wonders of the world, of times and people that Aidan could barely imagine. Musky smells and winking masks hinted at ancient treasures down the halls and up the stairs.

"Can't you hear Doc explaining everything in here to us?" Iris gawked at an ancient Etruscan tomb with fresco paintings on the walls, bronze statuettes, gold jewelry, and everyday objects a dead person would need in the afterlife.

A young white woman smiled warmly at Aidan. Her wavy hair hung below her buttocks. Intricate lace looked scratchy at her neck. Dragonfly earrings dangled to her shoulders, and she smelled of spring wildflowers. Redwood frowned, but Aidan, in a decent mood at last, returned the smile.

"Sir, I know you, don't I?" she said.

Aidan shook his head. "Well, Miz—"

"Fredericks," she offered.

"Miz Fredericks, I've never had the pleasure of your acquaintance."

"Oh, I am sorry to be so bold. I saw you in a motion picture, sir."

"Miz Fredericks, you seem no stranger to boldness." The hint of jealousy in Redwood's voice tickled Aidan.

"He's a star," Iris said. "I've seen all his pictures three, four times. And my sister's the toast of Chicago vaudeville." Redwood snorted at Iris's praise.

"You were a wild *Injun* on a painted pony." Miz Fredericks's eyes darted uneasily between Redwood and Iris. "Glorious."

Aidan wanted to hush her up before she spoiled everything. "Good day to you."

"It took the whole cavalry to chase you down!" Miz Fredericks said, and a couple strangers nodded too. "You put up a marvelous fight, so fearsome and daring."

"That was *Warrior Blood*," Iris said.

Aidan shot Iris a deadly glance. "No, ma'am, that wasn't me."

"It wasn't?" Redwood said.

Miz Fredericks frowned at Redwood's hand on Aidan's sleeve. "I don't think I could forget your eyes, sir."

"I was the drunken skunk who fell off his horse in *The Battle of Deadman's Gulch*. They captured me, and I turned traitor scout for whiskey." He staggered like a drunk.

"You were wonderful all the same." Miz Fredericks was charmed by his rough manner. "So handsome and dashing. I can't believe I'm meeting you."

Sweat sprouted from Aidan's temples; his breath was a wheeze, and he was shaking, as if the delirium tremens were coming back. More people gathered near them, bright faces splotched red with excitement. A few scowled as Aidan clutched Redwood's hand. He was fixing to give 'em a lick with the rough side of his tongue, when—

"Sorry, ma'am," Iris said. "We got to go." She and Redwood pulled Aidan away from this eager fan and the fool strangers who were pushing too close. "Why you want to lie to that lady?" Iris asked.

Aidan cussed under his breath. He balled up his shaking hands.

Swallowing, his throat felt parched, but water wouldn't do no good. He punched a fat marble pillar. Pain didn't help. Making it up to Chicago sober was easy compared to—

"Who are you playing? Crazy Coop?" Redwood said. "You s'posed to left him back in Georgia." Her hand on his forehead cleared his mind a bit. He wanted a jug even so.

"Ain't so many folks going this way." Iris tugged at them.

As they continued on, Tlingit masks glared from dark alcoves. Totem poles loomed in the corners: giant-beak creatures, with eyes in their stiff wings, squatted on men whose tears were bright flames; the men crouched on grinning foxes who held fish in their paws. Aidan doubled over and shook his head.

"I hear 'em talking," Iris said by the fox. "Just don't understand the language."

Aidan walked away. Even magic Iris was making him sad today. The next hall was a Hopi exhibit—jewelry, kachina dolls, tools, and clothing—ancient Arizona history and just yesterday too. Aidan balked in the doorway. The room was jammed with well-dressed Chicago folk admiring old Indian ways.

"I don't need to see any more," he said.

"I thought this might lift your spirits." Redwood pointed at turquoise necklaces and beads. "Fallen skystone—"

"My stomach's feeling sour. I can't abide the air inside here."

They skirted the other Indian exhibits and left without viewing anything from Asia or Africa, without seeing butterflies, ancient animal bones, or meteor rocks. As they tromped down hard marble steps, Iris took Aidan's hand.

"I didn't want to stay neither," she said.

"You should come back," he muttered. "Take a good look-see without me."

In the museum Redwood had tried not to worry, but Aidan was no better at the Aviation Meet in Grant Park. A squad of buzzing aeroplanes zipped through the clouds, chasing red balloons for a six-hundred-dollar prize. Seventy thousand people filled the grandstands, hollering and carrying on. Too many were swilling whiskey or wine.

'Stead of watching the air polo, Aidan threw up in a bush where Iris wouldn't see and tapped Miz Subie's tin on his lips.

"You all right?" Redwood whispered. "Don't pay those people no mind." She wanted to say, in their moving picture, he wouldn't do nothing to turn his stomach. He'd play an upstanding Seminole farmer, brave and wise, *ancestor of generations yet unborn.*

"I'm fine."

Iris poked her. "Miz Harriet Quimby of California flew this morning and won a prize. Mademoiselle Hélène Dutrieu of Belgium can't fly yet 'cause her machine isn't ready." Iris dragged her feet, kicked at rocks, and sighed dramatically, as if Mlle Dutrieu's broken aeroplane was Redwood's fault.

"Can't tell who the pilot is, when they're high in the sky," Aidan said.

"Mlle Dutrieu is goin' take up women passengers day after tomorrow," Iris said. "She fancies that soon, women as well as men will be flying from city to city, even coast to coast. Can't I come back? Why I have to be at school, learning stuff I been knowing."

"Your grammar doesn't sound like it." Redwood laid out cold chicken, biscuits, and peach pie for a picnic. "You don't want folks to think less of you, shut a door of opportunity in your face."

Aidan jerked his head back, as if something slammed too close to his eyes. He sipped a cup of water. Iris picked at the peaches, scattering pie crust for pigeons. Redwood ate three portions of everything, rather than let food go to waste.

"I got two woebegone companions on my hand. What fun showing you anything?"

"Look!" Iris pointed to a long, pale green scarf fluttering behind the wings of an aeroplane. "That must be Miz Quimby." She jumped up and squealed. Dipping and wheeling, the plane wove arabesques in the red, orange, and purple clouds of sunset.

They walked home. Redwood didn't trust her full belly to the El or even a trolley on the ground. Aidan didn't need to be in close quarters with strangers. He was spoiling for a fight, snarling at anybody who looked at them. Or maybe he just needed some good loving. Iris enjoyed folks bustling through the streets or sitting in front of stores and apartments, playing games and talking foreign words. She danced into Reginald Jones's grocery 'cause she and Aidan were finally ready to eat something.

"Mr. Jones is a Georgia man!" Iris came out with three meat pies. "Living his Chicago dream. He knew Daddy and gave me all this food for free."

Reginald Jones, a middle-aged, brown-skinned man, smiled in the window at them. Aidan nodded. He and Iris chomped into their meat pies. Redwood was still too full.

A mile from home, they turned a corner and walked into a wreck. An elevated train had jumped the track and crashed into the street. The rusty nose dug a big hole in the asphalt. The tail of the wreck was still on the elevated track, leaning against the roof of another train car. A crowd of railroad men stood beside it, scratching their heads.

"Nothing to see, folks. Just go on about your business." Policemen shouted at gawkers and stalled automobiles.

"Good thing we walked," Redwood said.

"Nobody died," Iris said. "Just hurt real bad."

"You full of good news, ain't you?" Aidan said.

When they got home, Iris told everybody the adventures of the day. Clarissa smiled, and George too. Redwood complained of a stomachache, and Aidan looked sick enough to escape to the back parlor with her. Hoping for inspiration, she laid out a piece of white cloth on the floor. She lit four candles and set one at each corner with a bundle of dried fireweed and swamp iris. In the center she placed a bowl with tupelo berries, Culver's root, devil's shoestring, man root, and lemon rind. She sprinkled sugar in the bowl and set the last candle in the center. Aidan stood in the doorway, watching her lay out the *crossroads* spell, like he didn't want to come in.

"I'm sorry I spoiled your day," he said. "I don't know what come over me."

"Taking you to that museum—I just didn't think . . ." Redwood set the two furry acorns from the bur oak on either side of the bowl of herbs and then pulled him into the room, onto the cloth. "Tell me something good. Read to me from your book." She thrust his journal at him.

Aidan shook his head.

"No? All right, let me read to you."

He was fixing to resist, but nodded. She turned the pages till a title caught her eye.

WALKING THE STARS

Stories and songs are medicine too.

Big Thunder was of the Wind clan, one of the first clans to come out the mountains when the Master of Breath called the Indians from the navel of the Earth into life. Wind clan was whirlwind friend to Panther clan, clearing away giant roots so that his bigheaded brother could make it into sunlight. The other clans tumbled in after that, Deer, Bear, Corn, Bird, Potato, and all the rest. Big Thunder had to marry across the Fire. His first wife was Snake Clan. His second wife, Aislinn, was an O'Casey from County Cork. They married far across the Fire.

"Your parents are dead," Aunt Caitlin said to Aidan Wildfire. "You are Aidan Cooper now and nobody else. Those mountain people you lived with got taken by fevers and coughing sickness. You are strong stock, lucky. You take after Aislinn, and I love you as my own. Don't go running off, hiding in the swamp like a wild savage."

Aidan was young, and sadness was sharp nettles clinging to him, digging deep, drawing lifeblood. He missed his parents and the clan of mountain folk who had made the world home. Aidan cried in the night. He grew sick and pale, not from coughing or fever, but grief. Finally, when Aunt Caitlin couldn't get any food to stay in his belly, she took Aidan to Miz Garnett Phipps and pleaded with this colored conjure woman to hold her adopted son to life.

Miz Garnett sent George and Redwood to help their daddy in the fields. She had Aidan gather hairy roots for a healing brew. They watched it boil in a black iron pot. A dead smell filled the house. When darkness fell, Miz Garnett stood by Aidan on the porch. The moon didn't bother to come out. The air was a heavy blanket of heat. Aidan felt a chill in his heart all the same.

"Shooting stars." Miz Garnett pointed at streaks of light. "That's a sign for sure."

"What the stars got to say to us?" Aidan asked.

Miz Garnett sang a star song in Gullah Creole, and Aidan could only feel the meaning, a traveling song, a song for loved ones far away. "I knew your daddy since I was younger than you." She put a warm cup of the nasty brew in Aidan's hands. "His people and my people been 'round these parts for a long time. I got family over on the Sea Islands still."

"My daddy knew folks from everywhere," Aidan said, proud of who he come from for a moment. "Aunt Caitlin said I shouldn't talk about him."

"I'm a hoodoo, hearing underneath things, can't hide the truth from me," she murmured. "We can talk about your daddy and your mama too, if you like, just us. I won't tell nobody."

Aidan put the cup to his lips and drank the medicine down quick. It was sweet and frothy and felt good going down. His tongue tingled and his belly didn't feel so tight. Miz Garnett sat down in the rocking chair and opened her arms. Aidan crawled in her lap, like he was a little child, and they rocked together, slowly. He liked her hickory smoke, sweet magnolia scent. She wore an orchid in her hair— seemed it was growing there and not ever fixing to die.

"Your daddy told me a story once about the Milky Way." She pointed to the stars.

"The Master of Breath blew into the sky and made the white pathway," Aidan whispered.

"He told you too? Ain't that something!"

"Yes. The white starway leads to a City of Light where good people go, when they're dead."

"Gullah song tell a similar story. Your mama and daddy are there, smiling on you, hoping you have a long life, a good life, before you walk the stars to them."

"Aunt Caitlin don't believe in the Milky Way. Uncle Charlie neither."

"It's up there in the sky for us all to see, a prayer every night. A good story fill you up when you hungry, when you lonely. A good song take the hurting out your spirit. No harm believing in that." She gave him a wind-up music box. "Play this and think of the stars smiling on you."

"Stars smiling on you . . ." Aidan's words, Mama's words tasted like warm rain after a long winter drought. "She used to rock me in her chair too." Redwood placed the red leather journal in his hands. "Why you write these stories as if Aidan Wildfire was somebody you heard tell of?"

Aidan shrugged. "How my mama used to do."

Redwood picked up Garnett's music box from her nightstand and twisted the screw. The drum wouldn't turn anymore, so she hummed the "Swanee River" tune. Aidan squatted in the center of the *crossroad* cloth, looking right through Redwood to her mama and beyond, to Big Thunder and Miz O'Casey walking stars.

"She still talk to you when the sun go down?" Redwood sat next to him.

"Just a whisper now and then," Aidan replied. "I can't make out what she's saying."

"If she talking Sea Island Gullah, who can blame you."

He leaned against her. "Is this a good life we're living?"

"What you want me to tell you?"

"Tell me 'bout this picture we're goin' make."

Redwood's pulse spiked. "I've been thinking on it every day." The candles hissed and sputtered in a draft from the window. The flames died away, but came back again.

"Me too," Aidan said.

"Really?" Redwood rested her head on his shoulder. "A Sea Island romance. I'll play that Teacher everybody always wanted me to be. Course, the Teacher longs for adventure, longs to see the world. The Pirate almost drowns, but Sea Island folk save him, and he loves poetry, like the Teacher."

"I bet he writes his favorite lines in a journal."

TWENTY-ONE

Chicago, 1912

"Two years? Has it been two years since we met?"

Aidan stood with the Persian prince and Walter Jumping Bear in the back of a dingy, crammed meeting hall listening to Indians, full-and mixed-blood, from all over: Lakota Sioux, Seneca, Oneida, Arapahoe, Kickapoo, Ojibwa, Winnebago, Apache, and other tribes he could not name. The balcony creaked above his head as late arrivals stomped up stairs. Nobody else could squeeze in the back. Hundreds were gathered to discuss an evening of entertainment in support of the Society of American Indians. Walter wore a fashionable gray suit with a few feathers in his cap, but Aidan spied several imposing figures in traditional dress.

"I've been to California and the Olympics in Sweden and back," the prince said.

Aidan missed most of what he said next concerning Jim Thorpe, an Indian who won gold medals and got crowned king of the athletes. A Seminole man in a turban and a great coat belted with a bright blue sash walked under his nose, talking the language of his childhood. A short, soft-spoken fellow with close-cropped hair, he looked nothing like Big Thunder. Still, Aidan's chest heaved and his throat ached, for his daddy *and* mama lost to yellow fever, for a family he never knew marched off to Oklahoma, for his people hiding in the Georgia hills and Florida swamps, chasing freedom.

"Chicago is full of Indian people," the prince said as squabbles and skirmishes broke out in the unruly crowd. "Now different tribes making a big tribe together."

"Yes." Aidan wasn't sure if one big tribe was a good thing or even possible.

"Strength in a big gathering of folks," Walter Jumping Bear said. He and several other Lakota from the motion picture factory insisted the Society was Indians organizing and leading themselves. Aidan didn't feel part of any clan and hadn't wanted to come, but Walter was offering to act in Redwood's pirate picture with one breath while persuading him to come to the meeting with another. Walter was his true friend at the studio. How could Aidan refuse? The prince went where he pleased, of course, and looked as Indian as Aidan did.

"I don't live in a tipi," a gal shouted. She wore a purple swamp orchid in her hair, like Garnett. Her cheeks were high and her eyes fierce. "Neither did my *Maskôki* ancestors." She smoothed a white collar on a somber blue dress as Aidan, Walter, and other men eyed her. Women were sparse in this crowd.

"We are all tired of Wild West show Indian raids." Aidan surprised hisself by speaking up. "But who pays to see Creek farmers or a Lakota romance in Chicago?"

Walter leaned into Aidan and grunted. "If we walk away from their money, where is our victory? White men will play *Injun* without us."

The Creek gal smiled at their words and moved closer.

A large fellow in a finely tailored suit with a doctor's bag stood up. "Italians, Poles, Hungarians, they leave their old world behind and become Americans. They pay a price—they must give up their tongue, their ancient ways. So can we."

"We did not cross the great water and steal this land," Walter said. "We are home, why should we bury our spirits and act as if nothing is sacred, like white men do?"

"I am an Apache. You are a coward Sioux in a toy Indian show. I can lick you!" The large doctor waved an umbrella in Walter's face. Walter knocked it on the ground. Aidan gripped his friend's arm before he did anything else. "They'll keep us prisoners on the reservations till we are civilized," the doctor said.

"We need a vision to follow, or else we fight over nothing." The Creek gal touched Walter's shoulder. He heaved a breath and studied her.

A man in the balcony took the doctor's side. "The white man has beaten us all."

"Well, I am not yet conquered," Walter declared.

Everyone was shouting now. Aidan's head throbbed.

"Don't look so glum." The prince grinned at the spirited exchange and clapped Aidan's back. "I've seen two years of your vast country and found so many people who let themselves think . . . anything. This is a wonder."

A secretary at the podium called for order.

"I'm feeling poorly," Aidan whispered to Walter and his daddy, whose name meant something close to *brave wind,* but he hated this English translation, so no one spoke it.

"You are abandoning this boat?" Walter said.

"No, I just can't take . . ." Aidan gestured.

Walter's daddy spoke—he knew English, but rarely used it, so Walter translated. "Smoking a pipe with so many different Indian people makes his balls ache too."

Aidan laughed. "I'll do whatever show you want to support Mr. Charles Eastman and his Indian Society."

Walter nodded, disappointed all the same. "This evening we are not at our best. Come another time."

Aidan waved goodbye and turned to leave. The prince bowed to Walter, his daddy, and the Creek gal too.

"My father asks, what is your tribe?" Walter said before they could escape.

The prince responded in Farsi and the old man seemed satisfied with his answer.

"Why must *we* entertain *them*?" The Creek gal spoke in Aidan's ear. "Tell me this."

"Guess we should try entertaining ourselves too," Aidan said.

"I have seen you both in moving pictures." Her eyes lit up. "Is this a new plan?"

"Yes, ma'am, it is." Aidan glanced at Walter.

"I look forward to your next picture show then," she said.

"Me too." Aidan hunched his back and walked on.

She took his place beside Walter. "My name is Rose. I am *Hutalgalgi,* of the Wind clan." And then her voice was lost to the babble of the crowd.

"Mr. Jumping Bear has won her heart," the prince said.

"Hmm." Aidan barged through a knot of latecomers, out the door. Their faces looked open and eager. Aidan tried not to glower as he took off down the street. The prince chased after him, barely keeping up. Aidan wanted to run till his own heart busted. He wanted to get lost in the noise from the streetcars and belching automobiles and grind his spirit against the cobblestones. Actually, he wanted a drink. He wanted a whole jug. The firewater thirst was getting stronger every day.

"Not so fast," the prince yelled behind him.

Aidan slowed. "All day, I make fun of myself. Where is the dignity in that?"

The prince caught up. He was wheezing and sweating, despite the winter chill in the air. He considered Aidan as he caught his breath. "You should have sons by now."

Aidan halted. "Did you hear what I said?"

"You need heirs, then what matter these difficult moments in flickering images?"

"Here's your motorcar." Aidan waved 'cross the street at Mr. Mc-Gregor. "I think I'm goin' walk the rest of the way." He dug in his shoulder bag for Subie's tin.

"It's several miles. Dinner will be prompt tonight. Akhtar cooks for you all." The prince stepped in front of Aidan before he could rush off. "I don't mean to offend you."

"You don't have sons, sir." Aidan clutched the tin.

The prince wiped his damp forehead. "I've offended you. Please, accept my apology." He stood close to Aidan, saying nothing as sweat dried on both their cheeks. Finally he spoke softly, little more than a hiss. "I've tried many women. Not one could give me a son or even a daughter. Farah, Akhtar, Abbaseh, and I are happy even so."

Aidan was stunned at these intimate remarks.

"And you, Mr. Wildfire?" The prince's moist breath made Aidan blink. "What of you and Miss Phipps?" He shook Aidan's shoulder. "Do you think of another woman? Hmm? Is it the cat that gets your tongue?"

"With me and Redwood, ain't no real worry 'bout children, sir. It's, well . . ." Redwood could barely stand Aidan laying a hand on her. But she wanted him all the same, as much as he wanted her. This was enough to make a man holler and cuss and drink and smash in the heads of anyone fool enough to ask stupid questions 'bout goddamned cats. Aidan took a deep breath. "The way of the world is against us."

"You can't believe this lie. The way of the world is always for you." He gripped Aidan's arm. "The way of men, now that can be troublesome."

Aidan sagged. "No, it's me. I let yesterday eat up too much of today."

Glass exploded from a building down the street. Aidan and the prince fell to the pavement as smoke billowed into the sky. Horses and motorcars almost collided. A dog whimpered. A bloody colored man jumped, fell, or was pushed out of a second-story window. It was Reginald Jones, screaming in the air. He hit the ground with a sickening smack, and Aidan closed his eyes. Reginald had come up from Atlanta and was making a good Chicago life. Clarissa had everybody buying from his grocery. The smell of burnt food filled Aidan's mouth. He spit out the taste and forced his eyes back open. People close by the fire hollered. The shower of glass had wounded a good many who limped, crawled, and staggered through debris.

Aidan and the prince struggled to their feet. Aidan coughed out smoke. The prince was wheezing, like he'd never catch his breath. A beat-up motorcar raced away from the catastrophe, darting through stalled traffic faster than even McGregor would drive. Pale skin and bright teeth flashed in fading sunlight. Rowdy white thugs in the front and back seats grinned at their handiwork. They almost ran down a few colored folk who were shaky on their feet. Aidan caught the driver's eye. He'd seen the man before, a big, red-nosed fellow, who'd been having a set to with George.

"What?" the prince asked. "What do you see?" Flames painted the air smoky red.

"Nothing." Aidan made sure the prince was standing fine and then ran toward the fire. He almost collided with a Chinaman. "Sorry," they said in unison.

"People are still inside," a wounded colored woman screeched, blood drizzling from her ear. "I can hear 'em in there but nothing much else."

Everybody heard them as the building collapsed. Aidan followed two men to the door, but the heat forced them back. Wind encouraged the fire to race through the grocery and grab hold of the Chinese laundry on one side and the colored bank on the other. Laundry workers and bank clerks watched with stony, soot-covered faces. Inside the grocery, folks screamed for Jesus's mercy as fire ate into them. Aidan raced back and forth, looking for an opening in the wall of flame and smoke. The ground burnt through the soles of his shoes to his feet. Shots rang out, and voices inside grew silent.

A black horse, his eyes spooked wide, his teeth gnashing dirt, dragged a junk wagon down the cobblestones and scattered the crowd.

Aidan jigged 'round the wheels toward the door. The prince gripped his shoulder and stopped him. "What is done cannot be undone," he said. "But you need not share their fate."

"What was that?" Redwood stood up from her chair in the back of the club meeting room, scratching at her dress. The boned bodice and stiff lace chaffed. Her hat weighted her head down. "Did you hear that?"

"No," Clarissa hissed as several heads turned their way. "Sit. It's nothing."

Redwood couldn't hear anything now. "Maybe it's nerves."

Clarissa pulled Redwood back in her seat and looked anxiously 'round the room of prominent colored women—college-educated, professional women: social workers, doctors, truant officers, teachers, and the wives of important colored men, women who now thought less of Clarissa 'cause of George, and Redwood too. A singing, dancing wonder didn't belong in a respectable family, a hoodoo witch neither. Chicago was no different than Peach Grove on that. Redwood was a fool for dressing up and coming here. These fine ladies would never support her artistic adventure. How could a pirate moving picture *uplift the race*?

"They're just about to call on you," Clarissa whispered.

"Naw, it'll be a while," Iris said to Abbaseh, who frowned. The prince's third wife wore no veil and from her expressions followed what was said quite easily.

Mrs. Powell, the club president, was making introductory remarks. That might last fifteen minutes. "Over sixty percent of our women in Chicago work in laundries or as domestic servants, but too many of our girls are walking the streets in gaudy attire."

Abbaseh was a foreigner forgiven her brassy yellow and pink. Iris had no excuse wearing gold slippers, a green-and-gold hat, and Redwood's bright red Oriental robe with a gold feather design. At least she and Redwood both wore dresses.

Mrs. Powell continued. "Too many of our young men are gambling and drinking their lives away and offer no shelter for our young women."

Prickly heat burned Redwood's cheeks. Foul air made her choke. A scream, coming from a few streets over maybe, twisted her gut. Iris sat up straight, listening to something other than Mrs. Powell too. Trouble flitted 'cross her face. She clutched Abbaseh's hand. Redwood darted past Clarissa for the windows, trying to figure what trouble they were feeling. She pulled back heavy drapes and looked out on the street. The new electrically operated traffic lights blinked on and off. Motorcars and horses were backed up beyond the intersection. Nothing else to see.

"I didn't realize you were in such a hurry." A flustered Mrs. Powell frowned at Redwood. "You all recognize Sequoia Phipps from her many appearances onstage and in moving pictures too."

Disapproving murmurs rippled through this elegant set.

"I got a show tonight." Redwood didn't, but her lie cooled a few hot faces.

"I believe she is here to speak for poetry, that we should add poetry and artistic training to our educational and vocational plan," Mrs. Powell said.

"For poetry, are you?" A very dark woman with sleek, straight hair piled in storm clouds sneered. Redwood remembered her as a volunteer at the settlement house. "More likely, she's speaking for singing and dancing and cutting the fool. Negroes waste too much time on that already. Or perhaps you will tell us how to jinx white folk off our backs."

"Wait now, that's a trick worth knowing," Clarissa said. A few women nodded.

"You aim to teach us hoodoo conjuring?" the dark woman said.

"Wilma, hush. I've seen you at Mambo Dupree's," Clarissa said. "You too, Bessie."

"I haven't said anything, but I do have a question." Bessie was a wiry, fretful woman who followed behind Wilma, trying to do good. She'd worked the settlement too. "What makes you think you can tell a story that anybody wants—"

"Or needs," Wilma added.

"Or needs to hear?" Bessie chewed her lip. "What I mean is, who needs to hear poetry, if you've come up from Georgia, Mississippi, and you're hungry and poor and got gambling in your soul and violence in your heart?"

A reporter for the *Broad Ax* wrote furious notes.

"Remember, ladies, Miss Sequoia Phipps is our guest." Mrs. Powell had taken her sweet time admonishing Wilma and Bessie for their rude interruption. "She will answer your questions later. Right now, let us welcome her."

Half-hearted applause died out before it got started. Iris squeezed Redwood's hand. Clarissa gave her a pat as well. Abbaseh bowed her head over a smile. Redwood crumpled her prepared speech and left it on the chair as she strode to the front of the room. It was like going to church, when George used to say, *"Smile at them hinkty fools, Red, and you be surprised."* She let anger at Wilma and Bessie drain away and looked into everybody's eyes, trying to see to their hearts, trying to feel full of their goodwill. As Mrs. Powell listed her many appearances and accomplishments, Redwood offered her warmest smile, full of sunshine and swamp breezes.

"I cannot speak for poetry." She acted modest, mimicking Clarissa. "I cannot speak for singing and dancing and telling good stories." They looked surprised. She wasn't what they expected. Even if a few women still frowned, most everybody else leaned forward. "It's what I do, like easing someone's pain if a leg is cut or broke, or bringing a baby into this life. Who can tell you what it's like to give birth?"

All the mamas and grandmamas in the room murmured and nodded at this.

"Being onstage is a conjuration for sure. There's magic in show people, I won't deny it. Why would anyone come see a show if there wasn't? Don't we *believe* in actors more than someone walking by on the street? 'Cause there's a poem in your body up onstage. Ain't there—I mean, *isn't* there beauty and magic in an osprey soaring high? Don't it make your heart feel free? But I can't tell you what that means. You have to come see me or do it your ownself if you don't like my shows—or *even if you do.* We make the world up, in our dreams and in our songs. Would you have a life with no music, no poetry, and just the factory snarling at you, just the blood and guts on the killing floor or dirt and filth running down the laundry drain? Would you have nothing but chicken-coop comedies and Wild West lies?" She paused. All the clubwomen held their breath. A good improvisation meant surprising yourself with truth you knew when you heard it. "I say, why only a rock smashing through the window of our dreams or flames burning our hearts down? Will we get anywhere if that's all we can see? Singing and dancing we turn ourselves into what we want."

Feeling faint, she gulped the glass of water sitting on the podium. "So I invite you all to the Ace of Spades Hotel. It's not a den of iniquity or whatever you're imagining, but a good place to feel alive. We're putting on a show tomorrow at midnight. Go on and be scandalized if you want—and come anyhow."

The clubwomen stared at her, stunned.

"Will you soar for us?" Bessie asked, sounding genuine, hopeful even.

"That's all I got to say. The show will answer your questions." Redwood hurried down the aisle. The skin on her back was burning up.

"Thank you for that lovely invitation," Mrs. Powell said.

"Something's wrong," Redwood whispered to Clarissa.

Iris agreed. "Something bad happened." She and Redwood headed out the door. Abbaseh scurried after them. Clarissa grabbed her things and followed.

Redwood, Iris, Abbaseh, and Clarissa paraded into the Dry Cleaning and surprised George. Iris threw her arms 'round his neck and hugged him like she hadn't just seen him this morning, like she'd almost lost him for good.

"Y'all fancy ladies coming to check up on me?" He hugged his sisters, squeezed his wife a good long measure, then tilted his head to Abbaseh.

"Do you need checking on?" Clarissa asked.

George laughed too hard at this.

"I had a bad feeling," Redwood said. "Somebody was walking 'cross your grave."

"I'm still alive, Red. Don't go hammering nails in my coffin." George patted her hand. "Nobody can spook you like your ownself."

"I seen the baron. He the one spook me," Iris said.

"You would have been proud of your sister today," Clarissa said.

"I wrote Red's speech all down. I'm making a record of our lives." Iris strutted and hopped 'round Abbaseh.

"Don't all talk at me at once," George said. "I can't hear nothing."

"Your sister spoke at the club meeting, it was beautiful to see," Clarissa said.

"She invited all the ladies to Spades for tomorrow night," Iris said. George chuckled. "That'll be something."

"I'm goin' do it, George," Redwood said. "You don't think I can, but you're wrong."

"You mean the pirate moving picture?" He slipped behind his desk. "You been talking 'bout it long enough."

"It takes a lot of conjuring!" Iris said. Serene Abbaseh nodded.

"I'll bet." George picked at a stack of papers. "Them ole backcountry hoodoo spells don't work so well on hardheaded businessmen. You got to deliver the goods."

Redwood put a hand on his pile of receipts. "You haven't seen my shows in awhile. I'm not just a clown, somebody's joke."

Clarissa set George's hat on his head. "We're collecting you and taking you home."

"I got plans." He pointed to the back rooms. "Work to do."

"George Phipps, you are coming home tonight," Clarissa said. "Miss Akhtar is cooking food from her homeland. We will all show up and dine like a decent family."

"Well, you got Sis in a dress. I guess I don't have to work till dawn."

The streetwalkers were skinny and ragged. One gal barely had any hips to shake, and her tiddies looked hard. Aidan stood under a glowing streetlamp and shivered in the cold air off the lake. Winter was coming. Maybe even snow this night, and these poor gals were still showing bare skin.

"Don't stand there scowling at us. You'll scare the other prospects away." This one had legs as long as Redwood's, but she was pale as ice and her hair was bloody red. "Or maybe you think you're enough to handle us all." She had an Irish accent, not as strong as Aislinn O'Casey, but Aidan could hear the lilt all the same.

"I don't know what I think, ma'am." Aidan had been half the night digging through rubble, pulling out charred bodies, trying not to think.

"Honey's my name. Are you a Christian reformer come to show us the error of our ways?" Her breath was sour. She smelled musty, like a rag that never dried out.

"Wasn't planning to get here. Just walking," Aidan said. "Trying to find a bit of green, some fresh air."

"A fancy man such as yourself must have a wife," Honey said. "Bet you need more than her, don't you?"

Wet sloppy snow fell on her neck. She didn't shiver how he did, probably used to the cold. After the heat of the fire, Aidan should have been grateful for the north wind and ice from the sky. He wasn't. He longed for a warm swamp storm, some hot rain to rinse his ashy mouth. The other women scattered, leaving Aidan to Honey.

"Why aren't you home, snuggling with her?" she said.

"Coincidence I run into you. Wasn't looking for company." Aidan started to leave.

"Don't go." Honey's fingers grazed his sleeve.

He pulled his arm away, but halted. "Is your name really Honey?"

"Let's have a drink, darling," she said. "Your pockets look full. I know you can afford to buy us one wee drink."

"I don't drink, ma'am. Used to, but not no more. Not a drop."

"Have I found a saint then? Am I wasting my time?"

Aidan pulled money from his coat pocket. "I ain't a saint." He placed twenty dollars in her hand. Her pale face flushed at this wind-fall. "I appreciate a hardworking woman," he said. "Find yourself a warm place."

She balled the money up in her fist. "I got a warm bed big enough for two. And a private bottle we could share." Honey smiled, like she wanted him, not just his money. "You're a handsome fellow. Not my usual customer."

"Really?" Aidan smiled too. "Who's to say you don't have a knife at your bosom and wouldn't rob me blind in that warm bed?"

"Same as a ride on the Ferris Wheel, darling. Danger's half the fun."

Aidan chuckled, almost feeling good. "You remind me of someone."

"This is a cruel world. Snatch comfort where you can." Honey touched his arm again. He didn't pull away as she purred at him. "What's she like, your ladylove? Tell me how to be and I know I can be just like her. Close your eyes and all the parts feel the same. It'll be just like doing her, so you won't have to feel guilty or sad or lonely. I'll do what she won't do, but it'll feel just like her."

Aidan was late. The ballroom of the Ace of Spades Hotel was jammed and they were supposed to go on in five minutes. He never came home last night. If Iris hadn't said Aidan was fine, Redwood would've been worrying all night and all day. If she set her mind to it, Iris could look out and *see* people, even if they were far away. She didn't recognize where, but she *saw* Aidan standing by dark water, shivering in cold snow, and talking Irish to someone. That was yesterday. Redwood didn't want to ask Iris to spy on him too much. It wore Baby Sister out. Besides, knowing wasn't always better than not knowing.

Redwood stood behind the audience, stretching her tight calf muscles, telling herself Aidan deserved a woman who could be a woman with him even if just for a night. Didn't she love him no matter what? If you loved somebody you wanted the best for them.

"Are you all right?" Saeed asked.

"Cramp."

"I meant you and him."

"I don't know."

"We can go on without Mr. Wildfire, can't we?"

"I guess."

"Sometimes I am jealous of him."

"Oh?"

"More than one way to feel that someone is yours." Saeed squeezed her hand.

"We have enough of our own routines to fill the time."

"You don't want to though."

Redwood blew air out her lips. "It took us over a year to put this show together. Where is he? This is our night for theatre magic."

"Magic? Good. Aida Overton Walker is in the audience."

"I thought she was in New York on Broadway." Redwood's heart pounded. The leading lady of colored theatre, *His Honor: The Barber, Salome,* sitting out there somewhere to see their little show? "Are you just saying that?"

"Why would I do that? I hear she's come incognito, in her husband's clothes."

"You see her?" Redwood peered at the audience. "Where is she sitting?"

The crowd, cheering and laughing for the comedy act, was the usual mix, rowdy working folk taking a night out on the town. Aidan's Indian buddies from the motion picture factory teased Walter Jumping Bear and an Indian woman on his arm. Nicolai and his camera crew cussed at the lights and cranked away. Saeed's family and Mr. McGregor sat among tourists hunting down exotic entertainment. Saeed's handsome friend, a union organizer name of Carl or Corey, drank black coffee from a tiny cup right next to Prince Anoushiravan. Club ladies nibbled sweet cakes and sipped bright beverages. Bessie Harris wore a somber gray dress and was sitting proud. Plump Mambo Dupree flaunted bright red satin robes. She sat beside a skeletal old gent in black, stabbing at her food with a large knife and gulping rum. A hot *Loa* was riding her tonight. A few women were dressed as gents but their faces were cloaked in shadows. Redwood spied two men who could've been Doc Johnson and Subie's nephew, Clarence, but with Nicolai's lights glaring up and her blinking away tears, she lost them in the crowd.

"You shouldn't be crying. That'll make you too hoarse to sing." A hand on her shoulder had her almost jumping out her skin.

"How you sneak up on me like that?" She turned and hugged Aidan, so fiercely it would've knocked someone else over.

"Where have you been?" Saeed asked. "You shouldn't do her, *do us* that way."

"Sorry, there was that fire at Jones's grocery yesterday."

"You were there!" Redwood got a whiff of smoke from him. "You saw it." The grisly scene raced over his face.

"Tell us later. At least you're in costume," Saeed said.

Aidan and Redwood both wore Seminole patchwork coats belted at the waist, and Saeed was dressed as a fine Persian gentleman.

"We got us a full house," Aidan said. "Five hundred souls and no cooning tonight."

"Are you a little bit happy at least then?" Redwood whispered to Aidan.

"Why only a little bit?" He pulled out Subie's tin.

"You run out of that powder a long time ago." She jabbed his ribs, smiling.

"Don't know if the powder was the cure, so I don't dare throw this ole thing away. It's my good luck." He touched the tin against his lips and the music called them on.

Saeed led their dance through the aisles. He leapt from the back of a chair onto a table without stepping in food or knocking over any drinks. The clubwomen at his feet squealed with delight. Mambo Dupree waved her knife, warning him not to stomp her pork ribs. He danced from table to table, while Aidan and Redwood ran onto the rickety stage. Redwood dropped her coat to reveal flowing pants and a loose blouse. She swirled like a storm rising. Saeed sprang from a front row table right at Aidan, landed on his shoulders, and pushed up into a handstand. Aidan sank down a bit at the impact, but held Saeed easily. The audience hooted and applauded.

Redwood circled the men singing *I've been climbing, climbing Sorrow Mountain* in Farsi. Shimmy-shaking, she lifted Saeed's left hand and he balanced just on the right. As he pushed off toward the ground, she danced up Aidan's left thigh to his right shoulder, stepping on Saeed's shoulder when he hit the floor. The piano player slapped a sultry rhythm on an hourglass drum. The guitarman blew a Persian flute. The fiddler bowed a few high notes, wavering 'round the melody like a hummingbird's wing.

Facing away from the hushed crowd, feeling a thousand eyes on her back, Redwood dipped down and then vaulted up off the men's sturdy bones. She soared through the air, the fabric of her costume billowing like glorious wings. Aidan and Saeed glanced up at her, stunned. The drummer and the fiddler halted. After a few shrill arpeggios, the flute player lost his breath. Redwood floated above their heads, no wires holding her up. She soared a good while for Bessie, for Aidan and Iris, for everybody. *Isti siminoli,* free as a Seminole, she twisted herself 'round to face the audience and landed back on Aidan's and Saeed's shoulders. Each man grabbed a hand, and she cascaded down to the floor. The piano man handed Aidan his banjo. He and Redwood left dancing to Saeed, while they sang in close harmony:

I've been climbing, climbing Sorrow Mountain
I've been climbing, climbing desperate days
Have you seen that dried-up fountain?
And all those folks lost in a maze?
I've been climbing, climbing Sorrow Mountain
This time around, I'm coming down
This time around, I'm coming down

At a front row table, Iris, Clarissa, and Abbaseh applauded. Walter Jumping Bear and his lady were on their feet, shouting. Prince Anoushiravan, Farah, and Akhtar smiled politely. Mambo Dupree waved her knife, and a white woman in a gray suit was so excited, she knocked over a cold drink. It was the lady from the El! Nicolai and crew captured quite a show in their cameras. Milton threw roses at the stage. Eddie was slapping his hands together and so busy talking to George, he was still clapping when everyone else had stopped.

After five songs, three dances, and two encores, after cheers and toasts, and Bessie and a few club ladies pressing money in Redwood's hand for the picture, after Mambo Dupree saying, "Blessings on you from Erzulie Dantor, no sweetie goddess she, a dragon of love, burning you free," Redwood and Aidan slipped out the back to an alleyway.

"Next time you get it in your head to fly . . ." He wanted to be mad, but she caught a grin.

"I'm a magic gal, ain't I? Got the devil in me too." She switched her hips at him. "You didn't think I'd fall, did you?"

"No, but that ain't the point, is it?"

"I talked myself into flying last night. Promised to do magic if you showed up." She stepped close. "Had the feeling for a snowy egret." She wanted to kiss him, wanted the taste of him in her mouth, but 'stead of being bold and courageous, she folded her arms over her bosom. "So what couldn't wait till we got home?"

"There'd be too many folks nosing 'round and walls closing us in," Aidan said. "I just wanted dark and shadow and the stars."

"Moon's hiding behind the clouds." She squinted. "Is that dark enough for you?"

"I suspect."

"Akhtar's mad at you. She cooked a big meal, but wouldn't serve anything since you wasn't there."

"Oh. That is too bad." He scratched his jaw. "I'll make it up to her."

"She promised to do it again tomorrow. So you better be there. And Iris has been writing up a storm. She want to put a Seminole farmer in our moving picture. I said fine, but she had to talk to you." Redwood was fixing to chatter on, but he looked ready to crumble into ash and blow away. "You all right?"

"Reginald Jones's grocery burning down, I heard them folks on fire, dying."

"I felt it. Just didn't know what was wrong."

He cleared his throat and spit out soot and smoke. "I got a look at the ones who set it. White fellows, roughnecks."

She pressed against his chest. He flinched. She didn't pull away. "Don't let them bad men haunt you."

"I dug through the rubble for the dead and then I don't know. Boneyard baron chased me 'round all night. Thought I'd freeze to death in the snow, till—" He hauled a bottle out of his shoulder bag, whiskey most like.

"What you doing with that?" She ran a finger down the glass.

He held up a second bottle. "My mama used to say, *If it's drowning you're after, don't torment yourself with shallow water.*"

"You still have all those voices in you." She closed her eyes and let the sound of him touch her. "Tickles me all over."

"Ain't you goin' yell at me?"

"You tole me fussing and cussing don't do no good."

"I said fighting, but you right."

"I'm so glad to see you. Couldn't cuss you, even if you deserved it. I thought you wasn't coming. I thought maybe you was gone for good."

"Without a word? Without a fight?" He looked ready to fall over. "You don't know me better than that?"

She clutched him. "I didn't say it made sense."

"I ain't in no hurry to leave you."

"But if I let you go?"

He threw the bottles against a wall. Shattered glass came back at them. They danced away, not quickly enough. A splinter lodged in Aidan's thumb. "Damn it. Goddamn it." It wasn't like him to cuss in front of her. She pulled the glass, pulled the pain, and then held his hand in hers. "I love you, I do, Miz Redwood," he whispered.

"And I love you too." She kissed his hand. It was rough and blistered. She drew her tongue 'cross his palm and each finger, tasting salt, sweat, smoke, and blood. "I don't tell you, but I feel it all the time." She put his cold hand on her warm bosom.

"What good is keeping that all to yourself?" He held out a box cut in the shape of a comet. The tail was silver threads and blue-violet feathers from a swamp hen.

She brushed it with her fingers. "You made this?"

"Yes, ma'am." He set it in her hands. "I know how you like shooting stars."

"When you have time to do that?"

"Better than drinking the night away."

"I hope you didn't kill no bird for those feathers."

"No. That bird had just come to the end of her days."

Redwood shook it. "What's inside?"

"You got to open and see."

"I don't know. I don't think I can."

"What you 'fraid of?"

"Breaking your heart."

Loud voices filled the dark. Aidan cussed soft this time so she couldn't hear.

"This ain't exactly the most romantic spot," she said.

Eddie and George tromped down the alley, arguing. Seeing Redwood and Aidan, they got quiet. George's hand was wrapped in a bloody handkerchief. Blood from a cut under his eye drizzled down his cheek.

"I thought you left fighting back in Georgia," Redwood said.

"They don't let you be a man nowhere," George said. "I have to fight."

"You *like* fighting, George," Aidan said. "You like smashing in a face, bringing a cracker down to the dirt. Am I lying?"

"You got it exactly." George smirked.

"That won't make you a man," Aidan said softly.

"And you goin' tell me what will?"

Redwood stepped between them. "I know how hard it is for you, Brother."

"Do you?" George looked over to Eddie's sneering face. "Even colored don't want you to stand up. I gotta fight for every inch."

"We can still make our own place in the world, be who we want." Redwood touched the wound on his face.

"Leave it." George grabbed her hand. "Let it heal on its own."

She struggled free. "What you want with scars? Ain't you mad enough already, you got to look at your ugly pain every day?"

"Just 'cause you done slipped the noose, you act like this world ain't trying to hang us all," George bellowed.

"How you know what noose I slipped or ain't slipped?" Redwood said. "You don't know nothing 'bout me. Too wound into yourself."

"You laying up in my house with this cracker saying that? I don't care how much wild *Injun* running through him."

"Let's go." Aidan pulled Redwood away from George.

"Wait." She halted. Aidan was wheezing like an automobile. George had fire on his breath too. "Nicolai offered to shoot any moving picture we dream up. No charge. I got more than half the money for my picture."

"So?" Eddie laughed. "You ain't goin' make no money after it's done."

"You got as much power as Mama ever had, more really," George said. "But you can't make the world turn your way. Only a crazy man would *believe* in that."

George banged into Aidan as he and Eddie walked away. Aidan grabbed George's arm. They faced off, nostrils flaring, teeth gritted. "Them crackers you hate so much ain't the only ones telling the story," Aidan said and let George go.

Back at the house, 'stead of romancing Aidan like she planned, 'stead of opening her shooting star and getting more of the taste of him in her mouth, Redwood fretted over George, over herself too. Was she still a naïve fool trying to make the world turn her way when danger was coming that could burn them all?

"You think he worries over *you* like this?" Aidan paced their back parlor room, a lion, roaring to tear the place apart.

"He's my brother and somebody walked 'cross his grave. Iris saw the baron."

"Whatever he's up to, it's a deadly game." Aidan shook his head. "But he ain't looking out for you. He ditched you in a swamp to go make a fortune killing birds."

"He come back to look for me that time!" She sank down on the bed, holding Aidan's box against her bosom, the swamp hen feathers trailing into her lap. George made her spitting mad, but she couldn't give up on him, not yet. "I won't be selfish to suit him. Mama said to watch over each other."

"And you and me?" Aidan shouted.

"Shush! You 'llowed to wake the dead," she hissed. "George is easier to sort out." She gripped Aidan's hand as he stumbled by. "Up all night, you ready to fall on your face."

"I can't stay in this house."

"I know. I know."

"George is . . . who he is. I ain't talking against him. He got a heavy load. He just ain't the only one. I can't stay under his roof." He was ready to pack his things and leave.

"Just till the moving picture's done."

He shook free of her. "Who knows how long that will be?"

"Not long." She reached for him again. "Don't you want to do our own story too?"

"Of course." He dodged her fingers. "Then we take Iris and we go. They got land out west *and* moving pictures. The prince say it's beautiful country."

"Out west? I don't know."

"They got hills and valleys and good farmland. They got a sky so big, it make your head reel trying to see to the end. I know how to make things grow and I . . . could make you happy out there. I know I could."

She jumped up. "You make me happy, Aidan, right here, right now. Happier than anyone deserve. It's my fault we got troubles."

"No. It ain't just you." His hands shook. "Things getting too hard to take sober. I can't stay in this house, playing the wild *Injun* savage or the drunk Irishman." He dropped on the cushions in the window seat.

"Who's asking you to do that?" She sat beside him.

He was shaking and cold as ice. "You didn't hear those screams."

"No." She leaned her forehead against his. He went dead still. "So tell me. Everything. How we used to be."

She wrapped warm arms 'round him and pulled a blanket over them both. Squirming, he fought tears and ended in a coughing fit. When that passed, she laid his head in her lap and stroked the tight strings of muscles running down his neck.

"Ten, fifteen people," he said, tears flowing now. "Dying in fire."

"That many?"

"Maybe more. Can't say who all was shopping. Shelves fell and blocked the front door. Stairs collapsed on people coming from the second floor and blocked the back. They couldn't get out. They just couldn't get out. Nothing left but to burn up or suffocate. Somebody had a gun, so I guess, well, there were shots, but they didn't all get to go quick. And me just standing there, wringing my hands. All I ever do."

"Hush. You a good man. The best I know. The evil you seen ain't your fault."

That made him cry more. "After the fire, I thought I wanted a woman so bad anybody would do. I need a drink to get that started. Truth be told, I was on the run, heading for a jug. But that was no good either."

"You just tired and lonely. I'll sleep here. Keep you company in your dreams."

"Ain't enough room on this window seat," he said.

She curled 'round him, hot for once against his frosty back. "Grown man need tender too." She pressed her storm hand to his cheek.

"Seem like I usually make your skin crawl."

"That ain't you," she whispered. "You know that."

"It's real hard being with you and not being with you."

"I promised myself, if you showed up at Spades tonight, I'd fly, in the show. But when it come time, when I felt the cue, I wasn't sure. I thought I might fall. But you a conjure man, always get me to trust my magic, get me to soar."

Redwood rubbed Aidan's back till he was warm, breathing deep, till he didn't fight sleep no more. She let the rumble of his chest and the rhythm of his heart fill her. And then she joined him in dreams like she promised.

TWENTY-TWO

After falling down a studio canyon all day, Aidan's muscles throbbed and his stomach hollered to beat the band. He stumbled over George's mail and dry-cleaning receipts stacked in the vestibule. The prince gripped his arm and broke the fall. Iris got the papers in order while Akhtar ushered everyone to the mysterious meal she'd been making for hours, days actually. The delicious aroma of spices and herbs was familiar, but Aidan only recognized one dish he'd eaten on the prince's train car. The table looked like a tapestry that should hang in a museum.

"In my country we do not have the same custom of surnames as you do here," the prince explained to Clarissa.

"Oh dear. I am ignorant of your ways." She flushed. "I don't want to be rude, sir."

"*Mokhalafat.*" Akhtar pointed to plates of fresh herbs, flatbreads, and white cheese and yogurt. "*Khoresht sabsi.*" She had thrown kidney beans, green onions, dried limes, and lamb into a pot with all sorts of herbs, spinach, and parsley, and then served it on top of rice. "*Tahdigh* . . . Iris."

"The sweet bottom of the rice pot is for Iris," the prince translated.

Akhtar brought out skewers of meat for each plate. "*Kabab koobideh.*"

"That is good." Aidan had taken a bite in the kitchen—beef ground up with onion and fragrant herbs.

"Everybody help yourself. That's how they do in Persia." George filled his plate.

The dinner party was in the dining room, despite the early winter chill. George was burning a fortune, heating every room in the house to impress his guests, business associates Dr. Harris, Mr. Powell, and their wives, women from Clarissa's club, one a doctor her ownself.

They were very fair-skinned colored people who exchanged nervous looks over the food. George presided at the head of the table near his colleagues. Clarissa sat at the opposite end. Saeed, the prince, Farah, Akhtar, and Abbaseh sat close to her. Redwood and Aidan were in the middle.

Akhtar poured Aidan pomegranate juice, and George lifted a glass of Persian wine. "To Miz Akhtar's fine food." Everyone drank to the cook, who blushed. George raised his glass to the women. "You ladies look good enough to eat too."

Iris was the only one to giggle at this. She also wore a fancy dress and lurked in the hallway, listening in on the grown-ups, too old to be in bed and yet too young to be at this table, according to Clarissa. Aidan would've had her sit next to him.

"You've traveled all over, sir," Clarissa said when the meal was pleasantly underway. "I'm glad you and your family stopped in Chicago before going home."

"Abbaseh's English is very good now. She can converse with you." He turned to his third wife, the musician, poetess, and his boldest companion. "Speak."

Everyone stopped eating to look at her. Embarrassed, she picked at her vegetables.

"Won't you say something?" Clarissa said sweetly.

After a moment Abbaseh spoke with only the faintest Farsi accent. "Did you know my name means lioness?"

"It suits you," Aidan said as Redwood smiled.

"Tell us about your moving picture project." Abbaseh turned to Redwood.

"Iris is helping us write a scenario," Redwood replied.

"Don't get her started on that." George stuffed lamb and kidney beans in his mouth.

"Poetry's good for the spirit," Mrs. Powell said. "We can stand tall with poetry in us."

"A motion picture is quite an undertaking for a colored woman," Dr. Harris said.

"Hope is always a guest at our table," Clarissa said. "We have high hopes for the colored woman."

Dr. Harris scrunched up his mouth and nodded politely.

The prince nibbled olives. "Yes, this is a young nation."

"And a flawed one," Mr. Powell said.

"But with great potential," the prince said quickly.

"Redwood need to do a picture to uplift the *white race*." George chewed a piece of flatbread. "She need to take all that talent and power and do *something* worthwhile! They burned down Reginald Jones's grocery and the colored bank standing next to it."

"I saw it." Aidan was seeing it again. "That Chinese laundry's gone too." He closed his eyes on images he'd rather not conjure up and focused on speaking the prince's name right. "Anoushiravan and I were there."

"Seeing it, that's nothing." George waved his hand at Aidan. His voice hardened. "Think of burning alive, your breath on fire and your heart sizzling away."

Aidan shuddered.

"George, please, we're eating," Clarissa said.

"Think of colored lives ruined. Hardworking people losing everything they got."

"It was a bitter sight." The prince drank down his wine.

"Something like that is happening to a colored business every time you turn 'round." George poured more wine.

"I've made a wonderful dessert." Clarissa smiled at everyone.

"I know 'bout losing everything you got," Aidan said, "the old times, the future, just living on the run, moment to moment."

George nodded. "Exactly, but you'd think the colored man had nothing better to do than go see my sister cut the fool in—"

"It's not the same ole story they make us do," Redwood said.

Aidan squeezed her hand under the table. "We goin' make a picture nobody seen yet."

"Wonderful," Clarissa and the clubwomen said as a chorus.

"I gave some money," Mrs. Harris said.

"I was against it." Dr. Harris chuckled. "Bessie is always doing good deeds behind my back."

Saeed turned to Dr. Harris's skeptical face. "I play a pirate and Aidan is a wise—"

"Did he graduate from the coon academy too?" George sneered. "Or do *Injuns* get their own schooling?"

"George!" Clarissa was so flustered she couldn't say anything more.

"What, my dear?" George's lips were drawn in a tight smile.

In the awkward silence, Farah worried over the teapot. Aidan picked at the last of his *Kabab koobideh,* but his hands were shaking so, he dropped the fork into saffron rice. He stood up slowly, feeling like a wounded bear, cornered into fighting.

Redwood almost threw her knife at George but stabbed a fat fig instead. "Don't make fun of who I am, Brother, of who I try to be, of the people I love." Everybody looked uncomfortable 'cept for George. He wanted this fight. "I know you and what you do. Even so, I stand by you." Redwood laced her fingers through Aidan's trembling ones. George smacked a fly buzzing near his plate. Redwood jumped at the impact. "Don't push me away."

Aidan looked her in the eye. "You stay and finish. The food is delicious. The company is grand, but I'm feeling poorly. If you ladies will excuse me."

Redwood started to protest, but Abbaseh grabbed her other hand. Aidan slipped away into the hallway, shaking with rage.

Iris snagged him and whispered, "You can't pay Brother no mind."

Aidan whispered as well. "When he jab at Redwood, I could just go wild."

"But you won't." She sure had faith in him.

In the dining room as Farah poured tea, Abbaseh talked again. "My husband will not give money for moving pictures, but I give this to you." She offered a ring to Redwood. Precious stones sparkled against gold. Iris stifled a squeal. Aidan fell on his butt. Farah and Akhtar murmured in Farsi. They seemed as shocked as everyone else.

Redwood gently folded Abbaseh's hands over the ring. "I can't take your ring."

"Of course you can," the prince said. "It's hers to give. Isn't this a free nation?"

"Indeed it is." Clarissa set down her napkin and stood up. All the men stood quickly. She headed for the kitchen. "I need your help, George."

"In the kitchen?" George asked. "Why you send that gal home early if you need help?" She did not reply. He muttered something and after a moment followed behind her. The men sat back down.

"Come on." Iris dragged Aidan down the hallway to the kitchen door. "Don't want to miss this." She crouched to the side in dim shadows and peered through a crack.

"You listen in on everything, don't you?" Aidan hissed.

Iris put a finger to her lips, then his.

In the kitchen, George paced. "This is my house. I'll say what I want."

Clarissa stood over a large chocolate confection, holding a knife. "The moving picture is the medicine I need to help your sister . . . be a full woman."

Aidan winced and hung his head.

George sighed. "Since when you going to a conjure woman?"

Aidan looked over to Iris, who shrugged at this.

George wagged a finger at Clarissa. "You been throwing my money away on that Mambo Dupree?"

"We have to *believe* in Redwood," Clarissa said. "With money—"

"Sis live in a dreamworld. I love her, but—"

"Are you going to let that Persian prince outdo you in your own country?" She sliced through the cake. "Hand me my mother's silver platter."

"What?" George screwed up his face.

"It's on the third shelf." Clarissa pointed.

"He ain't no prince. He's a rug merchant. Iris made that up." George stood on a stool.

Clarissa counted the slices. "They've raised most of the money."

George retrieved a brightly colored bundle from the top of the cupboard. "Here. Redwood and Aidan make more money than me."

"I know that's a lie." Clarissa unwrapped the platter and laid the chocolate pieces on it. "Redwood is ambitious, like you, and Mr. Wildfire believes in her."

"He laying up in her bed, ain't he?" George licked chocolate from her finger. "Hoodooed like the rest of 'em."

"Don't be so crude. He has his own magic too." She wiped George's mouth with a cloth. "People don't know it's a scandal unless we tell them."

"Who don't know that cracker be up in her bed?"

"I deny vicious gossip." Clarissa kissed the chocolate on George's lips. "Besides, Mr. Wildfire's an Indian."

"He wasn't Indian when we was growing up. You always take his side."

"I do not. You're just unreasonable." Clarissa cleaned the knife.

"Tribes down home in Georgia—Choctaw, Chickasaw, Creek, Cherokee, and Seminole—owned us, lived off our sweat, just like white folk. All them Indians claim when God made the races, when he cooked them up from fine clay, the black man came out burnt and foolish and good for nothing but slaving."

Iris stared at Aidan with wounded eyes.

"Mr. Wildfire doesn't believe such nonsense any more than you believe tales of pagan savages scalping innocent people!"

"Aidan Cooper was an Irish redneck when they raped my mama and hung her from a tree to burn."

Iris's fingers dug into Aidan's flesh.

Clarissa's eyes brimmed with tears. "Are we just the horrible things that happen to us? Is that all we are, George?" She wiped her eyes on the cloth from the platter. "Investing in a motion picture is better than fooling ignorant white folks out of their homes and charging poor Negroes five times what they can pay."

George's face fell. "Red tell you 'bout that?"

"What do you mean to do, George?" Clarissa picked up the platter and walked toward the dining room. "Your sister needs a loan from you, that's all."

George followed her. "I can't take it when you both gang up on me."

"So say yes."

In a cold attic room under the eaves, Aidan tucked Iris into warm blankets.

She pulled him onto the bed. "Three girls jumped me on the way home."

"What you do?"

"'Stead of whipping them good, I ran all the way to the prince's railroad car."

"Now, you shouldn't go bothering them . . ."

"Miz Abbaseh say I can come anytime. We talk about everything."

"I didn't know she spoke English till tonight."

"Miz Abbaseh's teaching me how to hide in plain sight."

"That's a good trick." He kissed her forehead. "You go to sleep now."

"I'm not one bit tired." Iris clutched him. "I want a story. Like when I was little."

"I thought you was too old, too sophisticated, for Georgia tales."

"Not if it's good." She tugged his sleeve. "You know lots of good stories."

"Didn't sleep much and I've been scalping white folk all day. I'm tired, honey bun."

She put her head in his lap. "It's not *you*. Brother George just don't like *white folks*."

"Good reason not to."

"But you ain't like—"

"Good sense not to trust a stranger right off. Color of the skin tell you a lot."

"Don't tell you nothing for certain. Look at you."

Aidan sagged. "If you look too hard, you might not like what you see."

Iris sat up, startled. "What you goin' do?" She threw her arms 'round his neck. "Take me with you." She knew what he was thinking before he did. "Please don't go off and leave me here. Aunt Clarissa and Brother George want to turn me away from myself."

Aidan pulled her off his chest and looked into her eyes. "I don't know where I'm going just yet, but when I get somewhere, I'll come back for you."

"And Redwood too?"

Aidan sputtered. His eyes darted 'round his head.

"Seminole farmer in the motion picture was her idea. She figured you wouldn't argue if you thought it was my idea."

"What you say?"

"You can marry Sis if you can't wait for me. I know you love her."

Aidan stood up and shook his head.

"I was jealous at first. Where am I ever goin' find someone who'll love me just how I am? But I talked it over with Miz Abbaseh. She say, love is generous."

"She's right, but—"

"You can't pull your own pain," Iris said. "I ain't a hoodoo *yet,* but Aunt Subie say a good conjurer should help lead people back to themselves when they be lost." She sighed. "Redwood's so worried you might just give up on her."

"How you know that?" He hunched under the eaves.

"Iris got her nose in everything." Redwood stood behind Aidan with a candle. He would have jumped at her coming out of nowhere like that if he wasn't so weary. "She be chasing through dark nights snooping behind me."

"You won't tell me nothing." Iris tried to pout. "So I have to find out for myself."

Downstairs Aidan shivered by the drafty window seat. He packed clothes and books in his battered traveling bag. Too sad for words, he set a row of wooden aeroplanes on the bed and then watched Redwood swaying in the breeze.

"Say something. Don't just burn a hole in my skin, staring," she said.

Aidan shrugged and wrapped his banjo in an old blanket.

"You ain't goin' take the case I give you?" She fingered her mama's music box. "More than half this money is yours."

"That money is for the moving picture." His eyes swept the room. "George is right."

"George is an ornery cuss. It runs in the family. He takes a mountain of patience."

"I'm a coward," Aidan said simply. "Don't argue."

Redwood bit her lip, hard.

"I been meaning to give Iris this." He handed her *Of One Blood: Or, The Hidden Self* by Pauline Hopkins. "That was a good story."

She set the book on her desk. "Nicolai thinks we can start on the film next week, after Thanksgiving for sure."

"That's good news." Aidan gathered his things.

"Money might run out 'fore we're done."

"I suspect we'll just keep on going." He trudged to the door. "I think maybe Walter will let me stay with him, while we do the picture."

"He's a good friend to you."

"What you thinking?" Aidan said just out the door. "Talk to me."

"I want to tell you don't go. I want to hold you here. But I love you too much."

Aidan wanted to shout, *come with me*. "The aeroplane with the lady pilot is for Iris." He headed over the soft Persian carpet and out the front door.

The moon was a sliver on the horizon. Aidan pressed his lips together against the snowy air. He put one foot in front of another, his mind so blank he didn't notice which direction he headed till twenty minutes from George's house.

Even so far, he felt Redwood's sad eyes stabbing at his back.

BOOK VI

And your very flesh shall be a great poem.

—Walt Whitman

TWENTY-THREE

Shooting the Moving-Picture Play, Chicago, 1913

Nicolai was wrong. They couldn't start filming after Thanksgiving. On a screen, Lake Michigan would do fine as the Atlantic Ocean off the Georgia Sea Islands, but not with thin ice crusting the surface, bald trees in the background, and snow spitting from a heavy white sky. They had to wait out winter and a cold spring to shoot *The Pirate and the Schoolteacher* in summer. The long holdup should've driven Redwood wild, what with money disappearing, respectable folk breaking promises or outright cheating the production, and then missing Aidan every blessed day, even when he was standing right next to her. But who could blame the man for getting out from under George? Indeed, Redwood would've left with Aidan, 'cept he was running from her as much as from George. And who could blame him for that either?

Redwood was a whirlwind, going too fast to feel sorry or stew in heartache.

Colored folk, escaping Jim Crow nightmares in the south, were hitting the rail and busting into Chicago's Black Belt. More and more families were stacked on top of each other in rickety tenements fixing to fall over when the El rattled by. Redwood was mending broken bones, broken hearts, and hiring hard-luck cases to build costumes and properties. These ex-Southerners knocked themselves out day and night to turn their world right side up. They flooded the schools, factories, shops, and docks with hope. Of course, these hardworking dreamers were looking for good times too, for a colored pirate picture show on a Saturday night. Redwood was goin' do 'em proud.

Aidan, costumed as a respectable Irish businessman, bargained with stingy merchants for cloth, paint, wood. The lilt on his tongue was charming and threatening. He got the price they needed and carpentered what they couldn't buy or borrow. The man fussed over every joint and nail, till each platform, stick of furniture, set piece was sturdy and looked good too.

At first, out-of-work Eddie refused to act the villain in a scenario written by fourteen-year-old Iris. He didn't see why Saeed should play the lead. Aidan wanted to throttle Eddie, but Iris promised Eddie swordplay and acrobatics on land, sea, and horseback in his final scene, and Eddie relented. Milton was happy to play a minister, just to be performing again, 'stead of working in the Dry Cleaning. George Jr., Ellie, Belle, and even Frank were thrilled to be cast with Iris as Redwood's pupils. Clarissa clicked her tongue over the propriety of a pirate romancing a teacher, yet agreed to play a good Christian woman if the scenario ended in a wedding. Walter Jumping Bear wanted a love story with Rose of the *Hutalgalgi,* Wind clan. Rose had acted in Shakespeare at boarding school in Pennsylvania where they *Americanized* Indians. She never liked the boarding school; still, she loved acting.

Iris worked all these wishes and demands into the scenario without a fuss. After Aidan moved out, 'stead of pitching a fit, Baby Sister was a moving picture wonder—organizing much mess, smoothing ruffled feathers, keeping peace and calm. She was never too tired for one more task. Iris conjured a convincing character at school too. Teachers couldn't tell her from the model students. She spoke any grammar they wanted and didn't pout, fight, or slink out in the night, chasing behind haints. Even so, Redwood was like to have lost her mind.

Iris wanted a lion to chase the villains and eat them for the climax.

"Even bad men shouldn't have to pay with their flesh," Aidan said to her, laughing. "Where we goin' find a lion to playact for the camera?"

"I can't wrassle with no big cat." Redwood might as well have been wearing a corset, her breath was so shallow. "I'm at the end of my tether with the likes of Eddie, fancy-pants Nicolai, and all these unskilled folk who don't know diddly 'bout theatre magic." Aidan laughed on, and Iris wagged her head and said mm-hmm. Redwood could tell she wasn't giving up on the lion idea. "We should get us a big cat to eat the landlords charging more for rent than folk can earn," Redwood muttered.

Iris put her hands on her hips and jutted her jaw out. "You mean Brother?"

Redwood didn't have nothing to say to that. At least Aidan stopped laughing.

"I'll talk to him," Iris said, rocking her head back and forth.

When the weather finally warmed up, Nicolai's crew ran off with arc lights, mercury vapor lamps, reels of film stock, and new cameras. The police didn't bother to investigate. Redwood put on silk and satin, painted her face like a brilliant sunset, and hoodooed Mr. Payne out of a terrible cough. In return she got replacement equipment for cheap before he moved his picture factory to California. Yet, what good were the cameras or building the sets or rehearsing if they didn't have folks to take the pictures and develop and process the film? After chasing hinkty white professionals for weeks with no luck, Nicolai balked at hiring two colored cameramen and an Indian apprentice to replace the thieves, supposedly 'cause he hadn't worked with them.

"They've done vaudeville, Wild West shows. They're good," Redwood said. Nicolai wouldn't budge. When she threatened an all-women crew, suddenly he was persuaded.

On a sunny day, Lake Michigan was vast and bright blue, magnificent with white-capped waves kissing golden beaches. Picture perfect. Mr. Powell, George's lawyer, had brokered an affordable lease on a grand filming spot. Crooked, windswept trees presided over shifting dunes and reminded Redwood of Sapelo, where her mama's people come from and some of Aidan's people too.

The lake, however, could also be a temperamental prima donna. Along the end of May, golden sand turned glassy as a demon storm dumped snow on their location, weighing down green branches and freezing buds and blossoms. The Baptist church set got ruined. They didn't have much time for repairs or any money to hire extra crew. So, the second frosty night, Redwood laid out a *crossroads* spell, a devotion to the spirits of this watery place. She should've done this first thing. As she blew incense in the four directions, Aidan hung glass bottles in the trees. The sound startled her, still she wasn't surprised. The church set looked brand-new. He'd been working both nights. Redwood waved. He nodded. She'd let him go, but he hadn't gone far. The bottles tinkled against icy leaves and the dark spit snow in her face. Watching Aidan, hope warmed her cold fingers. She tried to forgive every mean, ornery body and sweep away old pain. She

stepped close to him. Fogging the air white with deep breaths, he lit a
new fire, and they took a moment to celebrate first fruits. She silently
promised the lake to do no harm and asked the *crossroads* spirits to
open the way.

"Why you grinning?" he said finally.

"Forgiveness is the sweetest revenge."

"Hmm." He closed his eyes.

In the morning, the snow melted and the lake returned to early
summer glory. Frostbitten buds perked up in sunshine, looking ready
to pop. Everybody was rehearsed and raring to go—no magic-miracle,
just hard labor.

One day scrambled into the next, and even George was impressed
with their enterprise. Mr. McGregor drove him out to their remote
location as they were finishing up the first week of shooting. Eddie's
villain stabbed Redwood's schoolteacher and she collapsed in Pirate
Saeed's arms.

"Mr. Minsky said you were shooting the end," George said. "You
can't end your picture like that!" He looked to Aidan as if for help.
Redwood snorted at this and marched away. Before she could take off
her schoolteacher dress or untie the scarf on her head, George offered
her a handsome sum, which she didn't have to repay if they lost everything. She was so stunned, she tripped over sand. Aidan waved at Mr.
McGregor and vanished, leaving the negotiations up to her.

"Hold your money, George," Redwood said. "We're fine now."

Mr. McGregor pretended not to listen in, but she saw his ears perk
up.

"What's wrong with my money?" Her rich brother cut a fine city
figure in his white suit and summer straw hat. The withering look on
his country face still called a fire-breathing dragon to mind. "I know
I'm an ass sometimes, but you can't hold that against me when I'm
trying to help you, damn it."

"Is that supposed to be an apology?" Redwood rolled her eyes. "I
shouldn't put up with you, I really shouldn't. For Mama's sake I have,
but you ain't my only family."

"I didn't throw Coop out. I . . ." The fire on his breath went to his
eyes. "Reginald Jones was good people. I knew him back home. I put
up the money for his grocery shop."

"God rest his soul, but you staked Mr. Jones and not your own sister?"

"Reginald had a family, a legitimate business. And they burned him and his dream." George sighed. "Maybe they were hitting at me going after him."

"So why get mad at me? At Aidan? Like we hitting at you too. Maybe they were going after Mr. Jones! You ain't the only colored success rubbing white folks wrong."

"How come you didn't go with Coop when he left?"

She sputtered. "Why'd you leave me back in Georgia when you first come north?"

"I don't know." The wind picked up. He blinked away dust. "Let me help you now." They stared at one another till McGregor sneezed. "We're too stubborn, you and me." George clenched a fist. "Why end your picture so sad? Why you want to get run through with a sword?"

"I don't know." *Killing goes both ways. Dying is your own business.* "You don't know how low I feel sometimes. Nobody do."

"You don't tell anybody!" He gripped her shoulders like when they were young. "I'm not trying to make you do what I want. Just seem like you want to hurt yourself and . . . I don't understand."

"Don't always know what spell we're casting till after it's done."

"Ain't that the truth."

"When the picture's finished, you could maybe see to it that people line up, pay their dime to watch what we've done."

"That's what I was thinking." George grinned. "We'll do it same as a road show." He was suddenly more excited than she'd seen him in months. "I looked into it."

"Uh-huh." When it came to money, George had to know everything. "Well, ain't you goin' tell me?" Her stomach growled. She couldn't remember when she ate last.

"Motion pictures are putting traveling stage shows out of business." George pulled her into the automobile, out of the lake breeze.

"Theatre folk can't hardly find good work no more." Redwood sighed. "Pekin Theatre's been closed almost two years. Magic Lantern Theatre 'bout to go dark too."

George set a picnic basket on the fine leather seat. "The Magic's showing moving pictures, no more vaudeville shows."

"That makes you grin?"

"Vaudeville going down is good news for us. They'll be desperate for pictures. We can do special engagements of *Pirate* in colored theatres, or matinee and midnight shows in white theatres if we have to." He unwrapped a spicy-smelling something. "We'll make more money that way." He offered her bread and juicy sausages.

"How?" She filled her mouth with one bite, swallowing before she got a good taste.

"'Stead of selling a print outright, we get the box office." George always had a good scheme. "Charge two bits, so they know it's worth something."

"Two bits? For a picture show?" She filled her mouth again. "Who can afford that?"

"For a dark hero and a brown-skin sweetheart, for the best seats— high-toned coloreds will, and working folk too." He handed her a cloth for her greasy face. "Saeed looks colored, all right? Besides that's how *they do*. Some producers charge a dollar."

"Just 'cause that's what *they do*, we gotta do it too?"

"We can't get stuck in the past. This is the future we're talking." He glanced out the automobile at the Sea Island cabins sitting near Lake Michigan. "We're practically in Wisconsin, ain't we? Lake so wide, can't see to the end." He turned back to Redwood, a somber look on his face. "I dropped the rent, okay? I was spending half my profits evicting folks anyhow. Then you go setting my wife against me and Baby Sister too."

"Clarissa and Iris got minds of their own."

"Me charging less don't change nothing. You can feel better taking my money is all."

"George, George. What we do really does matter." She hugged her ornery brother. "Even if it don't change everything. Like you say, we be making the future, now." She stepped out of the automobile and swallowed a burp. Eating too fast gave her indigestion. Mr. McGregor beamed at her. "Thanks for the dinner," she said.

"You never take care of yourself, Red." George nodded at Mr. McGregor, who started up the engine. Brother loved having a white man drive him. "We can talk over the ticket price later. I don't see white folks making big money and us not. Tomorrow's s'posed to be a better day." Before she could answer, Mr. McGregor sped off, doing twenty miles per hour for sure.

"What better day?" Redwood was 'fraid to look in the future. Something bad was coming, down in Chicago. It lurked 'round the corner, under burnt-out street lanterns, in sagging doorways and cracked cobblestone streets. She closed her eyes and the El shot off the track, wheels spinning sparks in the dark and setting the air on fire. Angry faces shone in the flame light, dirt-poor folk, supping on somebody else's misfortune. Redwood didn't speak her fear to George. He'd laugh. Clarissa would quote the Bible 'bout poor folk and tell her not to be so dramatic. Baby Sister was too young for such a burden. Aidan would've understood, yet she just couldn't bring herself to tell him.

With days of fine weather, *The Pirate and the Schoolteacher* got ahead of schedule. Redwood avoided thinking on *afterward*. Rising every morning and doing good work filled her up, pushed away sadness. She drove folks crazy though, doing a scene over and over, till each step, gesture, and expression looked grand, till broke-down cameras were jury-rigged and running again, till the sun up in the sky cooperated. They all grumped at her 'cept Aidan. She'd turn from a sour spat over *doing the scene again* and catch him grinning. At the breaks, she spied him in a canoe on the lake, playing his banjo, jotting secrets in his journal, and chuckling.

"I'm writing down the movie," he said to her curious eyes one afternoon. "Words last longer than film. Play a picture enough, it wears out. Read something again and again, it just get better."

"You sound happy," she said.

"Look who's talking." He gave her a devilish swamp grin.

Did her good to see him this way, and whenever Clarissa or Iris asked how was she *really*, she'd reply, "I'm having the time of my life." It was only half a lie.

When they had just a few big scenes left to shoot, Redwood got nervous. *Afterward* was getting too close. So when blue-black clouds rolled in from the northwest on her twenty-sixth birthday, she didn't start cussing with Nicolai. She smiled as the sun got swallowed, the lake turned gray, and a wildcat wind chopped up the waves. A rained-out day meant another sunny one to look forward to, more time to figure out the ending, more time before *afterward*.

"Happy birthday." Milton caught her staring a hole in nothing. A bushy gray beard matched the frosty hair on his head. The minister suit made him stand up and stride. "The older you get, the more honey you need to taste sweet, the duller the colors of sunset, and the shorter each minute of your life. Memory starts looking better than right now. You're too young for all that." He still read her like a favorite poem. "Life's ahead of you, not behind." He slipped a book into the pocket of her costume. "*The Autobiography of an Ex-Colored Man*—an anonymous tome, but it's good. Thanks for this show."

"Thank you." She hugged him close, smelling coffee on his lips, tobacco too, and the oil she gave him to ease his joints. "Thanks for all the shows, for seeing me through."

Milton strutted away, glowing at the edges. Redwood undid her boots and thrust aching feet in the lake. Cold-water waves lapped her toes and churned sand to froth.

"Somebody in a lion suit and mask?" Iris surprised Redwood from behind. Despite her schoolgirl costume, she was such a grown-up young lady now. "Like *The Wizard of Oz*. Mr. Saeed would make a grand lion, or even Mr. O'Reilly. Nobody would have to get hurt, and we wouldn't torment a real lion."

"Why you so set on a lion eating the villain?" Redwood said. "Explain me that and maybe we can do something."

"Why you get stabbed to death? And then they all get off with their lives! That ain't right."

"You're as bad as Brother. This world ain't right."

Iris did a heavy stage sigh and stomped away. Redwood envied Baby Sister's innocence, her free hold on life. It was spooky how, almost grown-up, Iris didn't lose her wild self. Raindrops hit Redwood's eyelashes, and she blinked off hard thoughts.

"If it's storming over there, Nicolai, it'll be storming here soon. We have to stop."

"See why all big companies leaving Chicago." Nicolai stood over her and then shouted a string of Russian, probably more cussing. "In California, warm sunny days all year. No Mr. Edison beating sets, clobbering cameramen. Nobody pinching lights."

"No one clobbers you here." Redwood sighed. "Not yet. No one cares what we do."

"Mr. Edison is not joke, Sequoia." Nicolai always used her stage name. "Edison want to squeeze everything in his fist, strong-hand us all. But I hear this Cecil B. DeMille fellow making *The Squaw Man* in California." He squinted at the clouds coming faster now, covering the sky. "I could be working his picture, making dollars and dollars every day." Fat drops broke on their faces.

"*The Squaw Man*?" Redwood shook her head. "From the play?"

"A real Indian—Princess Red Wing—playing the squaw."

"Killing herself for a white man." Redwood snorted. "Everybody has *real* Indians and *real* colored people too."

"Is dime-novel foolishness, I know, but no snow, no rain, and—"

"Then you couldn't complain and you wouldn't be happy."

Redwood pressed Nicolai's arm and turned to go as Aidan paddled to shore in a canoe. He wore a white shirt with loose sleeves and full dark pants. His hair was pulled back, and a turban of purple and orange cloth was set at a jaunty angle. His hair puffed at the open center. Hanging from his waist were his daddy's alligator pouch and *Maskóki* hunting knife. Redwood felt an ache between her thighs; she ran her tongue over dry lips. Aidan wouldn't be nearly so handsome and colorful onscreen.

"I've got to run," Redwood said to Nicolai. "See you tomorrow."

The clouds burst open right on them.

"My destiny . . . dark storms." Nicolai covered his camera and motioned to the crew. "They say you are a witch with a bright dream, and I am blind cameraman."

"You know what you've seen, Nicolai," Redwood said. "You faced the lioness, looked her in the eyes, didn't flinch at her fangs."

"*Nyet*, my dear Sequoia, that was you, a brave actress with bright destiny."

Where'd he get that from? Destiny didn't seem bright, but dull and cold. Brave? She was a coward, 'fraid of her own self. Needles of rain stabbed her. High brown waves pounded the beach. Nicolai's crew cradled bulky cameras like babies and ran to vehicles borrowed from Clarissa's crowd.

Aidan heaved the canoe beyond a breakwater. "Still want to touch the fury?"

"Ha!" she replied.

Brave and powerful was an act she'd been playing since Jerome Williams broke her apart on a dirt road in Georgia. Back then and now too, she acted as if she could just get up from anything and go on. Yet every time she turned 'round—staring out filthy windows on the El, pulling weeds from the herb garden and smelling fresh dirt on the roots, looking at the moon sailing along the starway or hanging in a morning sky—she missed Aidan so bad she wanted to scream. Yesterday, helping a new life tumble into this world, buying a book from Mr. Kaufman's shop, listening to Nicolai explain a new gadget, she wondered, what would Aidan think? Didn't she have umpteen articles saved for him? She pulled them from her bag and tossed them in the rain.

JAPANESE IN SEATTLE ARRANGE TUSKEGEE SCHOLARSHIP
WANAMAKER EXPEDITION RETURNS AFTER OBTAINING THE ALLEGIANCE OF ALL INDIAN TRIBES
WILLIAM FOSTER'S ALL-COLORED RAILROAD PORTER A SENSATION, BUT DISTRIBUTION A PROBLEM
LADY LIBERTY TO BE JOINED BY INDIAN CHIEF IN NEW YORK HARBOR

Aidan collected the soggy newsprint, poking his fingers through a few articles. He stuffed the paper inside his shirt. She threw more at him.

AIDA OVERTON WALKER, BROWNSKIN SONGSTRESS TAKEN ILL
ANTI-MISCEGENATION BILL PASSES HOUSE
ILLINOIS WOMEN CAN VOTE FOR THE PRESIDENT BUT NOT THE GOVERNOR

Redwood had nobody to talk to like Aidan, nobody to fight with over Martians, poetry, over what Dr. Dubois or Mr. Eastman meant. Aidan helped her make sense. Maybe he felt something bad coming too. Maybe he didn't need her to be brave and powerful no matter what.

"What's on your mind, 'fore the rain washes us away?" Aidan grabbed the last paper floating in the rain.

ARE THOSE REALLY CANALS ON MARS?

"Pauline Hopkins made her plays come true for colored people, and this year Zitkala-Sa did the *Sun Dance Opera* in Utah with *real* Indians. Who ever heard of a Sioux woman writing a grand opera? She did it though, for her people. I'm not the only woman trying for . . . a bright destiny."

"You're the one I know." Aidan moved close.

"I'm jealous of Iris. Brother think I slipped the noose. She's the one."

"Yes, Iris goin' live in the future we hoped for, worked for." Aidan looked through the rain into the coming days. "Can you see her? Meeting a delegation from Mars, making sure we don't make the mistakes of yesteryears?"

Redwood nodded and drank tears down the back of her throat. The trouble between her and Aidan was her fault, and she could fix it. She could go on and be intimate with him. Even if she didn't feel nothing or her skin started crawling, she could *act* as if it was the time of her life. Everybody said *Sequoia Phipps was a great performer*, said *that Sequoia could act anything*. If it was torment for Aidan to be close and not close, she'd perform like Elaine at the Cherokee Bordello, only she'd do it for love, not for money.

"I'm goin' fly," she said. "I'm warning you."

"When?"

"I don't know. But watch out." She skipped off.

"Wait!"

Aidan ran to keep up with Redwood. She was a streak of color in gray fog, an aeroplane 'bout to take off in a day made night by a storm. It was a good ways to the road where the borrowed vehicles were parked, which Aidan didn't usually mind. He and Redwood were always the last to go. He relished a few moments, walking alone with her at the end of the day. They didn't talk much, too worn out, too skittish. Still he treasured the words they traded. Storms usually didn't make him no nevermind either. Today he wanted to cuss the muddy road, the sharp wind, and the greasy rain off the lake—half water, half factory spew. Chilly rivulets were running down his back, splashing his behind, making his muscles clench. Redwood was prickly too, static popping off her skin, out her hair. He knew her like the back of his breath. She was holding something back. Or maybe that was his energy crackling between them—so much he wasn't saying, and he should've been able to tell her anything.

"Wait!" He gestured at the news articles dissolving in his wet shirt.

"All right." She stopped.

As they used their bodies to shelter his hands from the driving rain, he smoothed out the newsprint pages inside the covers of his journal.

Are Those Really Canals on Mars? dissolved in his hands.

"It's all ruined," she said.

"Not yet." Hurrying the journal into his shoulder bag, Aidan thought he heard thunder clapping, but no lightning flashed in miles and miles of blue-black sky. A bear came crashing through the thorny bushes, moaning and rearing up on its haunches. Aidan grabbed Redwood and thrust her behind him. The bear half-heartedly slashed at them with stubby claws. Aidan fended off the clumsy attack with a slap on the nose. The bear danced this way and that, desperate for a tree to climb—nothing 'cept scrub bush and spindly grass back toward the lake. Trees were a good run away and hardly taller than the bear. Aidan sang a few burra-burras and heya bobs.

"Bears don't scare me, like those guns." Redwood pointed down the dim road.

Aidan could just make out three men and three rifles zigzagging through dunes. "Damn it!"

The bear sneezed, scratched its nose, and sat down, hidden from the trackers by the bushes. A mournful expression had Aidan wondering if bears could weep. Redwood, after not touching Aidan for weeks, leaned her thighs, belly, and tiddies against him. She just let go into his back, lying down on him. Whistling breath through her teeth, she laced chilly fingers 'round his chest and pressed her face into his wet hair. Something was brewing with her. Aidan was cold, soaked, and too tired for any *stuff*. Woman picked the worst moments to let him know she wanted to try lovemaking again. Something or somebody was always in the way. The bear blasted them with sour breath and chewed out a sound, asking for help, no doubt on that.

"I can't," he muttered to the bear at his feet and the woman at his back.

"You feel so good," Redwood whispered.

All Aidan wanted was to get back to Walter's place. He'd turned a storage hall into a cozy bedchamber. Walter was off romancing Rose most of the time, and Walter's daddy didn't mind Aidan banging on the banjo in the middle of the night. Sometimes the old fellow told stories that Aidan didn't quite understand, even when he begrudgingly offered up a little English. Listening to Lakota tales, Aidan would fall into a good sleep and dream deep till morning, without hankering for a drink or worrying on anything.

"I'm not right yet. I want to be strong for you. I want to be a whole man, not a broke-down drunk." Aidan wasn't sure Redwood could hear him mumbling in the loud rain.

An engine backfired, and Nicolai drove off in one of the borrowed trucks. Wheels growled in the muddy gravel. The frightened bear made fearful noises and curled up in a mound. A paw was mangled and bloody.

"Damn it!" Aidan said again, and then cut off a string of cussing.

Redwood took a step 'round him toward the bear. Gurgling almost like a cub drinking from its mama, Redwood waved her storm hand toward a second transport truck. The animal cocked a big head to the side and, favoring three paws, bounded through dense foliage right for the motor vehicle.

"He's wearing a chain on his neck," Aidan said.

"A she-bear—ain't wild, just real sad," Redwood said.

Iris threw back the flap of the storage truck like she'd been expecting company. She stepped aside and the bear gamboled in. Gazing from Iris to Redwood, Aidan laughed.

"Baby Sister and I can speak heart-to-heart sometimes." Redwood smirked, as if getting caught in a scheme. "Iris is just showing spirit. You're all for that."

"What'll we say to these fellows?" Aidan squinted at the trio toting guns and scurrying in circles, a regular comedy act, and getting closer.

"You'll think of something." Redwood pressed her wet body against his soggy shirt. "A she-bear at the beginning of the picture would work as well as a cougar."

Aidan sighed. "I don't have the heart to turn her over, either."

Redwood brushed his cheek with her fingers, then left him to deal with the hunting party. He crashed through the bushes away from the truck, making enough noise to wake the dead. When he was sure the three hunters were rushing his way, he shouted and hollered and carried on. "My god it's a bear. Bear! Bear!"

Luckily, under dark clouds and buckets of rain, wasn't much clear vision. The downpour made a mess of the tracks, and a bear on all fours would have been hidden in the bushes. Aidan pointed the men back toward the lake, claiming the fearsome creature had raced past him. Bears were fast, and who'd believe the truth anyhow? "Claws just missed me!" They swore this was a dancing bear and not all that dangerous. Aidan eyed their rifles and backed away. They slogged on in the mud.

Aidan climbed over the tailgate and into the back of the truck. "A fugitive from a traveling sideshow." He didn't know whether the bear stench filling his nose was fear or funky relief. The animal sat in the corner atop worn-out costumes, watching the three humans warily. Aidan couldn't fault her for a low opinion of them. They were acting crazy. He turned to Iris. "Where were you all morning? Did you turn that bear loose?"

Iris's eyes got big, but she didn't answer.

"Those men will come back when they don't find her or any tracks," Redwood said.

"What's got into you?" he asked Redwood, not talking 'bout the bear. She knew he wasn't and clamped her mouth tight.

"Don't worry on that now," Iris said. "Hurry and drive us away. Please. They're mean to bears, you can see."

They all stared at the frightened creature. Redwood sat down by the bear, not too close. She kept her head low and her hands folded. After only a moment, the bear scooted close enough to put her wounded paw right in Redwood's lap.

Iris tugged at Aidan's arm. "Don't she remind you of Star?"

"Who?" Aidan said.

"That bear from back home," Redwood said.

"All right, all right," Aidan said. "When the picture's done though, we find a place to set this bear free." He leapt out the back, hurried to the front cabin, and started the engine. Despite expert lessons from Mr. McGregor, he didn't like driving, especially in a storm. The road was a stream of slime, but they couldn't just wait for those fellows to come back and find them with the bear.

Zigzagging through mud and stones, he made a fast getaway.

THE PIRATE AND THE SCHOOLTEACHER

Nicolai Minsky and his valiant camera crew, Oscar Jones, Henry Wilson, and Freddie Fastfoot, braved the wilds of Wisconsin and tempestuous Lake Michigan to capture many wonderful scenes for *The Pirate and the Schoolteacher*. And although they shot the beginning after the end and all the other scenes out of order too, this was how the moving picture play came together onscreen for audiences far and wide.

The camera eye opened up to Hog Hollow, a Sea Island town off the coast of Georgia. A sailing boat bounced on stormy seas and lovely Schoolteacher Redwood set down her chalk on a mound of books. She stared mournfully at the open water through her classroom window. Her pupils—Clarissa and George's kids and Iris—exploded through the door to gather seashells.

Rose, playing a Seminole woman, tended a garden behind the school and smiled at the children running by. Wildfire, a Seminole farmer and Rose's brother, strode into his cabin with a deer over one shoulder and a bow over another. Following him, Walter Jumping Bear, also a Seminole farmer, dipped a carved wooden spoon into a bowl of *sofkee,* a dish made with corn hominy and meat. In a gesture of welcome and goodwill, Walter drained the deep spoon.

Outside, Milton, the Baptist minister, dragged himself through the sand with a Bible against his chest and a heavy weight on his shoulders.

TITLE: Without money for taxes, everyone in Hog Hollow might lose their land.

Clarissa, a good Christian woman, watched Milton from the church. Coming upon flowers strewn on the church steps, Milton broke into a weak smile.

TITLE: Hope is always a guest at our table.

A wave crashed against the now shipwrecked boat. Sailing men struggled between rocks, waves, and broken boards. On shore, a black bear chased Pirate Saeed, a salty rogue in tight breeches and puffy white shirt. A sword dangled from his hip. Desperate for escape, the Pirate dashed into frothy water, slipping and sliding, while the sure-footed bear gained on him. Animal and man ran across the path of Farmer Wildfire, now dressed in a voluminous beaded coat. Wildfire drew his mighty bow, aimed, and felled the bear (who could always be coaxed to roll on her back for honey from Iris's hands). But alas, Pirate Saeed was dragged down by a fierce, low-riding current. Wildfire threw off his coat and jumped in the water after him.

On the beach with her young charges, Teacher Redwood rescued a red leather journal floating in on a wave. She traced watery words with her finger as they washed away in the salty ocean brew. The back pages of the journal were dry and the words safe. Reading the sayings and poetry, Redwood sighed and dabbed her eyes.

TITLE: The afternoon knows what the morning never expected.

Struggling over slippery rocks, Wildfire managed to haul Pirate Saeed to the beach. Heaving deep breaths, the Pirate hugged his rescuer, grateful to be alive. Teacher Redwood waved at them from down the shore.

Meanwhile Walter and Rose sat in a canoe, eating smoked fish. An orchid rode the waves toward them. Walter plucked the flower from the water and offered it to Rose. She set the flower in her lap as wreckage from the sailing ship floated by. Startled, they searched the sea with wide eyes. Drowning men flailed against choppy water. Rose gasped and pointed.

TITLE: "You must save them!"

Walter wedged the canoe between rocks and, joined by his daddy, also a Seminole farmer, he dashed into the water. Rose scrambled to the beach. Walter and his daddy battled fierce waves to drag waterlogged sailors, Eddie and a seedy-looking Gang, to safety. Rose and Teacher Redwood ministered to the gasping men on the beach. The red leather journal rode in Redwood's pocket. Overjoyed at the sight of it, Pirate Saeed staggered toward her and almost passed out at her feet. As she bound his bleeding forehead, he touched the journal in her pocket. She smiled.

TITLE: "Yours?"

Pirate Saeed stood up slowly, finding his land legs. He took the journal from her hands and bowed. When the lovely Teacher cast her eyes on this handsome, poetry-loving Pirate, romance sparked between them. He pressed the red leather to his heart and kissed her hand.

TITLE: "Wildfire saved me from drowning. You rescued me from heartache and misery."

Later, inside the church, the Teacher served the Pirate a warm mug. Clarissa, the Teacher's good friend, wrapped him in a blanket. Minister Milton shook his head as he walked by Eddie and his dastardly Gang, who dripped dark water on the wooden pews. A sword and pistol tucked in Eddie's belt flashed in a sunbeam. The Preacher halted behind the Teacher, touching a scarf that trailed from her waist like a stream of clear water. He loved her too, and Friend Clarissa saw this with a mournful sigh. A collection box sat below the altar, stuffed with Sunday's offerings—all the hard-earned coins of the congregation.

TITLE: Still not enough to pay the taxes!

Eddie eyed the money. Pirate Saeed followed his greedy glance and scowled.

Outside the church, Wildfire paced as Rose and Walter talked. The Pirate emerged, wet, but warmed by a mug and the love of a good woman. Wildfire grabbed him by the shoulders. The startled Pirate clasped the hilt of his sword. Walter offered him dry Seminole clothing—much like his own. Relieved, the Pirate handed the Teacher his journal to hold as he slipped behind a bush. Wildfire and Walter laughed and dragged him to the cabin. As they entered, Wildfire offered a wooden spoon of *sofkee*. After a moment's hesitation, the Pirate emptied the spoon down his throat. Wildfire and Walter grinned as the Pirate drank a second spoon.

Meanwhile Eddie and his dastardly Gang slipped into the empty church. A candle burned under the cross. The collection box sat behind the altar. The Gang laughed and danced as they emptied coins and bills into a leather bag. Eddie cinched the pouch tight and tied it to his waist.

Coming out the cabin behind Wildfire and Walter, the Pirate strode into the garden. Teacher Redwood smiled shyly at him in his dry Seminole clothes. Her pupils did a rhythmic tap dance welcoming him to Hog Hollow. Minister Milton joined in with a turkey buzzard jig. Balancing on one leg, his arms flapping like great wings, he bent over and picked a handkerchief from the ground with his teeth, so like Mr. Buzzard pecking flesh. The Pirate set down his sword and applauded. After only one false start, he did Mr. Buzzard's dance with Milton. The children jumped up and down in glee. The Teacher's melancholy was put to flight. When she beamed at him, Pirate Saeed boldly pulled her out to dance. She resisted only a second, and then they whirled and spun to everyone's delight. At the end of the dance, the Pirate fell to his knee and clasped her hand to his heart. Despite his roguish nature, he loved her too.

In the church, Friend Clarissa held an empty collection box. Frantically, she searched near the altar for the money. Despairing, she ran outside and pulled the Minister and Teacher away to show them the empty box. Teacher Redwood covered her mouth.

TITLE: "We are lost. The taxes! Oh! Oh!"

Rose frowned and pointed to behind the church. Walter and his daddy also noticed Eddie and Gang crawling out a back window. They raced away. In anguish, the Pirate buckled on his sword and ran off in hot pursuit. The Teacher pressed the back of her hand against her forehead.

TITLE: "I am betrayed."

Eddie and Gang ran through sand dunes, stumbling over one another. The moneybag banged against Eddie's sword. Suddenly the Gang scattered like leaves in a breeze. Behind them raced an angry Pirate Saeed, followed by Wal-

ter and his daddy. They all darted through waving grass at a
furious pace toward the shore.

On the beach, water lapped at sand, and crabs scurried
every which way. Milton jumped from behind a rock and
gripped Pirate Saeed, who looked daggers at Eddie and
Gang escaping.

TITLE: "We saved you, offered hospitality, and this is
thanks?"

Minister Milton waved the collection box in the Pirate's
face, and the two men struggled. The Bear, who wasn't shot
dead after all, loped toward scurrying crabs. An arrow was
stuck in her shoulder and waved about with every move.
Seeing the Bear approach, Minister Milton abandoned his
fight with Saeed and turned to run. Twisting and turning
in sea grass, he got tangled in his feet and fell—a splendid
comic turn. The Bear sniffed Milton's hind parts and, un-
interested, plunged into the water. Pirate Saeed leapt over
the Minister to chase Eddie, who lifted the moneybag in
triumph. Hands on her hips, Teacher Redwood blocked the
Pirate's way. He somersaulted to avoid crashing into her.
With a desperate look at Eddie racing away, he turned to
face her. She flung the journal at him. Pirate Saeed caught
it. He opened to a page and pressed this into her hand.

TITLE: Tell me whom you love and I will tell you who
you are.

Teacher Redwood's heart almost broke, but could she
trust him?

Walter's canoe tossed in the waves, looking like an escape plan. Eddie and Gang converged and ran for it. Wildfire popped up in the canoe. The Gang ran away except
Eddie, who waved his gun, ordering Wildfire out the boat.
As Eddie got in, the boat collided with a rock and splintered. Eddie leapt clear, but his gun went flying through
the air. It landed near the bear. She pawed the weapon and
lobbed it toward Wildfire. Eddie dashed through the water
to the beach. Wildfire wrestled with the bear, who finally
released him to chase fish. Wildfire scrambled after Eddie.

The Gang raced down the beach on horseback now. As they overtook Eddie, a stout fellow leaned down and pulled him onto the saddle behind him. Wildfire barely missed getting run down by the thundering horses. They galloped on toward the Pirate and Teacher, who were still fussing with each other. Minister Milton sank to the sand in front of the empty collection box. Rose and Friend Clarissa shook their heads sadly. Teacher Redwood's pupils shrieked and danced in circles. It seemed that all was lost.

Eddie and Gang, their horses' hooves pounding the sand, were almost upon the Pirate and the Teacher. She faced the galloping beasts down and wasn't about to budge. Pirate Saeed pushed her aside, leapt on the last horse, and knocked off the rider. Wildfire gripped the fellow and hogtied him. In this fashion Saeed leapt from horse to horse and unseated each member of the Gang. Wildfire and Walter subdued all the thrown riders and tied them up before they could catch a breath. Finally Saeed jumped on Eddie's horse. They struggled and then flew through the air, leaving the riderless horse to gallop on down the beach.

Pirate Saeed and Eddie did a most acrobatic fight on the beach, tumbling and somersaulting around punches and kicks. Teacher Redwood, Minister Milton, Walter and his daddy, Wildfire, Rose, Friend Clarissa, and all the Pupils ran down sloping dunes to surround them. Eddie pulled his sword and slashed at Saeed, who rolled away quickly and pulled his own shiny weapon. Everybody gasped and fell back as the two swordsmen parried with deadly metal. Eddie's Gang, tied up in the rising tide, struggled to no avail.

Ruthless Eddie threw sand in the Pirate's eyes and threatened the crowd. He stabbed at Pupil Iris, slicing a bow from her dress. In a mad dash to save her, the Pirate slashed Eddie's arm with his sword, but lost his balance. Pirate Saeed's sword tumbled into the water. Wildfire pulled Iris out of range, as a gloating Eddie closed in on the unarmed Pirate. He was about to run him through when Teacher Redwood thrust herself between Eddie's blade and the Pirate's throat, saving him from certain death. Again the crowd gasped as Eddie's sword pierced her body. Stunned, Eddie backed away from his weapon in the wounded Teacher. The blade had plunged through the red leather journal and under ribs. Pirate Saeed grabbed the sword and caught her as she fell. Eddie looked around wildly. The others mobbed him before he could flee. Pirate Saeed clutched his brave beloved and cried up to the heavens.

TITLE: "I fear she is not long for this world!"

Later, inside Wildfire's house, Redwood lay in a bed, wrapped in white bandages. Dr. Harris stood over her, shaking his head. She clutched the journal of good words that had not saved her, but merely postponed the worst. Clarissa leaned into Minister Milton and covered her face. Dr. Harris picked up his bag and left solemnly. All stood around the bed. Pirate Saeed fell onto Redwood's body, begging her to not leave him. She stroked his head and looked to the stars.

Rose threw open the door. Mambo Dupree dressed as Erzulie Dantor, the hot *Loa* of love, danced into the cabin. She traced two *vèvés* on the floor—a heart with a sword through it and two crossroads intersecting—and called to the spirits of love and of death to ride her. Mambo Dupree brandished a machete and cut the air over the bed. She sprinkled charms and blessings.

TITLE: "I have only a little bit, but together, you all have plenty magic!"

Mambo Dupree danced out the door toward the sea. Sitting up, Teacher Redwood held out her storm hand. Candles in the room burst into flames. Everyone gathered close to the bed. A fire spirit blazed around the room, and no one could say what or who she was. Later, Nicolai and crew would claim the haint as camera magic, but everybody saw her leap from the fireplace and burn brightly over the bed. The Bear loped by the open door, a big fish in her mouth. She stopped in the doorway and dropped her supper, as the fire-haint flew out over her head. Spent, Teacher Redwood sank back into the bedding. Her eyes fluttered shut.

Pupil Iris stomped her foot and pointed to the night sky.

TITLE: "The stars are dim. She can't find the City of Light. She won't die tonight."

Somber faces told another story. Clarissa wept against the Minister. Despairing, Pirate Saeed stroked Redwood's peaceful face.

TITLE: "I would give all the treasure in the world for the light in her eyes!"

Valiant Iris refused to cry or sing a funeral song. She danced for the spirit of the dead, for the spirits of love, for the light to come back to Teacher Redwood's eyes. Who dared hope with her? The scene faded to black.

Some days later, inside the church, Rose, Walter, his daddy, Wildfire, and the pupils all in fancy dress, stood in the pews. They held flowers, and tears streaked a few faces. The Minister dabbed his eyes at the altar, reading from his Bible. He displayed a rich chest of treasure—gold coins, silver goblets, strings of pearls.

TITLE: "Our prayers have been answered. A gift from the sea! Hog Hollow is ours."

Friend Clarissa offered a bouquet of orchids to a bride wearing a dress as delicate as prairie smoke and fog. This was no funeral after all. Accepting the flowers, the bride turned. She was none other than Teacher Redwood! She had not died! Her smile and eyes were light. Pirate Saeed stood beside her at the altar, wearing a patchwork Seminole coat and turban. They kissed.

TITLE: Tell me whom you love and I will tell you who you are.

Between them, they clasped a bedraggled journal of good words—a heart with a sword through it, a *vèvé* calling to spirit Erzulie, *Loa* of love.

The image irised to black.

TWENTY-FOUR

"I can feel the moving picture again when I read this." Walter waved Aidan's journal in the air. "Everybody will love seeing this kind of story." The candle on the round table flickered. "Iris and you-all put our lives into that scenario."

"Iris is mostly to blame," Aidan said. Toting the rocker he'd made as a wedding gift for Walter and Rose, he squeezed through the back door into Walter's tight little kitchen.

"You finished that already?" Walter said.

"I felt the pattern in the wood, just made it come through. That don't take no time." Aidan set the rocker by the stove. Orchids bloomed on the back and along the arms.

"Rose loves those swamp flowers." Walter smiled. "Thank you."

"Easier than trying to carve the wind." Aidan reached for his journal.

Walter held on to it and sat back in his chair. "Your father was *Hutalgalgi,* Wind clan too." He stared at Aidan. "This book is full. You've got a lot of good stories to tell?"

"Writing myself down, it's—a hoodoo *tonic* spell." He paced 'round the table. "I thought I'd let Iris and . . . Redwood read it all tonight."

"Good." Walter shook his head. "I don't understand you two."

"Red and me went too fast when I first got to Chicago. We had to learn how to be with one another again." Aidan stumbled over pots and baskets lurking in the shadows. The sun had gone down an hour ago. "Don't you like electric lights?" He watched the shadows from candles play on the ceiling.

"Sometimes I do, sometimes I want a flame." Walter brushed away bits of food and set Aidan's journal on the table. "Sometimes I don't pay the electric bill on time." He shrugged. "This is not important."

"Now that *The Pirate and the Schoolteacher* is done, Red and me are going to California, or Oregon, or Washington," Aidan said. "We're taking Iris too."

"What are you running from?"

"I don't know that I'm running *from* anything." Aidan considered the empty jars lined up on the counter, waiting for the vegetable harvest. "Liquor cross my mind now and again. But I close my eyes, and it's empty bottles full of amber sunshine."

"That's wonderful, but have you talked to Redwood?"

"We talked before, before I left George's."

"What if she's changed her mind? Rose changes her mind all the time. We can't decide anything." Walter tried to laugh as if he'd made a joke. "Can't stand still with a woman. You got to change."

"They're making moving pictures in California. There must be vaudeville too." Aidan's head throbbed. "I want to dig in the dirt again and make something grow. Raise a family." He sank into a chair. "I need room, trees, a dark night, just for a while. And if we don't like it, we can come back. Where's Chicago going?" He rubbed his face and then squeezed his hands together. "Carving some difficult piece, no use digging away on a mistake. You get yourself a fresh piece of wood and—"

"What?"

"You love Rose, don't you?"

Walter smiled. "She makes me feel like a good man." He clutched Aidan's arm. "But I will miss you if you ride away." He paused, searching for something. "You know how to believe." Walter released Aidan, pleased with this.

"I'm your friend, even on a distant coast," Aidan said. "And I'll miss you."

"I don't farm," Walter said. "But perhaps—"

Aidan's heart pounded as Walter pondered his *perhaps*. "You and Rose could come, see what else to do." Aidan gripped Walter. "Raise hell for Indian people out there."

Walter sighed. "My father would like to see the Black Hills again. We could cross this way one more time." He nodded. "What are you going to do with the bear?"

Aidan chuckled. "Iris wants to take her with us when we go west, but—"

"So, it's only Redwood you must persuade."

"I feel something from her. Maybe she's ready to—"

The rocker moved back and forth of its own accord and startled Aidan silent. He and Walter watched it. *"Boneyard baron rock an empty chair."* Aidan quoted Miz Subie. An orchid on the chair gleamed in moonlight. Seeing that, he jumped up from the table.

"You didn't bring that flower. What is it?" Walter stood up too.

"I'm not sure." Aidan opened the back door and saw a flash of fire disappear 'round a corner. "I gotta go." He stuffed the journal in his shoulder bag and plucked the orchid from the chair. The petals were hot. The chair went dead still. As he rushed out the door and down the street, the tang of burnt flesh filled his nose and mouth.

The end of a good show with good players was always sad, but the gloom Redwood felt, now that she had reached *after the film*, was worse than usual. Dread had been dogging her for weeks, and not just over what she and Aidan were goin' do. Today at the screening in Nicolai's office, dread hit Iris too. Baby Sister flitted 'round like a dragonfly, pestering everybody till finally Aidan told her to sit down and be quiet. And still Iris twittered louder than the noisy projector, during the whole show.

The Pirate and the Schoolteacher looked grand and sounded grand with musicians playing along. Redwood hated to admit it, but George was right. Everybody cheered for the Schoolteacher coming back from the dead, for a dark hero and his brown-skin sweetheart. Who could deny their picture show would be a success? Mama used to say, *Stories and songs are powerful medicine. A good story fill you up when you hungry, when you lonely, help you find your way when you lost. A good song take the hurting out your spirit.* George and those hinkty club women were wrong—nothing naïve or foolish 'bout believing in stories.

After the screening, Clarissa hugged Redwood then disappeared quickly. Milton was out the door complaining of aches and pains. Fidgety Iris ran off behind George. Saeed offered to celebrate with Redwood, but she let him go paint the town red with Corey, his union man. Aidan rushed off too, with Walter, saying they could talk in the morning; they could plan. 'Stead of hauling Aidan off somewhere quiet for a talk right then and there, Redwood said, "Fine, fine." She shouldn't have let him slip away.

Nicolai lifted a glass of strong spirits. "Now, it is out of our hands."

Taking a shortcut home from the trolley, Redwood turned down a dim alley. A tall figure, little more than smoke covered by a colorful cloak, blocked her way. Like a highwayman from an old-fashioned romance, he declared, "Stand and deliver!" She backed up and opened her eyes wide. The alleyway was empty. Night had fallen.

Redwood tried to soak away nightmare images. After the bath, she slipped into a blue silk gown Clarissa gave her and watched the moonrise from her window. It looked like Mr. Noyes's *ghostly galleon tossed on cloudy seas when the highwayman came riding*. Redwood stepped away from the window, shivering inside and out. *Haints don't bother you, 'less you believe in 'em*, Mama always said. *Hear me? Don't be so hardheaded. Don't hug anger to your heart.*

"I ain't mad at you, Mama," she whispered. "I mean, I was, but not really, just mad at a world so mean you had to—" Redwood cried softly. "But see what I've done. Just like I promised!" She smiled and wiped away tears. "What I always wanted to do."

Nicolai had made several prints of *The Pirate and the Schoolteacher.* George was goin' pay for more. Her copy sat on top the books she'd boxed up, two reels in a metal case, glittering in moonlight—magic. They'd called up much magic. Nicolai captured their conjuring on film. Soon projectionists would set their spells free into the world. A thrill raced up her back, delight at her dream come true, and then fear. Something bad was coming, a train jumping the track or the moon falling out the sky. A blot on tomorrow, and what could she do about it? She moved to close the shutters.

A wooden box, carved in the shape of a comet, perched on the window seat. The tail was silver threads and blue-violet feathers from a swamp hen. Redwood picked it up and drew the feathers over her face and down her neck. A sweet ache spilled over her. Some secret thing inside rattled. The sound tickled her too. Aidan gave her the comet-box last year, but she'd never opened it. If tomorrow might not come, if something horrible was to claim her this night, she'd better burn her candles and open her secret treasures, now.

Lighting a red scented candle and setting it in the window, she undid the clasp of the comet-box. Her hands trembled as she slid the round cover to one side. In the box was a bright yellow bead and two cracked seashells wrapped in a brown-and-black feather. The bead was actually a mosaic of yellow, gold, and white. Redwood squealed as she remembered the pounds of beads and hammered gold jewelry hanging on the necks, waists, arms, and ankles of the Dahomeyan women at the Chicago World's Fair. The feather was something Aidan found at the Wild West show before they rode the Ferris Wheel. The seashells, though, were a mystery.

She kissed the bead and stroked the feather. Here was proof. "We were really there."

She put a shell to each ear. The ocean whispered a windy chant, urging her to get up and move. What if she and Aidan didn't make it to the morning? Redwood set the treasures back in the comet and slid the lid shut. She pulled on Aidan's old shirt and pants and set his cap on her head. She tied a stream of blue silk to her waist. Her red *mojo* bag hung 'round her neck. Walter's place was an hour or so, walking and taking the trolley. She could stay with Aidan there till they decided where they were going next. And if they only had one more night, it would be together.

Rustling in the garden startled her. A stiff breeze blew the candle out, and red wax dribbled down to the window-seat cushions. Redwood peered outside into the shadows. The boneyard baron flung the colorful cloak into the high branches of the maple tree. He stood below it, an icy wind in a long black coat. A scarf of white mist curled 'round his neck. The baron tipped his black top hat at her. "Stand and deliver!" Sparkly teeth caught a glint of moonlight and froze in a scowl.

Redwood shuddered. "You been following me." She stared in his blazing eyes and didn't blink as pain seared into her. "What you want?"

On each of the baron's skeleton fingers, a silver ring dripped blood. He pointed dagger fingernails at a flash of light in the distance. Redwood winced. The baron set his velvety hat on his bright white skull and sauntered away from the maple tree. Every step he took was a fresh grave. She felt warm flesh whither and heard anguished souls wailing, but she couldn't read the headstones. The baron turned back to glance at Redwood and then faded into the silver lining of a shadow.

Redwood rubbed her aching eyes and pulled on Aidan's brogans. She ran through the house from top to bottom. Iris's room was empty. The other children were visiting their cousins. George was working late and Clarissa had gone to take him supper. She called the Dry Cleaning but couldn't get a connection through the switchboard.

Redwood wished she was good at cussing, like Aidan. She longed for a foul stream of it. Nothing came. She dashed out into the middle of the street, trying to feel the right direction to take, trying to see the baron as a warning of danger to come, a danger she could stop. She ran and ran, till her bones rattled and her muscles burned, till the streets and the people were gray shadows behind the baron's top hat and cane, till she didn't feel her feet touch the ground, running toward—

TWENTY-FIVE

Fire, Chicago, 1913

Blistering flames scorched the cool moonlight. The letters on PHIPPS DRY CLEANING: CLEANER THAN NEW melted away. Aidan saw this several blocks away. Pale men on dark steeds pounded the cobblestones and raced past him, old nightmares on the prowl. Aidan cussed loud and long. His heart hurt, blasting blood into cramped leg muscles. A bullet ricocheted through the alley, singing a high sharp melody. He picked up speed. Fire engines, volunteers, and onlookers were illuminated in a shower of flickering light. A steam engine pump was sweating and wheezing like an asthmatic ole geezer.

Aidan collided with Redwood, and they fell to the ground. His brain banged into his skull, and he almost passed out. Redwood looked dazed too.

"You can't go back in there, George!" Clarissa shrieked. Her white smock was pink in the firelight. "It's a miracle you got out."

George dumped a man at Clarissa's feet and turned back toward the fire. She gripped his sleeves. "Let me go, woman. I'm to blame as sure as . . . if I struck the match." George shook Clarissa off, dodged a policeman, and ran back into the inferno.

Aidan and Redwood struggled to standing and staggered down the street.

"Nooooo!" Clarissa yelled.

Police dragged her and whoever George rescued away from the flames. Two geysers of fire-engine water evaporated in the heat as the blaze climbed to the second floor. A burly fireman gripped Aidan, and a volunteer blocked Redwood.

"If you go in there, you're cooked." The fireman shoved them back. He was strong and Irish from the lilt on his tongue. His red face was covered in soot, like a bad blackface job. Behind him, beefy policemen yelled at one another.

"Chemical fires are the worst!"

"Niggers take too many risks trying to make a buck."

"Naw. Somebody set this one."

Aidan wanted to turn 'round and run the other direction. He didn't need to see or hear or taste any more fire.

"My brother's inside." Redwood tried to push past the volunteer, a slim, midnight-dark man who wouldn't let her through.

The fireman gripped her shoulders with thick gloves. He spoke to Aidan though. "I'm sorry. But we can't let you—"

A shot rang out, and the Irish fireman knocked Redwood and Aidan to the ground. A firefighter operating a cranky pump crumpled. Blood spurted from a wound in his chest, turning his blond beard red. Several dark men dashed to his aid, but most of the onlookers scattered. Other firemen huddled against their engines and eyed windows and rooftops. Rescuers zigzagged 'cross the street, making it hard for the sniper as they carried the wounded man away. Back on his feet, Aidan heard desperate screams. He felt choked lungs and burnt skin as lives were cut short and dreams turned to ash.

"The whole street could go." Aidan grasped Redwood's storm hand and pulled her close. She shoved against him and then gave in to a bit of comfort. "A lot of colored businesses, ain't it?"

"What difference does that make?" Redwood said.

"That's why they set it on fire. That's why they're shooting," the Irish fireman said.

"I was 'fraid of that," Aidan said. Redwood wouldn't look at him.

"Somebody called us before the fire. We got here as it started. Otherwise . . ." The fireman wiped a runny nose. "Damn fools could burn the whole city down."

"Fire don't care 'bout color, don't care 'bout nothing." The colored volunteer wrapped a wet handkerchief over his mouth. "Poor white folk living 'round back. Fire'll eat them too."

He and the Irish fireman ran to the abandoned pump. They banged and cajoled it into working again. Water gushed into the Dry Cleaning, and the fire died back. A fourth and fifth pump belched water too. The fire cringed and spit, smoked and fizzled. Aidan wished they could dump the whole of Lake Michigan on it.

"Why did George run back in there?" Clarissa huddled on the

ground behind a motorcar. Mr. McGregor sat with her. Milton lifted his head from her lap and hacked his insides into the gutter as Aidan and Redwood stumbled toward them. "It's not George's fault. He didn't set this fire." Clarissa pounded Mr. McGregor. "Why do they do us this way?"

"She's out of her mind. Help me," Mr. McGregor said, stepping aside.

Redwood bent down and stroked Clarissa's face and hair. "George ain't dead yet."

"Are you sure?" Clarissa calmed down at Redwood's touch. "You're a conjure woman seeing underneath things, right? Do you see George alive?"

Redwood nodded and took Milton's hands, pulling his pain. Milton groaned relief.

"Look," Aidan put an arm 'round Clarissa, "they're getting this fire under control."

Clarissa glowered at thin streams of water grazing bright banners of heat.

"Beat it back enough, a rescue unit can go in," Aidan said.

Smoke billowed and steam hissed. "It's almost under control," McGregor said.

Aidan watched the flames retreat, 'fraid to hope, 'fraid not to.

Clarissa wiped Milton's face. "Can you speak, Mr. O'Reilly? Please, tell us what you know. Anything."

McGregor handed him a flask of something strong. Milton took a swig and coughed up black smoke. "A gang of white men, roughnecks, I'd never seen before."

McGregor exchanged glances with Aidan. "Go on," Aidan said to Milton.

"They were drunk and fighting with George and Eddie about some bad business—Reginald Jones's grocery getting torched. They said they didn't know who did that and then I don't recall what . . . Fire and glass flying." He drank another swig. "George can hold his own with fisticuffs, but arson? They had torches, and I don't think they realized what an inferno they were setting. One white fellow burnt himself up . . . I tried to get out, but they were shooting anybody who stepped out the front door. Folks pushed me back inside, a stampede.

Hooligans knocked Eddie on the head, got me in the gut. I couldn't breathe. George pulled me out. He said he had to go get Eddie . . ."

"Eddie? George went back for Eddie?" Clarissa sounded disgusted.

"Your husband's an honorable man," Aidan said.

Milton nodded. "He saved my life."

"George do what he think is right." Aidan squeezed Clarissa. "He's a brave man."

"I know." Clarissa would have preferred a coward this night.

Redwood stood up from Milton. "Did you see Iris in there?" she asked.

Aidan gasped. "Iris?" Felt like somebody jabbed a hot poker through his heart.

"I don't know." Milton's eyes darted 'round his face. "I couldn't really see anything after the fire started." A fire engine pump rattled to a halt. Its geyser of water fizzled. "These firemen aren't trying to fight this fire, they figure, let it burn." He was crying.

"Iris was cross-tempered all day and hounding George." Aidan searched Redwood's face. "You and her speaking heart-to-heart?" A rumbling explosion sent new plumes of flame into the inky sky. "What you know?"

"They running out of water." Redwood's eyes were silver slits.

Aidan couldn't think straight. "Not Iris."

Chemicals from the storage room exploded in a fireworks display of reds, blues, and greens. "Who's going to live through that?" Milton said.

"Isn't there something we can do?" Clarissa hissed.

"They don't want us to get ahead," Milton said. "They'll murder us all—"

"I don't care about advancing the race right now, Mr. O'Reilly. I just want my George alive." Clarissa clutched Redwood. "Your sister too, if she's in there."

"She is," Redwood declared.

Aidan watched the fire coming back to life like he was dry wood burning, like he was a dead man. He sank onto hard cobblestone, not sure how he'd ever get up again.

"If you can do all those things you say," Clarissa dug her fingernails in Redwood's flesh, "if you can fly and blow the breath of life into a little baby, can't you do something to save my ornery George and your sweet Iris?"

"I'm goin' try." Redwood stuffed her hair under an old cap of Aidan's. She squeezed her red *mojo* bag and spoke Sea Island Gullah words, sounding like Miz Garnett. She traced a cross on the ground, spoke to each direction, and strode by two firemen, too busy wrassling with leaky hoses to pay her no mind.

Aidan scrambled up beside her. "You fixing to walk into that firestorm?"

Redwood cut her eyes at him. "Don't know what else to do. Gotta improvise."

"I'm coming too." Aidan held out the orchid. It was still warm.

Redwood put her hand on top of his.

Even when good raconteurs tell a tall tale, folks don't believe everything happened quite like they say—unless of course they were there when the wild story happened. Still, crazy events might feel like a waking dream. That's how walking into the firestorm was for Redwood, and Aidan too. Gripping hands, they prayed to the Master of Breath, to the spirit in everything. They offered all the treasures they had in the world. They offered their lives in exchange. For Iris and for George.

Something popped, like a banjo string breaking in the middle of furious plucking and picking. Aidan and Redwood groaned at the painful sound cracking in their ears, and then they heard nothing else. It was as if they'd gone deaf. Clarissa talked on to Milton and McGregor, but the sound was lost. The screeching crowd and rattling engines were also silent. Even the roaring of the fire was gone, and the blaze itself slowed down till it was stock still, a red and yellow flag caught in a north wind.

The fire-haint that Nicolai claimed as camera magic busted through a cloud of dusky ashes drifting over the street. This time Redwood got a good look. The haint's hands were balls of fire. Strands of smoke trailed from its head like a comet's tail. Silver sparks pulsed from an iron heart. Ruby eyes glistened as the haint swooped out of hot, dead air. Long legs, graceful moves, a woman's form, someone dead, but not gone, charged right at them.

"Mama?" Redwood said, shaken to her bones.

"Yes, indeed. Miz Garnett," Aidan said.

They could hear each other and see the haint plain as day.

Garnett Phipps was shades of black and white, like the photo from the Chicago Fair, like how Redwood might look in ten years or after she was dead and come back as spirit. Garnett plucked the orchid from their hands and stuck it in her swamp-grass hair. She smiled polished stone teeth and sauntered toward the fire. Her dress was foamy rapids on a muddy river, racing from her neck to bare feet and back up again. She sported turtles under her feet—fancy high-heel slippers, swimming her 'cross the cobblestones. Lightning bolt earrings flashed at the trolley line. A necklace of stars pulsed against dark velvet skin. Pale riders galloped past her into the Dry Cleaning. The horses screamed and hollered. A tall figure rode a sweaty black stallion—Jerome? Before Redwood could be sure, he'd disappeared.

"Demons on their last ride!" Garnett said. She beckoned to Redwood and Aidan and glided by firemen into the burning store. Damp ground sparkled where she'd walked so easily. Moving against the moment, against time gone still, took great effort for Redwood and Aidan. Each step was a mountain to climb, a bad dream to scale. Their lungs labored as if breathing mud. Two turkey buzzards flew to the busted doorjamb, lazily folded long wings against their backs, and eyed them.

"Ain't rotting yet!" She and Aidan spoke together.

Miz Garnett was an unexpected answer to their prayers. Nothing to do but follow her, so they stepped into the ruins. The Dry Cleaning could have been an enchanted land caught in the spell of a powerful sorcerer. Aidan passed his hands through fragments of burning cloth, shattered glass, and exploding dust suspended in the air. Redwood touched plumes of smoke tangled over a charred body. The heat had left the paralyzed fire—everything was cool to the touch, cold even. The light was pale as moonbeams. A patron, worker, or firebug had been a few steps from escape when flames seared him. From his grim, twisted form, agony in death was clear; however, it was impossible to tell exactly who was walking the stars to greet his ancestors. A shudder passed from Redwood to Aidan.

"Don't linger!" Garnett called out, "This way." Her voice was wind and hissing steam. "Alive, you die. You go through the gates, beyond good and evil. You look for the life that follows death." Hoodoo logic to puzzle on later. Garnett's turtle shoes gushed swamp water as she strode toward the boneyard baron. He flashed diamond teeth. Blood dripped from smoky eyes as he tap-danced on shards of metal. Garnett jigged by him and slipped so quickly through the enchanted ruins she was a blur. "Hurry!" she called.

"Yes." The baron waved his diamond-tipped cane at Redwood and Aidan. "Hurry! You ain't got all night—just a few stolen heartbeats."

Aidan and Redwood tried to keep pace with Garnett. They picked their way 'round blackened vats and stooped under ceilings fixing to fall. They scrambled over gaping holes in the floor that dripped fire to the basement. Sidestepping blown-out windows and a cloud of glass, they headed for the back of the building. The baron's tap-dancing faded. They lost sight of Garnett and would've been frantic but her wet trail glistened. Swamp grass clung to burning splinters. Foamy river mud splattered broken glass. They paused for a labored breath by a bullet crashing into a pillar. Showers of blood reached for the walls from a body hidden under the rubble.

"No time yet to mourn the dead." Garnett circled an overturned claw-foot tub. "I'd give anything to turn this world right side 'round." Turtles at her feet snapped.

"We're over here," Iris said, near Garnett, though out of sight.

A surge of *E-LEC-TRI-CI-TY* pulsed through Redwood to Aidan. They wrenched sluggish muscles into a run. Iris's voice was thin and scratchy, filled with smoke and strain, but such a relief.

"Where are you?" Redwood shouted. "Is George with you?"

"We're coming, honey bun," Aidan shouted too.

The tub leaned against a wall of rigid blue flames. A split beam was wedged against its claw feet and half the ceiling had fallen on its sturdy back.

"I can't lift it up," Iris said.

"You goin' be all right," Aidan said, as they lurched over jagged debris.

"I knew you'd come. I knew it." Iris's lips were swollen and split. Sooty hair, singed silver at the tips, puffed out a topknot braid. The cast-iron tub had shielded her from fire, but trapped her too. Redwood gently clasped her bruised hands and covered her face with kisses as Aidan tried to pull her leg free.

"What you doing, running into fire?" Redwood scolded. "Scaring us to death?"

George and Eddie lay beside Iris, unconscious and also pinned under the back lip of the tub. A thin layer of ash cloaked them. Trickles of blood oozed from George's nose and mouth. Redwood put a finger to his lips and then to Eddie's too. Still breathing, the men lay just beyond cold tendrils of fire and smoke.

"I'd give anything at all, everything." Color flooded Garnett's cheeks. Her smoky eyes and swamp-grass hair turned rich brown. She smelled of hickory and magnolia. Her river dress was still and clear. She opened her stone teeth to speak again and Redwood whispered with her. "Y'all watch over each other." Garnett smiled and vanished.

"She is a good spirit," Iris said. "I followed her the way I do sometimes, to here."

"Are you hurt?" Redwood probed Iris gently.

"No. I'm just stuck."

Aidan strained, but Iris's leg was wedged cruelly between a cross brace from the beam and the side lip of the tub.

"Brother tipped it over, trying to save us, but—"

"We'll get you out." Aidan wiped his eyes and heaved brittle rubble off the beam. Redwood clawed at it too. They cleared what they could. Wood caught turning to a lick of fire, shattered on the floor like glass.

"Miz Garnett's gone now. She can't bargain with me no more." The baron chuckled. "Save yourselves if you can." His voice came from nowhere in particular.

"Let's lift it," Aidan said.

"All right." Redwood wiped stinging sweat from both their eyes with the river of silk at her waist. Squatting underneath the splintered wood, with much groaning and grunting, they lifted one end of the massive beam onto their shoulders. It rose half an inch above the claw feet.

"Get out of there, honey bun," Aidan said.

"I still can't move. Something's caught," Iris said.

"I'll hold this," Aidan said to Redwood. "Don't argue. Get her out."

Redwood slipped from under the beam. A blood vessel busted in Aidan's eye, turning it purple as Redwood stooped down, untangled Iris's leg, and pulled her free. She quickly shouldered the beam again. "Let's shove it to the side."

"It's a good foot till it's clear," Aidan muttered and then added, "sure."

Iris kicked at rubble in their way. Aidan was blinking blood and puffing ash. Shaking something fierce, he and Redwood inched the beam away from the tub. Iris shoved it as well, till they cleared the tub's back claw. Aidan howled "HEADS," like in a theatre. They all let go at once and jumped away as the beam clattered to the floor. It bounced onto shifting rubble, slid down a hole, and disappeared into darkness.

Aidan's arms hung funny from his shoulders, a rag-doll man. Blood dripped down Redwood's sleeves. Iris wobbled on a bruised leg, but stayed upright.

"We did it," Iris said.

"Yes," Redwood and Aidan said.

They laughed for no good reason, 'cept they were happy to be alive together.

"Tub looks heavy," Redwood said.

"All three of us?" Iris whispered.

"Let's do it 'fore I pass out," Aidan said, "and you ladies would have three strapping fellows to haul out." His gallows humor lifted their spirits.

As if doing a dance routine from the moving picture show, they each gripped a leg or a lip of the tub and on the same beat, lifted the back of the cast-iron behemoth off of George and Eddie. It weighed nothing compared to the beam. With surprising ease, they let it tumble to the floor. While Aidan and Redwood caught their breath, Iris leaned down to George. "Spirit wanted me to warn you, but I called the fire company first, so I got to you too late," she said. "I'm sorry."

"He's still breathing, ain't he?" Redwood said. "Don't be sorry yet." She touched each man at the crown of his head, trying to call them to their senses, but for the moment, George and Eddie had slipped beyond her weary reach.

Aidan lost his balance and grazed a flame, which, although slow as swamp current, was moving again. He drew away quickly, a welt rising on his arm.

Redwood tested the flame. "It's getting hot again. We gotta move." She appraised the unconscious men. "You carry Eddie, he's heavier. Iris and me will take George."

"All that way?" Aidan said. They squinted down the hall toward the front door. It seemed miles and miles to go.

"Isn't there a back door?" Redwood said.

Aidan heaved Eddie onto his battered shoulder. Iris gripped George's legs; Redwood reached under his arms. They lifted him, then faltered. George was a big man who enjoyed the good life. His hefty legs slipped from Iris's bruised hands and thudded on the ground. Redwood fell down on her behind, cradling George in her lap.

"I can't hold him." Iris fought tears.

"That's all right." Aidan leaned Eddie carefully against the tub. "Help me put George on Red's shoulder. Easier to carry that way."

"That's right. We can do that," Redwood said.

"Okay, okay," Iris mumbled. She and Aidan gripped George and heaved him, belly down, onto Redwood's shoulder. She staggered under the weight, but held him. Iris clutched his legs from behind, taking enough weight for Redwood to walk.

As fire crept 'cross the ceiling, crossbeams listed and burnt wood sagged. Aidan wrangled Eddie over his shoulder again. "Let's get going." He sagged at the first step.

"Watch out for that hole!" Redwood yelled. Too late.

Aidan tottered at a fiery drop to the basement. A wave of shimmery heat smacked his face. Eddie slid forward on his shoulder and stole his balance. Redwood reached for Eddie's leg and missed. Aidan strained against gravity to no avail. He and Eddie were falling toward blackness. Iris shrieked as a beam toppled. Aidan's shoulder slammed into hot wood that broke his fall. Redwood gripped Eddie's leg and tugged them back.

"I got you. I'm not letting go," she said as Aidan got his footing.

"Yeah." He spit blood in the hole and, before pain or fear registered, hurried for the back door.

Redwood and Iris followed as beams crashed behind them. Splintered wood exploded and shattered glass finally hit ground. The fire was no longer enchanted.

A young fellow with corn silk hair and gray eyes stood in the doorway brandishing a gun. "Get back." When Aidan charged on, the fool stepped into the burning store. Was he one of them that torched Reginald Jones's grocery? "Go on back! I mean it, or—"

"Or what? You'll look me in the eye and shoot me?" Aidan grimaced. The fire gathered speed; smoke ran over collapsing walls. "How many bullets you got left?" He headed for the gunman.

"Wait!" Redwood said. She and Iris tried to match his pace.

"You're not getting out this way!" A lick of flame caught the gunman's jacket. He stared at it, stunned. The ceiling above him groaned. "Stop." As he waved his gun, burning wood rained down. Aidan staggered back. A bullet ricocheted out the back door. The fellow flailed and screamed, tried to scramble away, but the fire swallowed him up. It was a horrible sight—no way for a body to leave this life. Aidan couldn't tear his eyes away.

"Come on." Redwood tugged at him. "We can't get out that way."

The front door might as well have been Mars. Pain came back to them all with the heat. Flames singed hair and burned raw skin. Blistering air scorched their lungs. Leg muscles protested; torn shoulders screamed. Smoke made it hard to see a foot ahead. Eddie's glassy eyes stared into another world, and George groaned with each step. Limping, Redwood set shaky feet in fading turtle footprints. Garnett's glittering path was patchy, almost dried up.

The way into hell was always easier than the way out.

Boards cracked and crashed as the floor in front of them gave way. Terrifying screams plummeted to the basement. Redwood halted. A three-foot chasm separated them from the door. She looked at Aidan. He shook his head.

"We're not getting out, are we?" Iris said. "I can't see it. Just smoke in the dark."

"Conjure woman make a way out of no way," Redwood said. "We got to jump."

"How we goin' jump with . . ." Iris stopped herself.

"Just see the other side and—" Gripping George tightly, Redwood backed up. "Run!" Without a moment for thought or protest, she and Iris leapt over the hole. Their impact sent more of the floor to the basement. Redwood almost lost her grip on George as they hustled to solid ground, but Iris steadied her.

"What you waiting for?" Redwood yelled to Aidan. "Soar!"

"You the one soaring, I'm—"

"I won't listen to you talk yourself down."

He closed his eyes and ran. If this was the end, he didn't want to see it.

The hot floor seared Aidan's feet, and rather than stumble onto his face, he just kept running. Dead bones, hissing smoke and spitting sparks, tripped him up, and he fell to one knee. A hot gun barrel broke through flesh and bruised him to the bone. He yelped as blood soaked his pants. Eddie's hair brushed against shattered glass as Aidan lost his grip. "Damn." Aidan tried for a breath and got smoke. Beside him Iris leaned her face on Redwood's sweaty back. Redwood's legs shook so bad, she almost dropped George.

"I see the door," Iris said. "We're almost out."

The heat was unbearable. Aidan tried to stand up, but Eddie had gotten heavier. Aidan's trembling muscles gave out. "You all go on—"

"No. Get up," Redwood said.

"Two steps, that's nothing," Iris pleaded.

"Nothing?" Aidan grimaced at the dead bodies below him. "This fool's got a gun, and that one's holding a torch. They called down catastrophe." He coughed more smoke. "These fellows been haunting me half my life. I seen 'em ride in here."

"They ain't riding out to chase you no more," Redwood said.

A shudder racked through Aidan's body then knocked into Redwood too.

"You can't just get up from everything and go on." He felt he might black out.

"I know. I know," Redwood said. "But—"

"What's wrong with you two?" Iris screamed. "The hard part's done. The baron's trying to trick you." Pillars gave way. The building was collapsing on itself. "We can't stop at the damn door with freedom in sight."

"You hear what Iris say. We *believed* in each other this far."

Sweet Iris cussing cleared his head. "Okay, okay." Aidan gritted his teeth and forced his weary self back up. His knee almost buckled, but Eddie's head smacked his groin. One pain blotted out the other.

So much smoke, they couldn't see where they were going. Two steps could have been a hundred. They walked on fire with no air to breathe, *believing* more in the open door than the world burning down.

A thunder crack, and the dream broke.

Redwood, Aidan, and Iris stumbled out of the Dry Cleaning with George and Eddie. The fire was burning furiously again. Eddie's shoes went up in flames. The Irish fireman doused them all in cold water as they laid George and Eddie as far from the Dry Cleaning as they could walk.

"Let me pass. That's my family," Clarissa said. "Thank the Lord." The colored volunteer cleared the way for her and Dr. Harris with his medicine bag. Clarissa fell on George. "You foolish man." Rocking him, she looked up to Aidan and Redwood through teary eyes. "And Iris too! Thank you. Bless you."

A shot rang out, and everyone ducked. A rifle fell from a rooftop and a yelping sniper retreated to darkness. Policemen scurried after him. Mr. McGregor held a smoking pistol in his hand, ready to take another shot.

"When I was a bad man, I had a good aim."

Redwood trembled all over. Trouble had come, fire too, but this time, her family wasn't on the run, mourning a loved one snatched away to Glory. This time, no wild man ripped her apart and scattered her spirit. Baby Sister hovered over George, squeezing his hand and chattering away. Aidan heaved breath like he wanted to sob, but a mouthful of smoke and soot wouldn't let nobody cry, not even for joy. This time, they all come through. So why did her heart feel so heavy?

"Folks still in them tenements back there." The colored volunteer scanned the alley. "Immigrants, just off the boat, can't speak English, 'fraid to lose what little they got."

"So go back there and evacuate that street." The Irish fireman sent two tattered men with the volunteer to cover a block of buildings. "I can't spare no more," he said to Aidan and Redwood's bleary eyes. "Why you looking at me that way? Be thankful."

Dr. Harris stood up from George and Eddie, almost smiling. Clarissa scolded George softly as Dr. Harris wrapped Iris's leg in a gauzy bandage.

"You-all should be dead. I would've never believed it, if I hadn't seen it myself." The fireman rubbed his chin. "We got us a low-down crime and a miracle, all in one night."

"Fire ain't over yet." Aidan croaked worse than a broken banjo string.

Redwood screwed up her face. "Ain't no telling how far it'll go."

The blaze licked at the next-door barbershop and reached for buildings out back. In the red glow, the boneyard baron tap-danced on wet cobblestones and grinned at the souls 'bout to join his number.

"Don't feel bad, lad." The fireman patted Aidan's back. "You're brave and foolish and lucky too."

"I'm not brave, sir. That's her." Aidan nodded his head at Redwood.

"I ain't as brave as everybody make out," Redwood said.

The wind picked up, encouraging the bold flames. "A proper rain is what we need, not this bluster and blow." The fireman escaped to a sputtering pump.

"Blow hard enough, couldn't you blow it out?" Iris shouted at his back.

"This ain't no candle." Aidan hunched a shoulder, then growled at the pain. "We can't give the fire this whole block."

"We can't run in those buildings and carry everybody out." Redwood mopped blood from his knee.

"Not this time. I can't—" Coughing stole Aidan's words, 'cept for—"I won't."

He limped away from her into the street. If Redwood thought their ordeal was over, she better have another thought coming. "We pulled through." She clutched him. "Don't we get to be happy, feel good? Just for one second?"

"My *Sikwayi*." Aidan slumped against Redwood and kissed her forehead. "That posse has been riding me and riding me."

She pressed her lips against his and through the smoke and sweat and blood tasted the good in him, the Aidan she loved.

"I won't be haunted by what we didn't do." He stood tall. "Baron already got his due tonight. He don't need no more."

"What you say?" The baron waved his cane at Aidan's throat. Aidan didn't flinch.

Redwood stepped between them. "We ain't 'fraid of you," she said.

"He's a fool can't do nothing but get burnt in guilt, but you—try me, gal." The baron smashed his diamond-tipped cane into the cobblestones, splitting the road open. "Do a *death-defying* spell if you dare, for strangers who wouldn't know you to thank you. Pass you on the street, spit in your face." He tap-danced on shattered stone. "These crackers would spill your blood for nothing, on a dare, to feel good." The baron caught her in secret thoughts. "You hoodooed, gal. *Any weapon you carry, any hate you hold will use you.*" He cackled Miz Subie's words, raised his long arms and spun 'round in a furious jig. His long black coat was an empty void where light died and left not even a shadow.

"Is he gone?" Aidan said.

Redwood saw only the glare of fire and a bright starway in the black of night. "Baron's a challenge, a *crossroads* spell, but this fire is how people do each other. A cracker come running toward me with a torch, I could break his neck, snuff his spirit, and go after his whole family too, till ain't nobody left to come after us."

Aidan wagged his head. "That don't even sound like you."

"Don't tell me who I am."

He flung battered arms 'round her and winced.

She wanted to fight him and his comfort too. "After everything, it's hard to still be me."

Aidan fixed her in his eyes. "I used to think if I wasn't such a coward, I'd've gone after those men what strung up your mama. George would've killed 'em, but he didn't know who they were, but I did. I could've gotten them bastards in their sleep, in the shit box, on the road to church, and who would've known? I don't mean to cuss at you, it's just . . . When they come riding me, and Miz Garnett's voice was on the wind pleading for mercy, I drank, 'stead of doing murder." He opened his palms to her. "Is that what she wanted? Their blood on George's hands, on my hands?"

"Why you never tell me this?" Redwood backed away from him.

"Is that what you want?" Aidan stepped close again, his hands stretched out to her.

Redwood blinked away tears and shook her head.

"I didn't tell you 'cause I was a coward who didn't do nothing, just sat in a tree and watched Miz Garnett suffer and die. I didn't tell you 'cause I couldn't bear to see me so low in your eyes. I didn't tell you 'cause I wanted you to love me."

"I always loved you. You were just one boy, up in that tree. What happened to Mama ain't never been your fault." Redwood let Aidan press his palms to her cheeks. "What happened to me neither." They stood silently, skin close, breathing each other's breath, tasting each other's spirits. "I just hauled off and broke Jerome's neck," she whispered. "I didn't mean to kill him, but I was glad to see he couldn't come at me no more."

"What else to do 'cept protect yourself with everything you got?"

"I was glad I snatched the life out of him. What kind of person be feeling that?"

Aidan laid his cheek against hers. He was feverish hot on her chilly skin. "You a good person, Miz Redwood, the best I know. No evil in your hands. No evil in your heart."

"Secret feelings—I don't even tell myself. Nightriders been haunting me too."

"What you goin' do now? That's what I want to know. That's who you are."

Redwood balled up her storm hand and pressed it against his chest. "Conjure woman can run through fire and not get burnt, but—"

"That won't put it out." Aidan finished Miz Subie's saying.

"Mama's hoodoo saved us all, but I ain't her. I don't want to die so everybody else can go on living."

"Fine by me."

Standing at the crossroads, her heart still heavy, but not aching so bad, Redwood gripped Aidan's back and was shimmy-shaking with him to the middle of the street. She pulled the river of silk from her waist and threw it up in the air. As firemen called out warnings, the sash opened up into a bright blue shimmer above them. Redwood's breath turned cold as snow. Her sweat was flecks of ice. Redwood and Aidan were as surprised as everyone else when—

A monster storm ripped 'cross Lake Michigan, bellowing in their ears. The fire fed on powerful gusts of air and ballooned high and wide. A flock of ghostly clouds, bloated silver specters rode in on the whirlwind—like when Redwood was a child in Peach Grove, dancing on the hillside with Aidan, reaching for fury. This haint battalion laughed flashes of crooked lightning and battered the skyscraping fire with cold water. Fat torrents hugged each flame and flicker. The fire bucked and heaved; it whined and groaned; but the downpour turned roaring heat to great tents of white smoke and thin columns of steam. Not a flame escaped. Water raced down streets and alleys chasing every last spark.

Just as the monster storm might have drowned them all in a mighty flood, Redwood reached out her hand. Aidan clutched her wrist. A dark spiral mass rose above the ruined Dry Cleaning store, a whirlwind, twisting and turning the clouds, smoke, ashes, and steam into tighter and tighter spirals above Redwood's trembling palm. The monster gale blew itself to nothing, to a dark swirl 'round a floating feather, and Redwood squeezed her fist shut.

TWENTY-SIX

Healing, Chicago, 1913

Most newspapers didn't report the Phipps Dry Cleaning fire. If they did, there was a line or two 'bout brave Chicago firefighters and risky chemical storage. Even the colored press was silent, not wanting to spread hoodoo tales or help the white folk think Negroes were careless or had truck with haints and devils. People gossiped though, claiming the fire was a curse and the storm a miracle. Didn't the fire engine company get a call *before* the catastrophe even sparked? Surely the spirits of Lake Michigan were watching over, taking care, since only the Dry Cleaning burnt to the ground, and George Phipps had insurance and a second shop just about to open. Neighboring brick buildings come through almost unscathed. No patrons had been on the Dry Cleaning premises when the calamity began. Not one of George's employees was stranded inside or got shot running to safety. Brave firefighters and volunteers who were wounded mended good as new. The fire chief concluded that the burnt bodies retrieved from the rubble were the very men who set the fire. The cowardly fellow shooting from the rooftop drowned in a puddle in the back of a truck.

Iris saw more trouble on the horizon: fire and race riots in the coming years. Chicago was a violent town. People went missing every night. So many dead poor folk—police claimed there was no time to track down the next of kin. Still, somewhere tears were shed, funeral laments sung, and a bitter ache gripped the hearts of those left behind.

Even bad men shouldn't have to pay with their flesh.

After the fire, after stopping time, calling a rainstorm, and holding the whirlwind, Redwood fell into a stupor on the wet cobblestones and could not be roused. Aidan's shoulder muscles were all torn apart, and the pain finally hit so hard, he couldn't gather her up. He fell on his knees beside Redwood, rocking back and forth and muttering crazy talk.

"She's exhausted," Dr. Harris declared. "You're a wreck too, Mr. Wildfire, and it's no wonder."

Aidan didn't know what came out his mouth. By the look on Dr. Harris's face, it was bad.

"I know what to do," Iris said, calming Aidan a bit. "Don't you worry."

Dr. Harris sent a protesting Aidan home with Walter. Wrapped and splinted and woozy as a drunk man, Aidan couldn't put up much of a fight. Walter brought him to George's house first thing the next morning to look in on Redwood, but she was still dead to the world. Aidan was beside hisself till Iris made another dose of Miz Subie's special brew—the one that brought Redwood back after the *Chicago Fair* spell. Iris poured it down Redwood's throat before being dragged off to school.

Dr. Harris threatened to send Aidan to the hospital in an ambulance if he didn't promise to go back to his bed and stay there. Watching the gentle rise and fall of Redwood's chest, Aidan barely listened to him.

Clarissa said, "George is doing splendidly, but he asked to see you, Dr. Harris." She opened the door to the hallway. When the good physician left, she patted Aidan's hands. "Iris tells me that conjuring can tucker a person out, what with stealing heartbeats and all."

Aidan raised an eyebrow at hoodoo talk coming out Clarissa's good Christian mouth.

Clarissa smiled. "I don't understand of course, but if the good Lord sees fit to let us help one another this way, who am I to argue?"

Aidan nodded at her sensible logic.

Clarissa's lips were close to his ear. "Doesn't Redwood need all her power for herself right now?"

"Yes, ma'am, but—"

She had a cool hand on his hot head. "You need mending too."

"He won't listen to anybody," Walter said. "I told him already."

Clarissa touched his sweaty neck. "When Redwood wakes up, she'll be angry if you haven't taken care of yourself."

Aidan wanted to scoop Redwood up and carry her away, but just standing and holding his own bones up hurt like hell. "Tell her—"

"I will." Clarissa laughed, bottles tinkling in the breeze. She stretched her long neck toward him, swaying sultry hips this way and that. She was a woman used to getting what she wanted out of ornery men, out of everybody.

"What?" Aidan said. "What you got up in your sleeve?"

"Don't worry," Clarissa whispered. "You haven't lost her." She opened the door for him. "I called Mr. McGregor. It won't do for you to bang around in the trolley again." She helped Walter sit Aidan down in the automobile. "I don't want to see you abroad again until you're well." She smoothed his hair and boldly kissed his forehead. George was a very lucky man. "Do I have your word?"

"Yes, ma'am."

Mr. McGregor drove off at a moderate pace till George's house was out of sight. Clarissa wasn't fond of anybody speeding.

"Did you hear?" Aidan grinned at Walter. "I haven't lost her."

And then Aidan couldn't tell you what happened for several days.

George had an easy recovery. Every time Redwood lifted heavy eyelids for a second, he was sitting by her bed, dragon wings unfurled, hot eyes filled with tears. Indeed, he sat with Redwood through the night and into the next day, till she opened her eyes all the way and rasped a few words 'bout the sun hurting her head. George kissed her cheek with dry lips and was out the door like a shot.

Clarissa closed the curtains at the window seat. "Is that better?"

"Yes." Redwood's voice was rusty and the sound surprised her. She frowned.

"Don't be mad at George," Clarissa said.

"I ain't mad at him."

"He feels terrible about what happened."

"He can't tell me that?" Each word came a little easier to Redwood.

"He's blaming himself, so hard . . ."

"That gang of hooligans come spoiling to burn George out." Redwood pushed up on her elbows. "Chicago ain't no place to be a man . . . or a woman."

Clarissa lost half her color. "Why are you talking George's line?"

"No, I mean, we got to fight for that place, make it up as we go."

Clarissa sighed, relieved. "Granddaddy said freedom will take everything you got and then some more."

Redwood tasted Miz Subie's medicine in the corners of her mouth. "Iris did a cure."

"I can't hardly get her to school, can't get her to sleep, she's so busy fussing over you."

"Aidan was here." Redwood looked under the bed. His *Maskóki* hunting knife was lying beneath her, cutting through pain.

"I didn't see him leave that," Clarissa said.

Redwood blinked. "Everything's all right, isn't it?"

"Mm-hmm," Clarissa said softly. "Almost everything."

"Don't worry on me. I feel grand."

"Still the time of your life?"

"Yes. The very best time."

Clarissa stroked Redwood's hand and glanced at the boxes of books, the bare walls, and the bound stacks of letters and papers. "Whatever will we use this back parlor for?"

"What'll I do with no good friend such as you?" Redwood hugged her fiercely.

Clarissa gasped and dabbed her eyes. "Save your strength."

"How will I bear it?" Exhausted, Redwood fell back into the bed. "Will you miss me too?"

"You will be a very good correspondent, writing with excellent grammar, and you will visit whenever you can. When my children are grown, I will visit you, wherever that may be." Clarissa wiped Redwood's damp face. "I won't scold you or Iris about wearing men's clothes. You'll bring fat babies into this world, maybe even one or two of your own. There must be a sister club out in the wilds of California or Oregon, and you'll persuade them to poetry. You'll make more moving pictures or something magical. You will think of me, and I of you whenever we minister to those less fortunate." Clarissa sighed. "And you'll love Aidan like a good woman should."

TWENTY-SEVEN

The Premiere, Chicago, 1913

The Magic Lantern Theatre was all fixed up, restored to its former glory inside and out. Clean walls, comfortable seats, and new velvet curtains put the audience in a good mood. A heavy chandelier with a thousand lightbulbs and twice as many dangling crystals flickered up and down. The fiddle player tuned to the piano. The show would start shortly. Even so, waiting was driving Aidan wild. 'Stead of sitting with everybody else in fancy box seats that were practically onstage, he paced in the wings and itched the back of his neck. The thick white screen, perched at the edge of the orchestra pit, quivered in the commotion everybody was making backstage and in the audience. He hated watching hisself in a motion picture. It wasn't the same as playing a song and feeling the crowd with you or not. Nothing to do if the audience turned sour, if you lost their hearts—the film would just keep on rolling.

Waiting to hold Redwood in his arms afterward, that was murder too. Aidan hadn't made love to a woman for too long. He felt clumsy, rusty, *out of practice*. Course he never loved anyone how he loved Redwood, and she wanted him the way he wanted her. He could feel that, even with that trick on her body. So no matter what demons were still haunting them, no matter what alcohol spooks or stray nightriders were trying to get under their skin, they were goin' fly west to make a bright destiny together, till they walked the stars to Glory.

Aidan slipped out the stage door and took a breath of air. The chill of fall nipped him, and he pulled his Seminole patchwork coat tight. Posters for *The Pirate and the Schoolteacher* were plastered on the outside wall. A line of mostly colored and Indian patrons (though some white folk too) went clear 'round the block—a lot of people he knew, and a lot more he didn't.

"I'll be damned." Aidan blinked and rubbed his eyes. Doc Johnson and Clarence Edwards hurried through the heavy doors behind Mambo Dupree. "Those rascals!"

George and Clarissa stepped out of Mr. McGregor's motorcar. Clarissa wore an Oriental gown of Redwood's—as scandalous as she'd ever get. George sported a flashy dress suit and carried a bouquet of roses. An angry wound wriggled 'cross his cheek.

"Good evening," Clarissa said before Aidan could escape them.

"How do." Aidan took off his hat to her.

"Clarissa tells me, you and Red be taking off after the show," George said. "Iris too."

"Can't be a burden on you forever," Aidan replied mildly.

"You know, it ain't better out west. California's no promised land," George said.

"Redwood don't like roses much." Aidan shook his head at the flowers.

"I'll see you inside, George." Clarissa squeezed her husband and patted Aidan's shoulder. They watched her enter the crowded theatre. Aidan refrained from telling George his wife was a beautiful woman.

"Ain't nowhere different for colored." George turned to Aidan. "They string you up and burn you out in Georgia, in Chicago, in—"

"Your sisters saved you." Aidan stepped close to George. "They loved you through fire. Can't stop a man who got folks like that on his side."

"Ha! A bullet, a torch, stop anybody."

"Well, not this time, huh?"

George groaned. "I don't know why, but she love you. Love her back, or else . . ."

Aidan held out his hand. George shook it quickly and entered the theatre.

Pirate Saeed gathered Teacher Redwood in his arms. The fiddle player and piano man struck their last chord. The chandelier showered light on the dark room. In the wings at the edge of the curtain, Aidan held his breath.

"That was the Ace of Spades show times a million!" Iris sprinkled him with rose petals and danced, happy and bright as a shower of shooting stars. Fifteen and going on forever, she was an old soul and a brash young colt. He grinned at her, busting with pride. Iris shouted something else to him. The audience was clapping and hollering back and forth so loud, Aidan didn't catch what she said.

"They liked it, I guess, and arguing over it too. Red will be pleased." He ducked into the shadows as Prince Anoushiravan, Abbaseh, Farah, and Akhtar marched by. They'd come all the way from Persia to see the moving picture and were probably hunting him down. Everybody would be trying to grab him or Redwood for a word, a slap on the back, a bouquet of flowers. The stage was strewn with every color of rose.

Aidan had an orchid for Redwood.

"Where's your sister hiding?" he asked Iris. "I haven't seen her since—"

"I'm right behind you," Redwood said.

"Y'all should keep better track of each other." Iris ran off.

"Isn't it grand?" Redwood smiled at the stage and the new crowd pouring in. "Some folks are just goin' turn 'round and see it again."

"I can't tell you how proud I am," Aidan said. "We ain't settling for anything. We're doing a spell to make the world we want."

Redwood flushed at him bringing up childish dreams, but she didn't deny what he said. Aidan looked her up and down, letting his eyes feast on her wild woman, scandalous style. She wore silk pants that come in at the ankles and billowed 'round her full hips. An embroidered belt rode high on her waist, playing up her strong shoulders and full tiddies. Chains of silver and glass beads were slung below her waist, accompanying each move, each breath with a jingle-jangle. Embroidery circled the flowing sleeves of her silk blouse and purple turban. Her hair was dark storm clouds framing her face. The yellow mosaic bead from the Dahomeyan women dangled on a slim chain in the hollow of her neck. Nobody but Redwood was dressed as a Persian gentleman and an African queen all at once. Lest his nature rise too much, Aidan swallowed slowly and drew cool air through his nostrils.

"You smell like a spring rainstorm. What's that you putting in your hair?"

"You like that?" She leaned in close. "Abbaseh brought it to me from Persia. S'posed to drive a man wild."

"You don't need no oil to do that." He kissed the back of her neck. She shivered at his boldness. "You got your own sweet scent." He slid his hands through silk to bare skin at her waist. They stood a good while taking measure of one another with the theatre humming behind them. "Come with me to the lake," he said. "Sprinkle some goober dust. Iris got something planned for us later." Aidan pulled Redwood out the stage door.

The sun was setting on Lake Michigan. The sky and water were purple violet, the air warm and sultry—all sign of fall had been banished.

"Indian summer," Aidan said. "A warm sigh from the Master of Breath to let us know he has not forgotten us."

Sitting in the canoe, if he slit his eyes, for a moment they slipped back to Georgia and were riding dark water through the Okefenokee Swamp. He opened his alligator pouch and sprinkled dirt into Redwood's hands. She clutched it tight. He emptied the last of it in his own hand. It was cool and made his palm tingle. Glassy meteorites sparkled.

"Miz Subie say, if I want to really play my banjo"—his hair fluttered 'round his face as the wind picked up—"if I really want to make good music, I gotta spread the last of this with you."

Redwood's eyes had taken on the purple of sunset. Her skin looked golden. "Well, all right then." She held out her hand with his. "You got to play for me tonight."

"Yes, ma'am."

They blew the goober dust to the four directions. The wind carried it far 'cross frothy waves. The Master of Breath carried the dust out to the stars.

Redwood hurried with Aidan through the cavernous train station, done up for a party more than for travel. Iris had told them to arrive three hours before their departure. She had insisted on fancy dress and high spirits. Redwood had no idea what scenario Baby Sister was conjuring, but she and Aidan indulged her. Folks coming and going from the world over cussed and gawked and smiled at them. Redwood lapped up the barrage of languages, the sweet smells and foul sweat, the coppery taste of blood and the sour tang of wine. She beamed at eager arrivals to the promised land, at despairing refugees and hopeless drifters, at wide-eyed seekers of adventures just like themselves.

"We're show people," Redwood explained to curious faces as she and Aidan strutted and swirled their way through the bustling crowd. Redwood hummed the song they'd rehearsed for Iris. Aidan had slung his banjo 'cross his back, and it buzzed and twanged in tune with his laughter and her singing. Battered soldiers and bone-tired laborers brightened at entertainment gracing their path. A little girl applauded their act and did some fancy footwork. Dusty travelers tipped their hats and offered snappy steps too. For a delicious instant, the station crowd turned into swooping osprey, elegant buzzards, and playful otters. Hardly nobody really *believed* what was happening to them. And after Aidan and Redwood passed, folk just settled back down to coming and going. Yet every once in a while in the days to come, these good people would hop or soar and feel as if they could just get up and do anything.

She took Aidan's arm. "A *bright-destiny* spell!"

When they reached the prince's private train coach, no one was there to greet them. Redwood hopped up the steps, peeked in the door, and holding a finger to her lips, beckoned to Aidan to look in as well.

In candlelight, spicy-colored fabrics and lavish cushions glowed like an autumn sunset. Iris wore flowing Persian pants and strands of beads over a Creek top Rose had given her. On the floor, she drew a heart with a sword through it, pierced but unbroken—a *vèvé* to Erzulie, *Loa* of love. With eyes closed and arms stretched out, she sat down cross-legged on an azure Persian rug. An arabesque of voluptuous blossoms, prancing horses, and swooping birds surrounded her. At each corner of the rug, a red candle burned, dripping wax on rose petals and orange peels. Aunt Elisa's sweetgrass basket presided at the head of the rug. It was filled with prairie smoke, spiderwort, and rattlesnake master. White seashells—one that Aislinn O'Casey gave Aidan on Mount Enotah and one that Garnett Phipps had carried from Sapelo Island— were nestled in a brown feather.

Iris whispered Sea Island Gullah words that Redwood couldn't make out. The rug floated up a few inches off the ground and hovered, rippling in an unseen current. The candles spilled fire that didn't burn. Redwood gasped and Aidan let his mouth hang open too. The rug sank to the ground and Iris laughed. *"They shall never become blue."*

"Did you tell her 'bout Cherokee good fortune?" Aidan whispered.

"I didn't think you'd mind. Sister gotta carry our stories too." Redwood grinned. Baby Sister would fly aeroplanes, meet a delegation from Mars, and discover secret places in the heart. A *bright-destiny* indeed.

Redwood pulled Aidan back down to the platform. The prince and his three wives, Saeed and Milton, Walter and Rose, and Clarissa marched in their direction. Everyone in fancy dress, such a splendid parade—it was a shame Nicolai wasn't there with his camera. "Oh my." The back of Redwood's throat tightened. She squeezed Aidan's hand. Their family and friends would probably never be all together this way again.

"What is it?" Abbaseh held up a red pouch to Clarissa. "Can you explain this?" Her English was as precise and sharp as cut glass. Clarissa sputtered and tugged at her collar. Farah and Akhtar leaned in for an answer.

"Mojo, a prayer in a bag." Milton rescued a good Christian woman.

"A medicine bag, holding you to a promise." Rose pointed at Aidan and Redwood. "They're here!"

"How'd you all arrive before us?" Clarissa hurried now. She, Rose, and Abbaseh grabbed Redwood and tied a dark cloth over her eyes. Walter, Saeed, and the prince did the same to Aidan.

"I got the door," Milton said, as they led the blindfolded couple up the steps and into the coach. Abbaseh sang a haunting melody, and Farah and Akhtar accompanied her on stringed instruments Redwood didn't recognize.

"What are you doing to us?" Redwood said. She bumped Aidan's shoulder. "Do you know what's going on?" Aidan only shrugged.

"Together we have plenty magic," Clarissa quoted Mambo Dupree.

"I've unleashed the carpet's talent," Iris said, solemn as a Baptist preacher.

"What talent?" Redwood asked as Aidan, the prince, and his wives laughed.

"Hush, we're working a *traveling* spell." Iris patted Redwood's shoulder. "You've stepped onto a flying carpet. It'll take you to your heart's desire." And then she whispered in Redwood's ear. "Don't worry. Clarissa didn't tell nobody your secret. They just want to send you off right."

Iris guided Redwood and Aidan onto the rug and had them kneel opposite one another. Milton joined Abbaseh's song and it sounded familiar. Iris pressed Redwood's forehead against Aidan's as everyone circled them, all singing now.

"Go n-eirí an bóthar leat," Iris said in Irish. *"May the road rise up to meet you. May the wind always be at your back. May the sun shine warm upon your face and rains fall soft upon your fields. And until we meet again, may God hold you in the palm of His hand."*

Hands brushed Redwood's back and shoulders till the song ended. Each person whispered some secret spell and then headed out the door and down the steps. The coach was full of good conjure.

"Sing the song, then play a scene from a romance," Iris said. "And don't laugh. This is serious. Acting is powerful juju."

The door shut, and she was gone too.

"Baby Sister is something else!" Redwood's heart pounded like before a show. She was breathless and every bit of skin was alive. She swallowed on a dry throat. This was good. Actors needed a bit of nerves, otherwise they didn't care 'bout their routines and didn't really show up onstage.

"Are we goin' do this?" Aidan asked.

"Why not?"

Aidan leaned away from her and tuned his banjo. The melody he played was close to Abbaseh's, but his finger worked magic on the strings, pulling pain and tears and fear right out of her. He played swamp currents, lightning flashes, snow in May, the El jumping the track and streaking 'cross the stars. His music was the ancestors' voices whispering on the wind, the hustle and bustle of great grandchildren yet to come. When she was 'bout to bust, he started singing. Redwood set her voice close to his:

> *The water is cold, the water is deep*
> *Before I'm old, before the long sleep*

Into someone's heart, I'll set sail
And find what's lost, write a brand-new tale

Aidan set down the instrument. Redwood was trembling all over. With such a skimpy scenario, she didn't know how to feel or what to do. *Acting* meant reaching for truth, conjuring a world for yourself and your audience. *Acting* wasn't the same as lying, although you could lie while you acted. She didn't want to think on that too much.

"You always were a conjure man with that banjo, but that is the best music I ever heard."

Still blindfolded, she reached out and found Aidan's face. She undid the cloth over his eyes and ran her hands 'cross the ridge of his jaw and through the soft hairs of a beard that never came. She paused at his mouth and touched the warmth of his breath, the bumpy wetness of his tongue. His lower lip was slippery and smooth and made her sigh. The feel of him raced up and down her spine. Aidan gripped her wrist, startling her. He undid her blindfold. His watery eyes caught all the light. She could see clear through him, back to his ancestors, back to the beginning of everything and up to now. He was looking all the way through her too.

"You all right?" he asked. "You breathing funny."

What could she say? With him looking into her and her blood moving so fast, she was dizzy and prickly everywhere. "I want to be all right. You?"

He breathed a warm swamp breeze onto her cheek and shook his head.

"Clarissa, Iris, and them trying to take the trick off my body."

"Uh-huh." He ran his fingers down her face to the bead at the cleft in her neck. She almost couldn't stand it. "Is it working?" he whispered.

"I don't know." She rested her face against his arm. "I thought of *acting* with you."

"Acting? What you mean?"

"If well . . . if I didn't feel," she gestured, "if I started disappearing on myself."

"Tonight ain't the only night. We got however long it takes." He tried to pull away but she held on to him.

"No. We can't let any more time go by." She wasn't feeling dull or blank, just on edge. "This is the moment we got! Let me make you feel good."

"I'm not goin' run away from you," Aidan said. "Even if we don't—"

"In our next moving picture, I want to fall in love with you." She opened his shirt and stroked his chest. The hair under his arm tickled her. She tickled him back with her tongue. "Do a scene like this."

"Like what?"

"A love scene." She kissed the gooseflesh rising on him. "Let's try it." Aidan cut his eyes at her.

Redwood put her storm hand over his heart and felt it beating underneath the bones. And then her own heart was throbbing between her legs. "When I was a young gal, sixteen or seventeen, I imagined you kissing me, touching my secret spots." She pulled off his shirt. "I imagined touching you, too." Getting him out of the pants was a feat—she was fumbling at buttons, and he seemed clumsy as all get-out. After freeing his left leg, she left a tangle of black wool bunched from his right knee to his feet. "I had you hollering how Daddy did, when Mama got him good and couldn't get him to shush 'cause she was so busy hollering too."

"In a picture show?" Aidan laughed. "With cameras running?"

She kissed the scar on his knee, where the nightrider's gun had burned him to the bone. "I felt bold and brazen, imagining you inside of me. Did you know that?"

"No."

Redwood held the weighty stones of his manhood till he groaned, and then lifted her arms. Aidan undid her belt and beads easily. He hesitated and then tugged on her blouse. Silk slid over her skin like river water. Since she hated corsets, her belly and tiddies were quickly exposed. He considered her in the flickering light. It had been dark that other time they were intimate. He touched the lion scars on her shoulder and ribs.

"My brave *Sikwayi*." Something come over him, fog rolling over the moon. "I ain't done this for a while. I ain't used to touching soft anymore."

Redwood laughed. It hadn't occurred to her that he might be as scared as her. "We ain't done this ever. We're making it up as we go."

Aidan laughed some of his tension away too. "I know how you like to rehearse."

"We can do this scene over and over again."

Aidan kissed the scars on her ribs. He ran his lips and tongue 'cross her tiddies, over both her nipples to the other smooth ribs, enjoying her shivers and squeals. Then his tongue was in the cleft of her neck stroking down to her navel.

"Making a crossroads sign, huh?" she said. "A *good-loving* spell." As he did it again, she didn't fight the sweet ache that was spilling all over her.

He set a purple orchid in her hair. "Miz Garnett gave that to me a long time ago, but it ain't wilted," he said softly. "You still with me?"

"Yes. You feel much better than I imagined." She rubbed her lips against the inside of his thigh, making her own sign. His muscles were taut; the skin was smooth; dark hair was silky and curled near his swelling manhood. He tasted salty and earthy, like thunder root.

"So where are these secret spots?" he said.

"Why should I tell you? You got to search. You might find something I don't even know 'bout!"

Aidan kissed her storm hand. His lips were hot on her cool palm. He found quite a few spots that she'd never known of and got her to hollering. Of course she was hoodooing him too, with every touch, so he wasn't one bit quiet hisself.

"Free people," she said. "How do the Seminole call it?"

But she remembered and they spoke the words together.

"Isti siminoli."

AUTHOR'S NOTE

I tried not to write *Redwood and Wildfire*.

The story came to me while I was researching and teaching courses on blackface minstrelsy, Wild West shows, vaudeville, and early film. I fell in love with the people coming up from Georgia and making a life on stage and screen in early twentieth-century Chicago. These performers were tricksters, magicians, shape-shifters. The richness, complexity, and brilliance of their lives dazzled me. Here was a treasure trove of exciting stories that hadn't been told, that were too good to keep secret! Yet I resisted writing a historical novel. My first novel, *Mindscape* (2006), was Afro-futurist science fiction. My second novel would be too, I thought. But my great-aunt and grandfather were in my head, haunting me, insisting that I tell this story! I made excuses: "I write about the present, the future. I don't know enough history." My elders replied, "You're a professor, aren't you? Don't professors do research?"

Well, yeah, but I wasn't sure I wanted to write about the turn of the twentieth century. Students often didn't understand why any self-respecting African American would act in blackface coon shows or why Native Americans played in Wild West shows. Students hoped they would never have taken part in such demeaning and destructive productions but feared they'd have been grateful to land any roles. My question was, how do you survive these soul-shattering circumstances with your humanity intact? Redwood and Aidan regaled me with their secrets, challenges, traumas, and good times. So I tried to have these ancestor tales ghost around the lives of other characters in a near future novel. I wrote over 140,000 words, but it wasn't working.

"Well, you've done the research." My great-aunt and grandfather were still haunting me. "What's stopping you now?"

I couldn't know enough. OK, women were busting out of their corsets, riding bikes in pantaloons, and making movies. Alice Guy-Blaché (French) made the first fiction film. Zitkala-Sa (Yankton Dakota Sioux) was writing opera; Aida Overton Walker (African American) was helping to invent the American musical comedy; Lillyn Brown (African American and Iroquois) wore top hat and tails and sang the blues dressed as a man; Lillian St. Cyr, known as Princess Red Wing, and James Young Deer (both Winnebago) produced, wrote, directed, and acted in over a hundred films. There were more women film directors in the early twentieth century than right now in the twenty-first! Still, nobody talked to the women to understand who they were, what they dreamed, why they told stories onstage or -screen. Nobody asked what their lives were like, their intimate moments, their fears and joys. Scripts had been lost and so many films had disintegrated! I felt as if I grasped after ghosts, spooks, haints who would dissolve under close inspection.

My elders laughed at me. "Girl, you're a speculative fiction writer, so speculate! Write what might have been. Clear away all that willful amnesia. The future is about recovering the past!"

I gave in. I pulled Redwood and Aidan's story from the 140,000 words and wrote a screenplay. That became an outline for the novel. On a writing retreat at Blue Mountain Center, I wrote *Redwood and Wildfire* to celebrate folks like my great-aunt and grandfather who faced impossible choices. I wrote the novel to offer myself hope. The present wasn't making me happy. A catalogue of disasters danced in my head: assaults on land, sea, and air; human misery on the rise; flora and fauna reeling. The future looked even worse. But how the hell would I have survived in 1910?

I speculated on what might have been. I imagined African American and Native American theatre and film artists surviving more oppressive social constraints than what we were facing in 2007, and still they maintained their humanity and expressed themselves eloquently. In the subjunctive text of what might have been, I offered myself and my readers a bridge to tomorrow. I imagined the folks who made me possible going against horrible odds to conjure a world they believed in. These ancestors had good times, love, and triumphs. They had vision. They did what had to be done.

By 2008 I had a draft of the story I wanted to tell on this world! Then lo and behold it was almost impossible to find an agent or a publisher for the book. Sending out the manuscript, I was told: *Redwood and Wildfire* is great work but there's no audience for "such unfamiliar characters and different storyline." There are "so few characters for the general audience to identify with." The characters were confusing and weird, so "I only read to the end because it was so well-written." Huh? And one white male agent had the nerve to tell me that I didn't know African American culture, that I didn't know my own idiom. In 2008, I faced the same dilemma my characters had faced a hundred years before me. I was caught in the stereotype warehouse! The stories I wanted to tell were supposedly peculiar, alien, confusing, and definitely not "universal."

I was at a SF&F convention, Wiscon or Readercon, and I spoke with another BIPOC author who told me she was writing fantasy that featured dark-skinned people but wouldn't have any direct relationship to American history, to colonialism or imperialism because no one was going to publish that. Huh? Eventually, I found a wonderful agent, Kris O'Higgins, who still challenges and supports my work. Timmi Duchamp bought *Redwood and Wildfire* for Aqueduct Press and was surprised that a large publisher hadn't snapped it up. Of course, I could have assumed that something was terribly amiss in the writing, in the choice of "weird" characters, in my breach of Eurocentric fantasy with a hoodoo tale. My great-aunt and grandfather weren't having any of that. "You ain't about to give up on us, are you?"

No, I was not.

In 2021, this situation has shifted. We have made the way out of no way. So many more voices have spoken and been heard. Many BIPOC authors are telling universal stories based in our particular lives. There are editors who get the idioms that make the world home for us. In fact, we have invented a new world with the stories we tell. Audiences across the globe are eager for these stories and also writing their own. I am thrilled that *Redwood and Wildfire* has a new life in this landscape. I couldn't give up. My ancestors fortified me. *Redwood and Wildfire* was/is a celebration of the sort of vision and love we need to make it to the very next moment!

April 2021, Florence, MA

ACKNOWLEDGMENTS

Blessings on my agent, Kris O'Higgins, and L. Timmel Duchamp who weren't afraid to believe in this novel when I first wrote it in 2007. I pour libation to all the people who have supported my writing for the last fourteen years. You know who you are! Ama Patterson, Liz Roberts, and Sheree R. Thomas never let me give up. Without Pan Morigan and James Emery there would be no book. Thanks to Lee Harris and the folks at Tordotcom for giving this story a second life.

ACKNOWLEDGMENTS

Turn the page for a sneak peek at
Andrea Hairston's next novel from Tordotcom

Available Fall 2022

Public Display

"Books let dead people talk to us from the grave."

Cinnamon Jones spoke through gritted teeth, holding back tears. She gripped the leather-bound, special edition of *The Chronicles* her half-brother Sekou had given her before he died. It smelled of pepper and cilantro. Sekou could never get enough pepper.

With gray walls, slate green curtains, olive tight-napped carpets, and a faint tang of formaldehyde clinging to everything, Johnson's Funeral Home might as well have been a tomb. Mourners in black and navy blue stuffed their mouths with fried chicken or guzzled coffee laced with booze. Uncle Dicky had a flask and claimed he was lifting everybody's spirits. Nobody looked droopy—mostly good Christians arguing whether Sekou, after such a bad-boy life, would hit heaven or hell or decay in the casket.

"Why did Sekou give that to you?" Opal Jones, Cinnamon's mom, tugged at *The Chronicles*. "You're too young for—"

"How do you know? You haven't read it. Nobody's read it, except Sekou." Cinnamon wouldn't let go. She was a big girl, taller than her five-foot-four mother and thirty-five pounds heavier. Opal hadn't won a tug-of-war with her since she was eight. "I'm not a baby," Cinnamon muttered. "I'll be thirteen next August."

"What're you mumbling?" Opal was shivering.

"Books let dead people talk to us from the grave!" Cinnamon shouted.

Gasping, Opal let go, and Cinnamon tumbled into Mr. Johnson, the funeral director. The whole room was listening now. Opal grimaced. She hated *public display*. Mr. Johnson nodded. He was solemn and upright and smelled like air freshener. Opal had his deepest sympathy and a bill she couldn't pay. Dying was expensive.

"Why'd you bring that stupid book?" Opal whispered to Cinnamon, poker face in place.

"Sekou said I shouldn't let it out of my sight." Cinnamon pressed her cheek against the cover, catching a whiff of Sekou's after-gym sweat. "What if there was a fire at home?"

Opal snorted. "We could collect insurance."

"*The Chronicles* is, well, it's magic and, and really, *truly* powerful."

"Sekou picked that old thing up dumpster-diving in Shadyside." Opal shook her head. "Dragging trash around with you everywhere won't turn it into magic."

Cinnamon was losing the battle with tears. "Why not?"

Opal's voice snagged on words that wouldn't come. She made an *I-can't-take-any-more* gesture and wavered against the flower fortress around Sekou's open casket. Her dark skin had a chalky overlay. The one black dress to her name had turned ash gray in the wash but hadn't shrunk to fit her wasted form. She was as flimsy as a ghost and as bitter as an overdose. Sekou looked more alive than Opal, a half-smile stuck on the face nestled in blue satin. Cinnamon inched away from them both.

Funerals were stupid. This ghoul statue wasn't really Sekou, just dead dust in a rented pinstripe suit made up to look like him. Sekou was long gone. Somewhere Cinnamon couldn't go—not yet. How would she make it without him? *Pittsburgh's a dump, Sis. First chance I get, I'm outta here.* Sekou said that every other day. How could he abandon her? Cinnamon brushed away an acid tear and bumped into mourners.

"God's always busy punishing the wicked," Cousin Carol declared. She was a holy roller. "The Lord don't take a holiday."

Uncle Dicky, a Jehovah's Witness, agreed with her for once. "Indeed He don't."

"So hell must have your name and number, Richard, over and over again," Aunt Becca, Opal's youngest sister, said. "This chicken is dry." A hollow tube in a sleek black sheath, she munched it anyway, with a blob of potato salad. Aunt Becca got away with everything. Naturally straight tresses, Ethiopian sculptured features, and dark skin immune to the ravages of time, she *never* took Jesus as her personal savior and nobody made a big stink. Not like when Opal left Sekou's dad for Raven Cooper, a pagan hoodoo man seventeen years her senior. The good Christians never forgave Opal, not even after Cinnamon's dad was shot in the head helping out a couple getting mugged. Raven Cooper was in a coma now and might as well be dead. That was supposedly God punishing the wicked too. Cousin Carol had to be lying. What god would curse a *hero* who'd risked his life for strangers with a living death? Cinnamon squeezed Sekou's book tighter against her chest. God didn't take a holiday from good sense, did he?

None of Opal's family loved Sekou the way Cinnamon did. Nobody liked Opal much either, except Aunt Becca. The other uncles, aunts, and cousins came to the memorial to let Opal know what a crappy mom she was and to impress Uncle Clarence, Opal's rich lawyer brother. An atheist passing for Methodist, Clarence was above everything except the law. Sekou's druggy crew wasn't welcome since they were *faggots and losers*. Opal didn't have any friends; Cinnamon neither. Boring family was it.

"I hate these dreary wake things." Funerals put even Aunt Becca in a bad mood. She and her boyfriend steered clear of Sekou's remains.

"The ham's good," the boyfriend said. He was a fancy man, styling a black velvet cowboy shirt and black boots with two-inch heels. Silver lightning bolts shot up the shaft of one boot and down one side of the velvet shirt. His big roughrider's hat with its feathers and bolts edged the other headgear off the wardrobe rack. "Why not have supper at home, 'stead of here with the body?" He helped himself to a mountain of mashed sweet potatoes.

"Beats me." Aunt Becca sighed.

Opal couldn't stand having anybody over to their place. It was a dump. What if there was weeping and wailing and *public display*? Aunt Becca glanced at Cinnamon, who kept her mouth shut. She didn't have to tell everything she knew.

"Some memorial service. Nobody saying anything." Becca

surveyed the silent folks clumped around the food. "Mayonnaise is going bad," she shouted at Opal over the empty chairs lined up in front of the casket. "Sitting out too long."

"Then don't eat it, Rebecca." Opal sounded like a scratchy ole LP. "Hell, I didn't make it." She needed a cigarette.

"Sorry." Becca pressed bright red fingernails against plum-colored lips. "You know my mouth runs like a leaky faucet."

Uncle Clarence fumed by the punch bowl. His pencil mustache and dimpled chin looked too much like Sekou's. "Opal couldn't see the boy through to his eighteenth year. I—"

Clarence's third wife read Cinnamon's poem out loud and drowned him out:

Sekou Wannamaker
Nineteen sixty-six to nineteen eighty-four
What's the word, Thunderbird, come a streaking in that door
A beautiful light, going out of sight
Thunderbird, chasing the end of night

Cinnamon joined for the final line:

What's the word, Thunderbird, gone a shadow out that door

"Hush." Opal turned her back on everyone. Maybe it was a stupid poem. "Sekou talked a lot of trash. You hear me?" She touched the stand-in's marble skin and stroked soft dreadlocks. "When he was high, he didn't know what he was saying—making shit up. Don't go quoting him."

Cinnamon chomped her bruised lower lip. "*The Chronicles is* a special book, *magic,* a book to see a person through tough times." She threw open the cover. Every time before, fuzzy letters danced across the page and illustrations blurred in and out of focus. If you couldn't stop crying, reading was too hard. The pages were clear now. The letters even seemed to glow. She dove right in.

Dedication to *the Chronicles*

The abyss beckons.

You who read are Guardians. For your generosity, for the risks you take to hold me to life, I offer thanks and blessings. Words are powerful medicine—a shield against further disaster. I should have written sooner. Writing might help me become whole again. I can't recall most of the twentieth century. As for the nineteenth, I don't know what really happened or what I wished happened or what I remember again and again as if it had happened. I write first of origins, for as the people say:

Cut your chains and you become free; cut your roots and you die.

Chronicles 1: Dahomey, West Africa, 1892—Stillpoint

Kehinde was fearless, an *ahosi*, king's wife, warrior woman, running for her life, daring to love and honor another man above Béhanzin, the king of Dahomey. She saw me come together in scummy water tumbling over smooth boulders, my eyes drawn from rainbows, feet on fire, crystals melting into skin. Momentum carried her through the cave mouth toward me as bright green algae twisted into hair, and I sucked in foam and slime to form lungs. Even if she had wanted to run from an alien creature materializing from mist, dust, and light, there was nowhere to go. Enemy soldiers rushed past our hiding place, bellowing bloodlust. Seeing me emerge into human form, Kehinde did not scream or slow her pace, but accepted the event, an impossible vision, a dream/nightmare unfolding before her as truth. Her disciplined calm eased my transition. Yet, nothing prepares you for the first breath, for the peculiar array of new senses or the weightiness of gravity. I was stunned by the magnetic field and the urgency of desire—for food, for touch, for expression and connection. The first experiences are paradise.

As I selfishly reveled in the miracles of this universe, in the delight of a new body, danger threatened at Kehinde's back: bayonets, bullets, and a hundred furious feet. She gulped the humid air and glared back and forth between me and the watery entrance. Her deep brown flesh was torn and bleeding as her heart flooded bulging muscles with iron-rich, oxygen-dense blood. An unconscious man was balanced on the fulcrum of her shoulder. He bled from too many wounds, onto the knives, guns, water gourds, ammunition, bedroll, food, wooden stool, palm leaf umbrella, human skulls, and medicine bags that hung from a belt at her waist. She settled the man against the damp earth. She kissed his eyes, stroked his hair, and murmured to him. Foreign projectiles were lodged in his organs. He'd soon bleed himself away. Abandoning him would have improved her chances of survival, yet she had no intention of doing this. Kehinde's spirit appealed to me at once. My body settled on a form close to hers.

She aimed a rifle at me. Later I would learn she was a sharpshooter, *gbeto,* an elephant huntress, a merciless killer of her enemies. In these first moments I understood the murderous device yet felt certain she would not set its lethal projectiles in motion. Too noisy, why give herself away to harm me, a naked being just coming to my senses? She could not fathom the risk I posed. Trusting me for the moment was reasonable.

I pushed her weapon aside with my still spongy cheek and bent to the suffering man. Kehinde shifted the rifle toward the cave opening and held a knife at my writhing algae hair while I ministered to him. If I knew then what I know now, I might have been able to save him. Perhaps it was better for me that I was so ignorant of human bodies. He might not have embraced a newly formed Wanderer, and Kehinde might not have become my guide. Lonely Wanderers fade back into the spaces between things or fracture incessantly until they are next to nothing.

"Kehinde," the man groaned and reached for her. "Somso . . ." I covered his mouth quickly. Kehinde dripped fragrant, salty fluid onto my face, silently urging me to act, to aid the broken man. With minor core manipulations, I eased pain, calmed turmoil, and gave them a few moments to share. The man came swiftly to his senses and gripped her calf. She thrust the rifle into my hand. I grasped it clumsily and monitored the cave mouth. I doubted my resolve and my accuracy—my bones were still gooey, my muscles rock hard. She crouched down, and they passed soft sounds between them, inhaling each other's breath. She never betrayed his last words to me, yet I'm sure he exhorted her to leave, to let him die with the hope that at least she had a chance to live. Kehinde shook her head, resisting his demand.

The people who carried her death in their minds raced again through the water outside our cave. The man heard them and clutched a blade at her belt. "Somso!" Insistent, he ground his teeth and spit this word at her, a name I would later learn. The sound made my throat ache. Someone splashed close to the entrance. Kehinde's heart raced. The dying man nodded at her and closed his eyes.

Kehinde sucked a ragged breath. "Somso," she said. Her hand shook as she forced her cutlass through his heart.

He did not cry out. My own heart rattled in my chest. Kehinde pressed her lips on his as blood burbled to an end. She wiped the blade on the damp ground and threw a wad of cloth toward me. Words rained down, a frothy hiss, barely audible, like steam bubbling through a hole. I understood nothing and waved the cloth at her stupidly. My new body was starving for language. I gorged on her sounds, gestures, smells; I lapped up the twists and turns of her nose and lips, swallowed the flashes of light and dark from her blinking eyes. Her expressions were tantalizing and rich, but sense would only come after more experiences. Abandoning me would have greatly improved her chances of survival. She had no intention of doing this either. I resolved to know her completely. Kehinde would be the *stillpoint* of my wandering on this planet.

A rash decision, but Kehinde was taking a similar foolhardy course. A storm of feet headed our way. She gripped my wrist and dragged me through the cave. We crawled on our bellies, twisting and turning through a labyrinth of darkness. Kehinde hesitated at an intersection of four tunnels. She lit a lantern, whispered *Somso,* and chose the narrowest opening. A distant spit of light might have been illusion. Just when I thought the walls would crush us, we tumbled out into a forest.

Kehinde lurched about dropping gear: umbrella, water gourd, bedroll, and several human skulls. How she chose what to abandon and what to keep was a mystery. She explained nothing. What would I have understood? She snatched the cloth I clutched stupidly, threw it over my nakedness, and cinched it with a belt. She reconsidered abandoning two skulls and wrapped them and bags of ammunition and food on the belt around my waist. Angry voices and clanking weapons echoed in the cave. Kehinde pointed to the bright orange star sliding behind trees. I mimicked her gesture. She ran. I followed, matching her cadence, stealing some balance. Luckily a new form yields quickly to the demands of the moment, to the first experiences.

Racing through dense forest over rock-hard roots, we kept a punishing pace until the star's bright light faded from the dome of sky. My lungs expanded, increasing their volume with each tortured breath. Indeed, my whole body strained to match the warrior woman's. I admired the powerful limbs, muscular buttocks, and indefatigable heart that she'd had years to develop. I had a few hours of struggle and pain to match her physique. Exhaustion accumulated in my cells; torn muscles generated more strands; my feet bled new blood. The trees sang comfort to me. Birds let loose battle cries, goading me on. So many strong chemicals assaulted us. My skin, tongue, and nose burned. Dizzy, I faltered, but the rhythm of Kehinde's breath and heart guided me through the maze of sensations. Our human pursuers could not fly across the ground as we did. Soon our sole companions were unseen animals and the wind.

We camped in cold moonlight on burnt ground. Kehinde had tools to make a fire, but resisted offering a sign of our location to her enemies, my enemies now. Nursing bloody feet, ripped muscles, and an empty stomach, I intertwined limbs under a scratchy blanket to sort and assimilate the first experiences. When Kehinde thought I was asleep, she hugged a dead tree stump and swallowed sobs. Distant creaks and rasps from the bushes made her flinch. She scanned the darkness for spies on her grief, for enemies about to attack. Pushing away from the stump, she spit and hissed, stomped intricate patterns in the dust, then obliterated them with furious swipes of a horsetail whip. She fell to her knees, threw back her head, and shuddered wordless anguish. As she forced herself back up, my eyes watered.

Spying on Kehinde felt wrong; yet, as I rehearsed her dance in the theatre of my mind, her love and anguish claimed me. I resolved to be a good witness.

My memories waver. Coming from another dimension and manifesting in this flesh form, who would not be uncertain? This drawing is what I make of that funeral night. It was a fevered moment. Such is life on Earth.

Guardians and Wanderers

"It wasn't a lie," Cinnamon whispered to the Sekou-stand-in half-smiling at her from his flower and satin fortress. "The Wanderer's like Daddy, an artist who sorta lost his mind."

Cinnamon stroked images of Kehinde dancing in the moonlight. The warrior woman was muscular and fierce, scary and beautiful. She was sad too, like Cinnamon, over losing someone she loved. Trees and bushes retreated from her, pulling in stalks and limbs, turning aside leaves. Animal eyes peeked from caves, nests, and prickly branches. Stars glittered above her, or perhaps a swarm of flying insects flashed fluorescent butts. Kehinde threw ample hips and brawny arms around like lethal weapons. Wide eyes were pulled into a slant by tight cornrows that covered her head in delicate swirls. Full breasts stood up on a muscular chest. Thunder thighs and big feet made a storm of dust in a rocky clearing. The drawing captured the Wanderer's fevered vision with photographic detail but was also dreamy like those painters Sekou loved, Marc Chagall or Lois Mailou Jones. The Wanderer was a good artist, showing how that night in old Africa had felt.

Despite the beautiful painting, it was hard to *believe* in an alien Wanderer *writing for his life*—to Sekou and now Cinnamon. Space aliens usually zoomed into big cities like New York, London, or Tokyo, and they came right now or on a distant tomorrow to conquer the world (mostly). Whoever heard of aliens going to Dahomey in 1890-something? Cinnamon looked up from the book. Opal was so embarrassed by a drug-addict son who'd maybe OD'ed on purpose that she almost didn't have a memorial service. Cinnamon resisted doubt. Sekou always dug up cool things nobody else knew.

"Good lord, what size are you already?" Aunt Becca waved a

chicken wing at Cinnamon. "You better learn to push yourself away from the table."

"I didn't eat much." Cinnamon hadn't eaten *anything*. Tears pounded her eyes.

Opal pulled Cinnamon aside. "Nobody wants to see that." She scoured away tear dribble. "You promised not to be a crybaby today. Sekou wouldn't want you crying."

"I knew him better than you did." Sekou wouldn't want Cinnamon to be sad forever, still he'd appreciate a few tears. "There's plenty he never told you."

"Your brother was no good. That's why he's dead this day." Opal poked the book. "I gotta dump that junk of his. Can't have it around the house doing us no good."

"*The Chronicles* is all true. Can't throw truth away." Cinnamon hugged it close. "The more I read, the truer it'll get. Sekou got it from a weird and wonderful Wanderer."

Opal wheezed. "Some homeless, trash-talking cokehead told Sekou that Wanderer lie 'cause—"

"No. Sekou said the Wanderer trusted him to keep several illustrated adventure, uhm, adventure journals of top, top secrets safe."

"Don't get wound up—"

"Can't have it drop on somebody who doesn't *believe*." Words flooded Cinnamon's mind from everywhere and nowhere at the speed of light, a story storm. "It's a, a treasure, priceless. We're talking about a Wanderer from the stars, I think, or no, wait, hold up." The floor tilted under her feet. Her tongue tingled. "A Wanderer from another dimension, from *the spaces between things*, come to chronicle life here on Earth. Without me reading, the Wanderer is dust! I'm a, a lifesaver."

"Lifesaver?" Opal snorted. "You wish!"

"I don't know if the extra dimensions have stars. Anyhow we're the Wanderer's *Mission: Impossible*. Only the Wanderer is like Buckaroo Banzai crossing the eighth dimension, and wait, I remember exactly: *A Wanderer from different stars traveling the spaces between things*. That's it. New pages can appear anytime. Sekou made me

Guardian of the Wanderer's *Earth Chronicles*—if anything should happen to him."

Opal stamped the tight-napped carpet. "Stop this motormouth nonsense."

Cinnamon couldn't stop. Consonants smashed into each other around whizzing vowels. "The Guardian should memorize *The Chronicles* in case the book is ever destroyed. Sekou worried about letting the ancient, marvelous Wanderer down. But he had me as backup, with my steel-trap memory. Hear it once, remember forever."

Opal gripped Cinnamon's face, digging jagged nails into her cheeks. "What did I tell you 'bout lying and making up crap? You're too old for that."

Cinnamon slipped from Opal's grasp. "Pages I don't read will disappear. Sekou said we're about to forget everything, but memory is the master of death!" Last week, standing in line for a sneak preview of a John Sayles movie, *The Brother from Another Planet*, Sekou had handed Cinnamon *The Chronicles*. He didn't say much beyond the life-and-death-Guardian bit. Cinnamon had to fill in the blanks. "*The abyss beckons.* Sekou said I should read to fortify my soul against Armageddon."

"You don't even know what Armageddon is." Opal pressed chapped lips to Cinnamon's ears. "Sekou was depressed and high all the time, and his baby sister was the only person dumb enough to listen to his crap."

"I don't see anyone from the other side of your family." Uncle Clarence crept up on them, sniffing flowers and eyeing sympathy cards. "Sekou was no relation of theirs—"

"Sekou's pronounced SAY-coo. And Granddaddy Aidan, Miz Redwood, and Great Aunt Iris are going to be here shortly unless they hit further delays." Riding story-storm energy, Cinnamon lied easily. "They were supposed to come yesterday. A freak blizzard ambushed them in Massachusetts."

Opal adopted a poker face; yet trial lawyer Clarence shook his head and wrinkled his nose, like lies were funky and he smelled a big one. His two grown-up sons sniggered in the corner. Their younger sister did too, and she wasn't usually mean. Sekou claimed people got mean in a crowd, even nice people. They couldn't help it—human beings tended to sync up with the prevailing mood. Sekou refused to hang with more than four people at a time. He hated handing his mood over to strangers. He and Cinnamon practiced throwing up shields against mob madness and other bad energy for when they might be surrounded by hostiles. Cinnamon tried to raise emergency fortifications, but sagged. Getting her shields up without Sekou was too hard. He'd left her alone, defenseless against *infectious insanity*.

"Miz Redwood is a hoodoo conjure woman, and she married herself an Indian medicine man," Aunt Becca explained to her boyfriend, who was a recent conquest and not up on the family lore.

"They never got married, not in any church," Clarence said. "Aidan is a plain ole Georgia cracker, no Indian anything—"

"Hoodoo?" the boyfriend said over him. "What? Like *Voodoo*?"

"Nah! Old-timey *real* black magic." Becca rubbed Cinnamon's hunched shoulders till they relaxed. "You know?"

He didn't.

"Not Hollywood horror, not zombie black folk going buck wild." Becca pursed her lips at Clarence and his grown kids. "They say old Miz Redwood can still *lay tricks* on folks who cross her."

"Rebecca, don't nobody believe that old-timey mess," Opal said. "Lies and backcountry superstition."

Cinnamon winced. Opal was syncing up with the enemy.

"When you get along to my age . . ." Becca's boyfriend didn't look old: handsome as sin, a little gray in a droopy mustache and powerful muscles pressing against the velvet shirt. "Going on strong is what you want to hear about."

That was two on Cinnamon's side.

"Devil worship and paganism." Uncle Dicky took a swig from his flask. His hand was shaking. Jitters broke out everywhere in this god-fearing crowd.

Clarence wanted to hit somebody. Becca shoved a plate of chicken and gravy-soaked biscuits at him. "Eat," she said. "Don't nobody want to be carrying this food home."

Opal pulled Cinnamon away. "Read your book." She sat her in a chair by a window overlooking a vacant lot and hissed, "Quit telling tales."

"Words are my shield too!" Cinnamon watched the sun head for the hills and cold fog rise off the river. A homeless man struggled with his shopping cart through dead weeds. "I know they're trying hard to get here. Nobody better tell me they're not."

"Your grandparents can't be running down to Pittsburgh for every little thing," Opal whispered. "They're old as the hills. You shouldn't be calling them up and bothering them."

"I didn't. They just *know*. They're coming to keep us company, 'cause we're sad."

"You're making up what you want to happen."

"They love us more than anybody, except Aunt Becca." Opal didn't deny that. "I'm their favorite grandchild."

"Only grandchild." Opal groaned. "How did I get stuck with a stupid optimist?" She sighed. "I'm hurting inside and out. You're not the only Guardian swallowing a flood of tears. Sekou put a knife in my heart every day, but I miss him too."

Cinnamon licked a bruised lip. "Sorry."

Opal scrutinized her. "You been fighting at school again?"

"No." Not *at* school. Cherrie Carswell and Patty Banks jumped her two blocks from school by the library, calling her the dyke from the black lagoon. Cinnamon thought they wanted to be friends. They had more bruises than she did. Nobody ever wanted to be her friend.

"I better not hear about you fighting. I couldn't take it." Opal staggered away. "Read *The Chronicles of the Great Wanderer* and let me have some peace."

"OK," Cinnamon said.

"What is he doing out there?" The funeral director cracked a window on December chill. "Move on, man," he shouted at the homeless man limping with his rickety cart through the vacant lot next door. "They got a shelter in East Liberty."

"East Liberty is a long walk, Mr. Johnson," Cinnamon said. "'Specially pushing your whole life on rusty wheels. He could hobble all the way there, and the shelter might be full."

Mr. Johnson turned from the window and scowled. Cinnamon clamped her mouth. She shouldn't fuss at someone her mom owed piles of money to.

Mr. Johnson marched toward the casket. "The family thanks you for coming." His voice was a soothing rumble. "Visiting hours are up in twenty-five minutes."

"Only twenty-five? We just got here." Clarence rolled his eyes. Opal couldn't afford to pay for more memorial time to impress him. Nobody wanted to be here a second longer anyhow. "A budget funeral," Clarence muttered.

"Driving a bus doesn't pay like telling lies in court for guilty people with money to burn." Cinnamon blurted this out fast.

"Where'd she get that from?" Clarence sneered.

"Cinnamon's a bright child, making up her own mind," Opal replied.

Becca's boyfriend gave Opal a cup of tea. Becca stuck out her jaw, put her hands on her hips, and kept Holy Rollers *and* Atheists at bay. Cinnamon opened the book. A breeze from the window flipped pages to just past the first drawing.

ABOUT THE AUTHOR

Micala Sidore

ANDREA HAIRSTON is a novelist, essayist, playwright, and the artistic director of Chrysalis Theatre. In her spare time, she is the Louise Wolff Kahn 1931 Professor of Theatre and Africana Studies at Smith College. She has received the International Association of the Fantastic in the Arts Distinguished Scholarship Award for outstanding contributions to the criticism of the fantastic. She bikes at night year-round, meeting bears, multi-legged creatures, and the occasional shooting star.